For Enrique,

D1528199

Heaven Below

Joan Lehmann

Lead on !

Joan Lehman

ISBN: 1-4392-3578-3
EAN13: 9781439235782

Photo Credits

Cover: Blue Sky Sailboat by Steven Pinker
Cover: Lord Baltimore Hotel by Fred B. Shoken
Author: by Doug McDonough

To order additional copies of this book, contact:
BookSurge
1-866-308-6235
orders@booksurge.com
www.booksurge.com for more information
Books may also be ordered through Amazon.com
For lectures, books signings or general inquiries, Dr. Lehmann
may be contacted at JoanLehmannMD@verizon.net

For Sonia,

My teacher and friend

Acknowledgements

Many thanks to family, friends and co-workers who have offered encouragement and support throughout the entire book writing process.

Special thanks to my editor, Sonia Linebaugh who took me under her wing, taught me to write and more importantly taught me to *like* what I write.

Thanks to my mother, Barbara Burton, who has tirelessly proofread and made corrections to each revision with a smile. Thanks to Doug McDonough who believed in my work and encouraged me to self publish. Thanks to Chrissy and Kirsten, my special German cheering section. Thanks to my children, Jenna and Lukas who gave me the gift of quiet when I needed to work and offered hugs when I needed them most.

Thanks to Dick Yuengling for permission to illustrate Pottsville's history with facts from his family business.

Many thanks to Jackie Thomas and The Radisson Lord Baltimore Hotel for providing historical facts, encouragement, hospitality and partnership in this project.

Thanks to Steven Pinker for his gorgeous, dreamy cover photo and to Fred B. Shoken for saving a bit of history through his photo of the Lord Baltimore hotel on the back cover.

Thanks to Nicole, Jacqueline, Tara, Julian and Helen, my Booksurge team, who made publishing the easiest part of the process.

I also want to thank my eleventh grade English teacher, Janice Baker, who taught me to write a five paragraph essay. I have never forgotten your gift that has helped me express myself on paper time and time again.

To love is to believe, to hope, to know;
Tis an essay, a taste of Heaven below!

Edmund Waller 1606-1687

Chapter 1

"Saturday's last whistle, thank the Lord Jesus Christ," muttered Sean. He lowered his shovel to the ground as if it were made of lead. It had raised calluses on his hands for the past six days, but now it was his friend as he leaned the weight of his body against it like a crutch. It was only when he stopped that he realized his right shoulder ached down to his hand until it was numb. The last car he loaded with coal was headed out of the shaft and it seemed an eternity for the trolley to return to carry him out of the mine. The ceiling was too low to stand and he spent most of his day stooped over to avoid hitting his head. His legs quivered like jelly, too tired to carry him out on foot. Still grasping his shovel, he dropped to his knees to wait. Thank God another long week was over. He closed his eyes and wished he had wings to fly from that dark loathsome hole in the ground forever.

While he waited, the foreman's words from Monday rang in his head. "Be thankful you've got a job," he said. "The mines have been closing left and right even before Black Tuesday. But by the grace of God, ours is still running three years into this despicable Depression."

Be thankful, he thought, trying to will it. But his joints creaked and his lungs were full of dust. At just twenty-four he had already put in ten years at one job or another, felt like twenty. The weeks got longer and the wages got shorter. I should be thanking the boss all right, thanking him for making me an old man before my time, thought Sean.

At last, he and his crew climbed into the trolley dragging their shovels and picks behind them. No one uttered a word because they were too tired to speak, and anyway, there was nothing to say. The ride along the track rattled their bones. As they turned the corner, the screeching of the wheels on the rails was deafening. Finally, as they neared the entrance, Sean caught a glimpse of daylight. He climbed from the car and like an old man, gingerly straightened his spine. As he lifted his face, he raised his hand to his brow to shield his eyes from the sun. He put out the lamp on his cap and pulled it from his head. His blond wavy hair contrasted with the black smudge on his face. He hung his cap on the peg at the door and exited the shaft. With the warm sunlight, life returned to his weary body.

"Hey, Sean. Will you stop off for a *taste* with us before heading home?"

The voice awakened him from his stupor. It was Patrick Donley. Pat had worked next to Sean for the past three years. Their crew called them the Mick Twins, because of their ancestry and because they tried to match each other shovel for shovel. Neither minded the teasing. It was better than being called a Molly Maguire. People had a long memory in Pottsville. No one had forgotten about the blood shed a few years back and some still held a grudge against the Irish. Sean would love nothing better than to throw back a shot or two, but there was a little less in his envelope each week. At this rate, he couldn't afford to squander even a penny at a gin mill.

"I'll pass. I'm gonna cash out and go home to my girls."

Patrick stood and stared at Sean, not willing to take no for an answer.

"Next time," said Sean firmly.

Patrick gave in and caught up with the others.

Sean moved to the line at the spigot. First he washed the grime from his hands. Then he glanced up at the mirror. His light green eyes shown through the greasy soot he washed from his face. He passed the cake of soap to the man behind him before moving to the next line to collect his week's pay. As he listened for his name, he wondered when the Depression would end, when he would see a decent wage so he could buy land for a house...

"O'Connell?"

...and when he would see the ocean.

"O'Connell!"

"Here, sir."

"Here's your week's worth, son," said the paymaster as he slid an envelope under the window.

"Thank you, sir."

The paymaster nodded and called the next name. "Altschuler?"

Sean stepped to the side of the line and opened his envelope. He counted the cash and change. There was fifty cents less than last week. His heart sank.

Just then, another miner realized there was less in his envelope too. "What the hell is this? How I'm feeding seven children with this?" he bellowed at the paymaster in his thick accent. His fists clenched as he stepped towards the window.

"Settle down, Kolinsky. You know I've got nothing to do with it. I got less this week too. We're all on the same boat."

"What boat? Must be Titanic. How do I get off?"

A few of the men snickered. But Kolinsky wasn't joking and so the laughing quickly ceased. After a moment, the big Czech backed away from the window and it was a good thing too. He could have broken a few bones if he wanted. But he knew it was pointless to fight. Things were bad all over. He grumbled a curse word in his mother tongue as he thrust his pay into his pocket.

Sean folded over his cash and shoved it into his pocket too. He tossed his jacket over his shoulder, picked up his jelly-bucket and started his walk home. As he walked, a car crept up behind him. He jumped when the driver blew the horn. The fellows from work laughed at their prank when he startled.

"Give her a big kiss for me, Seany boy," shouted Patrick.

"I'll see you bright and early Monday morning," Sean yelled over the roar of the engine.

"Bright and early, then."

The car stirred a cloud of dust as it drove past. As Sean walked, his thoughts turned again to the sea. He longed to be near the water, the green Atlantic his Grandda remembered and of which he had only dreamed. He'd never seen a boat, not a real one. He'd seen barges in the canal loaded with coal and rowboats on the lake. But Sean had never seen a boat under sail or a steamer or sternwheeler. He had clipped photographs of boats from newspapers and magazines since he was a child. Someday I'm going to build a boat, he thought. Someday I'll own one. But first he had to make it to the sea. He had a plan to get there, *once.*

When he was eighteen he left home and headed east. He set out to see the ocean to build boats or work on boats or fish. It didn't matter. He just needed to be on the water. He left his steel mill town and made it halfway across Pennsylvania to Pottsville before he stopped for the night. He got a room at the inn and went downstairs for supper. A waitress came to the table. Sean's eyes widened as she came near. When she asked him what he wanted to eat, he couldn't speak. He couldn't move. She had long brown curls and eyes that matched. Her face was fair and her cheeks were like roses. She glowed as she stood before him. Sean was sure he had died and this woman was an angel in heaven speaking to him. She spoke once more. He watched her beautiful lips move, her voice was like a song. Still, he was dumb. Her patience grew thin and she walked away in anger. "Fine, I'll be back when you've made up your mind."

"Wait," he cried. "I'll only eat if you will join me."

"But I've got two more hours until I'm finished," she answered.

"Alright, then I'll wait."

He watched her every move, the way she floated from table to table. Her skirts swayed and her feet scarcely touched the ground. His heart quickened whenever she glanced his way. She couldn't believe he would wait for her. At long last, she brought roast beef and potatoes and sat across from him. When he held her hand, he forgot all about the ocean. He took the first job he could get, as a laborer in the mines, shoveling five cars a day. Two weeks later, he asked the waitress to marry him and she did. Since then, six years had passed and he had still never seen a real boat, or the ocean for that matter. He was foiled by a pair of brown eyes. But how lovely those eyes are, he thought, and they're all mine. Sean never believed in love at first sight, until he saw Molly. He wouldn't have traded her for anything, not even the sea. Secretly, he still schemed to get there. When he had the chance, he whittled away on wooden toy boats and dreamed.

The couple rented half of a house from Molly's Aunt Abigail and Uncle Andrew, in Cressona, just outside Pottsville. Sean worried that he had yet to buy land. Saving money for their own place was impossible in those times but they needed more room for their little family. Their daughter was already five. She had curly brown hair and a fair face like her mother, but she had her father's *green* eyes. She was both of them and they were her world. But as happy as he was to have both his girls, he still wished for a boy. He longed for a son to teach what he'd learned and to pass on the family name—maybe even give him grandsons if he was lucky. Molly had been with child twice since Hannah, both were lost early on. But there was still time, plenty of time.

It was May and as he walked Sean took a deep breath of the country air. What a glorious day, he thought and what a shame he spent most of it underground. The trees were in full leaf and bright green. The sun felt good on his face. His step grew stronger when he neared his house. And though weary, his step got a bounce when he heard his curly girl's voice. With arms open wide,

Hannah called to him, "Papa, Papa. I'm so glad you're home." She raced down the hill to meet him. She was a sight for his sore eyes in her little blue dress and hair ribbons to match. Her face beamed when his eyes met hers. "Not as happy as I am to be home, sweet pea."

Sean dropped his jacket and lunch pail and bent down to wrap both arms around her. His clothes were thick with coal dust. The missus will have a fit, he thought. But Hannah didn't care. Though his arms ached from another long week of shoveling, he lifted her off the ground just the same. She was as light as a feather to him and he swung her 'round and 'round until they were both dizzy. They laughed, happy to see each other. Sean buried his face in her sweet hair that shone in the bright sun. His eyes welled with water as he squeezed her tight and felt her little heart beat next to his. A week's worth of misery was washed away by the touch of her hand. He kissed her tender cheek and lowered her feet to the ground.

"Hannah Jane O'Connell—why don't you have shoes on your feet?" he pretended to scold her.

"It's okay. Mama and I are working inside today."

Her apron and dress were covered with flour and now, smudges of black soot.

"Really? Working in the kitchen today, are you?"

"Uh-huh. We're making muffins."

"Oh no. Are they the kind I like best, with cinnamon and sugar?"

"Yep."

"Quick. Let's go get one while they're still warm."

He gathered his jacket and lunch pail and raced her to the house.

"Not so fast in those filthy clothes, Mr. O'Connell. The muffins are still in the oven. And anyway, they're for tomorrow after church, for those of us who go to church."

Poor Sean was foiled again, by the same pair of browns.

Molly's face was red and wet with perspiration. Her apron was covered with flour, like Hannah's. Next to the house, the wash waved on the line. Sean thought she was beautiful standing there smiling at him. He couldn't wait to get his arms around her, too. As he reached for her, she gently shunned him with her hand.

"Before you change out of your work clothes, would you bring an armload of wood? The stove is getting low."

"Of course, *my queen,*" said Sean with a wink to Hannah.

As Molly opened the door for him, the smell of fresh baked bread wafted to his nose. He inhaled deeply trying to taste the air. The bologna sandwich, apple and pint of milk he ate at noon were a distant memory. A pang of hunger hit his stomach and made him weak. His head began to spin. He bent over and leaned against his knees. The moment the nausea passed, the landlord, Molly's Uncle Andrew came to his door.

"Today's payday, ain't it, boy? Rent's due. I'd like to have my money now, if you don't mind," he said gruffly.

Sean's fists clenched and he gritted his teeth lest foul words fly from his mouth. He struggled to keep from taking a swing at the man who taunted him. Just in time, Aunt Abby intervened.

"My lord, Drew. Let the boy catch his breath. He just got home. He's never missed a week. Let him get his supper."

Andrew and Abigail Ashe. What a pair. Their voices sounded so much like Grandda's, Sean often wondered if they all came over on the same boat from Dublin.

Molly came to live with Aunt Abby when she was fourteen. She taught Molly to cook and sew and helped out when Hannah was born. Molly was the daughter Abby never had and she adored Hannah like her own grandchild. When Sean showed her the latest ship he'd carved, she told him he'd make a fine boat builder. She even slipped gooseberry tarts into Sean's lunch pail in summer.

Why did she settle for *Mr.* Ashe? He was the meanest-spirited man Sean had ever known. He complained about the weather, the food, the economy, even the President. Sean paid him rent, always on time. He split wood, carried water and mended his roof. Still he treated Sean like dirt under his shoes. Was Sean so different from him? Andrew labored in the coal mines, just like he did, for thirty years. Now that Andrew's bones hurt too badly to work, the two lived on Abby's piece work and the rent Sean gave him every week. Didn't he remember how hard it was to work to feed a family, especially in tough times? Was it the pain in his joints that made him ornery, or was he just a son-of-a-bitch? Mister was as mean as Missus was nice.

"I've got your money right here, Mr. Ashe," Sean said between his teeth.

He lowered the firewood to the floor and forced his grimy hands into his trouser pocket. Sean pulled out a wad of cash and passed it his way. Andrew tucked his walking stick under his arm and held out both hands for the money. He grinned as he wet his thumb on his tongue and counted every dollar. He turned on his heel and walked back to his side of the house without so much as a look. Sean felt his fists clench again. I can't stand the man, thought Sean. Sometimes I just wish a tree would fall on him or lightning would strike him. I don't need his taunting or his house for that matter. Every week Sean asked himself why he didn't spend his pay on three train tickets–to anywhere, to get out of that town to start a new life. They would have already gone if it weren't for the bond between Molly and Aunt Abby. Sean couldn't separate the two and little Hannah couldn't be happier. She was loved and doted on by two women. He decided long ago to tolerate this ingrate landlord and slave away in the mines until something better came along. He hoped it would come soon.

Chapter 2

Mmmmmm the smell of biscuits and bacon, the smell of Sunday. The O'Connells ate oatmeal and toasted bread most of the week, but Sundays were special. Molly got up early to make breakfast before church and then called up the stairs to rouse Sean from his warm, soft bed.

"Sean—food's getting cold."

"I'm coming, *darling*."

As he pulled on his trousers, Hannah, bounced into the room.

"Papa, are you coming to church? Mama says I can wear my new ribbons and we're going to have the muffins after."

"Why don't we eat a muffin right now?"

Hannah got a concerned look on her face, much too serious for such a wee one.

"Mama said they were only for church."

"Oh, I see. Well, c'mon now. Let's see what your mother has for us for breakfast. My belly is growling and I'm half starved to death."

Sean lifted Hannah onto his hip and carried her down the stairs. She held onto him tightly and he tickled her under the chin until she squealed.

"Breakfast will be ice. Now sit down, both of you," Molly said sternly. She was dressed in her Sunday best, a pink cotton dress with a flower print. It was mostly covered by a large white apron that came over her shoulders. Sean surveyed her thoroughly. With her back to him, his eyes drifted from her waist, past the curve of her hips downward past the hem of her skirt to her stockings and shoes with high heels. Then he noticed her dark brown hair was pinned high on her head with a few loose curls dangling down the nape of her neck. When she spun around to face him, with a coffee pot in one hand and a spatula in the other, she looked like a short order cook. Nevertheless, he admired her simple loveliness. Sean lowered Hannah to her chair and pulled out one for himself, but didn't sit. Instead, he continued to study Molly's form. The more attention he gave her, the more perturbed she pretended to be. He knew it was an act. It was just her way. She stood with her hand on her hip and a scowl on her face as she poured his coffee.

"I see you've got your work clothes on, Mr. O'Connell. No church for you today?"

"Dear Molly, when do you suppose I'll get time to fill the wood crib? There's nothing left of me when I get home from the mine. Sunday's my only chance and today the sun is shining. It's too much in the rain."

Molly was angry at first. After a moment of fuming, her anger turned to disappointment. She knew he was right. She couldn't possibly split all the wood and Uncle Andrew had grown too old to keep up with it. Aunt Abby wouldn't hear of a coal stove in her house. She had spent too many years beating back the black soot that stained the wash on the line and clung to the windows and who could blame her? Sean would have liked to sit next to Molly in church, but he had to keep two wood fires going.

"I know," Molly said sadly as she gave in to reality. She returned the coffee pot to the back of the stove and turned her back to him to pout. He moved toward her, pressed himself against her back and wrapped his arms around her waist in a single motion. He pulled her still closer to him, hung his head over her shoulder and kissed her softly on the neck. Her body relaxed and she closed her eyes. Her face softened and then sweetened with a smile. Perhaps she remembered the way they had loved the night before. He allowed his hands to drift from her waist to her hips. Then suddenly, she opened her eyes and freed herself from his arms. "Kindly behave yourself in front of our child, Mr. O'Connell. Now sit down and eat your breakfast," she said pushing him in the chest.

Sean flopped into a chair at the table next to Hannah. "I'm in trouble with your mother again, lamb chop." Hannah smiled back at him tightly grasping her fork and spoon. Her legs swung back and forth wildly under the table.

Molly was a fine country cook and Hannah and Sean gobbled down bacon and biscuits with blackberry jam as fast as she could serve them. She then basted three eggs in the hot bacon grease. She salted and peppered them right in the pan and slid them onto their plates. They stabbed the soft yellow centers with their forks and sopped up the yolks with another biscuit. When they finished their meals, they licked the jam and egg from their fingers and smacked their lips. Molly turned away from the stove and shook her spatula at the two like a school marm with a ruler. "What am I going to do with you two? It's like I never fed you before. Little piggies.

Don't forget to lick your plates clean too while you're at it," she said as she tossed the spatula into the sink.

Sean gave Hannah a wink and they lifted their plates to their faces and stuck out their tongues as if to abide her request. Molly quickly snatched their plates away and dropped them into the sink with the spatula. "Sometimes I think I'm raising *two* children," she squawked, still angry that Sean wasn't going with her to church.

It was a feast for kings, but it was over too soon. As hard as he tried, Sean couldn't stop worrying that when the mines finally closed, times would get even tougher and Sunday breakfasts like these would be a thing of the past.

"Molly. Hannah. We'll be late. Let's go," called Aunt Abby.

"Just let me get my sweater," answered Molly.

"Mama, don't forget the muffins."

Sean caught his little one by the elbow. He pulled her near him and whispered in her ear, "About those muffins, lamb chop. Do you think you could hold one back for your *dear old Dad?*"

Hannah knitted her eyebrows as the question rolled round in her little head. "Isn't that stealing? The preacher says stealing is a sin," she answered batting her big green eyes at him.

Sean paused for a moment and stared off deep in thought as he rubbed the stubble on his chin with his thumb. "Let's see now. Did those muffins come from our house?" he asked.

"Uh-huh."

"Well, then, that makes them *our* muffins doesn't it?"

She thought for a second. "Uh-huh."

"Now you can't very well steal from yourself, can you?"

"No sir."

"Alright then, I can't see the harm in it. And anyway, I never heard of anyone committing a sin with a muffin, have you?"

Hannah smiled until the dimples pressed into her cheeks and shook her head no.

Sean gave her a peck on the forehead and a pat on the breeches. "Now, off with you."

She raced to catch up with Aunt Abby and Molly. Her brown curls and ribbons sailed behind her. Sailing. That's where Sean longed to be. What a day for dreaming it was and what he wouldn't give to be on the shore. He stared off into space and watched the ships on the water in his mind.

"Dawdling again, eh? And wasting daylight," interrupted Uncle Andrew.

Sean startled at the gruffness of his voice. "I was just heading to the woodpile. Better sharpen the ax first I guess."

"Don't waste your time. I sharpened it yesterday. It's all ready for you."

"Thanks for thinking of me," Sean answered quickly and turned away from him.

"Don't get disrespectful, you. You're lucky you've got a place to lay down your head at night."

Lucky, am I? thought Sean. So lucky I have to live with a man who's a pain in my.....

Ax swinging was every bit as hard as coal shoveling but at least it was a change. Sean slammed the sharp edge into the first piece of wood he saw. It popped straight down the middle.

"Not bad. You oughta be an expert by winter," said Andrew.

Isn't it bad enough I have another long day ahead of me, but does he have to stand there and watch too? He has kept an eagle's eye on me working at this woodpile for six years. Go back into the house old man. Leave me alone, Sean thought to himself.

"I'm going for a little stroll."

Thank you sweet Jesus, thought Sean. After a few steps, Andrew turned and added, "I'll be back to check on you."

"I'm sure you will," said Sean under his breath.

Andrew walked off chuckling and talking to himself and leaned against his walking stick as he went. He called it his "shillelagh" but he had never hit anybody with it. He was too proud to admit it was really a cane to hold up his arthritic bones. Sean was happy to see him go but couldn't get his words from the day before out of his head. It was the same every Saturday. Sean barely got to see his pay before he had to hand it over to Andrew. The world would be a better place without the likes of him, he thought. Sean looked towards his direction and hoped at the very least it would be a *long* walk.

Sean chopped angrily at the pile of wood at first, but once Andrew was out of sight, he took notice of the fresh air and bird's songs. Every few logs, he paused from his work, closed his eyes and drank it in. He felt the sun on his back and enjoyed the breeze as it came over the hill heavy with the sweet scent of flowers and long grass. Even the smell of newly tilled soil with freshly spread horse manure from the fields was comforting. Though he worked nearly as hard on Sunday as he did the rest of the week in the mines, for a few hours, he had peace–and light. He was left alone with his thoughts and for this, he was thankful.

Two hours later, he ran his thumb along the edge of the blade. Dull. He wiped the sweat from his brow with his shirt sleeve and walked toward the shed. As he put down the ax, he became aware of his throbbing arm. Between the shovel and the ax, there was never a chance for it to recover. As Sean rubbed his shoulder, his thoughts drifted to earlier that morning. Molly was beautiful standing there in her dress and heels and holding her coffee pot. Maybe when she gets home, I'll take her upstairs for an afternoon *nap,* he schemed.

"What are you doing, lad? Why, you're just getting started."

Sean jumped at Andrew's words. His walk wasn't nearly long enough.

"The blade is dull. I'm going to run the whet stone over it."

"Nonsense. You're just stalling. This blade is fine. Have you been daydreaming again? You've barely got two day's worth," complained Andrew.

Sean stared in anger at the sizeable pile of wood he had split.

"Give me that ax. Let me show you how it's done," boasted Andrew. He snatched the ax from Sean's hand, swung it over his head and slammed it into a huge piece of wood directly over a knot. He had a hell of a time getting the blade out. He had to use a maul and a wedge to get the blade free. Sean offered with his hand to relieve him of the ax.

"Stand back, laddie. You could get hurt," Andrew teased as he waved Sean away.

Hurt? If anybody was going to get hurt, it would be *him*, thought Sean. He heeded Andrew's words and stood out of swinging range. Andrew lifted the ax over his head again. By now, his face was red and the veins stood out on his neck. He was a mad man, determined to split this knotted stump. He managed to get one small piece free. "Now she's coming."

He lifted the ax once more. But this time, he held it suspended in mid-air. His eyes bulged out of his head and his mouth hung open. He gasped for breath and slowly lowered the ax to the ground. Sean watched as Andrew balled his right hand into a fist and shoved it into the left side of his chest then dropped to his knees. Sean held Andrew by the shoulders and lowered him to the ground for fear he would hit his head.

"What is it? What's wrong?" asked Sean.

Andrew stared back at him with big unblinking eyes. He held his breath. Was he choking? Sean fanned him with his hat. What's happening? thought Sean. Dear God, what should I do? He stood up and looked around to see if there was anyone near to help him. He saw his neighbor working on his truck.

"Simmons, come quick. It's Drew!"

Mr. Simmons raced up the hill. "What is it, Sean?"

"He was splitting wood and fell to the ground and then he stopped breathing."

Mr. Simmons dropped to his knees and leaned over Andrew. "Drew, what's the matter? Say something, Drew."

Mr. Ashe closed his eyes. His body went limp. His fist uncurled, slid from his chest and fell to his side. The color left his face. Mr. Simmons pressed his ear against Andrew's chest. After a few seconds, Mr. Simmons looked up at Sean and shook his head.

"What is it? Is he…?

"He's gone, Seany. Passed on to the next world."

My God. It's not possible, thought Sean.

"What do you think—what happened?" asked Sean sheepishly.

"Probably a heart attack. I've seen it before. His ticker finally gave out. He just dropped dead."

Sean's thoughts raced. A heart attack? I didn't even think old Drew had a heart. God forgive me. I didn't mean it. He remembered all the times he hoped something would happen to Drew. This is all *my* fault, he thought. Oh, dear Lord, what am I going to tell Mrs. Ashe? They will be home from church any minute. What about Molly? She was never close to him, but she will hurt for her aunt. What about my little Hannah? She was so happy skipping off to church this morning. She's too little to see a dead body. I didn't see one until I was ten, when my grandfather died. It was horrible. I can't think. They'll be home any minute. What should I do?

"What should I do?"

"Well, we can't let him lay in the sun like this. Let's carry him over behind those trees in the shade," said Mr. Simmons

They laid his body on a blanket behind the shed. And none too soon, the women were just coming up the hill.

"I'll tell Molly and you tell Mrs. Ashe," said Sean.

"Me? You tell her."

"Please, Mr. Simmons. You've known them for years. She'll take it better from you. I've got to keep my little Hannah out of this."

Mr. Simmons walked quickly towards Aunt Abby, took her by the elbow and whispered the terrible news into her ear.

"Where is he?" she asked.

Simmons held her by the arm and shoulder, lest she faint from the news. "Over here," he said softly.

When Abby saw her husband's body in the shade of the tree, she gently pushed Simmons away. She had to go to him and see for herself. It was too painful for Sean to watch.

Molly saw Sean turn away. "What is it, Sean?"

"It's your uncle. He was chopping wood and his heart failed."

"Is he….?"

"We carried his body out back. You go to your aunt. I'm going to take Hannah in the house. She's too little for this."

Molly stood frozen with her jaw dropped. Then, she slowly nodded and walked towards Aunt Abby.

Hannah was a few steps behind, plucking dandelions from the side of the road.

"Hannah, what did you learn in church today?" Sean asked as he took her hand and quickly led her in the direction of the house.

"We sang songs and the preacher talked about sin and going to the fiery place," she said. "*Hell*," she whispered.

"Oh he did, did he?"

When they got inside Hannah said, "Oh, Papa. I almost forgot." She handed Sean her bouquet of wilted dandelions to hold for her as she reached into the pocket of her dress and pulled out her kerchief. She carefully opened it as a few crumbs fell to the floor.

"I didn't forget, Papa. I brought you a muffin."

It was too much. The burning in Sean's chest rose to his throat and reached to his eyes. Hot tears seeped from their corners. He never watched a man die. He tried to act like it didn't bother him. He couldn't stand Andrew, but he didn't *hate* him—not really. Sean felt guilty for wishing him dead. Was it his fault? Should he have taken that ax away from Andrew? He saw him struggling. Why didn't he? Did he secretly hope that Andrew would hurt himself, showing off like that? Was Andrew's blood on his hands? Sean never felt so helpless in his life, but it was too late. His tears changed from sorrow to anger. He was angry with himself, angry with how fragile their lives were and most of all, angry because life was so damn hard.

"What's the matter, Papa?"

"Oh, I think I got some sawdust in my eye."

Sean pulled back the kitchen curtain. Abby and Molly were kneeling on the ground and holding each other. They sobbed while Mr. Simmons stood over them and turned his hat round and round in his hands.

"Aren't you going to eat it, Papa?"

"What?"

"Aren't you going to eat your muffin?"

Sean lifted Hannah to the kitchen counter. He wanted a better look at her shining face, her innocence. She lifted the crumbling muffin higher with her tiny hands. It wasn't a muffin in Sean's eyes. It was really his heart she was holding. It was crumbling too.

He buried his face in her small neck and hid himself in her curls.

"Later, sweetheart, later."

Chapter 3

Cressona was a small town. News spread quickly about the fate of Mr. Ashe and soon neighbors appeared at the door bearing gifts. Abby was adored by those who knew her. She had perfect church attendance and provided flowers from her garden for the altar each Sunday. New brides received one of her patchwork quilts on their wedding day and if you were sick, you could count on a pot of her ham bone vegetable soup. Within hours of Andrew's passing, bouquets of irises and peonies, Mason jars of strawberry preserves and loaves of home baked bread filled the kitchen table. Over the next three days, the women brought stews, cakes and even a rhubarb pie. Hannah and Sean did their best to keep up with it, but poor Abby couldn't eat a bite. She was still in shock. Molly hardly ate either.

"I never got to say goodbye," Abby mumbled as she fought back the tears.

Mr. and Mrs. Ashe had been together over forty years. They never had children. All they ever had was each other and without him, she was lost. Sean hated to see her that way and tried his best to comfort her. He still felt guilty about what happened that day and wondered if Abby blamed *him* for not taking the ax away. He sent Hannah to sit on her lap from time to time. Abby held his little one tight like her own living baby doll. Hannah never squirmed or asked to get down. She stayed with her great-aunt as long as she was needed. Once, she even fell asleep in her arms.

With Abby in mourning, barely speaking or moving, Sean worried about Molly. She had taken over both sides of the house and kept two stoves burning. She did all the cooking and washing. She took care of all three of them, but she didn't look well. She was too pale. The roses in her cheeks had faded. She had few words and scarcely rested. Molly moved from task to task like a machine without ever looking up. Was she in shock too? Did she feel sorry for Abby? Did she miss her Uncle Andrew? Perhaps she was worried about the future and like Sean, frustrated that life was so unpredictable.

It was no use to bring up the matter. This was Molly's way, to keep busy and put on a brave face. After the funeral, she would be back to herself, hoped Sean. He kept busy too, shoveling twelve tons a day and trying to keep up with his household chores. In the evenings, he held Hannah and was determined to give Molly a little squeeze now and then—whether she liked it or not.

When it was time to bury Mr. Ashe, Sean had to fight with his foreman to get the afternoon off. The foreman argued that it wasn't *Sean's* uncle that passed. Sean reminded him that funerals weren't for the dead, but for the living. He needed to be there for his girls. At noon, he said goodbye to the other fellas and headed out of the pit.

"I'll see you in the morning," he yelled to Schultz over the noise of shovels and picks.

The foreman gave him a dirty look and waved him away with his hand. What a bastard, thought Sean.

There's nothing like heading off to a family funeral, pissed off and wondering if you'll have a job in the morning. Damn kraut.

In the church, Molly sat next to her Aunt Abby. They held each other and shook with grief. Sean couldn't bear to watch. His throat tightened and his eyes burned like fire. He looked away so that Hannah couldn't see him cry. Then he squeezed her little hand and buried his face in her soft curls. She held tightly to a rag doll Abby had made for her. As hard as Sean tried to divert his thoughts to the house, the vegetable patch, building boats and the sea, he couldn't drown out the preacher's words. He had attended a couple of funerals as a boy, starting with his Grandda's. His distractions then were thumbing through the Bible to look for profanities like *hell* or *damn,* or teasing a ponytail in front of him or tormenting a spider in the corner of the church pew. This time, however, he could find no escape.

The words from the Reverend Caldwell's mouth hung in the air:

"Ashes to ashes, dust to dust… The Father has called him back to the flock… The gates of heaven shall swing open to receive him… He has left his loved ones behind… The life ever after…"

The words cut into his belly like a knife. Why *hadn't* he taken away the ax?

He remembered the sad day they buried his Grandda. His ten-year-old brain tried to take in all in. He couldn't understand death then and he didn't understand it much better now. His own wedding vows rang in his head like yesterday: *For richer for poorer, for better for worse, through sickness and health, till death do you part.*

Till death do you part? Was that all there was? After they died, would they ever see each other again? I *will* see my Molly again, and Hannah, thought Sean. He couldn't hold back the pain any longer. A large tear dropped from his cheek to Hannah's hand.

She turned to face him and her eyes looked deeply into his. "Are you crying, Papa?"

There was no point in trying to hide it. "I'm afraid so. You don't think your father is a big sissy, do you?"

"No, your heart is just sad. It's okay, Papa."

He pulled her close and squeezed her until he thought he would crush the breath from her then quickly let go for fear of hurting her. He rested his chin in her curls once more. How could this five-year-old read his thoughts? It felt as though her soul was wiser than his as she comforted him. She is strong, like her mother, thought Sean.

"I would like the immediate family to come to the altar to pay their last respects," said the reverend.

Sean left Hannah sitting in the pew with a neighbor. He walked to the front of the church to take one last look at Drew. He stood next to Abby and held her hand. Molly held her other hand. Abby was shaking. The last three days had taken their toll. Sean lifted his eyes to see Drew for the last time. He was wearing the only suit he owned. Abby had put his glasses on his nose and his pipe in his breast pocket with a fresh tin of tobacco. His hair was reddish and he was balding in the front. His temples were nearly white like his bushy eyebrows. Sean remembered well the steely blues of the man who ordered him around and yelled at him. Now those eyes were closed, forever. Sean felt his throat tighten again.

Andrew had driven him crazy while he was alive, still Sean felt an overwhelming sadness at his passing. Perhaps it was the finality of death. Perhaps it was feeling sorry for Abby.

Suddenly, Abby became weak in the knees. Sean motioned for the preacher to close the casket. He and Molly helped Abby into a pew.

For the next few days, they all kept busy. Sean returned to the mines. Aunt Abby sorted through Andrew's belongings and separated sentimental things from those she would give away. She gave Sean Andrew's wool coat. It was sizes too big for him, but with times the way they were, he held onto it. Sean thanked her with a kiss on the cheek and hung it on a hook by the door for winter. Molly washed and returned all the neighbors' dishes without saying a word. Sean made up his mind that a week was long enough for the silence. Maybe she's waiting for me to talk to her first, he thought. We scarcely meet eyes during the day and she never speaks in bed. Is she angry with me? Tomorrow was Sunday. He decided he would leave Hannah with Abby and Molly and he would go for a little walk and a little *talk*.

The next morning, the sweet smell of coffee, baked apples and corn cakes floated up the stairs. As usual, Molly had risen early to cook breakfast and let Sean rest for another hour. After a long week of work, it was heaven to awaken to Sunday morning.

"Papa. Breakfast is ready." Hannah jumped into the bed with Sean. He tickled her ribs until she could scarcely catch her breath. He pushed her out the door long enough to pull on his pants and then raced her to the kitchen.

"Oh, it's you two. I was beginning to think wild horses were coming down the stairs," scolded Molly.

This time, Sean couldn't tell if she was teasing or really perturbed. He winked across the table at Hannah and they both displayed their best behavior. Sean put a dollop of apples on Hannah's corn cake and poured on some syrup. He reached across the table and cut up her cake. Molly seated herself at the table. Sean put two corncakes and a spoonful of apples on her plate. As he poured her syrup, she had a far away look in her eyes.

"Are you alright?" he asked.

"Yes," she said curtly.

"Can I get you some coffee?"

"No."

Her face was moist.

"You've gotten too warm working at the stove. Let me get you a glass of water."

"No, no—I'm fine—really."

Hannah and Sean shoveled down their corncakes. Molly never touched her fork.

"Do you know what these cakes need, Hannah?" Sean asked with his mouth full.

Hannah's eyes stared back at his for the answer as she chewed.

"A big fat sausage patty."

Molly shot from the table and threw open the door. Sean found her leaning over next to the oak tree with one arm firmly wrapped around it. He lightly rested his hand on her shoulder.

"Leave me be. I'll be fine," she growled. Then she clutched at her belly and vomited.

Sean panicked. It was one week to the day that Mr. Ashe dropped dead next to that very tree. What if he lost Molly too?

"My God, you're sick. Should I go and get the doctor?"

"Yes. You can get the doctor—in about seven months."

"Seven months?"

Yes, seven months. I think this one is a boy."

What? Had he heard that right? Boy? Could it be?

"Molly, how long have you known?"

"I've suspected it for over a month, but I didn't want to say anything until I was sure. I wanted to tell you last Sunday after church, but I couldn't. And it didn't seem fitting to give the news until Aunt Abby had some time of her own. I planned to tell you after church today, but well—you found me out."

"I've been so worried about you. You've scarcely said a word. I thought you were grieving your Uncle Andrew."

"I feel sorry for his passing. But to tell you the truth, I've been keeping my mouth closed for fear my breakfast would fly out. I'm miserable Sean. I've never been so ill in my life."

Sean was sorry she had suffered all alone that week, sorry she was so sick. He worried that it might not go well, again. Then his selfish side reared its ugly head. "How do you know it's a *boy*?" he asked sheepishly.

She shot him an angry glare. "You and your *son*, you are both responsible for my condition."

Her face softened and the color slowly returned to her face. "I'm not a fortune teller but I can tell you I was never so sick with Hannah or the other two that were lost. This has got to be the *son* you've been praying for," she said with a smile.

Suddenly, her eyes bulged and her face paled again. She leaned over and vomited once more. It was a joyful noise to Sean—music to his ears. Now that he knew the reason, he rubbed her back and grinned like the village idiot. His thoughts were far off. He was teaching him to throw a baseball. They sailed his little carved boats on the lake. Just as he was about to throw a fishing line into the water with his son, his dream was interrupted by Molly's sweet words.

"I can't believe you're smiling like a simpleton while I'm hurling my insides out." she complained.

This fishwife is not my Molly, thought Sean. She was really sick and tired–and pregnant. This was going to be a long one—he hoped. When her back was turned, the smile slowly returned to his face. At last—a son.

"Quick, Molly, let's go tell Abby and our little Hannah the good news."

"No, Sean, not yet. It's bad luck. It's too early. I've got to get through the first three or four months. What if I lose him, like the others? We'll have to wait until my belly swells and people start wondering about it. It'll be surer then. Promise me you won't jinx us. Keep it a secret, won't you Sean?" she pleaded with that pair of browns he couldn't resist.

Sean nearly burst at the seams. He felt like Santy Claus had just paid a visit and left presents under the tree but he wasn't allowed to open them. He wasn't sure if he could hold his tongue, but he knew she was right.

Hannah had just lost her Uncle Andrew. Losing a baby brother, too, would be too much.

He looked into Molly's imploring eyes and smiled.

"You make me the happiest man on Earth."

Molly's face glowed. Her eyes became moist. He stroked her hair with his palm.

"Of course, my sweet girl, I promise."

Chapter 4

The spring turned into one of the hottest summers anyone could remember. But in the pit, the temperature was the same year round–fifty-two degrees. For once, Sean didn't mind spending his waking hours in the mines and out of the blaze. The light was blinding as he emerged from the tunnel at five, but he wore a smile. His body was weary but his heart was glad because Molly was carrying their son. What a shame he was sworn to keep it a secret.

Everyday he wanted to brag to the fellas at work about his boy that was on the way. Every morning, he longed to whisper the news into Aunt Abby's ear, to take her mind off her grieving, if only for one happy moment. He wanted to take little Hannah on his lap and tell her about the baby brother that was coming. But no, he promised Molly and the last thing he wanted to do was bring bad luck. He'd like to think his superstition was rubbish, but he was as superstitious as they came. He was born into a long line of rainbow chasers and four leaf clover hunters. Daily, he steered clear of omens and asked for blessings from saints. A little part of him even believed in leprechauns. He was hopeless—and he knew it. Despite his promise, this news was too good to keep. He couldn't hold on much longer.

After another long week of shoveling, Sean started for home. Sometimes he caught a ride with a passerby, but that day he decided to walk. Two miles, after all, was a *short* walk to see his girls. By this time of day, the road was strewn with lumps of coal that had fallen from the trucks. The road would be clean again soon enough as the women and children gathered it in bushel baskets and feed sacks before nightfall. They toted it in wagons and wheelbarrows to burn in their stoves.

Sean was content to leave the coal camp far behind him. The houses were all the same, made from thin wooden boards that were rotted at the bottom from the snow in winter and the floods in spring. They each had a small porch on the front, the only place to get a breath of air in summer. But it wasn't fresh air. It was so thick with dust and soot that the houses had to be white-washed every year and the clothes that hung on the line looked like they had never been laundered at all. Such was the life of a coal miner and his family.

Besides mining and lumber, the only other game in Pottsville was the brewery—the oldest in the country. Used to be a man could get in line for a job there, but no more. Prohibition had put a hundred year tradition on hold and nearly ruined it. The new laws forced Mr. Yuengling to produce "near beer" which was little more than flavored water. Sean was only eleven when alcohol became illegal but folks who were used to the real stuff said there was nothing *special* about Yuengling's Special. Sales were so bad that his brother bought a herd of dairy cows and started making ice cream across the street. Ice cream instead of beer, no one could have believed it, but desperate times called for desperate measures. Everyone knew the old man still made vats of the good beer and stored it deep in the cellars, away from the watchful eyes of the Bureau. Of course he was afraid of landing in jail, so real beer was hard to come by and enjoyed only by his closest confidantes. The people of Pottsville smiled when Yuengling's ice cream trucks drove by, knowing fully some of them carried liquid refreshment as well.

The air seemed clearer and smelled sweeter with every step he took. Some of the houses in Cressona weren't much better than those in the coal camp, but at least they weren't so close together. There were big oaks and willows and fields of grass and buttercups instead of trash dumps and dirt roads. A man could raise a steer or some chickens or plant a little garden if he had a mind to. And his house, laundry and children were not covered with dust. Sean was glad for Aunt Abby's garden and something to see from his window besides more houses. Space was dear in the home they shared, but they had two bedrooms: one for Hannah and one for him and the missus. Some men who lived in the camp shared a room with five or six children, sometimes more. As his home came into view, Sean counted his blessings.

He came home to two women working in the kitchen. The church was selling cakes and bread to raise money for the widows and orphans of miners who lost their lives in the line of duty. Abby and Molly had slaved over the oven in the heat of the day. Pies and cookies cooled on the porch. Hannah sat at the table sampling a popover with blackberry jam. As he came through the door, the women looked at him as if they had seen a ghost.

"Heavens. Is it that late?" said Abby. "We've lost all track of time, Molly. I've got a canned ham we can fry up for supper. Help me take these tarts out so we can cook right here."

"We don't want to be any trouble. I can light my stove and heat a can of soup," offered Molly.

"Nonsense. This stove is already hot. You peel a couple of potatoes and I'll chop an onion. We'll make a nice hash. I think there's still some ketchup. We'll cook and eat right here, all of us. Now don't argue with your auntie. Sean, you go and get washed up. We'll have a nice supper, the four of us."

As the two women rushed around the kitchen, they both headed for the sink at same time and ran into each other. As their bellies and bosoms collided, Abby stopped in her tracks and stared at Molly.

"Dear Molly, you're putting on a little weight, aren't you? Lord knows you hardly eat a mouthful. How is it possible? Oh my goodness." Abby's mouth rounded at the corners into a smile.

Molly blushed and turned her eyes to the floor. Sean was afraid to say anything, but couldn't hold back the grin that spread across his face.

Abby put her hand over her mouth for a moment. When she took her hand away, she was beaming. "Well now, how far along are we? And how long were you going to try to hide it from your auntie?"

At long last, the cat was out of the bag.

"I would have told you sooner, but I was showing respect for you and Uncle and I didn't want to bring bad luck by telling too soon," Molly explained.

"Telling what? Telling what?" asked Hannah.

"Please, Molly. Can I tell her? May I do the honors?" Sean begged.

"You've suffered with the secret long enough. Tell her, Papa."

"What secret?" Hannah asked with her eyes twinkling.

Sean sat his lunch bucket on the kitchen table and got down on one knee in front of Hannah like he was proposing marriage to her. He gazed into her big, green, pleading eyes. "Your lovely mother is with child. You're going to have a baby brother," he said softly.

"Or sister," added Molly.

Sean never took his eyes from Hannah's. "Oh, don't worry. It'll be a brother, lamb chop. I've put in a special order."

For a moment, her eyes searched his. Then a smile spread across her face and her eyes glistened. She wrapped both arms around her father and squeezed him tightly. "Oh, thank you, Papa," she squealed.

"Hey, what about me?" whined Molly. "I'm the one filling this order."

Hannah rushed to Molly's side and hugged her around the waist. "Oh, Mommy, you're such a good girl. How did you know we needed a brother?"

"Your father has mentioned it once or *twice.*"

Abby surveyed Molly up and down, and then pulled her arms away from her sides. She inspected her belly once more. "Why, I can't believe I didn't see you were blossoming."

"You've had a lot to on your mind lately."

Abby rubbed her hand lovingly over Molly's abdomen. "You must be at least four months along. You've got a little melon growing in there."

Suddenly, Abby turned on her heel. "Sean, how the devil have you kept your mouth shut this long? You never could keep a secret."

"It nearly killed me."

Abby gave a low chuckle. She stood for another minute holding Molly's hands outstretched in front of her, gazing at her belly, smiling and thinking.

"A new baby in the house—sent by the angels from heaven," she said softly in her own little world. Then she came out of her trance.

"Alright then. Times a wasting. My babies are starving—*both* of them. Sean, get cleaned up for supper. Hannah, set the plates around the table."

Molly reached around to pull a large cast iron frying pan from the wall.

"Hold it right there, missy. There'll be no more of that. You've been on your feet all day. Put your bottom in that chair and I'll bring you the toast to butter. I'll man the skillet. And I want you to clean your plate tonight for a change. You're eating for two you know."

Sean looked around the room at these three, his little family. The dark cloud of mourning had finally lifted. Abby was glad to have something to be look forward to, a new little soul to meet and love. Sean leaned in the doorway drinking it all in, like Christmas morning, when Abby came after him. "Well don't just stand there like a boob, boy. Shuck off those filthy clothes and hurry back. We're having a baby. I mean we're having supper. I mean you know what I mean. Get going."

Molly smiled at Sean through tired eyes. The past few weeks had been hard on her. But the secret was out and hopefully the worst was over.

As the next few days passed, something changed. The invisible line that had divided their house while Andrew was alive vanished. Abby's things were on the O'Connell's side and vice versa. They never ate in their separate kitchens. Abby and Molly cooked together and they all ate in Abby's big kitchen. They had never been closer. The four of them shared food, wood, tools, whatever they had. They looked after each other. The women looked after the house and Hannah and the little one on the way while Sean worked at the mine. And even though Sean still gave Abby cash every payday, it didn't seem like rent. Sean felt it was his contribution to the cause.

Still, Sean worried. Molly was exhausted. Was it the baby or the heat? Was she sick? He wanted so badly for her to carry this child through the whole way. He wondered if there was something that could make her feel better, to give her back her roses. Was there something she could do to stay healthy while she was in her motherly way? When Molly went to bed, he slipped down to the kitchen for a glass of milk. Abby joined him at the table with her cup of tea. He was embarrassed to ask her about women and babies, but more afraid not to.

"Abby, does Molly look all right to you? I mean, is it the baby or should I take her to the doctor in town?"

"Molly is fine. She's just weary. A baby sucks the marrow from the bones. Ginger snaps and water crackers got her through the first part. She needs meat and greens to get her through the rest. Iron to get her blood up, that's the ticket. She gets some extra rest everyday, a little nap in the afternoon with Hannah, for the baby growing inside her. I've seen to that."

"I can't tell you how grateful we both are for all your help, Abby. We couldn't get along as well as we do without you."

Abby leaned forward, rested her hand on Sean's shoulder. "You're a good boy, Seany. And I love all three of you like you were my own. I should be thanking you, for giving this old bag of bones a reason to get up in the morning," she said with moist eyes.

Sean smiled back at her and then stared into his glass. There was a long silence between them. Finally, Sean mustered enough courage to ask her. "Abby, it's no secret we both want this child to make it. I felt so helpless when she lost the last two. I feel helpless now. Isn't there something more I can do to make sure she's alright? To make sure she doesn't lose this one too?"

Abby chuckled and patted the top of Sean's hand. "Oh, poor lad. I know how badly you want a son. But there are no sure things in this life. But I'll tell you what I know. You've got to try to keep Molly calm. No big highs or lows. Don't let her lift anything heavier than a water pitcher. As much as she likes to, don't let her carry Hannah. She's not the baby for long, so she may as well get used to it. And there is—well—one other thing."

There was another long pause.

"Well, what is it, Abby?"

"Well, it's not something *you and I* should talk about"

"Why not? You don't want her to lose him do you? What is it? I'll do anything."

Abby sat tapping the side of her cup with her fingernails. "How shall I put it? When the cow is bred, the bull is moved to another pasture" she said peering back at Sean over her glasses.

His jaw slowly dropped. He didn't blink. Abby continued to stare back at him. What the hell did she just say? "I'm sorry. Maybe I'm just stupid. I don't get it."

"Alright then. When you go upstairs at night, lay next to Molly with your arm wrapped around her waist, give her a peck on the cheek and say goodnight," she said confidently.

"I already do that."

"Oh, for the love of St. Peter. Are you going to make me say it? Dammit, boy. Stay off her. Keep your breeches buttoned. Do you hear me now?"

The blood rushed to his face. "Loud and clear," he answered softly.

Abby dropped her cup in the sink and twisted his ear from behind.

"Ow."

"That's so you don't forget," she said sternly. She kissed him on top of the head. "Goodnight." Abby walked to her bedroom chuckling and shaking her head. As the pain subsided from his ear, warmness spread over him. She is like a mother to *me* too, he thought.

He climbed up the stairs and slid into bed. He looked over at Molly as she slept, but he was far from it. It troubled him that they were still living in Abby's house. He promised Molly a house of her own when they were married, but was never able to scrape together enough money together to build one. Abby was generous and made them feel at home, but didn't Molly deserve a place of her own? Didn't their children deserve to play in their own yard? It would be difficult to try to move before the baby came. And anyway, Molly would need help, especially in the beginning, from her aunt. Still, some of his joy was fading. He wondered if Molly thought he was a failure. Living with her family was supposed to be temporary. It had been over six years. Maybe he *was* a failure.

He closed his eyes and tried to sleep, but his thoughts drifted to his grandfather. Grandda Joseph came to America as a boy, along with hundreds of other Irish. His forefathers were all fighters, but not in wars with names. They fought the government, the landlords and the Catholics. They even fought back the potato famine by surviving on fish and clams. But after countless decades of working the land, great-grandda knew no one in his family would ever be able to own it. He believed a man without land was nothing. He was tired of fighting in Ireland and decided to try fighting on the other side of the Atlantic. So he sold what he had and bought passage to the New World for the whole family including young Joseph.

They landed at Ellis Island and soon made their way to the mines of Eastern Pennsylvania in search of work. At the age of ten, Grandda Joseph went to work too, crawling into the tiniest holes for lumps of coal to fill their stove. Soon, he became a breaker boy and sorted the shale from the coal. As the years passed, he worked his way up the ranks from a laborer to become a miner. Somehow, he managed to feed a wife and six children. He survived the back breaking work, the fires, the cave-ins and the explosions. His family lived in a house owned by the coal company and he gave back most of his pay as rent. He worked everyday of his life, but never owned land. It was the black lung that got him in the end, at the ripe *old* age of fifty-two.

Grandda sent Sean's father to Pittsburgh to work in the steel mill when he was sixteen. The work was hard, but at least he wouldn't have to work on his knees ten hours a day and die with a chest full of dust. Sean's father's house wasn't owned by the steel mill, but he never owned land either. He could never save enough for a lot. His vice was the drink.

Da worked the steel over twenty years and he always thought Sean would join him. But Sean had other plans for his future. When he was a lad, Grandda took him on his knee and told him stories about the ocean. He told Sean how the green waves moved to and fro, and rocked him to sleep like a lullaby. His family lived on the shore and farmed and fished. Grandda passed on the sailors' tales of sea monsters and mermaids and told how men had made their fortunes and lost them all to pirates or storms. He remembered, as a boy, searching for seashells and gathering mussels for supper. As he grew, he helped his father on the boats. He loved the sea and remembered his fishing trips well. But his most memorable boat ride was to America. Grandda Joseph dreamed of land by the sea. He wanted a place where he could watch the ships, feel the sea spray and listen to the gulls on America's shore. It would be his gift to future generations. Sadly, after his voyage from the Emerald Isle, he never saw the sea again. His dream had become Sean's and Sean was determined to make it come true.

Sean was eighteen when his father died. His parents had been fighting over the money or lack of it. His mother complained that Sean's father drank it all away.

To remedy the situation, Sean's father went to the pub to drink some more. His body was found frozen, stiff as a board, a half mile from their house. Sean's mother barely grieved. The love had been lost long before. She was more bitter than sad from the way her husband had left her, penniless. In order to survive, she soon married another. Her new husband liked her, but he didn't like Sean. That's when he packed his bags and hitch-hiked east, bound for the Atlantic. He was headed for New York to see the port where his Grandda had landed when he was a boy. He longed to see the Statue of Liberty, the Empire State building and Coney Island. Then he would drift south to see the bathing beauties and the boardwalk in Atlantic City then continue down along the coast. He hoped to find work in a boatyard or a dock. That way he could buy a piece of land near the shore and watch the ships come in. Maybe he could even fish and gather clams, like Grandda. He was going to be the first O'Connell to own land in the *New World*. And he had it all worked out—all worked out.

Then, sabotage. Molly's brown eyes found him and a year later, along came little Hannah. He adored Molly from the start. Thinking about their first meeting—and their first fight, he drifted off to sleep with a smile.

The next night there was a torrential downpour. Thunder shook the house and the roof over the parlor leaked. A roasting pan caught the drip in the night. The next evening found Sean on the roof with a handful of shingles and a bucket of tar. He looked over his shoulder into the yard. He imagined Andrew standing on the ground yelling orders up at him. *Get some tar on that brush, boy. Space those shingles a little farther apart. Do you think I'm rich as Rockefeller?*

The thought of his voice made Sean cringe. He breathed a sigh of relief knowing Andrew was no longer there to torment him. Then a chill raced up his spine. *He is no longer here to torment me,* he thought. That meant *he* was the man of the house. All at once Sean realized he was solely responsible for these three women—and a baby on the way. What an order. They say the Lord never gives a man a job he can't handle. Sean wasn't so sure.

He summoned his courage and straightened his back. Diligently, he painted the tar onto the shingles. He had to find faith in himself. He and Andrew had mended, tended, fixed and patched every inch of that place several times over. Sean knew it like the back of his hand. They had braved heat, drought, hail storms and Pennsylvania blizzards. Sean was suddenly aware of everything Andrew had taught him and he was grateful. A strange feeling came over him. He missed Andrew. A pang of fear hit the pit of his stomach. He closed his eyes and mumbled a short prayer. He dipped his brush into the tar bucket once more. The Lord is with me, he said to himself. There is nothing we can't handle together—I hope.

Chapter 5

The next few months flew past. Abby buzzed around the house and garden humming to herself. She knitted booties and a sweater for the baby on the way. She sewed together scraps of fabric to make a little quilt for him. She whistled while she painted Hannah's old crib pale blue. Molly got her roses back and the sparkle in her eye. She picked flowers and vegetables with Abby and pickled cucumbers and peppers for winter. Sean and Molly took short walks after supper in the cool of the evening, held hands and dreamed of a house of their own. One Sunday, after church, Molly was too tired for a walk and went upstairs for a nap. Hannah and Sean sneaked down to the lake in the early afternoon. They found night crawlers under the rocks along the path and put them on their hooks in hopes of catching bass for supper. They never caught more than a few blue gills, too small to keep, but they loved their hours together. They gathered snail shells, tasted the nectar from honeysuckle and skipped smooth stones across the top of the water. After a while, they rested on a blanket in the shade of an ancient oak and had a *serious* talk.

"Papa, can we have a kitty? Mama's friend at church says I can have one, for free."

"Baby girl, it's all Mama and I can do to take care of you. And anyway, you have a baby brother on the way. Won't a brother be more fun than a cat?"

"I s'pose," she replied with a great sigh.

Sean was surprised she gave up so easily.

"Do you think Santa will bring me a kitty?"

"Great day in the mornin,' child. It's the middle of summer and you are already working Santa Claus. When does he ever get a rest?"

"I'm just thinking," she answered softly.

"Just thinking? Did you ever think that Santa's bag is so full that the kitty might get hurt under all those toys? And did you think the kitty might freeze to death flying on the back of Santa's sleigh all the way from the North Pole?"

Hannah got a sad, faraway look in her eyes. Perhaps Sean had gone too far.

"I guess it will be fun having a brother."

She paused for a moment deep in thought. "Mama will be real busy, huh?" Her eyes became watery and her bottom lip hung low in a small pout. The green monster was well on its way.

"Yep. Mama will be real busy, in the beginning. Babies are a lot of work. But she won't stop loving you and neither will I. You will always be our curly girl. You're getting big now, big enough to be mother's helper. Your mama *needs* you."

Hannah's face beamed. She began to buy into this baby business. After a moment, she spoke again. "Papa, do you believe in heaven?"

"What a big question for a little girl. What's got you thinking about heaven?"

"I'm thinking about Uncle Andy. Is he in heaven?"

Now there's a question. Sean had wondered about *that* himself. If *he's* there, then we've all got a shot at it, he thought. "Certainly. He's got a halo and wings and plays a harp. He's probably leading the angelic choir right now," he said with a hint of sarcasm.

"Will *we* go to heaven when we die?"

Sean's throat tightened. He had invested some time thinking about death lately too. He buried his grandfather and his father. Then he watched Andrew die in his arms. He worried about Molly and the baby. He wondered what life would be like without her, or Hannah. What would life be without Abby? She had helped them so much. Whenever there was an accident at the mines, he wondered what kind of life his girls would have without him. He had his doubts about heaven, but wanted to believe. He wanted Hannah to believe too.

"Yes. When we die, we all go to heaven, to live with God and the angels forever and ever," he said sincerely.

He pulled Hannah close to him and hugged her. He rocked her back and forth and drank her in. After a moment, his eyes drifted upward to the skies. "Oh, lamb chop. What a glorious lazy day. What I wouldn't give to have more days like this."

"Why can't we come to the lake everyday?"

"Because I have to go to work, to make money to take care of us."

Hannah hung her head.

"And Mama works real hard too, cooking and cleaning and taking care of us while I'm at work."

"Why do you have to work *so much?*"

"Because it's a hard life, little one. There's always a bill to pay or breakfast to cook or wood to split. It's a tough job to keep up with it all. You've got to work hard to have the best living."

49

She sat up, lifted her head and joined him in looking deep into the endless blue. "But Papa, it seems like sometimes the *best* living is when you do nothing at all."

Sean reached over, pulled her close and rocked her some more, rolling over in his head her words too wise for a child. He had nearly rocked himself to sleep when suddenly, Hannah broke free from his arms and jumped to her feet. "C'mon, Papa. The sun is going down. I gotta go help Mama make supper."

How did this tiny moppet make his heart swell like she did?

The summer cooled down into fall. Sean made a jack-o-lantern for Hannah and carved a kitten's face complete with skinny long whiskers and pointed ears. Her eyes twinkled when he made it glow with a candle on Halloween night. Come Thanksgiving, Abby cooked a dinner to boast about. She had a good year with her garden and graced their table with green beans, sweet yams, a golden turkey, homemade rolls, and her creamy pumpkin pie. When she said grace, a tear rolled down her cheek. They were all grateful for their blessings, but it was, after all, her first Thanksgiving without Andrew in over forty years. Sean squeezed Hannah and Molly's hands under the table. He was thankful for his little family.

After dinner, Molly and Sean chased Abby out of the kitchen. It was their turn. They cleared the table, washed the dishes and put Hannah to bed. Before long, Molly and Sean climbed into bed too. Their bellies were full and they were exhausted. Their bedroom was chilly compared to the kitchen and still smelled of roast turkey. Sean pulled Molly close to him in bed and spooned his body up behind hers. Her flannel nightgown was soft and he buried his nose in her hair. It smelled of the hot rolls and pies she had baked that morning. He rested his arm on her shoulder and then let his hand drift down to her belly. He let it rest there a moment hoping he would feel the child move inside her. Suddenly he felt a chill and quivered.

"Are you still cold?" asked Molly.

"Nope, warm as toast. I'm excited about the baby. It sort of hit me all at once."

She turned her head and gave him a peck on the cheek. He brushed away her hair and kissed her neck. She squirmed and turned away from him.

"Now you're giving me chills," she whispered.

Sean remembered Abby's words and put his cheek against Molly's. He pulled her closer. He gave her a gentle squeeze under her bosom and whispered in her ear, "Goodnight, love."

"Goodnight."

He held her until he felt her breathing change when she drifted off. What a wonderful day it had been and how glad he was to have this woman in his life. Somehow, with a word or a smile, she comforted him. When he looked into her eyes, he knew they belonged together. When they made love, they were the only two people on Earth. And when she lay next to him, soft and warm, she completed him. He wanted for nothing when they were together.

By the end of December, Molly's belly had gotten so big, she couldn't get close enough to the tree to hang the decorations. Molly read Hannah "'Twas the Night

Before Christmas," and sent her to bed to dream of eight tiny reindeer. She filled her stocking with an apple, an orange, some peanuts and an all day lollipop and collapsed on the sofa. Santa did not forget the wish Hannah made at the lake. Sean bought a toy kitten, black with white feet. He wrapped it in brown paper and tied it with a red ribbon and laid it under the tree. Then he reached into his pocket and pulled out a box of chocolate covered peanuts and put them in the stocking as well. Molly shook her head at him as he joined her on the sofa. Soon, Abby crept from her bedroom. She had made a blanket and dress for Hannah's doll. They were wrapped in Sunday's funny papers. She laid them under the tree next to the toy kitten and struggled to fit some taffy, a candy bar and some bubble gum into the stocking. "Between the three of us, Hannah won't have any teeth left," complained Molly. "Oh, you're only young once. And besides, she'll get another set. Goodnight, lovebirds," said Abby as she headed off for bed. Molly rested her head on Sean's shoulder. They gazed at the tinsel on their tree that glistened by the candlelight. The house was still. Sean let his hand drift down to her belly to feel the baby kick. Molly broke the silence.

"Sean, have you thought of a name for the baby?"

"I thought we were going to name him, Joseph, after Grandda?"

"That's fine, but what if it's a girl?"

"A girl? I thought we had all decided it was a boy. Abby painted the crib blue, after all. Besides, we have a girl. This one's a boy."

Molly stared back at him with a cynical look.

"What would you name her?" he asked.

"Well, I thought about Sarah or Josephine."

"Josephine? Then we can't name our boy Joseph."

"I know, but I was just trying to get your Grandda in there in case there *wasn't* another."

There was an awkward silence.

"Dear Molly, you can name her whatever you like, but can we save Joseph for a boy? I can always hope, can't I?"

She smiled and nodded. After another moment of silence, she started again. "Can we make her middle name, Abigail?"

Sean smiled. "I would love nothing better and I think your auntie would be in seventh heaven."

She squeezed his arm and let her head rest on his shoulder again. "Do you think we will always live in this town? I mean, do you think we will ever make it to the sea? Don't get me wrong. I know you are breaking your back at the mine. You must know I appreciate it. But every time I see a Black Maria drive by, my heart sinks. And if they don't bring your body home to me in a hearse, you are sure to get the black lung, like your Grandda."

For a moment, they were quiet, each deep in their own thoughts.

"I have always felt guilty, for ruining your plans to build boats. If it weren't for me, you would be on the water right now, doing what you dreamed of, instead of stuck in this poor little coal town."

Sean pulled her close and rubbed her shoulder. "That's right. You ruined my life. I have a job, a home, a woman who cooks for me and keeps me warm at night, a beautiful little girl who is the spitting image of her mother and a son on the way. My life is horrible. I don't know how it could get much worse. And it's all your fault."

Molly wrapped her arms around him. She began to cry and laugh at the same time. She knew he was right but she needed to hear it from him. The combination of exhaustion, Christmas and being in the motherly way made her giddy. She was sentimental and silly and Sean took full advantage of her condition and chuckled.

"Stop laughing at me," she whined like a little girl as she rubbed her face into his shirt. Sean tried to act like everything was fine, to convince her it was. But inside, he still worried what would happen to his little family if something happened to him. They heard about mining accidents everyday. Fires, floods from ground water, poisonous gasses and cave-ins maimed and took lives everyday. Last year, one of the men from his crew, got caught between two coal cars. The mule just gave out and let his load slide backwards. Schramm never saw it coming. The cart pinned him against another and crushed his ribs like matchsticks. The mule driver nearly whipped the animal to death to get him to pull the load off, but it was too late. Every woman on the street cringed when they saw the hearse and prayed it would keep driving past them. When it stopped at his widow's door, she collapsed. The men had to carry Schramm's body and his wife into the house. He left her with seven children. She had no money to pay rent to the mining company, so she, the children and their belongings were thrown into the street the next week. He gave fifteen years and his life to the mine. What thanks did he get? She took her brood east to stay with her mother. Who knew how they were making it? There wasn't much good in dwelling on it. There was nothing else Sean could do. Times were terrible. Some people lost everything when the banks failed and jobs were scarce. They were lucky to have a house that wasn't owned by the mines. The garden helped to feed them, but they couldn't make it without Sean's job at the mine. That's all there was to it.

"When you've had the baby and he is strong enough, let's talk to Abby about moving East. She has family in Baltimore. Now that Andrew is gone, maybe she'll come with us. The economy has got to turn around sometime. Maybe I can find a job building boats and we can live on fish for a while. Maybe we can get our own house with a yard for the children."

Sean saw the endearing brown eyes he loved looking back at his. This is what she wanted to hear.

"I like everything except the fish part. Can we have a chicken once in a while?" She was partly serious and partly teasing and was wearing Hannah's silly grin.

Sean made a promise he knew might be difficult to keep. It was nearly impossible to get a chicken lately or a turkey for that matter.

"Yes, sugar breeches. We'll have a chicken in the pot every Sunday."

It is so warm and wonderful to sit next to her and dream, thought Sean. His eyes wandered to the top of the tree. Perched on the highest branch was a little angel Abby and Hannah had made. The halo was made from a pipe cleaner and it had wings of tin and a dress of white tissue paper. It was holding a tiny hymnal made from a match book and had brown hair and green eyes, like their little angel. Sean and Molly fell asleep on the couch in each others arms that night. It was the best Christmas they could remember together—and the best slumber.

Chapter 6

January was fierce. The sky broke open and a terrible wind blew through the town. When the wind stopped, it began to snow. It was still flying the day Molly bent down to stir the embers in the stove and her water broke. It was five in the morning and Sean was getting dressed for another day in the pit.

As he came down the stairs, Abby stopped him dead in his tracks. "Hold it right there, buster. Just where do you think you're going?"

"To work, where do you think?"

"Like hell you are. We're going to have a baby today."

Sean's heart filled with joy and terror at the same time. He was fearful something would go wrong, like with the other two. But she was so far along this time. She had gone the whole nine months. They had done everything right. No, he wouldn't let himself worry. They were going to have a big fat boy and name him Joseph, after Grandda and….

"Christ Almighty, don't just stand there. Help me get her to the bed. Put a kettle of water on the stove. We'll need hot water and clean linens. Find me a string to tie the cord off," Abby ordered.

"Tie the cord off? Abby, you make it sound like *you're* delivering this baby. What about the doctor?"

"What about him? Have you spied outdoors, lad? We got another foot last night. We'll be lucky to get him here in time for the christening. Now do what I tell you, then you can see about the doctor."

They helped Molly into Abby's bed just off the kitchen. By the time they got her settled, she got her first labor pain. She squeezed Sean's hand until his fingers turned blue. He hated to see her like this and wished he could bear the pain for her. When it was over, her face was pink and moist. She smiled at him with tired eyes. It was going to be a long day, but a *good* day. Sean bent down and kissed her cheek, then her lips. Abby walked in with some sheets and caught them in a smooch.

"All right you two. It's that kind of nonsense that got her into this condition in the first place. Sean, I stoked the stove and filled the kettle, no thanks to you. I'll take over here. Now you can go and get that doctor."

Sean smiled once more at Molly. She squeezed his hand gently. "Go and do as Abby says. *We'll* be fine until you get back."

Molly put on a good face, but she was as nervous as Sean. When he turned to go, the curly girl was standing before him. "What's Aunt Abby yelling about?" she asked rubbing the sleep from her eyes.

"Today's the day we get a brother, lamb chop."

"When can I see him?"

"Probably not until after dinnertime, but we've got to have breakfast first. To the kitchen with you. I'll make you some toast and jam. Auntie is very busy."

Abby followed them into the kitchen to check the kettle. She took the loaf of bread from Sean's hands. "Are you still here? What about that *doctor?*"

She reached for the knife with one hand and pulled down a plate with the other. Abby was in full throttle. She scooted Hannah to the table to wait for her breakfast.

"Well?" she barked at Sean.

"I'm on my way, chief."

Sean grabbed his coat from the hook. Then he backed up two steps and leaned backward to peek through the bedroom door. He gave Molly a big smile from across the room. She smiled back and he was off.

He headed to the general store but it wasn't open yet. Mr. Flynn was shoveling snow off the porch. Abby was right. They had gotten nearly another foot overnight.

"Great day in the morning, a little one on the way, you say. Let me see if I can get Doc Patterson on the phone," said Flynn. Sean stood and read the labels on the canned goods on the shelves as he waited for the storekeeper's return. He hoped Molly was alright. He hoped the baby was alright. Right now, most of all, he hoped he could find the doctor.

"Doc is at Bill Reynolds' place. His mother caught the pneumonia and he's looking in on her. Mrs. Patterson says he stayed out there last night on account of the weather. No point in trying to call Reynolds. He hasn't got a phone. You'll have to get word to him another way," said Flynn.

Sean thanked him and trudged through the snow towards Mr. Reynolds' farm. After half an hour, Mr. Casey came by with a horse and sled, loaded with firewood. He was headed that direction and said he would get the word out to Doc that he was needed for delivering a baby. Sean made his way back home. By the time he got there, he was starving and his feet were frozen up to his knees.

Abby was frazzled. "Any luck, boy?"

"Doc's out at the Reynolds place. I got word out there by Mr. Casey."

"The son of a bitch. Men are never around when you need them," she rattled.

Sean checked on Molly. She was already exhausted and had fallen asleep between contractions. Sean crept back into the living room to keep Hannah company. She was sitting on the sofa wrapped in a blanket. She had put her doll to bed in the chair and her arm was wrapped around her toy cat, Boots.

They sat on the couch together for the next few hours and watched Abby race frantically in and out of the bedroom. They listened carefully for a knock at the door. Just before dark, Abby shouted at the top of her lungs, "He's here, he's here."

Sean jumped up and peered out the kitchen curtains hoping to see the headlights on Doc's sedan.

Abby caught him by the arm. "No, not the doctor, you knucklehead. Your son. Hannah, you keep a watch for that doctor."

Molly was lying in Abby's bed soaked in sweat. Her hair was plastered against her forehead. Sean looked for the baby, but didn't see him.

"Where is he?"

"God almighty. Lift her back and heave her forward. We've got to push him out yet. He'll be out in three shoves," cried Abby.

"Shouldn't we wait for doctor?"

"This baby ain't waiting for no doctor."

"Here it comes again," moaned Molly. Her legs trembled like jelly.

"Close your mouth and push, lassie. Sean, help her."

Sean had never seen a baby brought into the world. Every couple of minutes, Molly got a wave of pain and pushed their child down a little further. It was terrifying and thrilling at once. Sean was nervous and he hadn't eaten all day. He grew weak in the knees and felt perspiration bead on his forehead, but he never let go of her hand.

"Papa, papa, somebody's knocking on the door."

"Blessed Jesus. Let him in, angel, let him in," cried Abby.

A cold gust of fresh air poured in from the kitchen door. Molly leaned forward to feel it on her face. Doc shed his coat, hat and gloves as he came in. "What have we got here? I almost missed the best part," he said smiling.

Abby was not amused. "Well, you missed the last twelve hours. I'd say *that* was the best part. Where the devil have you been?"

"Now Abigail, I got here as fast as I could. The weather is dreadful out there, and it looks like you've done a fine job."

Another pain grabbed Molly. "This is it," she groaned.

The doctor pressed her knees to her chest and Molly pushed until her face was beet red. Two more pushes and they could see the top of the baby's head. Doc struggled for a moment and then put a hand on each side of the head and gave it a gentle pull. The first shoulder popped out followed by the second and then the rest of the baby tumbled out behind them. Abby and Sean stood on their toes and looked over the doctor's shoulder to spy between the baby's legs. Both their faces lit up. It was a boy, a big fat boy. Doc rubbed him and dried him with a clean sheet. Sean kissed Molly on her wet forehead. The doctor quickly tied off the cord and cut it through with a knife.

"You did it, my sweet girl," said Sean.

Molly beamed. Her labor was finally over and they got the son they prayed for. Abby pulled a little bassinet over to the doctor.

"Not yet," he grunted. The doctor dried the child's face and pressed his lips to the baby's. Then it hit Sean like a brick between the eyes. He never heard the baby cry. "What is it, Doc? Is he all right?"

"Why isn't he breathing? Do something!" cried Abby.

Doc paid them no mind. He worked frantically. He forced air into the child's mouth with his own and slapped the child on the bottom. The baby never moved or made a sound.

"You've got to save him," pleaded Sean.

The doctor rubbed the child with a towel and forced more air into his mouth with his own. Finally, he laid his stethoscope on the child's chest. They all stood perfectly still, watching for the child's chest to rise and fall on its own and for reassurance from the doctor's face. The doctor took back his stethoscope without looking up. By then, the baby was blue and his arms and legs were as limp as the one's on Hannah's rag doll. The doctor looked into Sean's eyes and shook his head. Sean stared at the baby, gray and cold. Reality crept in. He had never felt so much sorrow in his life. Not even the passing of his grandfather cut so deeply. He heard soft sobbing from behind him. Molly. Poor Molly. Abby wrapped her arms around her shoulders. Sean leaned over and pressed his cheek against hers. The entire bed shook as she wept. She let out a loud moan of loss, of pain. Sean, too, felt the pain that pierced her heart like a knife.

"I'm sorry, Molly. The cord was wrapped around his neck–twice. He probably died during the birthing. There was nothing anyone could do. It was the Lord's will."

"Lord's will? Lord's *will*? What Lord? What God would let this happen to us?" bellowed Sean.

"Think about what you're saying," said Abby sternly.

The door cracked open slowly. "Can I see the baby?" asked a small voice.

Sean had forgotten all about Hannah. How was he going to tell her?

Abby quickly got between the door and Hannah. "He's not ready yet. Come to the kitchen and I'll make you some soup. You must be starving."

"I know this is hard," said Doc. "You are both disappointed and you have every right to be. But if he had lived, he would have been slow or crippled from the lack of oxygen to his brain. In a way, it's a blessing."

"A blessing? You think this is a blessing? Look at her," said Sean pointing at Molly. "Does she look like she feels *blessed* to you?"

The doctor looked down into his arms at the gray infant wrapped in his blanket. He lifted the baby to Molly's side. "Do you want to hold him, Molly?"

Molly didn't answer at first. Sean's sadness had turned to anger, then nausea. He couldn't bear to watch.

"It's easier to bear if you hold him first, then let him go."

She accepted his lifeless body from the doctor and held it next to her bosom. Tears poured from her eyes as she rocked him back and forth and hummed a lullaby. She mumbled a few sweet words, "Your mama is here, darling."

Suddenly, she stopped rocking. The bed shook with tears of grief. She looked into her son's face one last time and kissed his cheek. Then, she held out the baby to Sean. He didn't think he could do it, but her eyes wouldn't take no. He reached out and took him from her.

Sean held his son, outstretched from his body, gray and cold. Then he held him closer and kissed his forehead. When he looked at his face, he could see his father and his grandfather—and *himself.* He closed his eyes and said a silent prayer over the child. "Please God, we need a miracle. Let him breathe. Let him open his eyes and look at me. Let me feel his body move in my arms. Take me. Take me instead. Let my baby live."

Sean opened his eyes. The child lay still in his arms. It was too much. He handed the baby back to the doctor and wept. His tears turned from sorrow to anger. He was angry with himself for not being stronger. Men weren't *supposed* to cry.

"What shall I tell my little girl?" he asked the doctor softly.

"Tell her that her brother is in heaven."

Sean squeezed Molly's hand. "I'll go and tell her."

Molly nodded. As he let go of her hand, his foot slipped out from under him. He and the doctor looked at each other with surprise. Their eyes dropped to the floor. It was covered in blood. The doctor lifted the sheets and looked down at Molly's thighs. She was lying in a crimson pool.

"Good God," said the doctor as he slid his hand inside her. Molly moaned under the pain and pressure. His hand scooped out large, bright red clots of blood.

"The afterbirth is completely out. I'm afraid she's torn."

Sean froze. "What the hell are you talking about?"

"Her womb is torn, son. She's bleeding to death."

Doc had been calm until now. He had no doubt delivered dead babies before. But now he was scared. "Quick. Let's get her out of this puddle. Get me another sheet."

The men changed the bed under Molly. The color drained from her face. She closed her eyes.

Abby cracked the bedroom door and poked her head in. "What's going on?"

"Molly's bleeding. We have got to try to stop it with pressure."

Abby shut the door tightly and tended to Hannah.

Doc put a pillow under Molly's bottom and another one over her belly. He put both hands over the pillow and leaned with all of his weight. He forced as much pressure as he could onto her womb. Molly let out a feeble moan of pain. After a moment, he checked again between her thighs. There were more large clots on the sheets. He leaned over her and applied more pressure. This time when he checked, there was less blood. Molly was a ghost and took shallow breaths.

Sean leaned over her and whispered in her ear. "Stay with me, sweet girl. We've already sent one to heaven this day. Stay with me. Stay with me and lamb chop. We need you. Be strong. We'll get through this."

She reached for his hand. She opened her eyes just for a second. "Tell Hannah I love her."

"Yes, love."

"Kiss me goodbye, Sean."

No, I won't do it, thought Sean. Not Molly too. This is all a bad dream. He bent down and gently kissed her icy lips. The last bit of color left her face. A cold chill raced up his spine. The doctor lifted the sheet once more. The bleeding had stopped. He leaned over her and pressed his stethoscope to her chest. Frustrated, he lifted Molly by her shoulders and shook her. "Molly, Molly. Can you hear me? Wake up. Open your eyes, Molly!" He put his ear on her chest and listened for a breath or a heart beat. After a moment, the color left his face. He lifted his head and with fearful eyes, looked to Sean.

"No. No. No. Come back, Molly, come back to me. Doc, you've got to do something. Get her to the hospital—do something!"

"It's too late. There's nothing anyone can do. I'm sorry, Sean."

Abby let herself in and closed the door tightly behind her so Hannah wouldn't see. Sean's eyes met hers. She held the corner of her apron up to her mouth to stifle her sobs. Tears streamed down her cheeks under her glasses. Her eyes never left Molly's face. She walked over and rubbed the back of her hand over Molly's cheek. Her body heaved with the ache of loss. This had been a long day, a day that was supposed to end in joy, not sorrow. She struggled to quiet her own weeping so as not to disturb Hannah eating her soup. Sean was numb. He didn't know anymore what he was supposed to feel and so felt nothing. He stood patiently, hoping to awaken from his nightmare. He stared into Molly's face, without blinking, waiting for her to take a breath, to open her eyes, to smile at him. But the longer he waited, the angrier he got. Slowly, the adrenaline moved up his spine, to his chest and neck. He must blame someone for this loss. What the hell good was this doctor? He let his baby die, then his wife, the only woman he'd ever loved. Sean's knuckles whitened in anticipation of taking a swing at the no good physician.

Abby watched his body tense and his fists clench. She took him by his right arm. "That'll be enough, Sean," she said wrapping her hand around his. "Molly's gone. We can't bring her back. We've got to say our goodbyes."

They held hands at Molly's bedside, talking in hushed tones to spare Hannah for as long as they could. After a few moments, Abby said, "Go to the kitchen. You've still got Hannah. Hold your *other* baby. You have got to think about her now."

The doctor let himself into the kitchen and washed the blood from his hands at the sink. As he put on his coat and hat to leave, Sean couldn't bear to look at him.

"I know you are angry, Sean. You have every right to be. I hope someday you'll forgive me for not being able to do more. I'll have to try to forgive myself as well." Sean lifted his eyes to see his, but couldn't speak.

Abby showed the doctor out into the frozen night. Sean sat next to Hannah at the kitchen table. She was pretending to feed Boots with her spoon. She spoke to him in her usual chirp.

"Can I see him, Papa? Can I see my baby brother now?"

Sean was still. His lips were silent. Moments ago, he wondered how he would tell Hannah her baby brother had died. It seemed like nothing compared to the task of telling Hannah her mother had died giving birth to him. A few hours before, Sean was the happiest man in the world. Now, he wondered how he should kill himself. No man can *live* with this much pain, he thought.

"What color are his eyes, Papa? Are they green or blue or brown?" Hannah chattered. "Where is he? Is he with Mama?" Sean's body shook with grief. He covered his eyes with his hand to try to stop the tears from streaming down his face when he broke down.

"Yes, lamb chop. He's with Mama."

Chapter 7

Sean never knew such pain existed. His chest was torn and his heart stolen. He felt he was bleeding to death, but his body refused to die. The only way out of his hell was to kill himself. Sean wasn't afraid to die. He was ready to join Molly and their son in heaven that night. But he must get it over with quickly before he lost his courage. First, he must have a plan.

I'll use a gun, he thought. No. Not honorable enough. A gun is the cowardly way out. A knife—that's it, the way the ancients took their lives. I'll die with the blood pouring from my flesh like my dear Molly. I'll go the same way she did with the life draining slowly from my body.

He went to the kitchen and took the butcher knife from the block. He slid open the drawer next to the sink and removed the whetstone. He carefully ran cold water over the stone and meticulously rubbed the knife back and forth over the gritty surface. The rhythm of its stroking calmed him. It spoke to him that the end was near. Soon, he would be released from his agony of this world to reunite with his beloved.

He focused on the work at hand and honed the tip as sharp as a dagger. That was the part that would first pierce his skin. He sat at the table and rolled the knife over and over in his hands. He held the blade to the light to see the glint of its silvery edge. He nicked his palm ever so slightly. Its sharpness brought a drop of crimson to the surface. Instinctively, he put his lips to his blood like an animal licks its wound. It had a familiar taste, salty and metallic. A sickening smile spread across his face. I am almost home, he thought. This will be easy. He slowly motioned back and forth with the tip of the knife across his throat. He had never seen a man die by the knife, but he had butchered many hogs. He knew exactly where to lay the blade to open the vessels. His eyes closed. He waved the knife slowly, slowly under his chin. Closer, closer, it spoke to him as it brushed against his skin. *Soon, you will sleep, my son.*

A few more seconds and it would be done.

"Sean, what in the hell are you doing?"

The spell was broken. His eyes popped open. The light and the pain flooded back in. He was discovered and his plan to escape was ruined.

"Give me that."

Abby snatched away the blade. "Are you out of your mind? What are you thinking, lad?"

"I'm thinking it's time to join Molly and the baby."

"What makes you think you'll go to heaven if you kill yourself? What if God won't take you?"

"What God? Is there one? Because if there is, how could he take Molly and my son like that? What sin did they commit? What sin did *I* commit? My boy didn't even get his first breath. And if there was ever an angel on Earth, it was Molly—*my* Molly. I lost half my family in the blink of an eye. What kind of God lets a little girl cry herself to sleep every night? Hannah hasn't eaten a mouthful of food in three days. There can't *be* a God. If there was, he wouldn't have let this happen. And if there is, he doesn't give a damn about us. Let *Him* burn in the hell He's made for us."

"Seany, think about what you're saying. It's blasphemy. I know you're hurt, but that's no reason to forsake the Lord. No reason."

"Well, I can't think of a better one."

Hannah heard the commotion and wandered in. "Papa, you're bleeding."

Sean rubbed his hand along his neck and felt a drop of wetness. "Yes muffin, I must have done it shaving."

"But your face is still stumpily," she said as she rubbed her hand along his face.

"Your father isn't finished yet. He was going to give himself the kind of shave that lasts a lifetime."

Sean gave Abby a dirty look and she returned it.

"What is all the yelling about? Are you fighting?"

Hannah looked worried. Sean looked at his curly girl. Her face was pale and long. Her eyes had dark circles and were swollen from crying. Her curls hung in her face. She had been wearing the same dress for three days, the one her mother ironed and laid out for her the day her water broke. Hannah refused to take it off.

"We're not fighting. Abby and me, were just having a little discussion."

"Abby and I," Hannah replied softly.

"What?"

"Mama says *Abby and I.*"

He smiled and slowly reached out to touch her shoulders. She glowed as her big green eyes stared back at him. But at that moment, they weren't really hers. They were *Molly's.* Molly wasn't gone at all. She was still there living in his little one standing before him–still

71

correcting his English. He thought he had finished crying, that there was nothing left to feel. But that wasn't true. He felt the tears coming again. He pulled the tiny girl towards him and held her. He found her, she was here all along. *Hannah* was his reason to live.

"You're right, kitten. *Abby and I.*"

Relief showed in Abby's tired face. "I'm going to heat some water for the bathtub, Hannah. Now go and get the clothes I laid out for you on your dresser. We're gonna get cleaned up for Mama."

Sean watched as his little one raced up the stairs. No other chest ever held a heart as pure as hers. He smiled as he watched her go. Then he heard a voice over his shoulder.

"As for you, Mr. Sean, there'll be no more of this nonsense. No more self pity. We've got a big job today. Only a yellow belly would kill himself before burying his wife and son. You've got to be strong for Hannah and yourself. And before this day is over, you need to make some apologies to the Lord."

She put a kettle on the stove and went up the stairs to tend to Hannah. As he sat in his hard wooden chair, the pain seeped back into his soul. Today is the day I have to bury the only woman I ever loved and the son I never got to love, he thought. He dragged himself to the sink to wash his face with feet of clay. How am I going to make it through this day?

The neighbors filled their home with food and gifts. He couldn't bear to look at them–the neighbors or the food. For the first time, he knew how Abby felt just a few months before. Their house had lost three of its members in less than a year.

When the doctor had left Molly's side, Abby chased Sean out of the room. While he went to Hannah to tell her about her mother and brother, Abby took away the blood stained clothes. She bathed Molly's body with a cloth soaked in warm water so her skin wouldn't feel cold when Hannah touched her. She cut the back of her own finest night gown, white cotton with tiny pink roses, and pulled it over Molly's shoulders. She combed back Molly's brown, curly hair and tied it with a pink ribbon. She washed the sweat from Molly's face and dried it. She lay in her death bed as white as snow, no drop of blood left in her body. Abby rubbed pink rouge into her cheeks to make her look more like the mother Hannah had known.

When it was time, Sean took the curly girl to see her mother. They stood next to the bed and sobbed together for twenty minutes. Then Abby sent them away. She didn't let Hannah see her brother. The baby was blue. It was too much for such a young child.

When it finally quit snowing, the ground was like a stone. The preacher said they might have to wait until it warmed up to bury the bodies, but there was no way Sean could abide by that. His friend Patrick and his younger brother came with picks and spades and the three dug a hole in the hard frozen ground deep enough for a coffin.

The mourners stood in the freezing wind at the cemetery. For fear they would all die of pneumonia, the reverend made the service short. The child was wrapped in the quilt Abby made and placed across Molly's chest so they could be buried together. Sean held Hannah close to him as she shivered in the cold. It was too much to bear so Sean's thoughts wandered to another time and place. It was summer and he and Hannah were at the lake. The sky was blue and the wind was warm. He tilted his head to feel the sun on his face. He closed his eyes and heard the crickets chirping. He got a bite on his line, a big bass, set the hook and started reeling him in. The fish was almost in his net when—a hand clamped down on his shoulder.

"I'm sorry for your loss, son. If I can help, you know where to find me."

"Thanks, Mr. Simmons."

What could he do? What could anyone do?

The next few weeks were strange. Sean was so weary at night, that he went to bed before Hannah. His brain woke up long before dawn. He dressed and escaped through the door before Abby awakened. He didn't want to see or speak to anyone. Abby was the same way after Andrew's passing. He now understood this part of mourning, the depression that consumes you.

The days were long at the mine. Some days he felt as hopeless as the mules that pulled the carts for miles in the dark. But some days the repetitive toil in the mine comforted him. He was content to have something to fill the empty hours. In a morbid way, he found comfort in the thought that he was underground, deep in the Earth, like Molly. I have a job that puts food on the table, he thought, and Abby to watch over my little girl. Most of all, I know I am blessed to still have Hannah. She was the only thing that kept Sean going those long weeks. It was too painful to think of Molly, when she was alive, too dangerous to open freshly healing wounds. No, it was *Hannah's* face he saw.

One night after Hannah had gone to bed, Abby cornered Sean in the kitchen. "Have you made your apologies to the Lord?"

"What apologies? Every day at the mine, all I can think about is losing Molly. I've decided there can't be a God or this wouldn't have happened. And if there is and He did nothing to stop it, who needs Him?"

"Sean, you can't mean it."

"I do mean it. And there's no heaven either. There can't be. I've seen no proof of it since I've lived on this Earth and my life *here* is hell."

"I just lost my husband too, remember. You're not the only one who's cried his eyes out for a loved one. It happens to all of us sooner or later. We're in the same boat, you and me. But I never lost my faith. How can you see all the miracles around you and not believe that there is a Creator behind it? Do you think the world with all its plants and creatures got here by accident? Not a chance. The Master was behind each and every one of them. He's an artist, I tell you. Only God in his heaven could create such beauty with warm flesh and blood and give man a brain, a beating heart and a soul. Not only is His artwork alive and breathing, but it can reproduce more life. He gave us that gift.

And if you're still not convinced, you need only look into your daughter's eyes. Weighing in at fifty pounds, she is the greatest miracle of all. She gives me the will to rise in the morning and face the day. When Andrew died, I thought I went with him. But this child gives me a reason to live. She should be your reason to live too."

Abby paused for a moment allowing Sean to think it over. She understood his pain only too well. After all, she grieved for Andrew *and* Molly.

"There's a little poem I learned in school a long time ago. I like to remember it from time to time:

The pearly gates,
The Father and Son.
Choirs of angels,
And the face of a loved one.
That is heaven above.

The kindness of strangers,
The kiss of a lover.
The birth of a child,
And the love of a mother.
This is heaven below.

I know heaven exists above and below and sonny boy, so help me God, you're going to know it too."

The next Sunday, Abby dragged Sean to church, whether the wood crib was full or not. He sat in a pew on the last row and listened to the singing. His buttercup fell asleep in his lap. A young woman sat on the other side of Hannah. Sean had never noticed her before. She looked at him and smiled. What did she see?

Was she thinking about a father's love for his daughter or feeling sorry that he had lost his wife? Did she notice the dark circles under his eyes or that his clothes were falling off him? Could she see through to his wretched soul that never stopped aching? She looked to be about twenty, just a few years younger than Sean. But he was far too old for her. At twenty-five, he had already loved and lost enough for a whole lifetime. No, I am eighty and she is a child, he thought. She can't possibly know what I am about. He gave her a weak smile and closed his eyes to join Hannah in dreamland.

Chapter 8

The tips of the leaves were golden and the air had grown cooler. It was the middle of September and nine months since Molly had passed. The tincture of time had begun to heal their wounds and mend their broken hearts. Abby tended her garden and it was as abundant as ever that summer. She and Hannah, with Molly's favorite apron tied around her, canned tomatoes and pickled beets. They even put up red plum preserves with the fruit from Mr. Simmons' tree. Hannah started school the first of the month. Abby found a pair of lace up shoes for her at the second hand shop. She cut the card board from a corn flakes box and slid it into the shoes to make them last through the school year. Then she rubbed brown polish into the toes until they shone. At the five and dime, she bought three pairs of new white cotton knee socks to go with them. Abby ripped the seams out of one of Molly's cotton dresses, the pink one with flowers, cut it down and re-stitched it to fit Hannah. Hannah wore the dress three days out of five, because it was Mama's. So Abby cut down two more.

Hannah was ready for the first grade, but was the first grade ready for her? Her teacher reported that Hannah "liked to share her experiences with the class" and that she had to ask her to be quiet and listen from time to time. That was no surprise. She had always been a chatterbox, a little busybody. With Abby's coaching, her handwriting was already better than Sean's and she climbed into her father's lap and read words from the newspaper. She hummed songs from Sunday school and had tea parties with her doll and Boots. There were no more tears at bedtime or nightmares that woke her. They had their Hannah again. She made their hearts swell. She gave them hope.

Each week got a little easier for Sean, too. He was able to sleep through the night and food got its taste back. He was able to smile again, though he still missed her terribly. Sometimes he still went to bed early, more lonely than tired, and prayed for a dream of Molly, so he could see her again. Sometimes he got his wish. He slept on his side with her pillow pressed against his back. He pretended she was there lying next to him. He longed to feel her body, soft and warm, next to his. He dreamed of the first time they met, at the inn. He dreamed of their wedding day and their wedding night. He remembered how she cried the first time they made love. He feared he had hurt her, but she said they were only tears of joy. The dreams were so real that he awakened with a smile on his face. Sometimes the smile lasted all the way to the mines. But eventually, reality always set in again. He was *alone.* The fellas at work told him he should look for another. Sean wasn't ready. Molly still had a hold on his heart and wouldn't let go.

The days grew shorter. It would be another cold Pennsylvania winter. Everyday there were more rumors that the mines would close. They were shutting down all around them. Thousands of men were out of work. The Depression showed no sign letting up. But what could they do? Coal was all there was in that little town. I will stay at it until they close us down, Sean thought. He had managed to put a few dollars away for a rainy day. He hoped it would never come.

Then one Saturday, it did.

The foreman gathered all the men together to give them the news they had all dreaded. "There's no need to stay until quittin' time. Just pick up your last pay and go. Good luck to you all and Godspeed."

Good luck? *Godspeed?* What else could happen? There is nothing in this life you can depend on, thought Sean. He collected his pay and stood in line at the store for bacon and flour. He tried to remember exactly how much money he had saved in the tin bandage box in the sock drawer of his dresser. He wondered how many days or weeks they could last. He decided to wait until after Sunday breakfast to tell the girls. But when he got to the house, Abby met him with a long face.

"I was going to tell you tomorrow."

"News travels fast in a small town, Seany. It beat you home."

"What the devil are we going to do?" he asked.

"We've got a place to live. I have a little money saved and you've got a strong back. We'll figure something out," she said confidently. But she couldn't hide the fear in her eyes or her hands from rolling nervously over and over each other.

It wasn't much of a plan but it was all they had. Sean was drained. Another long week of shoveling made his shoulder throb. He collapsed in a chair at the kitchen table. He leaned forward and held his right elbow up with his left hand. The pain in his shoulder let up a little when he took the pressure off it. He was still in shock and had mixed emotions about the news. He was afraid to think that he might not be able to put food on the table. At the same time, selfishly, he was relieved. He hated the mines and the past year, without Molly, had been the worst. All those hours in the hole sucked the life from him and he was ready for a change. He shucked off his filthy clothes and soaked in the hot bath water Abby poured for him. His head was dizzy. The past year had been unbelievable. He could have never guessed the twists and turns in the road that met him. This has been a crazy ride, he thought. I wonder where it will stop.

On Sunday, the preacher talked about faith, having faith in the Lord. The Lord *will* provide. Sean wanted to believe it. But how could he?

"Times will get better," said the reverend. "Surely the mines will open again."

The men shook their heads and the women cried. The newspapers painted a bleak picture throughout the country. It seemed the Lord wasn't providing for a lot of people. Sean tried to make sense of it all. After church, parishioners shook hands and said goodbye. They were moving to other towns to look for work. Sean couldn't understand why they gave up so quickly. Even President Roosevelt's weekly fireside chats weren't enough to convince them to stay and wait it out. Then he remembered most of their homes were owned by the mines and they no longer had a place to live.

Monday morning, bright and early, Sean set his sights on the lumber mill. The owner was a friend. When he got there, a group of men was already huddled around the door. He recognized most of them from the mines.

The owner shouted over the crowd. "I'm sorry, gentlemen. I wish I had work for all of you. I had to hire my own two nephews first. I'm sure you can all understand. I'm sorry."

The men grumbled as they dispersed, disappointed and desperate for work. They couldn't bear to look at one another. Sean walked over to the general store. Maybe he could make a little cash sweeping or stocking the shelves.

"I'm sorry, Sean. I know you're a good worker. But there are too many people who owe me money in this town. I've been letting them get by with credit. Now they'll never be able to pay me back. I can barely stay afloat. I'm thinking about closing the store and heading east myself," said Mr. Flynn.

Sean shook his hand and gave him a penny for a piece of licorice for Hannah.

He spent that afternoon splitting wood for Mr. Simmons. He gave Sean a peck of Irish potatoes from his garden as payment. For the next three weeks, Sean cleaned barns, split wood, picked pumpkins and dug potatoes with a spade. The neighbors were glad for the help, but none of them could give him cash. He returned home each night with baskets of apples, turnips, kale or a pail of brown eggs. Anything was better than the mines, but he needed a cash paying job. Each day, the struggle to find odd jobs was harder. The despair he saw in his neighbor's faces became his despair too. He walked for miles looking for work. There was none to be found. Everyday, more people left.

At the end of the day, he sat at the table and talked with Abby. "I've been thinking. The neighbors are all moving out. Maybe we should go too. I could find work a little further east."

Abby tightened her grip on her teacup. "Oh, you've been thinking, have you? Alright, then. Where will you go? Where will you live? Who's hiring? The entire country is in this depression. It took a little longer to get here because people still needed coal. But now they can't even afford that. It's no better anywhere else. All these folks think they are running away from their problem, but they aren't. It is going to find them wherever they go. We've got no where to run either. It is what it is."

She folded her arms across her chest in defiance.

"Well, I can't stand by and let my child starve to death. If you won't go, Hannah and I will go without you."

"Fine and where will she sleep while you are looking for work? What will you eat while you are on the road when you haven't got any money? Even if you do find work, and you won't, who's going to watch Hannah all day while you are gone? Have you got anybody, any family out east to help you with her? Have you thought about that?"

Her words cut to the quick. The worst part was he knew she was right. He sat in silence like a scolded child, and hoped the answers would come to him.

Abby moved toward him. She gently laid her hand on his shoulder. "Lord almighty, son. I know you've been through a lot. More than you should have been asked to bear for such a young lad. But you've got to use your head and think about what's best for your child. You are all she's got. We are a family now, the three of us. Fate put us here together. Can't you see it? I will take care of Hannah, do the cooking and cleaning and take care of you both. I've got a piece of land for gardening and a sturdy house. It's yours to live in as long as you like. You might as well say it belongs to you now. I have no one else to leave it to but you and Hannah and I'll see to that. You are our strength, Sean. We need you. And dear Hannah is the little ray of sunshine that keeps us going. We'll get through by our wits and God's will. Listen to the preacher, boy, have *faith.*"

For the next month, Sean wandered from house to house asking for odd jobs. They were few and far between. He shot a couple of rabbits and Abby made stew–but it didn't last long. Abby's canning from the summer was gone. She made biscuits as long as the flour held out. Everyday Sean got more frustrated and scared. He stood alone in the front yard and looked down the empty road as the sun went down. In anger, he asked out loud, "Lord, is this how it is going to end? First you took Molly and the baby. Are the rest of us are going to starve to death?"

Just then some fellas from work drove up in a sedan. It wasn't even dark yet but they were already drinking. "C'mon, Sean. There's room for one more. It's time to celebrate. Prohibition is over, *son.* We're going into town to the Shangri-La to get drunk and watch the girls dance," they shouted over the engine. "Yeah, Mr. Yuengling brought out the *good stuff* tonight. The whole town will be there."

Yeah, what's left of it, thought Sean. He had bad memories of getting drunk once or twice in his younger days on moonshine but he had never seen any dancing girls. His stomach got a sick feeling. His conscience wouldn't let him go. "Not this time, fellas," he shouted back over the motor.

Abby stepped onto the porch and surveyed the situation. "Go on, Sean. I'll watch Hannah. It'll do you good."

Sean battled with indecision. Abby smiled and nodded her head. Sean had one quarter in his pocket. What the devil, he thought, and climbed in.

The Shangri-La was nothing more than a rickety watering hole with a raised stage, a piano player and a long bar. But tonight was a special night. The men were drinking beer, *real beer*, so Sean had one too. The cold drink felt good on the back of his throat and when the alcohol reached his stomach, the warmth raced down his legs to his toes. He smiled when he realized what he had been missing all this time. When the dancing started, Sean realized he hadn't looked at a woman, not really, since Molly. The girls were young with white arms and painted faces. Their hair was short. Most were bottle-blonds. They had ribbons and feathers in their hair and wore dresses above the knee. They kicked so high, you could almost see what was under them. Sean tried not to look, but he couldn't help himself. By this time, the fellas were getting sloppy. But Sean wasn't interested in getting drunk and anyway, he was nearly out of money. He was spellbound with everything going on around him. When the music stopped, the men threw money onto the stage. The girls gathered the coins and stuffed them into their bosoms. Sean thought who has that kind of money to give away? He looked over at the men who were throwing it. They had dark eyes and wavy black hair. They shouted obscenities with their northern accents. He had never seen such fancy suits and patent leather shoes. Sean was sure he had never seen them around town.

One of them called out to a dancing girl. "Hey, sweetheart. Come over here and sit on my lap. Tell Santa what you want for Christmas."

She sat on his lap and wrapped her arms around his neck. They must be lovers, thought Sean.

"What's your name, cupcake?"

Maybe not. The waitress returned to Sean's table. "Can I get you another beer?"

"Yes, I'll have one more."

Sean hadn't been in a tavern or bar since he met Molly, but it was all coming back to him. "Ma'am, I'm sorry if I'm rude for asking, but how do those girls on the stage do? I mean, I see those fellas throwing money to them. What do they take in a night?"

"Well, every night is different. But on the weekends, they might take in four."

"Four *dollars?*"

"Yeah, I take in three during the week and four or five on the weekends waitressing. I'll go get your beer."

Four dollars? For prancing around a few hours? Sean shoveled coal ten hours for a less. How was it possible? When she returned, Sean bent her ear some more. "Do you need any help here? I mean, is your boss hiring? I could sweep up or pour beer."

"No, we don't need any more bartenders, but the boss is always asking for more girls. He likes to rotate the merchandise, get fresh faces in here from time to time, if you know what I mean. Not many girls will work in a place like this. My mother would kill me if she knew I was serving liquor."

"Pardon me, miss, but you don't, I mean, you don't have to—give any *special favors*, do you?"

"Certainly not. I'm a waitress, not a call girl. If that's what you're after, you'll have to talk to the manager."

She spun around angrily and hurried away. Sean was sorry he offended her. He didn't know much about these things and figured he would never know if he didn't ask. The next time she walked past, he apologized. "Miss, miss, pardon me. I am truly sorry for what I asked you. I wasn't accusing you of doing anything wrong. I am just curious—about your wages. I'm desperate to find work to feed my little girl."

"You and a million other Americans. Apology accepted. No harm done. What's your name, darlin'?"

"Sean—Sean O'Connell."

"Pleased to meet you, Sean. My name is Katherine, but they call me Kate."

"And your last name, if you don't mind my asking?"

"Flannigan."

Flannigan. A feisty Irish girl, like his Molly. He should have known.

"Too bad you don't wear skirts. We could use someone like you. You've got spunk. And you're kind of cute. I've got to get back to work. I make my money on tips. Nice talking to you, Sean."

The next morning, Abby made the last of the coffee. Sean wasn't used to alcohol and his head was busting. "A little too much juice last night, eh?" she teased.

She wasn't angry. After all, she was the one who insisted Sean go in the first place. "You had your first real beer, did you? I hear Yuengling sent a truckload of his best to Mr. Roosevelt as a thank you for making it legal again."

"The way my head is pounding, maybe he should have left it illegal."

"Ah, you're just not used to it. You know you are not the first to get a hangover. Drew liked to take a nip from the bottle from time to time."

"Abby, have you ever been to one of these *social clubs*? You should have seen the smoke and heard the laughter and the music. Everyone was talking at once and the drunker they got, the louder they got. The girls looked like painted dolls kicking up their heels on the stage."

"Hmmm, flappers," she grumbled.

"I talked to a waitress a little. She was nice."

"Was she pretty?"

"Who?"

"The waitress, who do you think, who?"

"Yeah, I guess. I didn't notice."

"Didn't notice? You went to a club and talked to a girl and didn't notice what she looked like?"

"I guess. It wasn't like that. We were talking business. I asked her what the girls make a night. She said three dollars for bringing the beer around."

"Great day in the morning, boy. That's what we need. Get your coat. Hurry lad. See if you can start today."

"Not so fast, Auntie. They don't need waiters. They want *waitresses*. And I didn't see any gentlemen on the stage, if you know what I mean."

"Oh."

They both leaned over their coffee cups and stared off into space.

"Well, you could always put on one of Molly's skirts and a little rouge and take a shot at it," Abby said with a giggle at the end.

"The waitress had the same suggestion. She said I was *cute.*"

"This waitress, did she have a name?"

"Katherine Flannigan."

"You got her name but you don't know what she looked like?"

Abby lightly rapped Sean on the back of his head. "Aye laddie, you are hopeless, completely hopeless."

Chapter 9

Hopeless. It was the truth. The snow began to fall. There was no work to be found or any prospect of the mines reopening. The rabbits had gotten scarce, so had the squirrel and dove. Sean took Andrew's gun far into the woods and shot a small deer, a yearling. Normally, when he got a deer, he gutted it and let it hang in the wood shed for a day or two to chill out, stiffen up and age before cutting it up into pieces. Not this time. Abby met him at the shed with a butcher knife and a big grin. She normally wrapped the roast in bacon and cooked it slowly until it fell off the bone. But there was no bacon to be had. She cut off a hind quarter and roasted it whole with onions. She wrapped the other one in brown paper and took it next door to Mrs. Simmons. They hadn't had meat in a while either. The young buck would feed them for a few days. But then what? Sean didn't know how much longer they could hold on.

For the next few days, Sean swallowed back his frustration until he felt he would explode. After Hannah was safely put away to bed, he let loose on Abby. "We're going to perish in this house with our ribs showing like skeletons. I don't know what else I can do. I can't get what we need to live. I'm—I'm useless."

Sean ranted on for twenty minutes. Abby listened patiently without saying a word lightly tapping her fingers on the side of her teacup. Her eyes had a faraway look. Finally, when Sean was finished, he plopped down into the kitchen chair. He threw his arms across the table and rested his head on them. He closed his eyes and exhaled a sigh of defeat.

A few minutes later, Abby's voice broke the long silence. "You're right. It's not working, lad. You've done everything you can. We've got to come up with a new trick. We can't go out this way, not with what we've been through. Hannah's dress is hanging off her. We've got to plump up our curly girl a bit."

Sean listened intently, his eyes still closed. He prayed that the next few words from her lips would hold the answer to their plight. He heard Aunt Abby open a kitchen cabinet and move dishes around. Then he heard the clinking of two glasses, like at a wedding party. The curiosity got the best of him and he lifted his head slightly and opened one eye. Abby had her back to him. She stood on her toes and reached way back into the cabinet. She pulled down a tall brown bottle, opened it and poured two fingers of the golden liquid into each glass. Sean rose to his elbows as she handed him one.

"It was damn hard to get decent liquor during Prohibition. I've been saving this for an emergency. Well, it's an emergency. Here's to you."

Sean was too surprised to protest. They both gulped it down at once. It burned Sean's throat down to his stomach. He began to choke.

Abby let out a deep belly laugh and slapped him on the back. "Ho, my boy. I see you are a stranger to the charms of Irish whiskey. It'll make a man of you alright."

"Abby, I had no idea you drank,"

"I don't, leastwise, not often enough. You forget. Abby was young once, cavorting, flirting and having fun. Even when we were married, Drew and I took a nip from time to time. Here. Have another."

She poured two more fingers into Sean's glass and he didn't mind.

"Maybe we should have a chaser. I'll get some water." Sean's voice was hoarse.

"Nay. It'll just dilute the effects. We're on a soul searching mission tonight. Firewater brings the truth to the surface." Abby poured herself another.

She tossed it back and swallowed hard. Her face became serious. It was time to get to work. "Now, have you asked the older ladies if they need help shoveling snow or tending to their woodpiles and the like?"

"They all need help. They have no way to pay. No cash and no food to spare."

She knew that already. She was just getting warmed up. Sean watched as her wheels kept turning. "Have you thought about selling firewood in town?"

"Same song. No cash or food to trade. The streets are full of firewood peddlers, but no one is buying. Those who can climb into the woods, get their own."

Abby wasn't daunted. She kept working at it. "Have you got any money left in your box?"

"All gone. I spent the last of it on shot for the rabbits and deer. All I've got is a few shells left. I feel badly that I haven't given you any money for rent in weeks. I don't know when I'll be able to pay you."

"What do you think, Sean? Do you think I would try to get blood from a turnip? You are doing the best you can. I ate that venison too, you know and the rabbit stew. You don't owe me a thing. We're even. Let's concentrate on where our next meal's coming from, shall we?"

Sean nodded and gulped down his drink. Whew. Easier than the first one, but still rough.

"We have nothing to sell. We need something to do–for someone who can pay..." Abby mumbled to herself and threw back another round. "I can wash or sew or cook. But I'm afraid we have the same dilemma. Nobody can pay."

She poured them both another one. Sean began to feel warm. The liquid fire burned from his stomach into his chest and spread down to his arms and fingers. His face felt flushed. Every muscle in his body relaxed. He was completely content, peaceful and his thoughts drifted away. He closed his eyes and thought of the ocean, the one he had never seen. He had been stuck here in this town for seven years. Maybe now was the time to move on. He gathered enough courage to think it out loud.

"We should move east. I'll take you and Hannah to the sea. I'll get a job in a shipyard, building boats," he said smiling, giddy.

It was a brilliant idea. Surely Abby would agree.

"What the hell's the matter with you? Can't hold your liquor? You're talking like a fool. Haven't we had this conversation before? It's the dead of winter. If we don't freeze on the way, we'll freeze when we get there. We've got no money for travel or food or lodging. You've got no job and no place to stay. You're talking crazy. Let me tell you now for the last time. Molly and your son are buried out in that cemetery. Andrew's body is lying right next to them. That's our family and *this* is where we belong. We are too old to run away from home. I'm going to die here and you are going to lay my bones between Drew and Molly. I'm not going anywhere and neither are you. I don't care if it kills us. We're not leaving. Do you hear me?"

Sean hoped her yelling wouldn't wake Hannah. He had never seen Abby like this. He sobered up quickly. They sat at the table, quietly, for a long time, determined to solve the puzzle before they went to bed. Abby kept pouring and they kept drinking.

Abby's tongue loosened with the liquor. She told Sean how she and Drew met and how their wedding night was a disaster. She was too embarrassed to let him see her naked. "It was awful. I wouldn't take my clothes off and he was too much of a gentleman to take them off me. Finally, after three nights of trying, he got some whiskey in me and they peeled right off. We could never make babies, but like Drew said, we spent a lifetime giving it our best effort."

Mother Mary. Sean couldn't believe what came from Abby's mouth. Her face was red and she laughed so hard she had to wipe the tears from her eyes with her kerchief. She couldn't bring herself to tell me to stay off Molly, Sean thought. Now she's telling me about making love to Drew. I've never seen her this jolly. Now I know why Drew kept this firewater around. It was the quickest route to get Abby in bed. Sean felt light as a feather. They both needed this.

After the laughing, there was an awkward silence. Sean broke it. "Abby, whenever you talk about Drew, he sounds so happy and fun-loving. I don't think I ever saw that side of him. He was either angry or his mind was somewhere else. Drew was always short with me. I don't think he liked me."

"Oh, there's where you're wrong, laddie. He wasn't really mean spirited. Andrew and I were not so different from you and Molly starting out. We came over from Ireland about the same time, on different boats of course, when we were children. Our families were looking for a better life here. But it was plenty tough in America too. My father was able to buy a small farm and make a go of it. It was all he knew. We never had much money, but we had a home and as long as the crops made it, there was food. Andrew's people were from the city. They didn't know anything about farming. When Drew was just a lad, he started in the mines. As hard as he worked, he never had enough wages to put away. His family needed every penny to survive. When we were married, we lived with my parents, in this house. Andrew didn't mind at first, but he wanted a home of his own. He took on a second job, working as a bartender on the weekend. The hours nearly killed him, but we were managing to put a little away by and by. Then one night, a fight broke out at the bar. Andrew was a strapping man and jumped over the counter to break it up. He grabbed the first guy, punched him in the jaw and threw him in the corner. Then the second guy came at him. He gave him a couple of punches and threw him in another corner. Before he could turn around, the first guy pulled out a pistol and shot Drew in the back. He dropped to the floor. He couldn't feel his legs. The bullet went straight into his back bone. The doctor said he would never walk again."

She paused a moment like she was reliving his pain. "But Drew wasn't having any part of it. We saw a doctor in Pittsburgh to see if he would take the bullet out. He wouldn't touch him. There was too much of a risk that it would paralyze him forever. I think Drew just willed the feeling back into his legs, then his feet and toes. He forced himself to walk a few feet with me and my father on each side of him. Da made him some crutches and soon, he could walk with them. Later he could walk with a cane. It was almost a year before he could walk on his own again. The doctor said it was a miracle. But it was determination. Andrew was never a quitter. He nursed himself back to health, day by day, step by step. Of course, by then, our dream of buying our own land was done for. I worked with my mother in the fields, raising and selling vegetables so we could feed ourselves. Drew got back on at the mines, but not with a shovel. He took care of the mules and repaired the equipment. He had learned a thing or two from Da, shoeing horses and sharpening the plow. Still, Andrew picked Da's brain every night at the dinner table about how to handle mules and how to weld or paint or bolt whatever needed to be fixed.

After the shooting, Andrew's back hurt him everyday of his life. And as hard as he tried to fight it, he missed work, sometimes days, sometimes weeks. You always knew when his back bothered him. He never said a word about it, but he was as mean as a snake. That's when I would pull out the Irish whiskey. It helped him forget about his back and at least he could sleep. His back pain kept us from saving money and kept him from ever working his way up the ladder.

He was a fighter, though. That's why they kept taking him back at the mines even though he was out sick so much. When my father died, the farm was sold and divided between my sister and brother. But he left us the house, so we would always have a place to live. So you see Sean, Drew wasn't naturally mean, he got that way from enduring years of pain. Worse yet, over time he grew bitter about the cards he had been dealt and watching his dreams slip away."

"I had no idea about Andrew's back. I feel sorry for what you two have been through. But I still don't think he liked me"

"Wrong again. When you married Molly and moved in, Andrew saw the spitting image of himself. You were young and strong and had big plans about buying land. You lived with family when you were starting out just like we did. Hell, you even lived in the same side of the house we used to. He saw in you another chance. He rooted for you and *envied* you at the same time. Your whole life was ahead of you and it was all over for him. He would never have children or buy his own piece of land."

"I have often wondered why you and Drew never had children."

Abby gulped down another shot and closed her eyes for a second. Sean thought perhaps he had gone too far. "It's none of my business. I'm sorry for asking."

She shook her head. "No Seany, it's OK. We were only married a short while when he was shot, hardly enough time to get in the family way. When the bullet lodged in his backbone, well, for a while, he had trouble even trying to pee. When he got his feeling and his strength back, he got control of his manhood again, if you know what I mean. But it was never quite right after that. The son of a bitch with the gun took away our future and our family with one shot. Eighteen months, he did just eighteen months for that crime. Self defense. How the hell can it be self defense when Drew took a bullet to the back, for Christ's sake? He didn't even have a gun. Damn lawyers. The son of a bitch did a year and a half. Drew and I paid a lifetime."

She poured them each another shot. She tossed hers back then her eyes met Sean's again. Her face was twisted in a scowl. She was still angry about it. She stared hard into her glass. After a moment, her face softened and her eyes grew kind again.

"He was no harder on you, than a father teaching his son and making him strong enough to take on the worst. He worked you to death to teach you to carry on after he was gone. Who else was going to see after me and Molly and Hannah? The reason he put you to work on the roof or the woodpile by yourself was because he couldn't do it anymore. His back wouldn't allow it. But he was too proud to let you know about his weakness. He was sick, Sean. And if it weren't for you working at the mine and paying us rent, we'd a starved. We had nothing but this place. Don't you see Sean? You took care of all *five* of us in those years. That's why Andrew was so crazy about getting rent from you. It was all we had for groceries."

It became clear to Sean. His anger and bitterness for the old man was melting away. He felt sorry for him and appreciated his plight. He felt like a lowly tenant when all along, he was the breadwinner who fed them all and took care of the place. He sat a little taller in his chair and felt good about myself, even proud.

"You're a good boy, Sean. I wish things could have been different. It was just his foolish pride. He could have asked for help instead of demanding it. He wanted you to respect him, not feel sorry for him. It was his way."

Abby sat quietly for a moment staring into her glass. Sean was sure the alcohol was wearing her down and soon she would fall asleep in her chair. Abruptly, she broke from her trance. "Sean, I've been working on something. It's time you saw it."

She walked to her bedroom and returned with a dress Sean had never seen before. "This is store-bought dress. I've had it for a long time. I never got to wear it. I've been working on it, shortening it a little and making it a little more, you know, modern."

Sean stared at it blankly. "It's very nice. Are you going someplace special?"

"It's not for me."

"Well, it's too big for Hannah unless you're going to cut it down some more." Abby gazed back at Sean with mischief in her eyes.

"Well, then who's it for?"

A smile slowly spread across her face. Her eyes peered deeper into Sean's. He sat dumbly with both hands wrapped tightly around his glass. He didn't know what was going on, but he had a feeling he wouldn't like it. Abby's face turned to disgust. "Are you blind, boy? Have you no imagination? It's for you."

"What the hell?"

"You are gonna go to town and serve beer and keep us from starving to death." Her smile returned and her eyes got bigger.

"Oh no. You have lost your mind, lady. There's no way I'm putting on a dress. I'll gladly starve to death first."

He pushed his chair back from the table. Abby never took her eyes off him. "Fine, then you'll be taking me and your little girl with you to the grave. There's nothing left, son. Don't you understand? This is our last card. The game's over. We're done. *You* have got to save us."

Desperate times called for desperate measures. But he wasn't sure he was desperate enough to put on a dress. "What will Hannah think? She'll be ruined for life."

"She'll never know. I'll see to that."

Sean still couldn't see exactly what Abby expected him to do. He began to worry out loud. "What if I'm found out? They'll put me in jail."

"I never heard of any law against dressing like a woman. Women do it all the time."

"The fellas will tar and feather me. Hell, they might hang me from the highest branch."

"Then they mustn't find you out." Abby shoved the dress into his hands. "During war time men have had to disguise themselves to sneak across borders and into enemy camps with letters and guns to save our country. They pretended they were something they weren't and they had to be good at it to keep from getting shot. They slept in the snow and walked miles, maybe even spoke different languages and cut throats to survive. Nobody's shooting at *you*."

Abby had her arguments all worked out. "All you have to do is put on a dress, act like a woman and serve beer to a bunch of drunks. You told me that club is noisy and dark. You won't even have to be all that good at it. Act like a woman, but think like a man. You know what they want. Give it to them. Beat them at their own game. Talk nice to them. Flirt with them, but be a lady. Don't let them put their hands on you, or the jig is up. Got it?"

Sean couldn't believe he was actually listening to her. Maybe he was even more desperate than he thought. Maybe it was the whiskey. Now he understood why she kept pouring.

"This is crazy. Flirt with men? I'm going to bed."

Abby never moved from her seat. "That's right, Seany boy, you sleep on it."

Just then, the kitchen door creaked. The mouse had stirred from her sleep. She stood propping the door open in her flannel night gown, rubbing her eyes. Her curls hung in her face. "Aunt Abby, I'm hungry. Can I have a biscuit?"

Abby's eyes flashed at Sean's. They both knew there was hardly a bite of food in the house.

"Well, we ate the last biscuit for supper. But I have half a glass of milk for you. Do you think that will do?"

Hannah nodded. They both watched as she drank the last drop of milk in the house. Sean turned his face away lest she see his face. His heart was breaking.

"Goodnight Auntie. Goodnight, Papa."

"Goodnight, angel," said Abby as she hugged her tight.

Without turning around, he said with a fatherly tone, "Goodnight. Now get back in your bed."

When she was gone, he turned to Abby. She knew the pain was eating him alive.

"We can do it, Sean. We can pull this off. It will be the train robbery of the century. The Lord helps those who help themselves, even if it means putting on a dress to feed your baby. Now get some sleep."

Chapter 10

Sleep never came for Sean. He tossed and turned for hours with nightmares about Hannah starving to death. As the preacher shut the coffin lid, he sat up in bed, soaked in sweat, his heart pounding. He felt his chest would burst. He could never let this happen to her. He'd walk through fire before he would let his baby starve.

Sean couldn't lie in bed any longer, pulled on his trousers and went downstairs. He was so stiff, he could barely move. He stoked the fire in the stove and put on a kettle of water to boil. He looked at his face in the mirror over the kitchen sink. Abby heard him and crept from her bedroom.

"I've never seen you come down so late. I was beginning to think you were dead. Was it the whiskey?"

"No."

She brushed the hair from his face. "You look like hell."

"Thanks."

"Well what is it then?"

Sean answered her with a blank stare.

"Oh. It's the little one," she said softly.

Sean looked away from her and stood holding himself up at the sink.

She made them each a cup of tea and then sat at the table. "Come, sit down. Talk to me."

Sean obeyed.

"Where is your head, lad? Are you considering my proposal?"

After a few moments, he shared his horrible dream with her. "I had a nightmare that Hannah had wasted away to nothing. I saw her pale face, her clothes hanging off her skinny arms and legs. I saw every rib on her little body. I went to her funeral and kissed her cold lips as she lay in the coffin. Just as the preacher closed the lid…"

"Stop it, Sean. I can't take it," Abby said and then she gulped down some tea.

I can't fail her," he said miserably.

"And you won't."

"No, I won't. But you've got to help me, Abby. You've got to help me pull this thing off," he pleaded.

She sat and smiled for a moment nodding her head. "Are you ready to put on a dress to get your bread?"

He looked her in the eye for a moment, thinking it over one last time. "Yes."

Go and get your razor. I'll heat up some water. It's Friday. You should be able to make some money tonight."

He stood for a moment more and watched her as she worked. He couldn't believe he was going through with this. There must be something else he could do.

"Go, now, before you lose your nerve. Get your razor."

Abby turned around and pushed him up the first stair. When he returned, he took a hot bath and shaved his face as close as he could. He slipped on a nightshirt and presented himself to Abby. She rubbed the back of her hand over his face, "Nice."

Then she pulled back his sleeve and the collar of his shirt.

"What the hell is that?"

"What?"

"You haven't shaved your arms or your chest."

"You've got to be kidding."

"No, I'm not kidding. You've got to shave at least to your elbow and your chest up around your neckline. Thank God it's winter or it would be worse. But we can only cover up so much with sleeves. I've got stockings for your legs. Your hair is blonde enough, but it's still there. A man will notice it under your neck as well as on your face. Get in there and try it again."

Sean spent the next hour trying to shave his chest and arms and cut himself several times. Shaving the left arm wasn't so bad. But making his left hand shave his right arm was nearly impossible. He wrapped a towel around his waist.

"Abby. Come finish this," he cried.

"Oh, quit your whining." Abby went rushing to his side to find him cold, wet and bleeding. She stood back to survey the situation and started to giggle. "My God, you're a sight."

"You're not making this any easier. This was your idea, you know."

"I know, I know, I'm sorry. Give me the razor. We'll see what we can do," she offered under her breath. When she had finished, she said, "Now, put on your shirt and sit over by the stove before you catch a death of cold."

When he had followed his orders, she draped a blanket over him. There was no money for a haircut and it had grown past his ears over the past few weeks. Abby dipped a comb into a glass of water and pulled it through his hair.

"What are you doing? I thought the idea was for me to get dry."

"Well, most of you *is* getting dry. Now scoot your backside a little closer to the stove. But we've got to get a little wave in your hair. I'll go and get my curlers and setting lotion."

"Your *what?*"

She returned with a bunch of female contraptions Sean had never seen before. Just then the curly girl returned from the neighbor's house and bounced in the door. Sean quickly covered his freshly shaven arms and chest with his blanket.

"Are you getting a haircut, Papa?"

He turned and looked to Abby for help.

"Yes, kitten. Why don't you go play with your little friend Dottie for a while longer," Abby said as she pushed Hannah out the door. "We'll have some dinner when you get back."

"That was a close one."

"Too close."

She spent the next few minutes rolling his hair in curlers. While the hair was setting, Sean took a peek in the kitchen mirror.

"My God, I look like a pantywaist, one of those *funny* guys."

"Put your arse back by the stove so your hair can get dry. I'll work on your hands."

Abby opened a little cloth bag with a drawstring at the top. She pulled out a brush and a file and a bottle of red polish.

"Uh—you don't plan on painting my fingers do you?"

"Do you have a better idea? These hands are going to need all the help they can get."

Abby brushed, clipped, filed and polished for what seemed like an hour. Sean tried not to look.

"Pretty rough work, but it'll have to do," she said under her breath. She slathered some sweet smelling lotion into his hands. "Try not to shake with these gentlemen unless you have to. And if you have to, just give them your fingertips. There's no way I can get all those calluses off your palms."

She rubbed in the lotion almost up to his elbow. His skin was still stinging from the shaving. The lotion burned like fire. He pulled his arms away in pain. "Is this necessary?"

"I told you, we need all the help we can get."

When she was finished, Sean waved his arms back and forth to dry off the lotion. Abby returned to her cloth sack for another torture device. "Now then, let's see about those eyebrows."

She took out a pair of tweezers, wiped them on her apron and began yanking the long, coarse hairs from his brows.

"Hell's bells, woman!"

"Hold still, damn you."

"What are you doing to me? Am I bleeding?"

"It just feels like it ought to bleed."

"How the hell do you women stand it?"

"You'll never know the things we do for *love.*"

She yanked another hair out. It hurt so badly his toes curled under. "Dammit, woman."

Abby kept steady at her work.

"How much more?"

"Be patient, lad. Beauty takes time."

"Dammit…ouch."

Sean grabbed her wrist to stop her from inflicting more pain. "If you thin my eyebrows down like a girl, how am I supposed to show my face in town?"

"Fine," Abby said under her breath as she tossed her tweezers back into her bag. "If you won't let me pluck them, then at least let me cut down a few of the wild ones with the scissors. Some of them are as thick as broom straws."

"Fine."

"Fine."

Sean couldn't believe he was doing this. He felt so *queer.* He held perfectly still and closed his eyes tightly for fear the tip of the scissor might put out his eye. What if someone saw him like this? He got nauseous thinking about it. Then the dream from the night before flashed through his brain. Courage flooded in. He sat up straight in his chair.

"Are you sure you're Irish? These look like the brows of a Scotsman."

Sean shot her a dirty look and she chuckled. "What's next?"

"You've got such nice green eyes. The kind women would kill for. Too bad I don't have some mascara to blacken those long eyelashes of yours."

Sean batted his eyes at her. Abby shook her head and hurried into her bedroom. She returned with a pair of stockings, a brassiere and some socks. Sean felt faint. He doubted he could actually go through with it.

"Slip your shirt off. Your nails should be dry by now."

She held the brassiere in her hands and studied his chest. "Put your arms up, way up." She reached around his middle and tried to fasten the bra behind him. He couldn't stand it anymore and started to giggle. His shaking made it impossible to fasten the bra.

"Hold still."

"I can't help it. You are tickling the daylights out of me."

The bra wouldn't fit. Abby got frustrated and stretched the bra around him so tightly, it nearly cut his skin.

"Son of a……"

"Got it. It's on now, buddy boy."

"I think you broke my ribs. How do you women *breathe* in these things?"

"Quit your bitching. We've got to batten it down tight. If it slips off then the socks fall out and there'll be hell to pay."

She adjusted every strap two or three times until she was satisfied. Then she stuffed Drew's wool socks into the cups against his chest.

"Hey, these things itch."

"The *real* ones itch worse, I can tell ya."

"How many are you gonna shove into these pockets?"

"They're called *cups*. And I'll put in as many as I damn please. We've got to get you stacked up a bit. You need something to get their attention. If they're staring at your bosoms, maybe they won't notice that mug of yours."

"Well, now. You really know how to hurt a girl, don't you?"

The two burst out laughing. Sean put his arms around her and hugged her tight. He made a point of pressing his woolen breasts against hers.

"Let's not get fresh, you scallywag. Anyway, the left one is bigger than the right and both sides are rather lumpy. Perhaps you should refrain from hugging any-one." She tried her best to seem annoyed with Sean, the way Molly used to do.

She reached down Sean's chest and pulled out a sock from the left side. She pushed Sean away from her and held him at arms length. She studied the left breast, then the right, then the left again. Then she let out a sigh of defeat and shook her head.

"All right then. Pull on your stockings. We might as well clip them to your bloomers. I haven't got a garter that will fit you."

Sean grabbed the top of the stocking, stuck in his foot and tried to pull it on.

"Whoa, whoa, whoa. What are you doing, son? You have to roll them up before you put them on. Your toe goes in the end first and you unroll them up over your leg. Didn't you ever watch Molly put on stockings?"

Sean thought for a moment trying to remember.

"No, I just helped her off with them."

"Scoundrel." Abby snatched away the stocking in disgust. She carefully rolled it into a doughnut. "Sit down," she said pointing to the kitchen chair.

She got on her knees, put his toes in and unrolled the stocking up his leg.

"I feel like Cinderella."

"Yeah, well you *look* like her evil step-mother. Now pay attention. You're going to have to do this yourself next time. My knees can't take it."

Next time? Sean shuddered at the thought.

"Now roll it on the rest of the way," said Abby as she struggled to get to her feet.

Abby handed Sean the other stocking and he stared blankly at it.

"Mother Mary, what am I going to do with you?"

She quickly rolled the other stocking up his ankle to his thigh. As she neared his groin, he pulled his leg back. When their eyes met, Abby laughed. "Oh Seany, you've got to be kidding. You're blushing for Christ's sake. I'm old enough to be your mother.

Sean began to laugh too.

"My God son, I've got underpants older than you."

Abby's eyes drifted upward to the clock on the wall. "Look at the time, Seany." Sean put his modesty aside and clipped the stockings to his underwear.

"Up with your arms again."

She pulled a petticoat over his head and then the dress. The waist of the dress got caught on his bosom and stuck there. "C'mon, work with me, son. Suck in your chest. Bend over a little. Shake the dress down. Hannah will be home any minute."

She yanked the curlers from his hair and brushed it out. She powdered his face, and penciled on new eyebrows. She rouged his cheeks and painted his lips red. Then she stood back to examine her work.

"Holy mackerel."

She pulled a soft pale green hat down over his head. "This will push those blonde curls in close around your face, so it won't look so broad." She tied a matching scarf loosely around his neck. "This will help cover up some of your manliness. That Adam's apple is a dead give away."

She looked him over once more. "Have you thought of a name?"

"A name?"

"Yes, yes, a name. You're not going to walk in there and tell them your name is *Sean*, are you?"

"Oh. No."

"Think, boy, think. We haven't much time."

"How about Elizabeth or Mary?"

"They're great names if you're a queen—or a ship. Pick something with a ring to it, something fun."

"How about Sarah?"

"Or Sally. That's it, Sally. You'll need a last name, too."

Sean glanced through the kitchen window. The shadows were growing longer. How long had they been at this?

"C'mon. You're daydreaming. Have you got a name?"

Sean watched the neighbor carry in wood for the night.

"Simmons."

"No. They'll think you're related. Too risky."

He was exhausted. He couldn't come up with a single thing.

"Well?" asked Abby impatiently.

"Well what? The butcher, the baker, the candlestick maker. I don't care. You pick something."

"Baker it is. It has a nice ring to it. Sally Baker."

Sean smiled satisfied that he had a name. Abby ignored his simple grin.

"Pleased to make your acquaintance, Miss Baker," she said extending her hand.

"Pleased to meet ya," said Sean as he gave her a coal miner's hand shake.

"Are you mad? You've got to shake hands like a girl. Just give them your fingers. Offer it timidly like you're not sure if you want them to touch you or not. Let the fingers dangle, like a dead fish. Lower your eyes and bow a little. The girls here are old school, some of them fresh off the boat. Now, then. Let's try it again."

"Pleased to meet you."

"Your hand is limp, but you still sound like a man. Falsetto, lad. Throw your voice up like you were mocking your mother."

"Pleased—hmmm, hmmm. *Pleased to meet you.*"

"Now we're getting there. Bat your eyes a little and act silly. Shift your weight nervously from foot to foot like you've got to pee."

Sean rehearsed his girl voice and stance. There was no time to waste. Abby watched and nodded, scrutinizing his every move and tapping her forefinger on her lower lip. "Now let me see you walk."

Sean held his arms at his sides and took a few steps.

"You look like you're heading to the mines, man. Remember? Now you're a *woman*. Give them their money's worth. If you want to get the tips, you've got to swing your hips. Watch this." Abby sashayed past him.

"You don't expect me to walk like that, do you?" he complained.

"Sean O'Connell. I expect you to do your best to bring home some money and put some food on this table. You've got to be convincing enough to get paid—and even more importantly, convincing enough to not get your *arse kicked.*"

She was right. He could be badly beaten if he were caught. Sean got serious and paraded back and forth past Abby while she shouted instructions the whole time.

"Your posture is atrocious. Your shoulders are rounded and you carry your fists in the front. You look like a prize fighter. You're all slumped over, son. Stand up straight. You're not in the mines anymore."

Sean struggled to keep up with the orders she gave at him.

"Chin up. Stop looking at your feet. Chest out. Shoulders back. Arms to your sides. Stand up straight. Swing your hips a little. Smaller steps—you're not shoveling coal tonight. Grace. Grace."

When she was satisfied, she stopped Sean with her hand against his chest. "Hold on a minute." She sprayed toilet water on his wrists and neck. It was almost more than Sean could stand. Still, he bit his lip. "When they give you a tip, smile, say thank you, bat your eyes a little and put the money in your bosom. You haven't got any pockets and no one will try and steal it from your brassiere. Take my coat and put on these long gloves. Maybe they won't notice your arms are too long for the sleeves that way."

Sean carefully draped her coat over his arm.

"Okay, laddie. You're ready. Wear your boots in the snow and mud. Here is a purse with a pair of slippers. Don't put them on until you get into town or you'll muss them up. If you stretch them, you should be able to get them over your feet. I'm afraid it's a long walk into town, but don't' worry. You can hitch a ride. They'll stop for a woman. Now, let me look at you," she said as she held him at arms length.

She lifted his chin with her finger. "How are you getting along?"

"I'm terrified."

"Me too, but I'm more terrified that I'm down to my last two potatoes and nothing at all to feed us tomorrow. You did say the lights are dim in this place, didn't you?"

"You can barely see."

"Thank you, Jesus. Now go and take a look in the mirror in my room, son, to see what you're working with. Be quick about it. Miss Priss will soon be coming up the walk."

Sean stood in front of the mirror afraid to lift his eyes. When he did, his heart stopped. For a split second, he saw his mother. What would she think if she saw him like this?

Abby crept up beside him and peered into the mirror over his shoulder. He felt her hand press on the small of his back and the other gently pull back on his shoulder.

When she let go, he felt his body slide back into its familiar posture. Patiently, she wrapped her leg around his and straightened his stance. Then she squeezed both his shoulders and pulled them back too, thrusting his chest forward again. Her finger lifted his face once more. "Chin up, lad—I mean, *lassie*. There's nothing to be ashamed of. You're a good father and a good provider and we need you now more than ever."

They stood staring at his image in the mirror together. Even through the make up, his eyes were dark and sunken, his face long from worry and lack of food. He was exhausted and the night hadn't even started.

To try to cheer him, Abby turned him round to face her and said, "You'll make the other girls jealous with that pair. Those are tits you can be proud of."

Sean managed a weak grin. Just then, they heard Hannah singing.

"Hurry, Sean. Here comes the wee one. Go out the back."

Sean's heart leapt to his throat. He started out of the bedroom, but not before Abby grabbed his wrist and thrust the purse into his hand. "Don't forget your slippers," she whispered as Hannah popped through the front door.

"Aunt Abby, I'm home." It was too late. Hannah's eyes grew wide as she spied the stranger darting out the door. "Who's that lady, Auntie?"

"Oh, that's Miss Baker. She's new to town and I was just having a cup of tea with her. Wasn't that right, Sally?"

Could he do it? Could he fool his own child? He was so nervous he got sick to his stomach. "*Hello there Miss*

Hannah. Your Auntie has told me all about you." He offered a limp hand and she gave him her little girl shake.

"You've got big hands. Papa has big hands, too. Where is Papa?"

"Well, uh, your Papa went into town to see about a job. He won't be home for dinner."

"What's for dinner? I'm starving." Sean's stomach tightened. He hadn't eaten all day. He felt another wave of nausea, but this time it was hunger, not nervousness. After a moment, he regained his courage. He was determined to never let his child go hungry again. Abby flicked her eyes at him in approval. He read the expression on her face and stood a little taller.

"I'll make some potato soup for you, sweetheart. Now go and wash up."

Hannah raced up the stairs to comb her hair and wash in the basin. Sean remembered throwing baskets of potato peels onto the compost pile when Abby made thick, creamy potato soup with milk and butter and bacon with hot biscuits on the side. Now they had been reduced to one or two potatoes per pot of soup made with water and salt and pepper–and no biscuits. Abby saved the potato peels to fry in lard or bacon grease for a second meal. Sean was suddenly weak from hunger. His knees began to buckle. He thought he would faint and just as his eyes closed, Abby grabbed him by the back of his coat.

"Steady, Sean. You can do this. Be strong," she whispered in his ear. "Have faith and the Lord will provide." As she patted him on the back, he regained his color. He nodded, clutched the satchel to his chest and stepped out the door into the freezing cold.

Chapter 11

A gust of wind nearly blew Sean off the porch. A few flurries swirled in the air. Sean looked up at the threatening sky and pulled Abby's coat tightly around him. He plodded head down, through the frozen air trying not to think about what lie ahead and—or how he looked. A few moments later, when he heard an engine behind him, he quickly spun around and put out his thumb. As the truck grew near, he saw it was Mr. Fitzgerald, his truck loaded down with milk cans. "Miss, get in here before you freeze to death."

Sean's face was already numb with cold. He was more than happy to oblige.

"The name is Fitzgerald. Pleased to meet you," he said offering his gloved hand.

Sean was quick to extend his hand, remembering only at the last moment to make his wrist limp.

"Sally Baker. Pleased to make your acquaintance," said Sean in his most convincing female voice.

He had known Fitzgerald for years. He helped him put the roof back on his barn after a wind storm. Sean prayed he wouldn't be recognized.

"Baker? I don't know any Bakers around here. Who are you staying with?"

"Mrs. Ashe." Oh no. Should he have told him? Sean hated lies.

"Oh. Is she kin to you?"

He couldn't help it. "She knows my mother from—way back."

"Too bad about Andrew. She's a good woman, that Abby. Where are ya headed?"

"Pottsville. I'm meeting a friend at the inn there." White lie number two.

"I go right past there. You shouldn't be walking in weather like this. You could freeze to death. I'll drop you off right in front."

"Oh, thank you. Thank you so much." Sean struggled to keep his voice feminine.

Sean worried that he'd have to walk the whole way. *The Lord will provide,* Abby said. His throat tightened. He was starving and tired and terrified with the thought of what he was about to try to pull off. The pressure was too much. Then he though of his dream of Hannah lying in a coffin. He couldn't stand the thought of a hungry child, especially his. Water welled in his eyes. Then he remembered the paint on his face. He couldn't risk the make-up running down his cheeks. How do women manage all this? he thought. He carefully dried one tear with his glove and fought back the rest.

"You okay Miss?"

"Yes, I think I have something in my eye. I'll be alright."

Fitzgerald was so intent on keeping the truck on the road, that he didn't notice Sean's voice wavering. At last, he dropped Sean off as promised in front of the inn. Sean waited for him to pull away before crossing the street to the social club. When he let himself in the front door, it was dark and empty. A woman's voice shouted from the back. "We don't open until six, but the inn across the street is open if you want food."

Sean's stomach growled at the mention of it. He would love nothing better.

"No, I'm not looking for food. I am looking for work."

As the woman came closer, Sean noticed how her wavy strawberry hair framed a pair of olive eyes. Two spit curls pressed against the temples of her moon shaped face.

"Well, we did have a girl quit last week, but I don't know if the boss is hiring. I can find him if you like."

"Yes, please." Sean's voice cracked and he struggled to clear his throat.

"What's your name, honey?"

"Sally. Sally Baker."

"I'm Lizzie Williams. Pleased to make your acquaintance."

She took him to the back and knocked at a door.

"Yeah?"

"Johnny, there's a new girl here, Sally. She wants to get on the payroll," she yelled through the keyhole.

"What can she do?" asked an annoyed voice from behind the door.

"What can you do?" asked Lizzie over her shoulder.

"I can serve beer, wait tables and clean up—I guess."

"She's a waitress," yelled Lizzie

"Give me a minute."

"Why doesn't he just open the door?" asked Sean.

"Johnny doesn't like us going in his office. I guess he's got private business. He counts the money and all."

It was difficult to concentrate on Lizzie's words over the sound of papers rustling and drawers slamming from behind the door. Johnny opened it only wide enough to slip through and closed it tightly behind him. He had a wallet in his hand, overstuffed with papers and nervously shoved it into his coat pocket. He was a slight man in a pinstriped suit. His eyes were dark and matched his mustache and thinning hair. His face was oily and pock-marked. He looked Sean over and then spoke to Lizzie as if Sean wasn't there.

"Well, she's got nice eyes, but kinda big through the shoulders don't you think? Definitely ain't no prize. Looks like she got that dress from her mother's closet but she's stacked in the front. I guess it all evens out."

Finally he looked Sean in the eyes. "You worked in a beer joint before, honey?"

"Well, no."

"Great. Just what I need—another amateur. I'm sorry, deary, I can't help you," he said shaking his head at Lizzie.

There was a crash at the end of the hallway. A man carrying a keg of beer had slipped in some water. He had held tightly to his cargo and fell onto his chest with outstretched arms. His elbows were scraped and bleeding. The three of them stared at him and he stared back with wide eyes trying to catch his breath.

"I'm surrounded by amateurs. Mop up that floor, Bobby, before somebody gets hurt," bellowed Johnny. It seemed to Sean it was too late for that.

Bobby carefully lifted his head and surveyed his injuries. Sean gave him a hand and pulled him to his feet. Then Sean grabbed the barrel, threw it onto his left shoulder and carried it to the bar. He swung it down onto the counter and headed for the door. He saw no point in staying where he was not wanted.

The other three stared after him in amazement.

"Wait. Wait. Hang on a minute. Where are you going, baby doll? You may be no beauty queen, but I never saw a woman heft a keg like that. You got moxy. I'll try you for a week. The girls on the floor make twenty-five cents an hour plus tips. You can start tonight. Make sure tomorrow you're here by five and plan on working until midnight. Maybe later if it takes longer to get all the drunks out of here. Nobody leaves until the place is spic and span—uh, what's your name again?"

"Sally."

"Welcome aboard, Sally," said Johnny shaking Sean's hand. "Okay, you guys, we open in less than an hour. Let's get this place ready. It's Friday night and this joint will be jumping," Johnny shouted waving his hands over his head as he retreated back to his office.

"Lizzie, you've got to help me. I don't know where to get started."

"Piece of cake. Sal. We keep it simple here at this *Shitgra-La* if you know what I mean. Alls we serve here is beer and bourbon. If you plan on sneaking a snort yourself, don't get caught. It's the best way to get the boot. Keep their glasses full and their ashtrays empty. Decks of playing cards are behind the bar. Most guys bring their own. Keep your eyes on the cash and don't let 'em walk without paying. Can you make change in your head?"

"Yes," said Sean not really knowing if he could or not.

"Good. Cause you're sort of on your own out here. You've got to pay the house for the booze and what's left is yours to keep. We draw from the tap and Bobby pours the shots. Sometimes he'll pull a beer for us if he's caught up. He makes his own tips at the bar, but I cross his palm with a little of mine if he helps me out. The faster he pours, the more I sell, the more I make. Are you getting the hang of it, Sally?"

Sean's head reeled trying to take it all in. "Yes, yes. I got it."

"Some girls use the trays to serve. I prefer to carry the mugs by the handles. Two or three in each hand is the limit before your arm starts falling off. This is a big place. It can be a long walk from the bar to your tables. The newest girl has to start at the station on the far end. Don't worry. You'll move up in time. Most girls don't last long."

Lizzie took Sean to the darkest section of the club. Abby would be pleased, thought Sean. "These six tables are yours. I know it seems like a lot, but if you move some of the chairs away, maybe you won't get so many customers your first night."

Sean studied the tables to figure out how many *more* chairs he could possibly pull up to each one. The more chairs, the more tips, the more food for his baby.

Lizzie started to walk away and then turned on her heel. "Oh, and when the fellas get too drunk, their hands tend to *wander*. But I'm sure your mother warned you about men when they've had too much sauce. Don't be afraid to take up for yourself, deary."

Sean found a cleaning rag and wiped down his assigned tables. He pushed a few more chairs around them when Lizzie wasn't looking. More girls began to file in. They complained about the cold weather and that their feet hurt already. Finally the patrons began drifting in, too. The men filled the tables closest to the bar. Tables near the stage filled next. The girls at those tables were soon serving drinks, flirting and laughing—and making tips. Sean could see his money slipping away.

When the next man entered, Sean beckoned to him, "Sir, this table is free."

He shot Sean a look, smiled and chose a seat closer to the bar. Time was wasting. Sean had to do something. He walked to the front and got the bartender's attention. He was a stout man with a few gray strands in his thick curly hair. His face was red and puffy. Sean remembered how red his father's face had been and decided Bobby was probably helping himself to the liquor.

"Bobby, spot me a beer. I'll make it up to you."

Bobby stopped rubbing ice over his bloody elbow, drew up a beer and slid it down the bar. "Sure thing, doll."

He gave Sean a wink. Sean returned it with a nervous smile. He wasn't quite ready to wink back at a *man*. Sean carried the beer back over to his section and stood on a chair. "Gentlemen, I have a free beer for the first man to guess my name," he shouted over them.

The men were amused and began to shout out women's names.

"Mary."

"Katie."

"Beth."

"Rose."

"You're as cold as this beer. Keep trying fellas." Sean threw his hip out to one side and flirted with them. Abby would have been proud.

"Dora."

"Tess."

"Sue."

"Nell."

From a distance, Johnny asked Lizzie, "What the hell is she doing?"

"The *amateur* is teaching us how to sell beer."

More men gathered round Sean each shouting names and trying for the free beer. Sean got down from his chair and held it out for a man to be seated. He pulled out chair after chair, inviting each man to have a seat in his section.

"Take a load off. Make yourself at home. Would you like to *buy* a drink while you're guessing?"

"Is it Jane?"

"No. Good try though. What's it going to be? A pint or a shot?"

Sean's tables filled quickly. He knew he'd have to pass some drinks around before they get bored. Sean raced back to Bobby. "Please, Bobby, I need six shots of whiskey."

Bobby nodded and poured quickly. Sean pulled six steins of beer from the keg. He carried a small tray with the whiskey in his left hand and six steins in his right. He passed the drinks around and collected the money. Then he raced back to Bobby with the money and drew twelve more beers. He had to hurry. My tables are full and *my boys* are thirsty, thought Sean. They were still shouting names at him as he got the last drink into the last man's hands. He climbed back onto a chair and made an announcement over the men still shouting women's names at him. "I'm glad to see you all here tonight. Unfortunately, no one has guessed my name, but you'll get another chance tomorrow."

There were a few grunts and boos, but mostly there were cheers. They had gotten caught up in the game and the antics of watching the new blonde girl race for their drinks. They soon forgot the distraction and got back to the main events: smoking cigarettes, playing cards, getting drunk and watching the stage for the entrance of the dancing girls.

Sean moved methodically from table to table collecting empty glasses and setting down full ones. He emptied ashtrays and pointed the gents to the water closet. Men slipped him nickels and dimes when he brought their drinks and some left change on the table after them. He remembered Abby's advice and slipped the change into his bosom. He continued to carry six beers in each hand every time he came from the bar. Nobody will get thirsty on my watch, thought Sean. He overheard one gent say to another, "She's not much for the eyes, but have you seen arms on that girl?"

"Yeah, she's twice the woman of some of these little gals," replied the other.

"She never wears down. She just keeps on coming with the drinks."

They both nodded. Sean beamed with pride. He was passing as a woman and filling his blouse with silver and no one was the wiser. He bent over to set down the latest brace of beers, when he felt a hand on his buttock. Instantly, the blood surged up his neck. He could feel his veins bulge. His hand tightened into a fist, but as he turned to knock his block off, he suddenly remembered he was a *woman*. Slowly, he unclenched his fingers, reared back his hand, and slapped the offender as hard as he dared across the face.

"The beer's for sale, but I'm not." The adrenaline made Sean's voice crack mid-sentence. No one seemed to notice as they stared back at the five finger marks Sean left on the man's cheek. The man struggled to stay in his chair. Sean feared he had gone too far. Perhaps the strength of the slap had given him away. A tear welled in the man's eyes but the smile never left his face. "You're a wild little filly, aren't ya?" he asked as he checked his mouth for a loose tooth.

The nearby men and waitresses began to laugh. Sean threw his voice up as far as he could. "Mother warned me about men like you." He sassed as he walked away with his nose in the air, twitching his hind quarters for good measure. He wrapped his hand around the first beer he saw. The cold stein felt good against his palm that was still stinging.

The night flew by so quickly, it was dizzying. At midnight, Johnny and Bobby chased out the last few stragglers. The women washed the ashtrays and wiped down the tables. Sean grabbed the mop and began washing the floor. Bobby firmly took the mop from his hand. "Give me that. This is man's work. Not bad for your first night, Miss Sally. You really used your head out there.

You're *my* kind of girl," he said as he placed his hand over Sean's.

Sean gratefully handed over the mop and gently pulled his hand away from Bobby's. Sean turned away, reached down his bosom and pulled out a dime and a nickel. "Here's what I owe you for that first beer. And thank you for your kindness, good sir."

"No. Thank *you*," said Bobby as he hastily cleaned the floor.

Johnny handed out wages to the dancing girls and the waitresses. "Here's two-fifty, Sally. You got here early and you passed out a lotta brew. Nice work, kid. See you tomorrow, cupcake," said Johnny.

Two dollars and fifty cents, thought Sean. And he hadn't even counted his tips. How many bits had he shoved down into his brassiere? His feet hurt up to his shoulders, but he didn't care. He slipped on his boots and put his slippers in the purse. He buttoned Abby's coat on tight. It was below freezing and besides, he couldn't' risk losing a single coin.

"Which way are you headed?" asked one of the girls.

"Cressona."

"Sorry, we're headed north," they yelled as their sedan sped away.

The earlier snowstorm had moved on and left a still, cold clear night. Sean could see his every breath, even the air from his nose looked as thick as smoke. Three-quarters of a moon lit his way and he watched his shadow in the snow as he walked. His feet were so cold he could not feel the road beneath them. His head pounded from hunger and his body begged for rest. Still, he pressed on towards home. The warmth of the woodstove and the softness of his bed were three long miles of icy roads away. He had walked this path hundreds of times, but never in the wee hours of the morning–and never in a dress. He pulled the coat tighter against his frozen legs. His head was spinning trying to remember all that had happened that night. The Shangri-La was a strange world he had never known. He searched his mind to see the faces of Lizzie, Johnny and Bobby. A smile tugged at the corners of his mouth when he thought what he must look like hefting a beer keg on his shoulder in a dress. He couldn't wait to count his tips. He tried to remember each coin that was given to him that night, but it all became a blur. His brain was befuddled by exhaustion. Nevertheless, with the money he made in those past few hours, his girls would eat for a few more days. He clutched his coat tightly once more, pulling the silver closer to his chest and smiled a frozen smile.

Chapter 12

By the last mile, Sean was not sure if his legs would make it. Not a single car drove past him that night. It was nearly two in the morning when he finally reached his porch. When he opened the door, the warmth of the kitchen made his face tingle. Abby must have risen in the night and stoked the fire. God bless her, he thought. His boots were covered with snow. His hands were so frozen he could scarcely take off his boots. He set them near the stove to dry. His stockings were soaked in sweat and his feet were red and cold. He gratefully stripped off the women's clothes: coat, hat, scarf, dress and petticoat.

A kettle of hot water simmered on the back of the stove. *Bless you, Abby.* He poured some of it into a basin with cold water and steeped his icy hands in it. He dipped the corner of a towel in it and wiped the paint from his face. When his hands were thoroughly warm, he set the basin on the floor and carefully put in his feet. Pins and needles jabbed at his toes and the sting shot to his calves. The pain was almost too much to endure, but he feared if he didn't warm his feet, they might suffer from frostbite. As he warmed a little, he realized he still had on the brassiere. He spread a dish towel on the kitchen table, lowered his chest over it and slowly unhooked it from the back. He couldn't risk losing the change on the floor or waking the girls with the clinking of the change. Those silver coins might as well have been gold from the way he smiled when he saw them. So many nickels and dimes–and even a few quarters, carefully, he counted his booty. He had two dollars and sixty-five cents in tips. With the money Johnny gave him, he had over five dollars. That was enough to feed them for a week. For this kind of money, he didn't care about his frozen feet or the loud mouth drunks. It was more than he ever made in a ten hour day at the mines.

He put on clean socks, trousers and a shirt and felt like himself again. He refilled the kettle and stoked the stove. He set three plates, forks and knives around the table and pulled down a small skillet. He wrapped a blanket around his shoulders and sank into the couch to doze until sunrise. He would be the first customer of the morning at the general store.

* * *

Sean was up to meet the first rays of sunlight through the window pane. A pang of hunger cut into his stomach like a knife. He pulled on his shoes and coat and got to the store just as Mr. Flynn began sweeping the snow from the steps. He gave Sean a long face when he approached.

Flynn was a short man, with strong arms and a round belly. His face was ruddy, especially when he was working. His mustache and few remaining strands on his head were gray. The long hem of his shopkeeper's white apron hung beneath his winter coat.

"Good morning, Mr. Flynn."

Nervously, Flynn began to sweep faster.

"I'm sorry, Sean. I can't give out any more store credit," he said without looking at him. Sean thought it strange. The store owner had never treated him this way before. Flynn had a gap between his two large front teeth. His words sometimes whistled when he spoke. It occurred to Sean that he looked like a red-faced, pudgy rabbit. Sean was undaunted. After a few seconds of watching him work, he tried again.

"I've got cash money today, Mr. Flynn. I'd like to buy a few groceries, if you're open for business." Flynn stopped in mid-sweep and stood upright. "Oh, I'm open for business, alright." He gave Sean a dubious stare over his glasses.

"What kind of money are we talking about?" he asked as he moved the broom in front of him and rested both hands on it. Seamus Flynn had owned the store as long as folks could remember. He also served as the postmaster, a notary and the justice of the peace. He made it his business to know everybody else's business. It wasn't too difficult, especially since he had a party line and listened to every call that came through.

"I've got—*a couple* of dollars to spend."

Sean knew he had over five dollars in his pocket. It wasn't a lie since he only planned to spend about half of it this trip. Flynn was suspicious. Nobody in town had any work. The mines were still shut tight. He wondered where Sean had gotten money. After a moment, he replied, "Sure, sure. Help yourself. You know your way around." He motioned with his hand to enter his store. Flynn rested his broom against the door jamb and followed him in.

Sean knew this store like the back of his hand. In minutes, he gathered a large bag of flour, can of lard, slab of bacon, dozen eggs, six apples, can of coffee, pound of butter, quart of milk and a five pound sack of potatoes.

"Great day. You must be rich. Did you inherit some money?" Flynn asked as he rang up the goods on the cash register.

"No," answered Sean as he put his groceries on the counter.

"Oh, I know. Did Andrew have a life insurance policy? Maybe Abby just got a check," he offered.

"Nope. No such luck."

Flynn rang him up slowly, still trying to pump him about where he had gotten the money. "You haven't been making any corn squeezings up in the woods there have you, Seany boy? I know you take your gun up there once in a while. Maybe you're doing more than shooting squirrels. I wouldn't blame you. Your secret's safe with me."

Flynn couldn't keep a secret if his life depended on it. Sean knew the minute he left the store the whole town would know he'd been in here with cash.

"No. I don't know anything about moonshine."

"Well what is it then, lad? Don't keep me guessing. Share your secret," he whispered as he put some of the groceries into a paper sack.

Sean ignored his question.

"What's the damage?" he asked.

"Oh. Uh, that'll be one dollar and seventy-two cents," answered Flynn as he came out of his trance.

As Sean dug deep into his pocket, he spied a jar of strawberry jam on the top shelf.

"I'd like to have a jar of that jam, too, if you don't mind."

"Fifteen cents," said Flynn adding it to the sack.

"One dollar eighty-seven."

Sean handed him eight quarters. Flynn seemed disappointed that he wasn't offered a large bill. Then he would have something to talk about. He handed Sean his change then lifted the paper sack to him but wouldn't let go. "But you haven't told me a thing, laddie. Where did you get the money?"

Sean hated secrets and lies. But what could he say? If he told Flynn he found work, he'd have the neighbors watching his house night and day with his comings and goings in hopes that they could find work too. He wished he had gone to another store, but it was too far to walk. Hunger pounded at his brain once more. He had to get something to eat before he fell to the floor–and he had to feed his *girls*.

"The Lord has blessed me with a little good fortune. That's all I can say. Thank you, Mr. Flynn and good day." Sean tugged the groceries from Flynn's hand, gave him a quick hand shake and grabbed the sack of potatoes from the counter.

Flynn slumped at the shoulders in disappointment. As Sean headed for the door, Flynn called after him.

"Hey, wait a minute, you."

Sean thought, what is it now?

"I'll get the door for you."

Flynn opened the door just wide enough to let Sean out and not let any more cold air into the store. With a sincere smile he offered, "Don't you spend your good fortune anywhere else. I've got everything you need right *here*."

Sean returned his smile just as a gust of wind slammed the door shut.

He rushed home to cook breakfast before the girls awakened. He considered the small skillet he had pulled down the night before. It wouldn't do. He replaced it on its peg and pulled down the biggest skillet they had. He used his best knife to slice through the bacon. His hand trembled so hard he feared he would cut himself. He didn't know if his shaking was from excitement or hunger. Nevertheless, Sean filled the pan with as many slices as it would hold and started a pot of coffee on the back of the stove. He poured some flour into the mixing bowl and started cutting in the lard. As he raised a cloud of flour dust he felt Abby's hand on his wrist. She took the biscuit blender from his hand.

"Give me that," she said taking the bowl away too. Abby's eyes beamed as she curled the bowl under her bosom and set to work. Her eyes became moist as she worked the dough. She added a few shakes of salt, poured in some milk and mixed it some more. Hastily, she cut out the biscuits and without another word shoved them into the oven. When the bacon was crisp, Sean beat the eggs with a little milk and poured them into the skillet with the hot grease, sprinkling salt and pepper over the top. The biscuits smelled heavenly as they baked. Sean thought he would faint from hunger before they were brown. Then he heard a small voice say, "Mmmmmm, Sunday breakfast."

"Lamb chop," said Sean softly. Hannah's curls hung over her brow and there was still sleep in the corners of her eyes. Sean pushed the hair from her face, lifted her warm cheek to his, kissed it and lowered her back to the floor. It seemed like days since he had seen her.

"Today, we'll have Sunday breakfast on Saturday, won't we?" Sean's voice cracked when he spoke.

Hannah smiled and nodded eagerly. "I'm hungry."

"And it's a fine thing, too," said Abby. "We need someone to eat all these scrumptious vittles."

Hannah and Sean extended their hands over the table for a biscuit when Abby stopped them mid-reach. Abby closed her eyes and bowed her head. Hannah and Sean bowed out of respect for Abby, but didn't dare close their eyes. They had waited too long for food like this. They both hoped that it would be a short blessing.

"Dear Lord, thank you for this thy bounty, for food for our bellies and for helping us take care of each other. Amen."

Sean gave Hannah a wink and their hands shot straight back to the biscuits. They wasted no time slathering them in butter and jam and devouring them with hardly a chew. Sean shoveled down his scrambled eggs and Hannah ate her bacon with her fingers and licked the grease from each one.

"Hannah Jane, where are your manners?" scolded Abby and motioned for her to use a napkin.

"Do we have to have manners this time, Aunt Abby? Sometimes it's fun to eat like a piggie."

Hannah and Sean froze in mid-feast for her reply.

After a moment, Abby replied, "What the devil." She licked the jam off her thumb and proceeded to lick the egg yolk from the back of her knife.

"May I have another biscuit, Papa?"

Sean spread on butter and strawberries and watched her gobble it up. Finally, his stomach was full too. By now, exhaustion was getting the best of him. He smiled with moist eyes, happy to watch his little girl eat—to finally get *enough* to eat. Suddenly, he experienced a wave of nausea. Sean bolted from the table and stepped out the door for some cool air. He had to sit on the porch for a moment until his head stopped spinning. Soon after, Abby poked her head out the door.

"You alright?" she asked softly.

"I don't know what happened."

"Well I do. You haven't eaten in two days then you ate all that rich breakfast in a matter of minutes. I can't blame you. Chin up. You'll feel better when it gets into your blood."

Sean stood up. He was already steadier on his feet. They both sat back at the table to finish their meal. Hannah was still seated at her place, licking her fingers. Abby cleaned her plate, sighed and leaned back in her chair. She held her cup to her lips savoring every drop. "Heavens, this coffee is good. It's been weeks."

"Papa, you've got jam on your fingers," scolded Hannah. Sometimes she sounded just like her mother. Sean looked down at the red polish on his nails and hid his hands under the table.

"Yep. I'll be sure to wash my hands after breakfast," said Sean as he looked to Abby for help. Abby giggled and almost spilled her cup. "Sweetheart, run along and get out of your nightgown. Auntie needs help with the dishes." Hannah nodded and ran up the stairs with enthusiasm.

"I haven't seen her with this much energy in days," said Abby.

"She was starving. She finally got–*full.*"

"We *all* did. How did you do it, Sean? All this food? How much did you bring in last night?"

"Five dollars and fifteen cents."

"Great day in the morning! That's more than the mines."

"For battin' me eyes and serving the liquor," he said way up high.

Abby stared into her cup. "You didn't spend it all– did you?"

"No, I thought I should save some back, for later."

"Aye, you're a wise man. Besides, folks will be getting suspicious if you are suddenly rich. We've got to be careful so you're not found out. Don't go flashing your money, son."

"What am I going to do about these?" Sean asked holding out his polished nails.

"Well, a little paint thinner will get that off, but then you'll have to paint them next time. When are you gonna work again?"

"Tonight."

"Good boy. Make hay while the sun shines I always say. But right now, you can barely keep your eyes open. You must be worn out."

"Yes ma'am. But it's a good thing I've got going. The boss says he'll try me for a week. I've got to be there tonight but I'll have to get some sleep before then. Can you keep the wee one quiet for a few hours?"

"Aye."

"I'll have to get up in a while to shave and roll my hair. Will you help me, Abby?"

"Aye."

"And Abby. Could you find me another dress? Maybe something with green to go with my eyes?"

"Now I've heard everything. Get your dainty derriere upstairs and get some beauty sleep. You're gonna need all the help you can get."

Chapter 13

That night, Sean put on a dress and headed back to the Shangri-La. He set up his tables and waited for the night to begin. As the door swung open with new arrivals, he started up the same name game he had played the night before. This time, the men were ready for him. Within two minutes, one of the gents guessed *Sally* and won a free beer. While the other fellows congratulated the winner with a pat on the back, Sean noticed he stared at him in a strange way. Sean wondered if the man recognized him. Or perhaps he had figured out that *Sally* was really a *man*. Fearful of being found out, Sean smiled and quickly darted the other way. A few minutes later, Sean noticed the same man staring at him again. Sean was sure he didn't recognize him. He stayed as busy as he could to take his mind off the strange glances. Sean made a game of how quickly he could get back to his tables with his drinks. More drinks—more tips. More tips—more vittles for his curly girl. By now, the stranger had gotten a couple of drinks under his belt. He smiled like a simpleton and winked at Sean. "For Christ's sake, he's flirting with me," said Sean under his breath. The strange man rose from his chair and walked directly towards Sean. "What can I get you sir, a pint or some whiskey?" asked *Sally*. The stranger grinned like a love sick seventh-grader and asked, "How does a fella go about getting a little smooch?"

Sean wanted to belt him. Once again, he had to remind himself, he was a *woman*. For a split second, Sean was impressed with himself that his disguise was working, until he felt a hand touch his thigh. Quickly, it crept up his dress. Sean grabbed his wrist.

"Hold it right there, buster. What kind of a—girl do you take me for?"

"I hope the kind that likes to fool around," he hotly whispered into Sean's ear.

Sean squeezed his hand hoping to break a few fingers.

"Ouch. Jesus," said the stranger as he pulled his hand away. "Are you trying to kill me?" he asked pathetically. For a moment Sean felt sorry for him and his face must have shown it.

"You got quite a grip on you for a woman. I like strong girls. They last longer," he said in a lusty voice as he puckered his lips for a kiss.

"I'm spoken for," Sean said as he grabbed the man by the wrist and twisted it until he bent at the knees in pain. Sean turned his body back to the direction from whence he came and gave him a good shove. "Nice try, big boy," grunted *Sally*.

What a way to start the night, thought Sean. He carried as many steins as his arms could bear and soon he was quick at making change in his head. It was Saturday night, after all, and everyone was in good spirits. After several fast runs to the bar, Sean paused for a moment to catch his breath. He watched as the main attraction, the dancing girls, did their act. Most were fair with flat chests and skinny legs. They wore scanty clothing and far too much make up. They reminded him of porcelain dolls. Most had hair as short as a man's. It was the latest style, but Sean didn't like it. A woman should have long hair, which falls loosely around her shoulders–like Molly's, he thought, and missed her. Over the music and jeers, Sean heard someone call his name. "Oh Sa-a-a-lly. How about that kiss?" He looked over to find that his admirer was so drunk that he could barely stand at the bar. Using one hand to steady himself, he used the other to blow *Sally* a kiss. At first, Sean was disgusted. Then a smile crept over his face. Perhaps he should take the drunken man to the privy with him and show him what was under his skirt. That would cure his infatuation, maybe cure him of women for life.

The night was over in a flash, much easier than the first night. Sean's take was just over six dollars. He was thankful, even relieved. He gave Bobby a whole dollar for getting his drinks up so fast. Sean considered it a payment of gratitude as well as an investment in the future. He wouldn't soon forget the favor. Bobby nodded and smiled as he folded the greenback and shoved it into his pocket. As Sean turned to go, he thought Bobby must have children too.

After another long walk home, Sean warmed himself by the fire and crawled into bed. The next morning, he handed his cash over to Abby. She bought a short list at the general store and put the rest of the money in a jar in the cabinet next to the Irish whiskey. "Sean, we've got to save as much back as we can. Who knows what tomorrow will bring?" He agreed. There were so many things they needed, but none so important as the next day's meal.

Sunday night, the club was closed. Sean wasn't disappointed. He slept until ten then brought in enough wood for the next couple of days. For supper, Abby cooked split pea soup with bits of carrots and ham. Curly girl filled them in about school as she reached for another corn muffin.

"We have our spelling test tomorrow."

"Don't you usually have spelling on Friday?" asked Sean.

"Yep. It got cancelled."

"Cancelled?" Sean asked as he peered over at Abby. Abby smiled and said nothing.

"Billy Hertzel took Tommy Dickerson's pencil, so Tommy hit him in the stomach. Then Billy busted Tommy in the nose and blood started coming out," explained Hannah. By now, she was nervously twirling her forefinger round and round the curl that dangled from her temple.

"The test was called on account of a bloody nose?" asked Sean.

Abby snorted.

"When Billy's sister, Patsy, saw the blood, she threw up in the middle of the classroom so Miss Klein had to get help cleaning up the place. The whole class had to go over with the second graders for the rest of the afternoon."

Sean lowered his soup spoon and shook his head.

"Wait a minute. How is it Billy and Patsy are in the same grade if they are brother and sister? Are they twins?" asked Sean.

"Nope. Billy failed. He's supposed to be in the second grade. Some kids think it's because he can't read too good. I think it's because he's a bully. I won't let him borrow my pencil because I know he won't give it back. And anyway, he uses the eraser end to dig wax out of his ears. He's just rude," said Hannah matter-of-factly as she stuffed another piece of muffin into her mouth.

Sean leaned over the table towards Abby with a confused look on his face.

"When do these kids have time to read and write?"

"Welcome to the first grade," replied Abby.

Sean looked over at Hannah and noticed her soup bowl.

"How about giving the muffins a rest and eating some of your soup?" he said in a fatherly tone.

Hannah dropped the muffin back onto her plate.

"Hannah is invited to a birthday party next Saturday," offered Abby.

"Can I go, Papa?"

"Whose birthday is it? Caroline's?"

"Nope."

"Susie's?"

"No sir."

Sean looked to Abby for help. "Marie's?"

A smile spread across Abby's faced. Hannah giggled.

"Tell him, Hannah. Go on."

"Jimmy Johnson."

"A boy?" asked Sean.

Abby nodded.

"Hmmmmmm, I see. Is Jimmy your friend?" asked Sean

"Yes."

"Or is Jimmy your—*boyfriend?*" teased Sean.

"Oooooh, yuck. He's *not* my boyfriend. He's just a friend. Well, he's not even really my friend. He picked his nose in class last week and the teacher caught him. She made him stand in the corner with a tissue in each hand so he would remember to use one next time. I guess you could say he's just a dumb old boy."

"I don't know, Hannah Jane. Pretty soon the boys will come a calling. Then you'll get married and have a bunch of babies and you'll spend all day changing stinky diapers."

"No sir! I'm not going to marry Jimmy Johnson."

"Aye. You're a smart girl, lassie. Stay away from men. They'll ruin your life," said Abby.

"Anyway, I hate boys."

Sean considered this as he sopped the last bit of soup from his bowl with his muffin.

"Then why do you want to go to his party?"

"Well—I'm pretty sure there will be cake. And maybe ice cream if his father can get some," she said with her eyes shining.

"That figures. What do you think, Aunt Abby? Should we let her go?"

"I suppose. But she'll need a present to take. Have you thought about a gift for your little friend?"

"Well, I could get him a coloring book and crayons or a cowboy hat or maybe a spinning top."

Abby and Sean looked at each other over Hannah's head. Even though they were a few dollars to the good, they were cautious about letting even a few pennies go out the door.

"Uh, have you thought about making him a present? Homemade gifts are the best," said Abby.

Sean tried to think of something Hannah could make and what there was in the house she could use. Then he got an idea. He went upstairs to his bedroom and returned with a little wooden boat he had carved.

"No, Sean. You work too hard on your boats," argued Abby.

"Really, Papa? Can I give him one or your boats?"

"It's alright. It's just a row boat. I have another one like it upstairs."

Abby carefully took it from Sean's hands and marveled at the ribs on the inside that made it seaworthy and the tiny oars he had carved. Hannah peered over her shoulder for a better look.

"Nice work," said Abby softly.

"It's amazing," echoed Hannah.

Sean beamed. It was just a little boat, but he put his best effort into it.

"But you know this is *Papa's* handiwork. You should put some finishing touches on it too, little one," said Abby with a motherly tone.

After supper, Hannah read from her first grade primer to her father. He could scarcely believe how much she had learned in such a short time. His eyes watered when he realized Molly had not lived to see her daughter go to school.

Monday was slow at the club, but Sean was grateful for any cash he got. On Tuesday, another waitress arrived early, like him, to clean and set up her tables. She had golden hair and blue eyes. Sean was sure he hadn't seen her before. He went about his business and she went about hers until they reached for the broom at the same time.

"Oh, you can use it first," she said handing it to him.

"Thank you." As he got a better look at her face, he could see she was lovely—her peach complexion, the sparkle in her eye, the life in her smile. Her pink lips moved but he....

"Are you alright?"

The spell was broken. Sean cleared his throat and tried to regain his composure. "How do you do? My name is Sally Baker." He offered his dead fish hand only this time it was trembling.

"Margaret Schmidt. My friends call me Maggie. Pleased to make your acquaintance," she said taking his hand. Sean felt the warmth flow from her fingers into his hand, arm, through his chest and up his neck. His face flushed and the blood left his feet turning them to ice. He became dizzy.

"The pleasure is all mine," Sean managed to say almost flirting.

Maggie looked back at him, a little confused, smiling and nodding before she let go of his hand.

The pleasure's all mine? You idiot! That's what a *man* says to a woman. Think. Think. "Where do you come from, Maggie?" Sean asked as casually as he could.

"I am staying with my great-aunt. She was widowed last year and my parents don't want her to be alone over the winter. It's too hard for her to get out in this weather. I don't know what she will do when the weather breaks. She shouldn't live by herself. She was sick the past few days so I had to miss work to take care of her. She doesn't like me working here, but it's the only job I could find.

"Are you from around here?"

No, I grew up in Maryland, south of Annapolis. But Pottsville has always been her home."

"Is that near Baltimore?"

"A ways south of Baltimore."

Sean was concerned about his prying, asking so many questions, but he had to know the answer. "How far is Baltimore from–the ocean?"

Sean's dream of the water rose up fast. He had kept it locked away too long. Had Maggie ever seen the ocean? Had she ever been on a boat? Did her father own a boat? In his mind, Sean was once again on his way to the sea. It called to him. All his longings since childhood rushed in.

"Baltimore sits on the Patapsco River. It flows into the Chesapeake Bay and straight into the Atlantic. The harbor is a busy place and so is the city. It's famous for its crabcakes and oysters."

"Crab cakes? You mean like with flour and sugar?"

"No, more like a patty of fried fish with crackers or a roll."

Sean tried to imagine it."

"Oysters? Do they look like the mussels my grandfather told me about?"

"Not exactly. But they're mighty tasty in a stew of cream and butter," she said with her eyes twinkling like two stars.

"I have always dreamed of living on the water," admitted Sean.

"I want a house of my own on the water too."

"Are you two going to clean up or gossip all night?" complained Johnny as he came out of his office.

Sean quickly swept the mud left by winter boots from around his tables then took the broom to Maggie. When she took it from his hands, one of her fingers touched his and the warmth crept up his arm again. He hadn't felt this way in years, not since he first met Molly. He didn't know he could ever feel that way again. His mind raced. He couldn't believe he found a woman who shared his dream of the water. He wanted to talk to her, be near her, and find out everything about her. But he couldn't. He had to lay low. He needed this job. He had to be silent—and wait. It was *miserable.*

The night flew not just because he was busy, but because he couldn't take his eyes off Maggie. Her skirt gently swayed back and forth as she waited on her customers. The shape of her body, her hips and her bosom lingered in his mind. The dimples in her cheeks and the pattern of her freckles made her childlike, innocent. When she was nervous, she twirled a strand of her hair round and round with her finger, like Hannah. She had a brown birthmark on the left side of her neck and Sean's lips longed to kiss it. Her eyes were sparkling blue diamonds and he wanted nothing more than to gaze into them. It had been over a year since Molly had passed and his thoughts had never left her. In every dream, he saw her face. But it was time for the mourning to be over. He wanted to love and be happy again. However, his chance for happiness had to wait. Maggie could not discover he was a *man.* Not yet. For now, he would have to love her from *afar.*

It was a long walk in the wind that night and Sean's heart was heavy. He felt guilty about looking at another woman. Still worse, he was trapped in women's clothes, not able, as a man, to look into Maggie's eyes. Most of all, he felt alone. It had been too long since he had enjoyed the company of a woman. His heart and body ached.

By noon the next day, Abby buzzed around the kitchen. She'd been out early that morning and had found a chicken to roast for supper. Sean remembered how he had promised Molly a chicken in the pot every Sunday the last Christmas they spent together. Abby had the radio in the front room playing loud enough for her to hear in the kitchen. She hummed along and sang the words when she knew them.

"I got rhythm. I got music—who could ask for anything more? Who could ask for anything more?" She fussed over the fat little bird, only partly dressed, resting on a sheet of brown paper.

"It's still got feathers."

"Huh? Oh, good morning, no, good *afternoon*, there, Seany boy. I got it fresh from the farm. Never mind about the feathers. Reach me the grabbers in the top drawer."

Sean handed her the pliers and she washed them in the sink. Then she plucked the pin feathers from the wings."

"Why don't you just cut off the tips? There's no meat on them anyway."

"Nonsense. The wings have the juiciest meat and crispiest skin. I like to use that little piece there to pick my teeth after supper," she said pointing to a nub on the side. "The wing is my favorite piece, that and the pug nose, the last part of the chicken to go over the fence," she said with a wink. "No, we won't waste a morsel."

"I haven't seen a chicken in this kitchen in months or even in the store for that matter. How did you get it?"

"Do you remember Mr. Tucker? He has a farm on the other side of town."

"Yes, but I didn't think he sold chickens anymore."

"He doesn't. But he keeps a few for himself."

"And?"

"And I had a life before Drew, you know? Tucker was, well, sweet on me in school. I went out to his place and told him I had my eye on one of his chickens."

"So you batted your eyes and got a chicken? The old girl's still got it."

"You bet I have. And since his wife is gone, I saw no harm in using a little charm."

"Charm for chicken. Well, well, well..."

"Charm and the tin of coffee I pulled out of my bag. He hasn't had a drop since the bottom fell out. When he saw that blue can, he caught this little birdie, wrung its neck and plucked it right there for me."

When Abby finished pulling out the last of the pin feathers, she rolled them in the paper she'd been working on and handed it to Sean. "Put this in the rubbish, mister."

"So it wasn't the eye-batting, it was the coffee that won the pullet."

"Horsefeathers. It was my irresistible charm and natural beauty that won us this prize. The coffee just sealed the deal." Abby laid the chicken on the cutting board and chopped off its neck with a cleaver with a loud thud. Sean leaned on his elbows and watched her. Her apron was speckled with blood, her forehead was beaded with sweat and a wisp of gray hair had fallen down around her cheek. She was right. She *was* beautiful—beautiful and happy. She rinsed the giblets and dropped them and the neck into a pan of water with salt to simmer on the back of the stove.

"Are you going to see Mr. Tucker again?"

She swung around and faced him, shaking her cleaver. "I have no interest in Mr. Tucker, just his chickens. I won't be going out there again anytime soon. It's a wise man who leaves a woman to her work when she's waving a knife around," she said teasing him. When he turned away, she tapped him on the back of the head for good measure.

She stirred her giblets once with the wooden spoon and added a little pepper. "That's going to make a fine gravy," she said under her breath. She rinsed her hands in the sink and wiped them on a towel. Then she dragged out a cutting board and large knife and commenced the chopping of the onions, celery and stale bread crusts for the stuffing. She hummed to the music on the radio once more. Sean found a chair at the table to sit and sulk. He folded his arms and rested his chin on them. Misery set in as he watched her work. She continued to hum and chop for a few more minutes before she noticed Sean did not share in her jolliness.

"What is it, lad? Are you sick?"

"Sort of."

"Good heavens. That's it. You're getting the flu or even worse, the pneumonia. I knew it would catch up with you sooner or later. I'll fix you some soup. Now get a hot bath and get back in bed until it's time to go to work. We've got to get you feeling better. Have you got a fever?"

"No, not that kind of sick."

"Oh. Have you got an intestinal problem? Do you need some castor oil?"

"No. God, no."

"Well is it your back, your feet, uh, uh a headache?"

"I'm all right."

"Well, you don't look all right. What's eating you? Tell me."

"I'm too embarrassed to tell you."

"Too embarrassed? Now what can be more embarrassing than putting on women's clothes and selling beer?"

Sean shot her an evil look.

"Oh, now Seany. You know I didn't mean it that way. My God, where would we be if you hadn't done it? We three would be laying up in the bone yard by now. You are doing a hell of a job keeping us fed. I just mean, if you can't tell your *old Aunt Abby*, then who can you tell? Haven't we been through enough together by now, lad?"

She was right. He couldn't stand aching all alone any longer. Still, he didn't know how she would take it.

"I met a girl."

"And?"

"Her name is Maggie."

"And? C'mon, boy. Don't make me drag it out of you. What about her?"

Sean looked up at Abby with pleading eyes and hoped she would realize what he was trying to tell her.

"Do you like this Maggie?"

"I'm miserable."

"Then you're in love," she squealed.

"Shhhhhhhhhhhh. Hannah will hear you."

"Seany is in *love*. How long have you been suffering, lad?" she whispered.

"I just met her last night."

"Smitten, are ya?" She sounded pleased.

"You're not angry?"

"About what?"

"About Molly?"

"Oh, laddie. You and I both loved Molly while she was alive and she will always be in our hearts. But she's gone now. It's been over a year. *I'll* never love another. Drew and I were together forty years. I'm too old to start over. But you, you are still so young. It would be a sin to waste your life grieving for Molly. You must love and *live* again. It's time."

Abby rested her hand over Sean's. "Here's the bigger question. Does she love you?"

"How can she?"

Abby looked at him blankly for a moment. Then she shook her head. A smile widened across her face. She held her sides and gave a low belly laugh.

"What? What's so funny?"

"I forgot. You are a *woman*. How could she love you?"

Abby looked at him through blurry eyes before laughing harder and harder until the tears were streaming down her face. It angered Sean.

"I fail to see the humor in this."

"Oh. Oh. I'm sorry. So sorry, Sean," she said gasping. "You know I love you like a son. Please accept my sincere apology. But you've got to see the lighter side of this. You, Sean, *only you* would fall in love with a woman who thinks you're a girl. Think about it. You are in your favorite spot, between a rock and a hard place. What the hell else can happen to you lad? What else?"

She grabbed his shoulder and pulled him close to her. Then she gave him a Dutch rub on the top of his head with her knuckles. Sean smiled too. After all, she was laughing with him. And she was right. Who else could get themselves in such a ridiculous situation? For a moment, they laughed together. Sean felt like a small boy, warm and content with her arms around him. He remembered how he felt when his mother held him, safe and *loved*. Abby was his mother now.

"Sean, you can't give in to this right now. You can't blow your cover. W*e* need this job. If you want to start dating, why not find a girl in town. Take her for a walk. Sit with her in church. Bring her home. I'll cook her my best dinner."

"Thanks, Abby. I know you would. It's not like I have a choice. You don't understand. My heart wants *her.*"

"Oh, laddie. That's where you are wrong. I do understand. Love is a maddening thing. We can neither make ourselves love someone nor keep ourselves from it. We can't go looking for it. It has to find us. And when it does, we are powerless against cupid's arrow. Andrew Ashe was a son of a bitch. But he was *my* son of a bitch. He was still chasing me around the house the week before he died. I know I'll never find that kind of love again, nor do I wish to. But you lad, you may be lucky enough to find it again, or maybe it has already found you. I doubt if you will have to play this charade for long.

Then you can meet her as a man and see how she feels," said Abby as she tightened her grip on his shoulder.

Sean got an idea. Eagerly he suggested, "Maybe I can go there tonight without women's clothes and sit and have a beer and talk to her."

"Nay. Don't chance it, deary. Someone is sure to recognize you. You'll be out of a job and maybe lose some teeth too, mind you. Don't risk it. We need the money. I know it's hard, lad. But you'll have to wait."

Scan watched as she rolled a piece of newspaper into a tight baton. She lit the end of it in the stove. She quickly singed the remainder of the down feathers from the chicken's skin and tossed the spent newspaper into the stove. He watched as she mixed the bread and celery with melted butter, rubbed sage and some of the juice from the giblets and stuffed it into the bird. Sean knew she was right. He got a sinking feeling again. Back to square one. But at least now Abby knew about his plight and he didn't have to suffer alone. Most of all, he didn't have to feel guilty about loving someone besides Molly.

Sean was still tired from the long night before. He folded his arms in front of him and returned his chin to the table. He watched as Abby carefully lifted the stuffed bird into the oblong roaster. She salted and peppered the skin and added a cup of water to the pan. As she opened the oven door, she turned her face away from the heat that wafted out. She talked to the chicken as she shoved in the pan. "I'll be checking on you in an hour or so to make sure you have enough water, little birdie. In the meantime, you'll get good and brown for Aunt Abby, won't you?" she said in a low, loving voice.

Sean smiled. What would we do without Abby? She shut the oven door and returned to the counter to brush the bread crumbs with the tip of her apron into her hand. Sean sat up straight and moved his chair a little so she could get past him. He noticed something from the corner of his eye that he didn't recognize. He squinted and leaned forward to get a better look. It was his rowboat. The girls had painted it with the same sky blue paint that was used on the crib. They had made a miniature picnic basket from a match box, a three pronged anchor from a paperclip and a fishing pole from a willow twig, complete with a line and a bright yellow construction paper fish with a penciled on smile hooked at the end. Sean's eyes welled with water. What's wrong with me? Am I just tired? After all that has happened to us, to this family, how can there still be so much love? Sean had thought that by going east, he would find a life, a home, happiness. But he needn't go anywhere to find those. They had been right there, under his nose, all along. He decided to stay right there in the kitchen a while, where it was warm and listen to the radio and watch Abby bustle about. He put his face back into his folded arms on the table and turned his nose towards the oven so he could smell the chicken cook. At that moment, he realized how lucky he was. He closed his eyes and smiled wide. For the first time, in a long time, he was content.

Chapter 14

It was painful–loving from afar. It was hard to give his customers a smile, when inside, he was aching. He wanted to look into Maggie's eyes, talk to her heart and put his arms around her. She had no idea how he felt about her. She didn't even know he was a *man*. He tried to lessen his suffering by keeping busy. He brought arm-loads of drinks to the tables, collected his money and took it home to his girls. For now, this family of three had enough food in their pantry but things were get-ting bleaker for so those without jobs. People packed up and left town, headed for the big city to find work and a place to stay. Many had to squeeze in with relatives. Lines at the soup kitchens stretched around the block. Folks waited their turn for bags of potatoes, flour and lard at the "giveaway office." Brawls erupted when the food ran out before the line did. The streets were lined with people trying to sell off their belongings for pen-nies on the dollar to buy food. Sean knew how blessed he was to take money home every night. He gave thanks at the table for the food, but secretly, he prayed for more. He wanted Maggie.

The next few nights at work, Sean paid more atten-tion to the men who frequented the Shangri-La. Some were local fellows. They were easy to recognize by the emblems on their coats and hats. They were miners, farmers, mill workers and the like. Sean tried to get a good look at them from a distance before they saw him, to make sure he wouldn't be recognized. If they were well-known to him, he steered clear, and asked the other girls to seat them at their tables. This was a small town, and even if he lost some tips, it was better than being found out. Some of the men were obviously from out of town. They were different, foreign-looking with big city accents. They spoke loudly and the profanity flowed freely. Most had coal black eyes and hair, like Johnny's. No work boots and coats for them. These guys wore fancy suits with ties and shiny leather shoes, rings on their fingers and expensive fedoras. Flashing their money around was a favorite sport and some were pretty sloppy drunks, spilling one beer while they yelled for another. One guy didn't even make it to the toilet and peed himself in his chair. And the drunker they got, the more obnoxious they got. Sean didn't like all the foul language around the waitresses, especially Maggie. He made it a point to ask Lizzie what she knew about them.

Once Sean posed the question, she looked over her shoulder to make sure Johnny was out of earshot and filled him in with a low voice. "Most of those guys come from New York, Cleveland and Baltimore—you know, big cities. No matter where they're from they all seem to know each other. Always hugging and kissing each other like a bunch of women. They're a tight crew, alright. They haul in the hooch and have "business meetings" in the back. The "board room" is off limits to the women. We all know they're playing cards and shooting craps. Johnny has to pay off the cops to keep them from raiding the joint. They're just hustlers. All shady, the whole lot of 'em. You wouldn't believe the money that comes and goes outta this hole. If you ask me, they got quite a racket going." Sean quietly nodded trying to take it all in.

"And believe you me, nothing gets between them and their money. They'll shoot a man for looking at them the wrong way." A chill raced up Sean's spine at the thought of being shot.

"They'll give you a nice tip when you bring their drink, but keep your distance. They got fast hands and they think they're entitled to feel you up after they pay you off. Know what I mean?" Lizzie's tone grew bitter. "They don't care about nobody but themselves," she said with a shaky voice. Lizzie dashed away to the bar for more drinks with tears in her eyes. Sean wondered what had happened to Lizzie. Maybe she had let herself get close to one of these men and he cheated on her—or broke her heart. Maybe it was Johnny.

It was another Saturday night and the place was packed. Seemed like on Saturdays the music got louder and the tips were bigger. Even the dancing girls got caught up in the spirit and kicked a little higher. Sean was in high gear too and kept the glasses full for his big table of *city* boys. As he brought the next round, one of them spoke to him. "I never saw you here before. What's your name, *missy*?"

"Sally."

"Wow, Sally. You gotta face only a mother could love, but you're well endowed," he said staring at Sean's chest.

Sean ignored him, but as he reached across the table to collect the empty glasses, the man grabbed Sean's behind. "You got a tight little ass, too."

Sean's hands clenched into fists, but he forced himself to remember, once more, that he was a woman. He swung around and slapped the man's face so hard it knocked him out of his chair.

"The drinks are for sale, but I'm not." Sean was not smiling.

The man jumped to his feet and slapped Sean in the face. Everyone at the table froze to see what would happen next. Sean's hot Irish temper flared and the adrenaline raced through his veins. His fingers curled into white knuckled fists. The dame act had to go. Sean gave him a quick jab with his left fist and followed through with a right hook, just like his old man had taught him. It didn't take much to knock him on *his ass,* since he was already three sheets to the wind. The man was out cold. His buddies were shocked and looked back at *Sally* in amazement. They lifted the man by his shoulders and dragged him to the back room. As they closed the door behind them, they still looked back at the waitress with the killer right hook.

The jig is up, thought Sean. I'm finished. Johnny marched quickly from his office towards him. Surely he suspected by now that *Sally* was a man. Johnny put his arm around Sean's shoulders. His body went limp. Here it comes. "You all right, doll?"

Sean swallowed hard. "Yeah, I'm fine."

Johnny turned his back to the office and turned Sean with him. His body began to shake as he snickered. "Holy shit, that son of a bitch picked the wrong broad to cop a feel. You got one hell of a punch, there, blondie." Johnny patted him on the back.

All at once, the adrenaline wore off and Sean stood there trembling, trying to compose himself.

Johnny squinted in the poor light and stared at Sean's face. Then he wiped his chin with his thumb. "Miss Sally, I'm afraid he cut your lip. You're bleeding a little."

Johnny looked around the room for someone to help.

Maggie came to his rescue. "C'mon, Sally, we'll get you cleaned up."

She took him by the hand and led him to the ladies room. He became nervous, hoping no "real ladies" were using the facilities. Up until now, in dire emergencies, he had relieved himself at the edge of the woods when he was sure no one would miss him. Maggie dampened a cloth at the sink and cleaned his swollen lip. It was the first time Sean had seen her face in good light. She's *beautiful,* he thought. He couldn't take his eyes off her while she fussed over him. "That bastard. First he grabs your bottom then he slaps you around. Who does he think he is? What an animal."

She pressed the cloth down hard over the cut to stop the bleeding. They stood in silence for a moment, far from the crowd beyond the door. In the quiet, he could hear his own heart beating. Maggie lifted the cloth away from his face and inspected his chin and lip. "I think it's stopped."

Maggie stepped back to look him over and suddenly raised her hands to the sides of her face in confusion.

"What? What's wrong?" Sean asked fearing the worst.

165

JOAN LEHMANN

He followed her eyes down to his chest. The brawl had taken its toll. One breast was up at his neck and the other was down near his waist. His brassiere had popped in the back and his breasts had *escaped*. As Sean desperately tried to straighten out the mess, Maggie's look of confusion turned to one of shock.

Sean tried to reassure her in his best falsetto, "Well, not all girls are blessed with God's bounty. I have to compensate for being so flat. I'm afraid it runs in the family."

As Sean struggled to adjust himself, a wool sock and handful of change fell out of the cup. Instinctively, Maggie reached down to pick them up. She was coming around, starting to feel sorry for Sean as he fell apart. Sean shoved them back down his dress but they fell out again. He reached behind his back and tried to fasten the brassiere through his dress, but it was impossible. Maggie couldn't stand to see him struggle.

"Here, let me help."

She unzipped his dress in the back and froze. "I've never seen muscles like this on a woman." She softly rubbed her hand over his shoulder and back. Sean's skin turned to gooseflesh, aroused by her gentlest touch. Quickly, Sean turned to face her taking his bare back out of her view. He was furious with himself that he had let his guard down, terrified she might guess he was a man and frustrated as hell because he couldn't get that infernal bra back on. His frenzied efforts caused his dress to slip down one shoulder. Maggie reached down for the collar to pull up his dress. She paused for a moment with a look of confusion. Had she felt the hair on his chest? She pulled back his collar a little further to

166

get a better look. Out of fear, Sean quickly stepped back snatching the collar away from her. The adrenaline had made his arms bulge. Their eyes met when they heard the cloth tear at his arm. Maggie turned slightly to examine the damage.

"You've torn your sleeve."

"It's all right," said Sean trying to convince himself. His masquerade was literally falling apart at the seams.

Maggie tried to pull the torn edges back together and felt the muscle of his bicep. "Wait a minute." She rubbed the back of her hand over his face. Her face showed anger as she pulled the scarf from his neck to examine his Adam's apple.

"You're not a woman at all—you're a, a man," she cried.

Sean panicked. He forced his hand over her mouth. "Shhhhh. Be quiet. They'll hear you."

Maggie's eyes widened like saucers. She struggled to free herself from him. Sean realized he must seem like a monster. Softly he whispered in her ear. "Please, Maggie, don't scream. If the guys finds out, they'll kill me. Please, just hear me out. If I take my hand away, do you promise not to scream?"

Maggie nodded and Sean slowly lowered his hand.

"You. You're one of those *funny* guys who gets a thrill from dressing like women, aren't you?"

"No, I'm not one of *those.*"

"Then what are you? What kind of man dresses like a woman to work at a beer joint?"

"The kind of man who can't find work–anywhere. We were starving. The mines closed weeks ago. We had nothing. I have a little girl at home. We needed the money to buy food. Believe me, I couldn't find any another way. I did it for her. I did it to keep her alive."

By the time Sean was finished, he was trembling. He hadn't fully recovered from the fight or the touch of her hand on his back or his fear at being found out. He couldn't think straight.

Maggie lowered her head and became quiet. After a moment she spoke.

"What's her name?"

"Who?"

"Your little girl."

"Hannah."

"What about your *wife?*"

"She died in childbirth. I lost my wife and my son the same day. That was over a year ago. All I've got now is my curly girl and our Aunt Abby. We are a family and they are depending on me."

"Do they know about–this?" she asked waving her hand at his costume.

"I would be mortified if Hannah found out. But Abby helps me get dressed everyday. It was her idea. She was starving too. We all were."

Maggie was still doubtful, but slowly coming around. Sean stood quietly with his eyes lowered, hoping that she would believe him and praying that she wouldn't give him away.

He became nervous, afraid that by now they were missed out front and that someone would walk in.

"Please, Maggie. You've got to keep my secret. It's the only way I can feed my family. And anyway, if you give me up, there will be hell to pay," he pleaded.

Maggie's serious look turned into a smile. "I knew it. I knew there was something different about you the first day we met. When you shook my hand, I could *feel* it. It wasn't just because your hands were rough. I could sense it. When my hand touched yours, the day we were sweeping, I got a strange feeling, like I was attracted to you. But I couldn't understand the way I felt, knowing you were a woman. I thought I was crazy. But I'm not. It was natural to be attracted to you."

As Maggie spoke, her face glowed. Then it occurred to Sean that she liked him too. A wave of emotion overcame him. It consumed him like a schoolboy's crush. He wanted to put his arms around her, to kiss her, to tell her he loved her. Then he remembered Abby's wise words. "Not yet." Sean extended his hand—this time like a man and firmly shook hers. "The name is Sean O'Connell," he said in a deep, masculine voice. "Pleased to meet you, *Maggie.*"

She smiled as she shook his hand. "The pleasure is all *mine.*"

Lizzie opened the door and stuck her head in. "Girls, girls, the men are getting thirsty out there. Did you forget about your tables? You okay, Sally?"

Maggie answered, "We've got her face cleaned up but her dress is torn. Have you got a safety pin?"

"Let me see what I've got in my purse," she said closing the door.

Sean took Maggie's hands into his. "Miss Margaret Schmidt, I have had my eyes on you since the moment we met. I can't stop thinking about you. I know it is awfully forward, but I would like to see you sometime, maybe buy you dinner. Of course, I plan on wearing trousers instead of a dress, if that's alright with you."

She said flirtatiously, "Why Mr. Sean O'Connell, I would be honored. I would love to see what you look like with trousers on."

They were interrupted by the sound of yelling out front. "The drunks are at it again," said Sean. Maggie nodded and the two slipped out of the ladies room to see the fight, but by now, everyone had frozen in their tracks. One of the out-of-towners was standing over the guy Sean had just punched. He was pointing a gun in his bruised face.

The gunman leaned in even closer to him. "Tony's been telling me for weeks you've been skimming, but I didn't believe him. I told him you were one of *my* boys, from the old *familia*. But this month, I came up short, real short. It's you, Vinnie. It's been you all along. You hurt me, Vinnie. You broke my trust, you broke my heart, now you're breaking my back. There's only one way to settle this, with blood. It's gonna be yours, not mine."

"Give me a chance, Joey. You got it all wrong," pleaded Vinnie.

Joey put the gun to Vinnie's forehead. Vinnie cried tears and begged for his life. In cold blood, the gunman pulled the trigger. Brains flew out the back of Vinnie's head as he dropped to the ground. Sean witnessed it all and played it once more in his mind, in slow motion. It was unreal, like a dream. After the gunman exited out the side door, the girls screamed and rushed out the front. Bobby slipped out the back. Johnny stood motionless with his back against the bar. Maggie stood at Sean's side, her hands over her mouth not blinking, not moving. Sean grabbed her firmly by the shoulders. "Get out of here. Go out the back door and find Bobby." Maggie obeyed, walking sideways slowly towards the door, unable to take her eyes off the dead man.

Vinnie's men, who feared they might be next, scattered like roaches. Johnny quietly slid back to his office. For some reason, Sean didn't flee with the others. Instead, he ducked back into the ladies room and watched through the door slightly ajar. He watched Joey's men pat down the pockets of Vinnie's coat and search under the tables and chairs.

"It's not here, boss," one of them said as the others shook their heads.

"Look in his car. Maybe he hid it in the trunk," snarled Joey and they headed outside.

A minute later, Sean heard two cars pull off. He waited a moment more to make sure they were all gone. He stepped quietly out to the floor where the dead man lay. He took a good look around to make sure no one was watching. Then, curiosity got the best of him. Like a kid who pokes a dead animal with a stick, Sean nudged the man in the back with his foot, to make sure he was really dead. Then he kicked him harder. When he was satisfied, Sean bent down over the dead man. This loud mouth Vinnie had been alive and sparring with Sean just a few minutes earlier. Now he, like Andrew, was gone forever. Sean paused a moment, considering once more, the finality of death. He bent down closer to examine his face. It was ashen with the start of a shiner over his right eye. Pretty good jab, Sean thought to himself. There was a small hole in his forehead, but the back of his head was nearly gone. A dark pool of blood streamed behind him.

Sean wondered why he was shot, especially like this, in cold blood. He could think of only two things, love or money. It certainly wasn't love. He wondered if Joey's men found what they were looking for in Vinnie's car. Sean couldn't stand to look at the back of the man's head any longer. He grabbed the man by his shoulders and rolled him over onto his back. As he moved the body, Sean heard a crinkling sound, like paper. He pulled the dead man's coat tight around him. It crinkled again. Sean rolled the man back onto his side, reached under his coat and ran his hand along his back. He pulled his shirt out of his pants to find a large envelope tucked into his waistband. He pulled the envelope out and re-turned the man to his back. Sean felt nervous wondering what the envelope held.

Within seconds, he heard a car pull into the front. The driver slammed on the brakes and he could hear car doors slam. It's the police, he thought. Or worse, maybe Joey and his men have returned. In a panic, Sean shoved the envelope down his dress and ran to get his coat, but he was too late.

The gunman busted in the front door. He stared at Sean in disbelief. "What the hell are you still doing here?" Sean couldn't speak or move. He felt his fingers tighten into fists still not sure whether he should fight or run. Joey waved his gun at Sean. He's going to kill me too, thought Sean. I hope whatever is in this envelope is worth dying for, one man has already paid with his life tonight. "Get out of here, you stupid broad," he said in disgust. Sean couldn't believe his dress had saved him.

He bolted out the back way grabbing his coat from the hook as he ran. He didn't dare stop to get his boots. He ran on the frozen ground in his slippers as fast as his legs could carry him. He heard a car approach. When the headlights grew near, Sean got out of the road and hid behind trees. He couldn't let himself be found by Joey's men—or the police. Besides, envelope or not, he must be a sight, half man and half woman by now. Sean hid behind a hickory tree, trying to catch his breath, feeling his heart would pound out of his chest and praying the car would pass him by. When it did, he could see it was a shiny new, black sedan—one of *them.* Sean's mind raced. After murdering a man, in a room full of witnesses, why aren't they high-tailing it back to Pittsburgh or Baltimore or wherever they came from? They had gotten their revenge on Vinnie. Surely the police are looking for them. Why had they returned to the scene of the crime? What is worth risking jail, or worse, for? Was it this envelope? Do they know who has it? Are they looking for *me?*

Sean continued home on foot. His mouth was parched and his feet were frozen. He wondered if Maggie made it home. Why hadn't he made sure she was safe? All he wanted was to be with her, wasn't that enough? Why did he have to meddle and worse, take the envelope? Surely by now, Joey knew he had it–and its precious contents. Now, he and Maggie would never be together. Surely, they would find him and kill *him* too.

Chapter 15

It took Sean nearly two hours to walk home. He hid behind a tree or fence post or snow drift each time he heard a noise or saw headlights. As he approached a screech owl in a tree, the bird's call nearly scared the life out of him. He was terrified, afraid they would find him and kill him. He had to make it home, to tell Abby what he had done. She'll help me, he thought. She'll know what to do–I can't think anymore. By the time he pushed open the back door, he was nearly frozen. His feet were cut and bleeding from the sharp edges of the ice on the road. The pain throbbed to his knees. He hobbled through the kitchen to put more wood into the stove, desperate to get warm. There was no time to heat water to wash the paint from his aching face. He was so cold that he trembled at the sink as he straightened the curls from his hair with a wet comb. He tore off his dress and got into trousers, a flannel shirt and socks as fast as he could. He pulled a chair close to the stove. Even as he warmed up, his body still quivered. It was hard to tell if it was from cold, hunger–or fear. He couldn't wait for daylight to tell Abby. He put the envelope on the kitchen table and knocked at her bedroom door. "I'm awake," she said softly. "You sound like an elephant in there. Have you been drinking?"

She came to her door still tying her robe around her waist. "What is it, son? You look like you've seen a ghost. What's happened?"

"I saw a man get shot dead tonight at the club."

"You poor thing. It must have been quite a shock."

"That's not all. I found this shoved in the dead man's pants," he said pointing towards the kitchen table.

Abby stared, motionless, at the envelope. Sean peered into her face trying to read it. "What is it?" she asked cautiously.

"I haven't looked yet. I thought we should open it together, but it must be worth killing for."

"And dying for."

Neither one of them could move.

"Well, shall we see how much trouble *we're* in?" she asked.

When she tried to lift it, it was heavier than she thought. She shot a confused look at Sean. She slid her finger under the flap, opened it and dumped the contents onto the table. Both their jaws dropped.

"How much do you think it is?" asked Sean.

"I don't know. I've never seen that much in my life."

"I've never seen a one-hundred dollar bill."

"Me neither," said Abby as she slumped into a wooden chair.

There before them laid five bundles of crisp one-hundred-dollar bills.

"I'm afraid to touch them," said Sean.

"One of us had better."

Abby picked up a bundle and began counting.

"Twenty," she mumbled.

They stared into each others eyes, too anxious and tired to do the math, each hoping the other would come up with the answer. Sean tried to focus.

"Two thousand…"

"Times five…" said Abby.

"Ten thousand dollars," they finished in unison.

Abby got a somber look. "They'll be here soon," she said softly.

"What do you mean?"

"This is a fortune," she said pointing to the stack. "If they go back without it, heads will roll. They'll hunt you down like an animal, Sean. You have got to run," she said firmly.

"What about you and Hannah?"

"Leave us here. What do they want with an old woman and a little girl? Go now, and pack a few clothes and be quick about it."

Sean struggled for another answer. "What if I just give them back their money, make it right with them?"

"No. They'll shoot you just for spite. You made them look stupid. You haven't got a chance, son. You've got to go."

"Why? Why didn't I run out that door with the others? Why did I roll over the dead man and find that envelope? Now I'm a thief."

"Everything happens for a reason and you're not a thief. You didn't steal that money. It was already stolen. You *found* it. The dead man was the thief and he paid for his crime with his life. The scum that killed him are all bound for hell. They don't need that money where they're going. What's done is done. Now's your chance. You've got to live by your wits, Seany. Outsmart them.

But be careful, son. Keep your trap shut about it. Hide it away until long after the dust settles. Pull it out a little at a time or someone will get suspicious. Put it to good use, lad."

Abby worked feverishly on a plan. She talked a mile a minute and her eyes shifted back and forth. She rubbed her hands over and over nervously as she gathered her thoughts.

"Wait a few weeks before you come back for Hannah, until things die down a bit. There's enough cash in that cookie jar to get us through until you can get back."

Sean stood with a forlorn look on his face.

Abby grabbed him by the shoulders and held him at arm's length.

"Now listen to me for once. Your luck is changing. Here's a chance for a new life for you and Hannah. You can be free from the mines, get out of this little town and finally see the ocean. You'll have your dream come true and yours will be a life worth living. Head for Baltimore. I've got a first cousin there. Sam Mulligan is his name. He's the manager of a ritzy new hotel in the middle of town. Oh, what's the name of it? The Lord Baltimore—that's it. It sits a few blocks from the water. You'll get to see your boats everyday. Tell him Abby Sue sent you. Now get your things and go," she ordered shoving the envelope of cash into his hands.

Sean ran up the stairs and packed a few clothes in a sack. He hid the envelope in the leg of a pair of trousers. He desperately tried to think of anything he could possibly need. The harder he tried, the more his mind went blank. How could this be happening? His whole life had been turned upside down. Abby said this would be a dream come true but it felt more like his worst nightmare.

When he returned to the kitchen, Abby handed him a paper sack. "Here's a few vittles and some other things you'll need. What a time to travel. It's freezing out there."

Sean knew only too well.

"Hannah's not upstairs. Is she sleeping in your room?"

"Aye. It gets cold up there. She is sleeping with me tonight."

Sean headed for Abby's bedroom, but she grabbed his arm. "What are you doing? It's the middle of the night?"

"I can't leave without kissing her goodbye."

"She'll cry her eyes out. You'll never get out of here. Let her be," ordered Abby.

Sean lowered his head and considered it but he couldn't stand it. "I've got to."

He tip-toed to her bedside and kissed his angel on the cheek. She was as warm as toast and soft as a kitten. "Papa, you're home," she said rubbing her eyes.

"Yes, but I'm afraid I'm off again. Papa has to take a little trip."

"Where are you going?"

"To find a new house for us by the sea. Will you stay here and take care of Auntie until I get back."

"When will you be home?"

Before he could answer, a car squealed into the yard. "Be quiet, kitten," said Sean as he peered through the bedroom curtains.

Two pairs of footsteps stomped onto the porch. A fist pounded at the door. Abby said loudly, "My goodness, who could that be at this hour?"

Sean's heart leapt from his chest. He listened as she made small talk at the front door. "Well now, it's been a long time since I had gentlemen callers, especially this late in the evening. What can I do for you fellows?"

"We're looking for a girl that works at the club in Pottsville, name of Sally. The milk man said she lives here, with you."

"Well, he must be mistaken. I am just a poor old widow living here with my grand-niece. There's no one here by that name. Sorry I can't help you gentlemen. I'll be seeing you out then."

"We're sorry to bother you ma'am."

Sean held his breath and waited for the sound of the door shutting behind them, but it never closed.

"Hey, wait a minute. Joey. Look at this dress. Didn't you say that dame had on a green dress?"

Sean's heart stopped. He had left the dress in a heap on the kitchen chair. He looked over at Hannah and put his finger over her closed lips. He shook his head for her to be quiet.

An eternity seemed to pass before he heard the next voice.

"Yeah, it's got a big tear in the sleeve—and a spot of blood on the front. Okay, lady, fun and games time is over. Where is she?"

Sean firmly put his hand over Hannah's mouth fearing what would come next, holding her close to him.

"Gone. She's an hour ahead of you. She took my sedan and headed north on the main road to New York

City. You'll never find her. Seems she outsmarted you boys, but from the looks of you, it wouldn't take much," gloated Abby.

"You'll hold your tongue, old lady, if you know what's good for you," said Joey.

"Hey Joey. Look at this picture. This don't look like the right dame. She's got dark eyes and long hair."

Sean realized they had found his wedding picture on the wall.

"No. That's not her. This dame had light colored eyes, green or blue and short blond hair. Hey. Wait a minute. Look at the guy she's with," said Joey.

"What? What?"

"This is her. I mean, this is *him*. He wore a dress at the club. Don't you get it?" said Joey.

"You two are even dumber than I thought. Christ almighty you can't even tell a man from a woman," teased Abby.

"Where is he? Where are you hiding him, Grandma? You turn him over and maybe we can make a deal. What do you say?" asked Joey.

In the distance, police sirens began blaring. "Dammit, these small town cops. How the hell did they find us? Quick, check upstairs," ordered Joey.

Sean heard footsteps fly up the stairs.

"Okay, lady. What's his *real* name?" asked Joey.

"Rumplestiltskin."

"Cute. Why I oughta…."

Foot steps barreled back down the stairs. "Nothin' up there boss."

The sirens wailed closer.

"What about *that* door? We never checked in there."

"It's my grand-niece. She's sleeping. I won't have you going in there and scaring the hell out of her. She's just a baby. Let her be," ordered Abby.

"Boss, we gotta get out of here. What about that door?"

"Forget the kid. What are we going to do with the old lady?" asked Joey.

"She's just an old lady. Leave her be. Let's get out of here."

"Yeah, an old lady who knows *she's* a *he* and where *we* are headed. The cops might catch up to him in New York before we do. We can't let that happen. There's only one thing to do," said Joey.

Sean carefully slid the window open, wrapped Hannah in a blanket and climbed out with her in his arms. He couldn't run, not with Hannah. They had to hide. But where? They only had one chance. He looked around and spotted an outhouse.

A shot fired in the house. The sound echoed in the frigid air forever. Sean tightened his hand around Hannah's mouth. They stared in horror at each other. There was another shot. Sean froze. He knew she was gone. There was no time to think. He had to hide Hannah.

"Lamb chop, we are going to play a little game."

"Now? Who are those men in our house? What was that loud noise? Where's Aunt Abby?"

"Too many questions, sweetheart. This is important. I'm counting on you. We are going to play hide and go seek. Right now, we are the hiders. We must do a very *good* job in hiding. Do you understand?"

"Uh-huh." Her eyes were afraid

"Those are bad men back there and if they find us, they might hurt us. I need you to be a big girl. Don't tell them where I am, no matter what. Do you promise?" he begged.

"Yes, Papa."

"Don't fail us, curly girl. It's a big job, but you can do it."

Sean opened the door to the outhouse. The ground was frozen. He lifted the bench lid and carefully climbed into the pit. Then he pulled the lid back over his head.

"Pull up your night gown and sit on the seat."

"What? You want me to *pee* on you?"

"No, lamb chop. Leave your underpants on. Pull your night gown down over your knees. Don't pee on me. Just make pretend. Hide me. Hurry now. If those men come near, don't say a word. Be still."

The sirens had almost reached their house. The men were running around the yard now, checking the shed and barn.

"What's that noise?" asked Hannah.

"Shhhhhhhhh, quiet like a mouse. *You promised,*" Sean whispered from below.

"C'mon guys. We've got to go. The cops will be here soon."

"I gotta take a leak," said one of them.

Sean heard his footsteps approach. He saw his life and the life of his child flash before his eyes. He would surely kill them both. The outhouse door opened.

"Excuse me, but I was here first," Hannah said with authority.

"Oh, sorry, sweetheart," he stammered.

Joey yelled, "Christ Almighty. You can take a leak in jail. Let's get the hell out of here!"

The rusty spring creaked and snapped shut. Sean was still holding his breath.

He could hear the car peel off as the sirens closed in. Sean started to snicker. He held his hand over his mouth. He couldn't stop it. When he was sure the thugs were gone, he laughed maniacally, giddy with relief.

"Can I pull up my pants now? My bottom feels like an icicle."

"Yes. Yes my beautiful baby," Sean managed through the laughter.

Hannah stood and lifted the lid so Sean could climb out.

"How did I do, Papa? They couldn't find you, could they? Did we win?" Hannah chirped away.

Sean was so exhausted that he could barely climb from the pit. "You're a tiger, brave like your Aunt Abby. Yes, baby, we won." The police had seen the sedan pull out. The sirens never stopped, but continued to sound as they passed the house. Sean wrapped his arms around Hannah and nearly squeezed the breath from her. He was sure they would have both been dead by now. His relief turned to sorrow as the sound of the gunshot flooded back into his head. He was suddenly weak in the knees and sick to his stomach. The woman who loved him like a son had made the ultimate sacrifice. He turned his face from Hannah so she wouldn't see his tears, but he couldn't stop his body from trembling.

"Papa, you're freezing. Let's go back in the house. "

"We have to wait until the sirens are far away. Then we can go inside."

They sat in the outhouse, she on his lap, shivering together.

Sean knew he had to get Hannah into the house and up the stairs without her seeing Abby's lifeless body. There was no confusion left in his mind. This was not a dream, it was his worst nightmare. He had only one purpose left, to get Hannah out of there alive.

Chapter 16

Sean lifted Hannah to his hip as they came through the door. He turned her head away from the kitchen and down upon his shoulder. Once they were upstairs, he dressed her in the warmest clothes she had: long underwear, snow pants two pairs of socks and pulled a dress over her head too.

"Papa, I'm burning up," she complained.

"Not for long. You'll be glad for every stitch of clothes you've got," he answered.

Sean put more clothes on too. He frantically looked around for anything he should take with him. As his eyes scanned the room, it occurred to him that he might never see this house again. As he rifled through the bureau, he found the pair of booties Molly made for their son. He quickly tucked them into his breast pocket. He wondered what he should take for a keepsake for Hannah.

"Lamb chop, hurry, get your favorite rag doll Auntie made for you."

He looked around the bedroom that Molly and he had shared. For a moment, it looked foreign to him. As he looked closer, the memories flooded in. He reached into the wardrobe for another flannel shirt. Molly's dresses were still hanging there, untouched, just the way she left them the day she died. He rubbed his hand along the hem of one of them. He lifted the skirt to his face and pressed it against his cheek. He held it to his nose and inhaled deeply, hoping to catch the scent of her. A water pitcher on the nightstand belonged to her grandmother, from Wales. It was porcelain painted with purple thistles and thin gold leaf trim, too fragile to take. There were six wooden boats he had carved berthed on the shelf over his bed. He wondered if he would ever build a real one. Would he ever make it to the sea? He was still pondering these questions when Hannah stomped into the room.

Sweet Jesus, he thought. How much time has passed? How long have I been standing here daydreaming?

"Did you find your doll, lamb chop?"

Hannah's arms were loaded down with five dolls, blankets and doll's clothes.

Guilt set in. What was he dragging this innocent soul into? "Oh, sweetheart. We must travel light. Take one and put the rest to sleep in your bed so they can stay warm."

"Fine, but I'm taking Boots, too." She pouted as she trudged off to her task.

Sean panicked. Joey and his men could return any time. As he started out of the room, a small wooden box caught his eye, Molly's jewelry box. He lifted the lid and found her mother's rosary carved from rose quartz, smooth and pink. Under them, he found their simple, gold wedding bands. Molly took off her ring when her fingers began to swell when she was with child. Sean took his off the day he buried her and laid it beside hers in the box. Back then, he was dead too. He quickly slipped the rings onto the rosary, tied it into a knot and tucked them into his pocket. I'll give these to Hannah, someday, he thought. Finally, he forced himself down-stairs.

When he reached the third step from the bottom, he saw her for the first time. Abby had fallen so that her shoulder was resting against a chair. Sean went to her and lifted her face to see her. His eyes surveyed the rest of her. Those dogs had shot her through the heart. Sean felt like a coward hiding in the bedroom with Hannah, but he didn't know what else to do. He felt spineless just the same.

Sean lowered Abby's shoulders to rest on the floor. He realized he could only find one wound, but there were two shots fired. He examined her legs and arms and checked her head and neck. Then he noticed there were buttons missing from the top of her nightgown. The cloth around her collar was torn. Those bastards had put their hands on Abby. He could feel the rage rise from his chest to his face. "Why Abby, Lord?" He asked as he lifted his eyes to the heavens.

He spotted a small hole in the ceiling's plaster. That must be the resting place of the other shot. He was puz-zled at first and then he realized *Abby fought back*. The old girl gave them a run for their money. She must have grabbed Joey's hand and forced him to misfire at the ceiling before he finished her off. His rage turned to pride. Atta girl, Abby. His throat tightened as he felt he was not worthy of her sacrifice. He took a cushion from the kitchen chair and rested her head on it. He took her right hand in his and kissed the back of it. When he rolled it over in his hand, he noticed blood under her nails. It made him smile. Abby still wore the locket around her neck that held photos of her and Andrew in their younger days. He unfastened the clasp and added it to the treasures in his pocket. Sean was torn when he saw her. He felt he should stay at least long enough to bury her. But her voice spoke to him, "Fly, fly like the wind, Seany boy. You and your little sunshine make a new life for yourselves by the sea. Leave my bones here to rest with Molly and my Andrew."

He took a bill from the envelope to leave on the table to pay for her funeral. Then he realized that if he left such a large bill, the whole town would know he took the money. He shoved the hundred dollar bill into his pocket. What else could he do?

The cookie jar. He carefully reached into the cabinet. The stone crock was heavy with coins and small bills. He sat the jar next to her body and scribbled a short note. "Please take care of my beloved aunt, Abigail Ashe."

Sirens sounded again. Joey and his men must still be near. Or maybe the police weren't looking for them. Maybe they were looking for *him*. Fear gave Sean a second wind.

"Hannah Jane. Get your boots on, now," he shouted.

On the kitchen table, he noticed the photo taken on his wedding day, the picture that had given him away. He looked into Molly's eyes. She *was* so beautiful. Time was wasting. He shoved the frame into the cloth bag and yelled for Hannah once more.

Hannah came down with one boot on. Sean forced her back to Abby as he shoved on the other one. She couldn't get her coat on with so many extra layers of clothes. Sean forced her arms in as she protested. He pulled her hat down over her ears and tucked her curls in away from her face. He fumbled with the strings as he tied them in a knot under her chin.

"C'mon, sweetheart. I'm afraid we've got to play hide and seek again."

"And we aren't going to let them find us, right?"

"Not on your life." Sean cringed at his words.

Sean swung the satchel over his shoulder and took Hannah by the hand.

"Are we going to hide in the outhouse again?"

"No, not this time. Just behind some trees if we see a car."

"Where's Aunt Abby?"

Sean held her head close to his chest so she couldn't see her.

"She's not here, baby. She's–*gone*."

Hannah stared back at him in confusion.

"There's no more time. We have got to go."

He pushed Hannah out the door and gave one last look over his shoulder. He noticed the laundry basket next to the stairs. It was full of Hannah's washed and folded clothes. He grabbed a big handful and shoved them into his bag. He had to take one last look at Abby's face. His throat tightened. He whispered, "Thank you."

It was a mile and a half to the train station in Cressona. Who would have believed he would be walking out in the cold again in the same night? Hannah's little legs got weary quickly. Sean couldn't feel his anymore. He hefted her onto his back and she wrapped her arms around his neck. At least it's not snowing, he thought as he trudged through the wee hours of the morning. It was not quite daylight when they reached the station. He sat on a bench and cradled Hannah in his arms while he waited for the station to open. Finally, someone slid open the ticket window.

"I'd like two tickets to Baltimore."

"Passenger train won't be around for another hour or so. But you can get your tickets now if you want."

Sean reached into his pocket, pulled out his money and passed it under the grill.

The clerk looked at it and blinked twice. "A hundred dollar bill. It's been a long time since I've seen one of these."

He looked at the front, the back and the front again. "It's not counterfeit is it?" he joked.

Sean's face didn't change.

The clerk looked Sean up and down in his coal miner's clothes. "Or stolen?" he asked.

Sean snatched the bill out of his fingers and shoved it back into his pants pocket. "Thanks anyway, I think we'll walk."

"To *Baltimore*?" called the clerk after him

Sean took Hannah by the hand and walked along the track until he found an open box car. He looked in both directions to make sure no one was watching him then he lifted Hannah by the waist and put her onto the train. "We're going for a little ride after all, lamb chop."

"But that man wouldn't give us a ticket."

"As it turns out, we don't need tickets after all."

Sean tossed the sack into the car after her and hoisted himself aboard. The car was dark and dusty, full of wooden boxes and feed sacks. Within a few minutes, the train started moving.

"Uhhhhhhhh."

Hannah clutched her father's arm in fear of the strange noise from the back of the car. Sean pulled her onto his lap. What kind of animal was it? A bear? A dog?

"Who the hell's in *my* car?" asked a rough voice.

"We don't mean any trouble but we need a ride," said Sean.

"We?" An old man emerged from the pile of feed sacks. He was covered with chicken feed dust. He moved towards them, toward the door and the early morning light, his eyes squinted against the slanted sun rays streaming into the box car. They were deep set and steely blue. His beard and mustache were peppered with gray. His face was brown and wrinkled and he was so thin even his baggy clothes couldn't hide his emaciation. Sean quickly surmised he was the result of many years of a hard life, sun, smoke and drink. He imagined the man was in his fifties even though he looked seventy. As the old man moved toward them, he was unsteady on his feet. He brushed the chicken feed from his coat and pants as he spoke. "You gotta smoke there young fella?"

"No, sir. I'm afraid not."

Hannah clung even tighter to her father.

The man dropped down to sit on a wooden crate and reached into his coat pocket for his pint. After a long draw, he swallowed hard and released a loud belch. He reeked of whiskey and smoke and had no doubt been a stranger to soap and water for some time.

"Excuse me," asked Sean politely. "Does this train go to Baltimore?"

"It's either going there or coming back. Look down the tracks. Is the sun on the right or the left?"

"Left."

The codger closed his eyes deep in thought. "Is it coming up or going down?"

"The train?"

"No, the sun."

How long had he been riding this train? "The sun's just coming up."

With eyes still closed, the man scratched his head then leaned against the wall to steady himself. His mouth gaped open and for a moment Sean thought he had passed out. Suddenly the man awakened and stomped one foot loudly on the wooden floor.

Hannah's whole body jumped. Sean was startled as well.

"Then we're heading south. Yep, Baltimore is on the way soze it is."

The old man stared at the two of them still blinking while his eyes adjusted to the dawn. "You got a pretty good sized knapsack there. Whatcha got in it?"

"Just some food and clothes."

"Where are you two running off to? Or should I ask, what are you running *from*?"

A wary Sean paused for a moment, not sure if he should divulge his plans.

"I'm going to look for work in Baltimore. There's nothing much left for us here."

"What about Auntie?" asked Hannah.

"Aunt Abby will be all right. She's–taken care of."

"When are we going home?"

"By and by, buttercup. By and by."

"I didn't catch your name there, young fella." The man leaned in for an answer. The combination of his breath and body odor was overpowering.

"I'm Sean and this is my daughter, Hannah."

"She's a pretty little thing. Dark though. Must look like her mother," he said as he took another look at Sean's fair features.

Hannah cupped her hand around her face to spare her nose from his stench.

"She's the spittin' image," Sean said proudly.

"Oh, where's my manners. John Louis Radzinski at your service. My friends called me Jack. I 'spect now you can call me Jack, seein's how I don't have any friends left." He chuckled as he extended his hand.

"Nice to meet you, Jack."

Hannah became bored with the introductions. She turned her face away from the strange man. "Papa, what do we have to eat?" she whined. The poor little bird was starving.

"Let's see what Aunt Abby packed for us."

Carefully, he sorted through the contents of the sack. Sean feared that Jack would sense from his facial expression that he was hiding something. Sean had a horrible poker face, and he knew it. But Jack couldn't care less about Sean's face. His eyes were fixed like a hawk's on the sack. He was starving too and already salivating.

"Do you think we should share our breakfast with our new friend?" Sean asked Hannah.

She returned the question with a confused look. What friend?

"I'll give you a drink from my bottle for one of those biscuits," said Jack as he leaned forward for a better look.

"That won't be necessary. We've got enough to share," Sean said handing him one.

Jack lifted the biscuit quickly to his mouth and nearly swallowed it whole. Sean wondered how long it had been since his last meal. He took a quick survey of everything Abby had packed for them: half a dozen biscuits, a canteen of water, a box of matches, two wedges of cheese, two apples, two tins of sardines, a sharp knife, two forks, two spoons and two tin cups. Why two? Did she have a feeling? Did she know he would take Hannah with him? In the bottom of the sack, he found a cake of soap and a little New Testament. Cleanliness and godliness. That was Abby.

The back of his throat tightened. He felt guilt for her death and missed her terribly already. Hannah looked hungrily to Sean. He cut a slice of cheese and placed it in the middle of a biscuit for her. Then he cut an apple in two and gave her half.

"Don't have anymore of those biscuits, do you, son?" asked Jack ready for more.

Sean handed him another one and he gobbled it down. He chased it with a long swig of whiskey, let out another belch and seemed satisfied. When Hannah finished, Sean offered her a drink of water and she was soon asleep. Sean was ravenous. He ate two biscuits, some cheese, a tin of fish and the other half of the apple.

"That looked like a pretty good apple," commented Jack.

Sean threw him the other one. Jack took out a pocket knife and cut off little pieces and slid them to the back of his mouth. Sean had noticed his black teeth, too wobbly to bite into an apple.

"How long does it take to get to Baltimore?"

"Who knows? Sometimes a day, soonest. Sometimes two. Depends, soze it does."

Two days? How would he feed Hannah?

"Depends on what?"

"We could get rough weather or an engine could break down. Might be some long stops, problems getting freight on or off and such. Hell, sometimes the cops stop the train to look for crooks and toss out the stowaways."

Sean's heart skipped a beat—he was both. He pulled Hannah closer to him and rested his face against hers. Jack sensed Sean's fear and added.

"Been a long time since I seen the police hold things up though."

"Does this train go *all the way* to Baltimore?"

"Doubt it. Probably have to change trains in Reading. That's fourteen whistles from here. Then you gotta change again in Wilmington. *That* train should take you to the big city."

"How will we know we're in Reading?"

Jack squinted at Sean. "You ever rode a train, kid?"

"Not like *this*," he said motioning his hand towards the contents of the box car.

"You two been traveling all night?" he asked as he watched Hannah nod off again in Sean's arms.

"Yeah, on foot."

"Ooooooo-weeeeee. Foot's a hard way to go. I prefer the rails myself. It's the only way to travel if you ask me."

Jack peered into Hannah's face and smiled. "Sleeping like a baby. I remember when I used to be able to do that. Look sonny, why don't you get some shut eye? It'll be a while before we get to Reading. I'll let you know. I'm gonna change trains too."

Sean didn't know whether to trust him or not, but it didn't matter. He couldn't hold his eyes open any longer. He slid down onto his back and rested his head on the sack. Within seconds, he was out. He dreamed of the Shangri-La and Maggie. He wrapped his arms around her and told her he loved her. Then they heard the shot and saw the body. He took the envelope from the dead man and slid the envelope down his dress. He ran forever in the cold night, snow crunching under his feet, dodging every pair of headlights. He was almost home when he was startled by a hand on his shoulder. Fear struck his heart. It's the police, he thought, or worse, Joey.

"This is it. We're getting off here. Get your little girl and come on," Jack shouted over the screech of the wheels braking on the tracks.

Sean's body was so stiff from lying on the floor, he could barely move. Jack jumped out of the train and Sean handed him Hannah still half-asleep. Sean grabbed his bag and hopped out too.

They walked to the other side of the yard and jumped another train that was just taking off for Wilmington. They barely got to stretch their legs.

"You got lucky," said Jack as they piled into another freight car. "I've waited hours to get on another train."

Hannah nodded off at once. "I hope my luck is changing. I lost my wife, my son, my job–my best friend and now my home. I hope Baltimore has got something better for me and Hannah. We're trying to start over again, the two of us."

"I know what you mean," said Jack. "My kids are grown and gone. I never hear from them. I'm a smitty by trade, a gunsmith. I used to have my own shop. When the banks failed, I lost my shop and my money. My wife ran off with somebody who still had some. I've been riding these tracks for two years, as far north as Canada. Why I've seen a moose as big as a draft horse. For a while, I slept in a cabin in front of a crackling fire on a bearskin rug. There's nothing better than roasted deer over a campfire or fresh fish from crystal clear lakes. I've picked pails of wild blueberries the size of dimes. They are mighty fine in a hotcake cooked over an open fire. I've been as far west as you can go, California, panned for gold, and found a little too. The summer days were long in the hot sun picking tomatoes and grapes with the Mexicans until I thought my back would break. At night, I drank some of the best wine ever made. The furthest south I've ever been is the everglades. In summer, it's so hot and humid your clothes stick to you like a second skin and the air is thick with magnolias. I've lived on oranges, pomellos and dates and drank the milk of green coconuts. Down there Spanish moss floats through the air and the trees have knees. The skies are deep blue and full of birds, snowy egrets, brown pelicans and bright pink flamingos.

JOAN LEHMANN

"You saw *pink* birds?" asked Hannah as she rubbed her eyes and face.

"Well, good morning, there sleepyhead. Welcome back. The pink ones are the strangest birds you never saw. They've got long, skinny necks, yellow legs and stand on one foot and curl the other one up under their wing. When they stand straight with their necks stretched, they're as tall as a man. When they go hunting, they swing their hook beaks back and forth in the drink and scoop up frogs and fish. Sometimes they snag turtles or little snakes. The place is full of them. Florida is full of strange looking critters: snakes, birds, lizards, gators..."

"Alligators?" asked Sean.

"Did you ever see one?" added Hannah.

"See one? Why young lady, I ate one."

"You ate an *alligator?*" asked Sean.

"Yep. You've got to eat him or he'll eat you. He's sorta chewy like a rubber band and tastes like nothing. It'll fill up that empty place in your belly but I wouldn't trade him for mom's roast chicken, if you noze what I mean."

Jack leaned over and tickled Hannah under the chin.

"The Seminoles have got a special way of rassling them down and suring them up. They jump on top of them and tie their jaws shut. Then they bind up their arms and legs. Next they carry them back to their camp in a hollowed out log canoe. They don't kill 'em till they get 'em home, a day away, soze the meat won't turn bad.

"What's a *Seminole?*" asked Sean.

"They're the last hold outs, the Indians that refuse to be corralled onto a reservation. They're still running wild, living free and picking off a white man every once in a while. Nothing you can do about it."

"Do you rassle alligators?" asked Hannah.

"Not a chance," answered Jack. "Too dangerous. I prefer the rapid lead injection method," he said as he gave Sean a wink. "That way nobody gets hurt, well, except the alligator."

Hannah wore a serious face.

"A few years back, me and some other fellas got hungry for fish. We took a skiff into the swamp. We didn't catch anything on a line, so we threw a net over. When I reached over to pull it in, something grabbed my left arm. It felt like a vice grip and tore the skin off me. It was a gator, alright. I let go of the net and went with the other hand for this."

Jack reached with his right hand to a leather sheath on his hip. He pulled out a large knife. The blade was every bit of six inches. He held it high and twisted it until the blade reflected the sunlight. His eyes grew wild and twenty years melted away from his face.

"Just as I whipped it out, the gator pulled me overboard. The other fellas couldn't get a hold of me in time. It was just me and the gator. I knew I only had one chance 'cause I would soon drown. He twisted me round and round in the water. I felt my arm snap in two. I took the knife and shoved it into his chest as deep as I could. I sawed it in and out down the length of his belly as far as my arm could reach. Finally, he quit thrashing. I managed to get my head above water for air. Even though the gator was dead, his jaws were clamped shut and wouldn't let go. I yelled for the other guys to pull me back into the boat before the other gators smelled the blood. We were too heavy to pull up together, so they held onto me and dragged me and the gator alongside the boat to shore. They had to use an oar to pry his jaws open to get my arm out. That gator, from the tip of his snout to the tip of his tail, was ten feet long."

"Ten feet?" asked Hannah.

"Yep, half as long as this here freight car. But he was just a youngster. I've seen them get up to sixteen feet."

Sean and Hannah sat quietly a moment, trying to take it all in.

"Did you eat him?" asked Sean.

"Nope. We ate fish that night. But I didn't let him go to waste."

Jack returned his knife to its sheath. Then he rolled up his left sleeve. His arm was badly scarred and deformed. He wiggled his fingers and flexed them into a fist. "Yep. Everything still works. That gator thought he got the best of old Jack. But Jackie Boy got the best of him."

He bent down and rolled up one leg of his denim pants and wiped the dust off his boot with the palm of his hand.

"I've been walking on him ever since."

Hannah and Sean leaned forward for a better look.

Sean chuckled. "Well, I'll be. Alligator boots."

"Genuine. Finest leather there is. Would you like to touch them, there, young lady?"

Hannah looked to her father for permission and then she timidly leaned forward and extended one hand out to his boot. She hesitated, not sure if she wanted to touch it.

Jack shook his boot at her and growled, "Arrrrrrrrrrrrrrrrrgh."

Hannah screamed in fright. Sean reached forward and pulled her back.

Jack threw his head back in laughter. Tears streamed from his eyes.

Hannah was so spooked, hot tears poured from her eyes too.

The old man felt badly when he realized he made her cry. "Oh, I'm sorry, there, young lady. I couldn't help myself. It's not often I'm around a youngin' to play a joke on. Don't be scared. That alligator was dead since before your were born. The only thing under his skin now is an ornery old cuss. Can you ever forgive me?"

Hannah clung to Sean tightly and buried her face in his shoulder. Sean turned her to face the man who had given her his sincerest apology.

"Yes sir," she whimpered.

"Atta girl. Come over here and touch this gator leather. You've never seen or felt anything like it. I promise I won't scare you again. If I do, you can box my ears."

Curiosity slowly overcame her fear. She released Sean and crept over to Jack once more. She leaned down and ran her fingers over the toe. Sean leaned over her and touched the boot too. He was surprised it looked more like fish scales than cowhide.

"That gator nearly killed me. I still have bad dreams about him. But at least I'm still here to dream."

Hannah still glared at Jack, afraid to speak to him after that prank.

"You're breaking my heart, little one," said Jack still feeling guilty.

He reached into his bag and pulled out a seed pod. It was large and furry and deep green. He handed it out to Hannah. She cowered from him. Jack reached forward and gently took her hand. "Can you feel that? Just as soft as a mouse. That's from a wisteria vine. I picked it up when I was down south last. Wisteria is a beautiful flower, purple like a cluster of grapes and sweet smelling in spring. I'm not sure why I picked it. I got no place to plant it. I guess I just like to feel the fur under my thumb. And maybe I still dream about a place of my own again."

Hannah cautiously rubbed the pod with her little fingers.

"Feel the bumps under the skin? Those are seeds. But they aren't ripe yet. The pod will turn brown and pop open to let the seeds out. If you keep it in your pocket, you'll know when they're ready. You'll *feel* it. Maybe you can plant them whenever you get where you're going."

Hannah slid the pod into her pocket.

"Thank you."

Jack smiled still deep in thought. "You know, as mean as they are, gators ain't the most dangerous critter in the swamp. No siree. It's not the poisonous snakes either. It's a little animal about that big," Jack said as he barely held his thumb and forefinger apart.

"The most fearsome critter is a mosquito. I got tore up by those little buggers in the glades. I near to died of malaria. Spent three weeks shaking with fever. It was worse than trying to mend that broken arm. I thought I was a goner. But well, here I am."

"Have you seen much of the East Coast?" asked Sean.

"Surest have. Been up and down the coast many times. Ate Maine lobster and tasted Vermont maple syrup. Had salty oysters from the Chesapeake Bay and seen the sand dunes where the Wright brothers played. I even dug a few bushels of peanuts in Georgia once.

"Have you seen New York City? Ellis Island? The statue of liberty?" Sean asked as excited as a child.

"You betcha. Big cities aren't for me though. Kinda rough like. Dirty. And too many damn people. Excuse me there, young lady for the cursing. I like being closer to nature where you can scare up some vittles when you're hungry. It's tough in the cities right now. Country folk don't know how good they got it if they can raise their own food and fish and hunt."

Sean knew it only too well.

"Have you been to Atlantic City?"

"Atlantic City? Surest. The boardwalk, the ocean waves, the sand, plenty of goodies to eat. And of course, the *beautiful women*. Every year, their bathing dresses get a little shorter and so does the hair. Pretty soon there won't be anything left of either," said Jack with a grin as he elbowed Sean.

"Oh, excuse me again, there, young lady," he said as he glanced over at Hannah.

"Seems like you've been everywhere. What's your favorite place?" asked Sean.

After a moment, Jack answered. "It'd have to be Florida. Warm, wild, beautiful–and plenty to eat. A little slice of heaven."

"So why don't you stay there?"

"I can't seem to stay put anywhere. My heart's not in it. I guess as long as the trains run, I'll be running with them."

When they got to Wilmington, Jack didn't change trains, but instead stayed on. "I'm headed to New Jersey. I gotta brother there. I'm gonna get me some clam chowder in Cape May. Damn cold there but it is everywhere—except Florida. Weather will be changing shortly though. You'll be south of the Mason Dixon soon. Good luck to you, Sean," he said as he shook his hand.

"It was a pleasure, young lady," he said as he tipped his hat goodbye.

Hannah and Sean waved as they watched the train pull off again. They followed Jack's instructions and jumped into another freight car. This time, finally, they were headed to Baltimore. The sun sank low in the sky and Sean knew they wouldn't make it before dark. Hannah was shivering by the time they arrived at Penn Station. In the icy air, the poor were trying to keep warm by burning wood and trash in barrels. Sean held Hannah close to him. They were poor too, but things had never gotten this bad for them.

Their eyes widened as they walked into the station. They had never seen anything like it. There were marble columns the size of trees and shiny tile floors. They found the bathrooms and made use of the modern indoor plumbing to wash off the boxcar grime.

"Papa, there was hot water coming right out of the spigot," she chirped when she emerged from the ladies room. And one lady in there had on a fur coat and another lady gave me a towel to wipe my hands and there was a big fluffy couch with flowers."

Sean hugged her and smiled. "I'm hungry, Papa. What are we going to have for supper?" They had long since emptied Abby's lunch bag.

They walked back into the night air. Sean hoped to see a restaurant or street vendor, but feared they were too late. A woman stood next to barrel, warming her hands over the flames. Her face was wrinkled with worry.

"Excuse me, ma'am. Is there someplace we can still get some food tonight?"

She looked him over and then Hannah.

"There's a soup kitchen two blocks down. You and the little one can still get fed. Hurry, they'll be closing the door soon."

"Thank you," he said as he lifted Hannah onto his hip and took off. I have ten thousand dollars in my bag but I can't buy a crust of bread, he thought. This must be part of my penance, for stealing. But God won't let Hannah starve. Her little fingers were like ice against his neck. He was determined to find something.

The soup kitchen was about to close. They just made it in time for a bowl of chicken broth and a piece of bread. It wasn't much, but they were glad for it. Sean asked the woman that served them where they could stay for the night. "There's a homeless shelter three doors down, but I wouldn't take a little girl down there. It's just for men. Pretty rough. Plus, you could get knocked in the head for your bag," as she pointed to his satchel. Sean lowered his head in disappointment.

"There's a catholic mission on Greene Street. But they close at dark. You can try there in the morning."

Sean thanked her for the soup and her help. Homeless. The words cut to his soul. But after all, that's what they were. "Where are we going to sleep tonight, Papa?"

Sean had no idea. His thoughts raced. He couldn't let her sleep in the cold. Then he got an idea. "We're going to sleep in the biggest bedroom you ever saw. It's got marble columns, tile floors and indoor plumbing"

Chapter 17

Suddenly, Sean feared the train station might close too. He couldn't wait for Hannah's little legs to keep up. He lifted her to his hip and raced back towards Penn Station. When the great doors swung open, he breathed a sigh of relief. He was even more grateful for the warmth of the indoors that hit his face. He found a wooden bench at the back of the building, away from the chilly entrance. He sat on the bench with his satchel behind his back. Hannah sat next to him and he cradled her head in his lap. She was asleep in seconds. Sean had just dared to close his eyes when he felt a sharp dig in his ribs. A policeman stood over him, poking him with his baton. Sean looked up at him, startled. It is over, he thought. They've got me. Sean started to raise his hands in surrender when the cop spoke.

"There'll be no more trains tonight. Move along. You can't sleep here."

Relieved, Sean slowly gathered up Hannah and his bag. He acted as though he was heading for the door while he surveyed the rest of the station. The policeman was herding a few other men out, but there were no women around at this late hour. When the policeman had his back turned, Sean quickly ducked into the ladies room. The sound of the policeman's bounding voice and the rapping of his baton on the benches echoed through the station. Still, Sean quietly pulled the door closed behind him. The room was especially warm and clean and smelled of soap and perfume. And there it was, the fluffy couch with flowers Hannah told him about. He turned out the light and lay on the couch with his back against the wall, the satchel under his head and the curly girl spooned up tightly against him. He wrapped his arm around her lest she roll off in the night. How good it felt to finally be still. As he closed his eyes, he felt his body sway to and fro with the jerking of the cars on the rail. The engine's roar and the clickety-clack of the tracks still echoed through his head. I have ridden the train all day, he thought. Now I am going to ride it *all night.*

The next morning, Sean was awakened by the squeaking of a cart's wheel. As it grew nearer, he could hear a woman humming. As he listened, he hoped it would go away, so Hannah could sleep a little longer. Suddenly, the door swung open and a hand reached in to turn on the lights.

"Ahhhhhhhhh! What are you doin' in here? I'm gonna call the police."

The startled woman was dark skinned and tall with wide shoulders and hips. She wore a faded blue dress and a white apron. Her hair was braided around the top of her head, like a woven basket. Sean imagined it to be a crown of laurel, like the Romans wore. It was as silver as the wire rimmed glasses that rested at the end of her nose.

Sean sat up quickly and Hannah's eyes widened. The nightmare of being homeless had returned. She turned towards her father and clung to him tightly. Perhaps she thought this woman would put them both in jail. Or maybe she was frightened because she had never seen a Negro.

"Please, dear lady. We mean no harm. We had no place to go. The mission was closed. I couldn't let my little girl sleep in the cold. Don't call the police. We'll be on our way directly."

Hot tears rolled down Hannah's face. She had been a little soldier up until now, but she couldn't bear it any more. "Papa, I want to go home. Please take me home," she cried.

"We can't go home, baby," Sean whispered softly into her ear.

She buried her face in his shoulder as he held her close. She was breaking his heart. This was all *his* fault.

The cleaning woman's eyes filled with tears too. She removed her spectacles and dried her tears with a handkerchief from her pocket. Sean noticed her hands were large and arthritic. Her palms were chaffed and red.

"You poor little thing. Now wait right here, both of you. Listen now, I mean it," she said wagging her finger.

Sean no longer feared she would call the police and so took the time to wash Hannah's face and hands in the sink. As he washed, he glanced at himself in the mirror. The guilt of putting Hannah through this made him sick. He couldn't stand his own image. In a few minutes, the colored woman returned.

"Now don't get yourself in a big hurry. Have a little breakfast," she said with her face beaming.

On the wash stand, she sat a dinner tray that held a bottle of milk and two of the largest blueberry muffins Sean had ever seen. His throat tightened. He was overcome with emotion, gratitude and self-pity. He could barely get out the words, "Thank you for your kindness."

"Thank you ever so much," chirped Hannah. "Can we eat them *now*, Papa?"

The woman retrieved the handkerchief from her pocket once more. "You all be careful now."

As she walked toward the door, her hair caught the first diagonal rays of sun that streamed in through the window high above the washstand. It glistened like tinsel on a Christmas tree.

"Did you see that?" asked Hannah.

"See what?" asked Sean.

"She was glowing."

"Yes, I saw it."

"I guess some angels have *braided* halos."

Sean stared back at the door in wonder. But he didn't wonder long. His thoughts were soon overtaken by the sweet aroma of the muffins. They were still warm. The blueberries were tart but the cake was buttery and tasted like cinnamon. Large crystals of sugar on the top crunched when he chewed them and melted in his mouth. He was so hungry, that he nearly swallowed his muffin whole. He thought of the wild man Jack with his biscuits and remembered the pails of blueberries he had picked. Then he noticed Hannah was enjoying her muffin too. Her face and fingers were stained with berry juice. Large crumbs had rolled down her dress and spilled onto the floor. Sean didn't have the heart to scold her for making such a mess. For a moment, she had forgotten about their plight and was in her own little heaven with sugar on her lips and warmth in her belly. She sat on the edge of the couch swinging her legs and humming. Sean became worried she would soil the upholstery with berries.

"Hannah Jane. You are supposed to eat it, not take a bath in it," he pretended to scold her as he carefully lifted her from the sofa, crumbs and all. "Little piggie."

"Papa, stick out your tongue."

"What?"

"Stick out your tongue!"

Sean obeyed.

Hannah let out a squeal.

He quickly turned to face the mirror over the sink with his tongue still out.

Hannah laughed once more.

"Fine. Want to see a *little piggy* with a blue tongue?"

Hannah quickly finished licking the blueberry juice from her fingers. Sean lifted her by the waist to the mirror. She giggled at all the sticky muffin crumbs on her face and at the tips of her ringlets.

"Go ahead."

Hannah stuck out her tongue and laughed at the sight of her reflection. She began to clown and make silly faces.

"That's enough, little monkey. C'mon now. Let's get cleaned up before she gets back."

Sean brushed the crumbs from her dress and set to work washing Hannah's hands and face. While she dried on a towel, he brushed the crumbs from the couch into his hands and picked up the largest crumbs from the floor with his fingers. He gave Hannah the last swallow of milk and rinsed out the bottle. Sean thought about the cleaning lady's kind gesture and fretted that he had nothing to give her in return.

"Hannah, step out of the door to see if she is coming. I'll be right behind you." Hannah hesitated, afraid to leave his side, even for a moment.

"It'll be alright. Now go."

When Hannah was out of sight, Sean reached into his pocket and retrieved the bill he tried to give the ticket master in Cressona. He carefully wiped the water from the corner of the sink with his shirtsleeve and placed the bill under the milk bottle. He stared back at the bill for a moment. It was a lot of money, but it's all he had. He hoped her luck was better when trying to find someone who could break a hundred dollar bill. Hannah and Sean slipped through the front door before the cleaning lady could return.

The air was cold enough to see his breath. The sky was clear and the sun shone brightly. March had come in like a lion and the lamb couldn't come too soon. Sean closed his eyes and turned his face to the East to feel its warmth against his cheeks. Hannah observed her father and followed suit. Sean felt a chill and tightened his coat around him. He put his arm around Hannah. No, spring couldn't come soon enough, he thought. When a porter caught his eye, Sean asked, "Can you tell me where to find the Lord Baltimore hotel?"

The porter surveyed Sean's wrinkled and soiled clothes skeptically. Sean realized he looked like a charity case. Nevertheless, he gathered his courage.

"I'm looking for work," he said confidently pulling the curly girl even closer.

The porter's eyes lowered to Hannah's face. His expression softened. She seemed to have that effect on everyone. With a change of heart, he suddenly raised his arm from his side and swung it round like a weather vane in a wind storm.

"Head that way on Lanvale Street. Then catch the streetcar at St. Paul. Get off at Fayette and take a right, left at Liberty, then left again onto Baltimore St. You can see the hotel from there. She's a beaut. About two miles from here. You can't miss her."

"Thank you, sir," said Sean as he tipped his hat and tugged at Hannah's hand.

"Papa, are we going to ride a streetcar? Oh, goody," squealed Hannah.

Her eyes glowed as she looked on all the people and buildings and cars around them. Hannah had never been in a city and to her it was as exciting as a circus. Sean was wary of the fast pace of the people and realized Baltimore was even bigger than Pittsburgh. He held her hand tightly fearing she would be hit by an automobile when they crossed the street. Sean remembered what Jack had said about cities and *too many damn people.*

"No sweetheart," answered Sean. "Wouldn't you rather take a little stroll with Papa and see some of the city?"

Hannah gave her father a disappointed look as she tagged along beside him. Sean knew if he couldn't buy a train ticket with a hundred dollar bill he probably couldn't buy a streetcar fare either. The two dodged people on the sidewalks and had to wait to cross at each street. They peered into shops and marveled at the shoes, coats, lamps and dresses. They dallied in front of a hardware store. Sean was intrigued with a shiny new ax in the store window. "What I could do with that!" he exclaimed. They passed five and ten cent stores, diners and fancy restaurants. When they got to the theater, Sean read out loud from the marquee to Hannah: "*Death Takes a Holiday,* plays at 7:30 pm." There were also two matinees at two and four, *Carolina* starring Shirley Temple. At the ticket counter, the glass was plastered with bulletins about the cartoons that were featured: *Silly Symphonies, Krazy Kat and Betty Boop* and there was a new star, *Popeye the Sailor.*

Sean pushed up his coat sleeve and flexed his forearm.

"What do you think? Just like the sailorman," said Sean comparing his muscles to the cartoon character. Hannah was not impressed.

"Papa, can we see the show?" she begged.

"Later, lamb chop. Papa's got to find a job and a place for us to sleep tonight, in that order."

"Why can't we just go home?" asked Hannah with a pout on her lips.

Sean pulled Hannah by the hand into the theater's alcove to get clear of the dozens of people bustling past. He got down on one knee and took his hat into his hand. He rested his other hand on Hannah's shoulder, held her at arm's length and looked her in the eye.

"Hannah, honey, listen to me. We *can't* go home. Not for a long time–maybe never. There are some bad men that want to hurt me and they know where we live. So please don't ask again. We can't go back."

Hannah's bottom lip quivered. Reality was setting in.

"But what about Aunt Abby?"

Sean took a deep breath. The sight of her body lying on the kitchen floor flashed before his eyes once more. It made him sick to think about it. He swallowed hard but couldn't get the lump from his throat.

"They can't hurt her anymore," he answered softly.

Hannah was dissatisfied with his answer. She stared at the ground for a moment and then lifted her eyes to Sean's.

"What about my dollies?" she asked with a tear in her eye.

"Did you put them to bed, like I told you?"

She nodded.

"Did you cover them up tight, so they won't get cold?"

She nodded once more.

Sean studied her face. It bore a mix of disappointment and exhaustion. There were dark circles under her eyes. He lifted her chin with his forefinger and gave her the most convincing smile he could muster.

"Then they are having a rest with Aunt Abby. They'll look after each other. Now be a good girl. Chin up. We are starting over again, you and me, and we are having the adventure of a lifetime. We are going to see or hear or taste something different every week. Will you be a good sport, be my traveling partner on this journey?"

Hannah considered the offer for a moment. Then a smile spread over her face and then she nodded her head enthusiastically. She wrapped her arms around her father's shoulders. Sean held her tight. For that moment, they weren't aware that people were walking past them or that automobiles were bouncing along and blowing their horns a few feet away. At that moment, they were the only two people on Earth. Me and my curly girl, we're going to get through this, one way or another, thought Sean.

Suddenly, Hannah pushed Sean away. "Papa, will the tooth fairy be able to find me here?"

Stunned, Sean asked, "Why would you ask a question like that?"

"Because my front tooth is starting to wiggle. It got wigglier last night when I ate the apple. Look," she said as she used her finger and thumb to wiggle her front tooth.

It occurred to Sean that all he could think about was food and shelter for them both and her concern was the tooth fairy. Even this tragedy couldn't stop childhood. He smiled, relieved.

"Yes, I'm sure tooth fairy will find you no matter where you are."

His throat tightened. Molly was missing this. "All right then. No more dawdling. Let's go to the hotel and meet Cousin Sam."

Finally, they turned left onto Baltimore Street. When they looked up, there she was, The Lord Baltimore Hotel. They had never seen such a tall building. It was magnificent.

"Look, Hannah, there she is, the place Aunt Abby told me about. That's where Papa is going to work." Sean said it like it was a sure thing. But it was far from sure. Sam Mulligan didn't know him from Adam and he was learning all too well that nothing in life was *sure*.

They looked up and up at nineteen stories of concrete and red brick, twenty-two if they counted the octagon shaped tower at the very top. The hotel was actually two towers with a few floors at the bottom joining them, like a giant horseshoe standing on end. There were huge arched windows, like on the side of a church, and an awning and flags flying on the front. They stood on the far edge of the sidewalk, close to the street, and craned their necks trying to see the whole thing at once. It made Sean dizzy. There was nothing like it in Pottsville or even Pittsburgh for that matter. As they reached the front, they watched the revolving door swing non-stop, like a merry-go-round, letting people in and out. As they grew nearer, they felt the warm air pushed out by the spinning glass and brass doors. Sean got up his nerve to jump into the door with Hannah but she pulled back against his wrist. "No, Papa, no! That door is going to eat us. I don't want to go in there." She pulled him back with all her might, terrified to go through the revolving doors. Sean offered to carry her and jump in together. She wanted no part of it and began to cry. "Okay. Let's see if there is a door on the other side," said Sean as he dried her tears with his shirt sleeve. On the other side of the building, Sean saw a concrete medallion of an Indian chief's head, with feathers. "Look Hannah, like Jack told us about." Before they could take it all in, a man in uniform approached them. He had a whistle on a string around his neck. His shoes were shiny and so was his smile. He tipped his hat and opened the door for them. As they stepped through, he put out his gloved hand to Sean. Surprised, Sean gave his hand a good shake and thought what a friendly town.

The lobby was enormous with speckled tile floors and brass joiners. The walls were pale pink marble with rust swirls. The supporting columns were marble too. Even the stairs were marble. Sean led Hannah to the nearest wall to touch the surface with his fingertips. Hannah joined him. It was perfectly polished and smooth and cool, like glass. Where the wall met the floor, there was a trim of black marble with thick white veins. Large pots were painted with birds and flowers and ferns and little palm trees grew in them. Deeply colored carpets in blues and reds with fringe along the ends covered the floors. The stairs had brass railings that shone like jewelry. Sean was surprised that the ceiling was like looking up into a flowerbed. There were deep blue octagons with gold blossoms in their centers. He shook Hannah's arm to get her attention then pointed to the ceiling. "Lamb chop, take a look at that." Her jaw dropped as she stretched her neck to see it. "Are they real gold? They look like rows of cabbages. My Sunday school teacher says babies come from heaven. Aunt Abby says they come from the cabbage patch. Maybe the cabbage patch is in heaven. Is it, Papa?"

"You are seeing it with your own eyes just like me," Sean said with a smile. Then Sean noticed the tops of the columns were gilded too. The balcony along the second floor had little shops: a coffee shop, a barber, a tailor, beauty salon and a shoe shine station. The doorways and windows were arched and the ceiling was so high, they felt like they we're in a church or castle. People stood waiting to be helped at tall counters in front of the revolving doors. Men in uniforms carried luggage to and fro. Telephones rang off the hook. There was another kind of bell as well. Sean figured out it was the elevators, five of them. He decided he needed to take a ride to the top floor with Hannah to look out over the whole city. Sean glanced down at Hannah when she squeezed his hand tighter. She was trying to steady herself, dizzy from craning her neck upwards. Just like Sean, she was trying to take it all in. She pointed to the massive brass and crystal chandelier suspended over their heads. Mesmerized by it she said softly, "Look, Papa—diamonds."

Sean knew it must be glass, but didn't utter a word, lest he break her spell. As his eyes drifted downward, he noticed an old-fashioned painting of a man. He stood straight, with his hand on his hip, holding back his black cloak and exposing his gold handled sword. There was a ruffled collar around his neck and his dark figure against the red background was regal. His head was tilted slightly and his eyes were piercing and confident. Sean took a few steps closer and read the brass plate beneath it: *Sir George Calvert First Lord of Baltimore.* Sean studied his face, his hazel eyes, brown hair, mustache and pointed beard. They made him seem fatherly. Lord Baltimore, the old bird himself. Sean looked down at his own clothes and suddenly felt small. What am I doing here? He became disheartened but soon gathered his courage once more. He knew what he must do. They got in the line at the counter. Sean became nervous as they waited.

"Checking in or checking out?" asked the clerk as he looked Sean over.

"Uh, neither. May I speak with Sam Mulligan?"

"He's awfully busy. Is there something I can help you with? Is there something wrong with your room?" he asked.

"No, I don't have a room. I'm looking for work. Do you know if he is hiring?"

"I should have known," said the clerk with disgust. "Follow me."

He took them across the lobby to a small hallway and rapped at the door."

"Yes, who is it?" a deep voice asked.

"There's a man here to see you about a job."

"What's his name?"

"What's your name?" the clerk asked turning to Sean

Sean hesitated for a moment. No one knew him here. This was his chance to start a new life. He could make up a name. No one would know the difference except him and Hannah—and God.

"Sean O'Connell."

"He says his name is Sean O'Connell," yelled the clerk through the door.

"I don't know any Sean O'Connell. Tell him I'm busy," answered the voice.

Sean's heart sank. This was his only hope. He panicked.

The clerk tried to lead him away from the door, but Sean pushed past him. "Abby Sue sent me," he yelled through the door.

Sean heard the sound of a chair scooting backwards and steps coming towards the door. The knob turned quickly and the door flew open. The man that appeared in the doorway was tall and broad like a barn door with bright blue eyes. He had white hair and a mustache that curled up at the ends. He was dressed in a dark blue suit and had a gold watch fob dangling from his pocket. The expression on his face was stern.

He looked annoyed. Sean guessed he had had enough of this conversation and was going to throw him out of the hotel himself.

"Abby Sue? Well, why didn't you say so? Goodness gracious I haven't heard that name in years. How is the old gal?" he asked as the corners of his mouth softened into a smile. He offered his hand and Sean gave him a strong shake.

"Pleased to meet you, Sean."

"And I'm happy to meet you, sir. But I'm sorry to report Aunt Abby has passed on. It was rather sudden."

"Oh no. That's terrible. What a shame. I'm so sorry to hear that."

Sean felt a lump in his throat. "I'm her niece's husband and this is her great-niece, Hannah," he managed as he looked down at the curly girl. Hannah quickly turned to Sean. "He has Aunt Abby's eyes."

Hannah offered her hand to Sam. "Pleased to meet you, Mr. Mulligan."

Sam beamed as he shook her hand. "Well, now, you look sorta like another little girl I used to know, a Miss Molly."

"That was my mama."

"Molly died in childbirth," Sean explained. "It was with our son over a year ago. He was already gone."

"It seems to me I heard about that through the family grapevine. I'm sorry for your loss, son. I'm sure it was devastating."

Hannah's smile faded. She got a faraway look on her face.

Sam broke the silence. "Well, what brings you to the big city?"

JOAN LEHMANN

"The mines are all closed in Pottsville. I headed this way to look for work on Abby's advice. She said you might need some help."

"What kind of work do you do?"

"I've worked in the coal mines and sometimes at the lumber mill."

Sam laughed. "Well, I'm afraid we don't have either here at the Lord Baltimore. Can you do accounting?"

"No, sir."

"Can you cook?"

"No. At least, not anything anybody could stand to eat."

Sam grabbed his belly and chuckled. "Can you sing or dance or tell jokes?" he asked teasingly.

Sean considered telling Sam that he could serve drinks in a dress. No. Never again. "Not good enough to make a living at it I'm afraid."

"Oh, laddie. Times are hard. Why, I've got fifty fellows who want every job that comes along. I'm sorry to tell you I haven't got anything for you. Maybe you could get a job at the docks loading ships," offered Sam.

"Sir, I was hoping, maybe….."

"Yes, what is it son?"

"Well, I don't know anyone here in Baltimore. I was hoping maybe you could help me with a job and maybe help find a place for Hannah and me to stay. We're all we've got left, each other, she and I. I'm afraid we're sort of fish out of water."

Sam looked at Sean with big fatherly eyes and said, "I'm sorry, son."

"I'm willing to work at anything. I've got a strong back and I'm willing to learn."

Sam stared back at Sean and with sternness and finality said, "I'm sorry."

Sean was in a state of shock. How could this happen? He had nothing else, nothing. They had come so far. Sean tried to gather his pride and walk away. But how could he? How was he going to take care of Hannah? They were homeless and they might as well be penniless. Sam was his only hope. What could he do? Then Abby spoke to him, "C'mon laddie, it's your last card. You cannot fail *her*." He took a deep breath to ask one more time.

"Mr. Mulligan, I…."

Just then, there was a commotion in the lobby. The three of them stepped around the corner to see what had happened. A bellhop, who looked to be in his fifties, was face on the floor with a suitcase that had burst open, and three others lying next to him. An older woman in a fur coat and high heels tried frantically to get her belongings back into to the suitcase. As the three of them approached her, she turned her face to Sam.

"Mr. Mulligan, you've got to do something about this," she said pointing at the bellhop like he wasn't even there. "I don't want to cause a scene."

But it was too late for that.

"This man is shamefully inebriated. This is embarrassing, a travesty."

Once she had everything back in her bag, Sam snapped it shut. "I'm so sorry, Mrs. Stein. Just give me a minute to straighten this out."

"Well if you don't, then I will," she barked.

Sam turned his back to her and put his arm around the bellhop's shoulder.

"Now, Ralph. How long have you been working at the Baltimore?"

"Two years."

"And how many times have I fired you for drinking on the job?"

"This will be the third."

"I've done all I can do. Three strikes and you're out, my man. I'm sorry. Go down to the mission and get yourself sobered up. You can come back next week for your things and your last paycheck," said Sam.

"Yes sir. And Mr. Mulligan, I'm real sorry." Ralph offered Sam his hand.

Sam secretly gave him a little shake. "Good luck to you, Ralph," he whispered.

When Ralph was several yards away, Sam shouted, "And don't come back."

Ralph snickered.

Sam and Sean carried the lady's bags to the front desk. "Call one of the fellas to take up Mrs. Stein's bags," he told the clerk.

"Mr. Mulligan, I'm afraid we're understaffed today. Four men called out with the flu and well, now we've lost Ralph."

Sam thought for a moment. "Fine, I'll take them up myself."

"Sam, I'll take them up. Let me help," offered Sean Sam hesitated.

"Well somebody do something. I'm going to be late for my luncheon," complained Mrs. Stein. To Sam's amazement, Sean lifted all four bags at once.

"Fine, you take her up, Sean. I'll watch the little one. Meet you in my office when you get back," said Sam.

When the elevator door opened, there was a colored man seated on a high stool. "What floor, madam?" he asked.

"The penthouse," answered Mrs. Stein.

Sean peered through the elevator doors as they closed to see Hannah being led away to Sam's office by the hand. She looked over her shoulder to give her father one last glance. Her face was a scowl. Sean blew her a small kiss and gave her a little wave. She turned away just as the doors closed.

Even the elevator was ornate. The walls were covered in cloth, the floor was tile and the ceiling had a brass lamp dangling from it. When it took off, it left Sean's stomach behind. He felt woozy for a second and his knees buckled slightly. As soon as his strength returned, he noticed the levers the colored man controlled. The three of them were silent, like in church. Sean thought how strange for people to stand so near each other and not speak.

"All the way to the top," said the colored man under his breath.

When they arrived, he forced the metal doors open. Looking down, he noticed the elevator had not stopped flush with the floor.

"Please, watch your step," he said as he offered the guest his hand and helped her over the gap. She reached in her purse and handed him a dime.

"Thank you, Mrs. Stein," he said and tipped his hat to her.

She quickly walked down the hall and put a key in the door. She swung the door open and said to Sean

"You can put them down there," pointing to a sitting room.

This wasn't just a room. It was a parlor and a bedroom and a bathroom and…

"That'll be all. You can go now," she said as she motioned for Sean to leave.

"Goodbye," she said as she handed him a quarter.

"Thank you," said Sean as she closed the door in his face. He didn't mind. He felt like he was floating. He'd never seen anything like this place. As he walked back towards the elevator, he realized the colored man was still holding it for him.

"You never been up here before, have you?"

Sean shook his head.

The man pointed to a window down the opposite end of the hall. "Take a peek over the city, over the harbor. Make it a fast peek. Boss don't like the help hanging around up here."

The view made Sean dizzy. He beamed as he looked over the rooftops and high above the smoke from the chimneys. Streetcars below looked like toy trains and the people looked like ants. There were so many buildings and streets and shops and–the harbor. His heart soared when he realized it was the closest he'd ever been to the sea. The river seemed to go forever into the Bay. He tried to imagine that if he squinted hard enough, he could see Ireland on the other side. His spell was soon broken.

"Hey you. C'mon. Before you get us both in trouble."

Sean ran back and jumped in with the elevator man. He quickly closed the door behind him. When the colored man pulled back on the lever, the elevator dropped like a brick. "It's faster going down," he said with a grin.

"I think we left my stomach up there," said Sean. "Or my heart."

"It's fascinating alright."

They rode the rest of the way in silence. When the doors opened, Sean offered the man his hand, "Thanks." The man looked past Sean, neither speaking nor nodding.

Sean found Hannah in Sam's office with a crayon and coloring book.

Sam rose from his chair. Sean smiled like a kid just back from the carnival.

"Well, how did you make out?"

"I must have passed the test. She gave me a quarter. At least I can buy Hannah some lunch," said Sean jokingly.

Sam didn't smile. The silence was uncomfortable. Hannah continued to color.

"Hannah and I had a nice conversation."

"I'm sorry about that. She will chew your ear off."

"No need to apologize. She told me about her mother and brother in heaven and Aunt Abby cutting down her mother's dresses to fit her. She also told me about eating fried potato peels for breakfast."

Hannah's eyes met Sean's. Sean was embarrassed, but it was after all, the truth. "The mines have been closed a while now. We have been getting by week by week–and sometimes day by day."

Sam looked down at the floor and shifted his weight from foot to foot. He nervously shoved his hands deeper into his pants pockets. "I forgot how tough it is to make it out there in the mountains. Heck, it's tough all over. But I've been spoiled, I guess. I think I was a little too hasty before. I don't have much to offer you in the way of a job. I'm almost embarrassed to suggest it. But if you would like to work as a bellhop here, I mean, for starters, I could use you. You'd be doing me a favor. I'm kind of short right now."

Hannah and Sean smiled at each other at the news.

"But of all the places you could have settled, why Baltimore?"

"Partly because of Abby, but mostly because I wanted to see the water. I have dreamed of seeing it my whole life. My grandfather was the one who planted the seed. He lived and worked on the water."

"In Baltimore?"

"No, Ireland."

"I see."

"When I took that lady's bags to the penthouse, I got to see the water from the top floor. I can't wait to go down to the docks and see it."

"That *lady* is the congressman's wife. I hope you two got along."

"Yes sir."

"And as far as the water goes, that isn't the sea. It's a river that turns into the bay, more fresh than salt. They sort of run together. Regardless, Sean, Baltimore is a big city. The dock can be a rough place, a place for industry, not tourists. I don't want you to get the wrong idea. It's not a resort, like Ocean City. You should take Hannah to a nice beach to see the water come summer."

"Yes sir. Sam, I won't let her down, or you, I promise."

"I know you won't. I guess Miss Hannah made me remember, family has got to take care of each other."

Sean looked down at Hannah who was still coloring away.

"The clerk that showed you to my office will put you in business. Ask him to find you a couple of uniforms and show you around. You'll need to start today."

"Mr. Mulligan, I don't know how to thank you."

"Hold your gratitude until you've done a few shifts and your arms are falling off. You might not want this job after all."

He sat back in his chair and looked over Hannah's handiwork. "My wife, Flo, loves children, particularly little girls. How about if I take you home at lunchtime and you can spend the afternoon with her? I'm sure she's got something for you to play with and she'll get Little Orphan Annie and the Singing Lady on the radio for you. What do you say?

"We have Little Orphan Annie on our radio. You've got her on your radio too?"

"Absolutely."

"Can Papa come too?"

Sam's eyes met Sean's. "Well, he could, but I think he would rather find his way around the hotel today, you know, since he's starting his new job."

"Can he come for supper?" asked Hannah.

"I'm sorry, Sam," apologized Sean.

"That's alright. It is a valid question and an appropriate concern. Sean, can you come by the house tonight for supper, around six?"

"Yes sir."

"It's settled, then."

Sam scribbled down the address on a slip of paper and handed it to him.

"Sean, you run along and get started. I have some paperwork to get caught up on and I bet Hannah has a few more stories for me."

Sean gave Hannah a hug and kiss. She pouted and didn't want to let go of his arm. "Now you listen to Mr. Sam. Be a good girl and I'll see you tonight," said Sean as he hurried out the door to find the clerk.

Things were starting to look up. Sean got his foot in the door. Was it because he volunteered to carry the bags upstairs or was it Hannah's charming stories and big green eyes? Maybe both. It didn't matter. Sean had his chance. As he walked to the desk, he saw a woman checking in with gray hair, worn swept up with hairpins, like Abby's. When she turned towards him, he hoped it was her. But of course, it wasn't. The lady smiled and walked away. It occurred to him that Abby was still here, watching over them. He took a deep breath as he readied himself to deal with the clerk that had been rude earlier. He stood straight with his shoulders back, chest out and chin up. He thought to himself, I can do this. And so their life in Baltimore began.

Chapter 18

The clerk held Sean's arms away from him and sized up his chest with a measuring tape. As he spun him around for another look, he mumbled under his breath. The clerk seemed thoroughly disgusted to have to deal with him. Sean didn't care—he had a job. Sean smiled as the clerk left his station to search of a uniform. A few minutes later, he returned with outstretched arms.

"These will have to do until you can see the tailor."

He showed Sean to the staff's quarters in the basement. Bunk beds were stacked three high and slim, tall lockers held each man's belongings. The rooms were small, but orderly and clean. A washroom with sinks, toilets and a big shower was just down the hall. Sean fought to fend off thoughts of home. This place was so crowded, so tight. He knew it was only temporary and it was better than sleeping in a train station or a park bench—or a boxcar. He surveyed his face in the mirror over the washstand. He couldn't believe Sam had hired him considering how rough he looked. Even a close shave couldn't improve his long face or the dark circles under his eyes. Sean retrieved the cake of soap and razor from his bag. Then he took a clean towel from the linen cabinet. It took him a minute to figure out how to work the hot and cold water, but when he did, he stepped into his first hot shower. Sean smiled as it warmed his aching body. First he washed away the grime and then watched as the soapy water flowed out through the little holes in the floor. When the dirt was gone, he set out to wash away his misery as well. He stayed there under the hot spray, until he was dizzy. When he turned off the water, he noticed the cloud of steam hovering just above his head. The mirror was so fogged he had to shave by feel. He remembered how precise he had to be the last time he shaved, when he had to put make up on before going to work. He shuddered at the thought. He tried on one of the uniforms. The jacket was little tight across the shoulders and the pants were too long. He felt like a monkey in the suit with its high waist and double row of brass buttons across the front. Yellow stripes ran down the outside of the legs. The get-up was topped off with a round cap held on by a string under the neck. It was ridiculous. But at least it isn't a dress, thought Sean, and now we won't starve. He wiped the last of the fog from the mirror and took a look at himself. He tried to tuck some of his hair under his cap. He hadn't had a hair cut in weeks. He headed for the stairs and suddenly, his stomach rumbled. He remembered how little he'd eaten that day. His blueberry muffin was long gone. Hadn't Sam mentioned something about chow? He followed his nose to a small kitchen and spotted a table with a couple of other bellhops. When Sean came near them, they pointed across the room.

"Tomato soup and cheese sandwiches today. We get fifteen minutes to eat. Take a plate." Sean grabbed two sandwiches from the tray and dipped them straight into the hot bowl of soup. As soon as he swallowed down the last piece of bread, he held the soup bowl to his lips and drank it down. When he finished, Sean noticed they were both staring at him. "Looks like you missed breakfast," one said as he handed Sean a napkin.

"I guess I was pretty hungry."

"Is this your first day?"

"Yep."

"You better get that hair cut."

"I know."

"Well, grab another sandwich. You're gonna need it. 'Cause when they ring that bell, our asses hop—get it?"

One bellhop found the head porter who spent most of Sean's shift showing him the ropes. Sean helped him load and carry luggage but the porter kept the tips. Pretty soon, Sean learned the routine and was left to operate on him own. The clerks at the front desk rang when they needed service. One bell was for checking in, two for checking out, three bells if more than one bellhop was needed. The luggage carts had tall arched bars. They were brass but might as well have been gold, the way they shone. They looked like something Cinderella rode in to the ball, a far cry from the rickety coal shuttles Sean had loaded. He learned quickly that bell hopping was just like waiting tables–it was all about the tips. He made nickels and dimes or sometimes, a quarter. On a really big job, with steamer trunks, he might pull in fifty cents. The more luggage he could squeeze on the cart, the more tips he made. It all went into his pocket and at the end of the day, he didn't have to share it with the bartender. It's was all *his.*

His body ached and his feet throbbed by the end of his first day. He tried to remember that it was better than breathing coal dust and breaking his back with a shovel for his pay. It was better than cramming his feet into slippers and pretending to be a woman five nights a week. He smiled at the thought. And it was a hell of a sight better than a bullet in his head like Vinnie–or in the chest, like poor Aunt Abby. His brain put things into perspective and he quickly forgot his aches and pains.

At 5:00, he headed down to the staff's quarters. The shower was calling his name. At that hour, the place was busy with other employees cleaning up after their shifts. When Sean got his turn, he was quick about it. Others were waiting in line and anyway, he couldn't risk being late for supper. He wondered how Hannah had fared that day apart from him. He put on his last clean clothes from his bag. He combed his wet hair away from his face. He tried to smooth the wrinkles from his shirt with his hand—but it was no use. His pants were frayed at the bottom and one knee had a small hole. After being surrounded by suits, dresses and furs all day, he felt like a hayseed. He realized he didn't even own a necktie.

Sam lived a short walk from the hotel in a tall, brick row house. Sean marveled at the flower box which held crocuses in bloom and a few daffodil heads that had sprung from the ground. It was decidedly warmer here in the city than in the hills. And anyway, he surmised it was the south facing wall of the house. A brass mailbox with "Mulligan" inscribed on the front greeted him. He started to knock on the door then realized there was a bell. As he pushed the button, he heard little feet race to the door. "Papa, papa, you're here!" Sam was close behind.

Hannah jumped into her father's arms and he lifted her and swung her around once before speaking to Sam.

"What a nice place you have here, Mr. Mulligan."

"Oh, you can save the misters for the hotel. Call me Sam. Come on in. The missus has been fussing over supper all afternoon. It will be ready in no time. I bet you are beat. The first day's the worst."

It was a nice house. There were cherry tables and ceramic vases and lamps. Paintings and photos hung on every wall and there was a large, swirling banister along the stairway. The carpets reminded Sean of the ones at the hotel.

"Well, it's so nice to meet you. I heard all about you from Hannah. I'm Flo. How do you do, Sean?"

Sean quickly removed his hat. "Pleased to meet you. Thanks for the dinner invitation. And most of all, thanks for looking after my little one today."

Before long, they were seated at the table. Sam sat at the head with Flo to his right. Hannah sat next to Sean. Hannah clung to Sean tightly and didn't dare let him out of her sight, afraid he would leave her again. A maid brought small, steaming bowls of soup to the table. It didn't look like much for someone who had been fussing in the kitchen all day. I'm starving, thought Sean. He carefully dipped in his spoon. The broth was thin and milky with butter floating on top. He found an odd looking piece of meat at the bottom of his bowl. Flo noticed his expression of confusion.

"Those are oysters," she said as she sprinkled a few little round crackers on top of his soup. "And these are *oyster crackers.*"

Then Sean realized what it was. "Is this oyster stew?"

"Yes, have you eaten it before? I was hoping to surprise you with something different, one of our local specialties," said Flo.

"I've never eaten it, but I've heard about it," said Sean as he sipped a little of the broth from his spoon. It was hot and salty and the melted butter stuck to the top of his lip. He scooped up an oyster and put it in his mouth. It was chewy and tasted a little fishy. Sean noticed that Sam had nearly finished his. Hannah sipped the broth and ate her little crackers, but refused to try the shellfish. Sam spied her bowl, empty except for three oysters lying on the bottom. He helped himself to them–all three in one spoonful.

Sean didn't blame him. He was still hungry too.

"Oh, Sam," scolded Flo.

"What? She's family, and besides, I'm not letting these babies go to waste." Sean couldn't believe it. After a long day of work, he expected more food than this, especially in such a fancy city home.

Hannah leaned over and whispered in his ear, "Watch this, Papa."

Flo reached for the dinner bell and gave it a gentle ring. The maid returned with salads and set a plate in front of each of them. Now I get it, thought Sean. She is going to feed us a little dish at a time. I just hope she keeps them coming.

"It's magic," said Hannah. "Every time she rings the bell, more food comes. Papa, you don't need to go to work anymore. We just need one of those bells."

Flo and Sam chuckled. "You can have our bell. It's making me fat," said Sam.

Sean cut into the wedge of crisp lettuce with his table knife. There was some light green dressing poured over it. It was odd looking, but delicious. "I've never tasted anything like it. This is good, Flo," offered Sean still chewing.

"Do you like it? It's called *Green Goddess.* It's made with fresh herbs. We had this salad dressing at the Garden Court Restaurant when we were in San Francisco. It was named after a play showing there. Why don't you have a signature dressing at the Lord Baltimore, Sam?"

"I'm not in charge of the kitchen. And anyway, we have the best crab cakes in town. That's good enough."

"But the Lord Baltimore doesn't settle for good enough. Wouldn't it be keen to offer a salad with fresh greens, tomato and cucumber? Perhaps a sliced hard-boiled egg, some bleu cheese and bacon? Oh and a sliced alligator pear?"

"Alligator?" Hannah whispered to Sean.

Sean shook his head.

Sam rolled his eyes to the ceiling for divine help but Flo ignored him. "The center could be a mound of cold crab meat with a dressing of mayonnaise, lemon and cayenne pepper."

Sean devoured his salad much faster than his soup.

"Does that sound good to you, Sean?" asked Flo.

Sean was afraid to get between these two, but after all, it was the lady who was feeding him tonight. With twinkling eyes, he gave her his Irish charm. "Good lady, I think it sounds *heavenly.*"

It made Flo blush. "That's it. You can call it the Lord is in His Heaven salad. That ought to top the Green Goddess."

"What a mouthful? There you go dreaming again, Florence. Who cares about salad? We men need food that will stick to our ribs, meat and potatoes, wouldn't you say, Sean?"

Flo leaned forward to better hear Sean's answer. Sean was in trouble. He knew better than to take sides. When would he ever learn to keep his mouth shut? He desperately needed a job, but he couldn't let down this lovely lady who was feeding him. He searched his brain for the perfect answer. "I grew up on meat and potatoes and I have to agree with Sam that I couldn't live without them." Sam sat back in his chair and beamed, victorious. Flo let out a sigh of defeat.

"But that was the best salad I ever had in my whole life and Flo's recipe sounds like a winner."

Flo folded her arms and looked to Sam with a great smile of satisfaction.

"Can I ring the bell this time?" asked Hannah in her baby voice.

"Certainly," said Sam as he handed it to her.

Sean liked the way Hannah rang the bell because this time a platter with a large fish, stuffed with sage dressing appeared. It was covered with a pale yellow sauce. Bowls of rice, peas and carrots and a basket of hot yeast rolls soon followed to the table.

Sam sliced and served. "You could leave the Hollandaise off the fish once in a while you know, Florence. I can barely get my belly up to the table now," complained Sam. He leaned over to Sean and grumbled," She puts some kind of sauce on everything."

"Oh Sam, you're exaggerating. And I won't leave out the Hollandaise. It's just not the same without it. Sean and Hannah, this is shad. I sent Sadie to the dock for it this afternoon. Shad bones are long and thin. When you cook the fish in a little vinegar, it softens them so you can eat bones and all. In early spring, the female shad are full of eggs, or roe. I had Sadie fry some for Sam." She pointed to a small plate at Sam's elbow. Sam speared a couple of lumps with his fork and put them on his plate.

"You have to cook them slowly so the sacs don't explode. If they pop, the eggs fly everywhere. You can try some if Sam will share." Sam muttered something and shoved the plate of roe Sean's way. The fish reminded Sean of trout from the river and the stuffing reminded him of Abby's chicken but Sean didn't dare touch Sam's roe. He needed his job too badly and after the salad discussion, needed to earn back a few points.

Between bites of shad roe, Sam pondered, "Too bad you can't make fish gravy. That would stick to your ribs."

Everyone continued to enjoy their meal until Sam again broke the silence. "You know Sean's right. That salad of yours does sound pretty good, Flo. Maybe you should talk to the chef about it."

"Really Sam?"

"Yeah, I mean it's got crabmeat in it. How bad could it be?"

Poor Sam, thought Sean. He's like me. He doesn't know when to stop when he's ahead. It didn't seem to bother Flo. She beamed and rang the bell once more. The sweet smell of vanilla and cinnamon reached the table before the maid. She placed a large glass dish of bread pudding, bursting with raisins in front of Flo. She cut large squares for each of them and ladled hot, sugary sauce over each slice, except Hannah's.

"This is hard sauce with bourbon. I made one bottle last nearly through Prohibition. But I let it flow a little more freely tonight for our special company," she said grinning.

"Miss Hannah, would you like to try a *little* taste?" Hannah shook her head. She couldn't be bothered with sauce. She eagerly spooned pudding into her mouth and didn't want to be interrupted. The taste was rich and creamy and melted in their mouths.

"The pudding was delicious, Flo, but you shouldn't have gone to all this trouble."

"Thank you, Sean. I'm glad to do it. We don't get company nearly often enough."

"I never had hard sauce. It was real nice."

"Another sauce," muttered Sam.

"Oh, be quiet you," fussed Flo.

"And I want to thank you, Sam, for giving me a job. I don't know where we would be without you."

Sam's eyes met Flo's. There was another short silence. "Uh, Sean, have you thought about where you are going to stay?" asked Sam.

"I have. I don't have enough money for a room yet, but Hannah and I can probably stay at the mission a night or two until I can find something better."

"Will tooth fairy be able to find me there, in case I lose my tooth?" asked Hannah clutching to her father's side. Flo folded her napkin and rested it on the table. She looked over to Sam and shook her head.

"Well, you know, Sean that might not be the best place for a little girl. Florence and I thought maybe she might like to stay here a little while, I mean, until you get on your feet," offered Sam. "Of course, she'll have to learn to like oysters," he said with a wink. Hannah's eyes got big.

"Stop it, Samuel. Don't tease her," said Flo as she rubbed Hannah's hand across the table.

Sean posed the question to Hannah. "Would you like to stay here a little while, until I can get us a place?" Hannah squeezed his arm tighter. "I know she must love it here. She's just shy and a little–attached to me. We've never been separated before. But I agree with you both. It would be much better for her."

There was another silence. Hannah hung onto his arm and leaned against him. They all listened when the clock chimed in the parlor. "I guess I better go and get a bed at the mission. I think it closes at 8:00. Can you tell me the best way to get there?"

Flo shook her head again. Sam cleared his throat and began to speak. "You know since I let Ralph go, there is an available bunk in the staff quarters. It isn't much and your room and board will have to come out of your pay, but you'll keep all your tips, of course."

Sean hesitated for a moment to consider the offer.

"You'll be much closer to Hannah if you stay at the hotel. Why don't you try it for a few days?" Flo nodded in agreement.

Sean thought some more, then a smile widened across his face.

"I don't suppose the mission has a hot shower."

Sam shook his head, "Probably not."

"Thank you, Sam. Thank you for everything," said Sean extending his hand.

"Don't thank me. I got a report from the porter this afternoon. You're a good worker, Sean. You are doing me a favor. It's six days a week, but I guess you're used to that from the mines," said Sam as he handed Sean a key. "This opens the side door, for the staff. So you can come and go as you please on your time off."

Hannah squeezed Sean's arm again and began to pout.

Sean crouched down beside her. "It's only for a little while and then we'll be together again," he said softly. So much had happened in such a short time, Hannah didn't believe him.

"I should be off now. I need to get some sleep so I can put in a good day's work for Sam tomorrow. Good night, lamb chop. Be a good girl. Thank you, Sam." Sean took Flo's hand and gently kissed the back of it. "And thank you, good lady, for a meal I shall never forget. I'm sure your salad will be a hit." Sean gave Hannah a quick hug fearful that tears would soon follow. As he walked back to the hotel, Hannah's face lingered in his mind. A wave of sadness came over him. He made a vow to have a room for them as soon as he could.

The next day was a long one at the hotel. There was a lot to learn and a lot to do. He carried so many bags he thought his back would break. He jingled the change in his pockets from time to time to keep his spirits up. He started at six and finished at four. He showered, changed back into street clothes and headed to the water while there was still good daylight. He had to see it for himself.

Sam was right about the "roughness" of the dock. There was smoke and diesel fumes. Some trashcans were overflowing, but Sean could see past all that. He stood on the dock and felt the cool wind on his face.

The clouds just over the horizon grew pinker as the sun set behind him. He walked on the piers and surveyed the boats moored there. He looked out over the Patapsco and admired the boats under sail. The men on the docks were busy loading and unloading boats before nightfall. Vendors sold their wares on the street. The smell of gasoline, trash, tar, cigar smoke and fried fish all blended together. This is a *real* city, thought Sean as he watched a barge loaded down with coal, head down stream. The thought occurred to him that it could have come from Pennsylvania, maybe Pottsville. It could have been mined by *him*. He had never given much thought to where the coal went after he loaded it into the cars. The world suddenly seemed smaller.

The Lord Baltimore Hotel was a world unto itself. It had 700 rooms and 700 employees. "A staff member for each room," was the slogan at the grand LB. There were cooks and waiters, tailors and launderers, chamber maids and custodians. There was a clerk on every floor who made sure every guest's need and desire was met. There was even a radio in every room–first class all the way. The LB had everything and everybody who was somebody stayed there. It was always open and those who entered through the shiny brass revolving doors left their other worlds, and the Depression, far behind them.

Before long, the hotel was as familiar to Sean as the mines once were. Soon, he knew every entrance, stairway and freight elevator. He learned to manage two or three guests at once to save time and make more tips. Sam gave him a decent hourly, but tips were where the money was, like when he waited tables. Hustle was the name of the game. He got a system in his head for keeping bags and room numbers straight. Salesmen went to the ninth floor. Most of them carried their own bags. If they didn't, they were pretty fair tippers. The big shots went all the way to the top floor. That was a mixed bunch, Sean soon learned. Some were generous and some tipped nothing at all. Sean guessed that was how they stayed rich, by keeping his tip in their pockets. In time, he could even recognize where people were from by the way they talked. They might be from New York, Atlanta or Boston. Some came all the way from Germany, England or France. Before long, Sean was making four to five dollars a shift. He counted the days until he could get a place for him and his curly girl.

Sean got Tuesdays off and so he sneaked Hannah out of school early those days to take her on adventures in the city to see and hear and taste something different every week, as he had promised. One day, they strolled down the shopping district, Howard Street. They window shopped and browsed through Hutzler's and Hecht's, Stewart's and the Hochschild-Kohn. They were amazed at the modern appliances in the department stores: electric stoves, refrigerators, toasters, mixers and waffle irons. There was even an electric coffee pot. Sean quickly pulled Hannah by the hand through the lady's department. He didn't want to look at curlers, make up, wigs, hats or pink nightgowns. His curiosity got the best of him and he hesitated a moment to glance at the new brassieres. When a saleslady caught his eye, he and Hannah quickly moved on. He paused to inspect the new electric razors. He rubbed the stubble on his chin and wondered if he would ever be able to afford one. When

Hannah became impatient, they moved on to the toy department. Hannah's eyes beamed when she saw the Teddy bears and china dolls with satin dresses. She held up a doll and pleaded with her eyes for it. Sean had to shake his head no. He knew he had to save every cent and anyway, she had Abby's doll. She settled instead for eight fat crayons, like she used at school. The highlight of their day was the escalator ride at Brager-Gutman's. Sean marveled at how steps could suddenly appear and disappear. Hannah thought she was at the carnival and made Sean ride it with her up and down ten times. Finally, a floor clerk gave them the eye so they quickly scooted out the front door.

Sean knew Babe Ruth had been born in Baltimore and learned of the restaurant his father owned on Conway and Little Paca. The newspapers reported that Ruth was all washed up, that he was coming to the end of his career, but Sean didn't buy it. He had been glued to the radio listening to "going, going, gone," since he was a kid. Some said The Babe was losing his edge because he drank too much. Sean refused to believe his hero was a drunk. And even if he was, he still swung the bat better drunk than the rest of them did sober. Sean had grown up a Pirate's fan and stood by them as they lost pennant after pennant. But when Ruth and Gehrig swept Pittsburgh four to three with their Murderer's Row in '27, he became a believer. Sean knew he would probably never make it to New York to see the Yankees play, but he might catch a glimpse of his hero and maybe even get his autograph the next time he came home.

Hannah couldn't care less about baseball. Instead, she begged to go to the zoo. One Tuesday, they visited the elephants, giraffes and lions. They both marveled at their strangeness.

"Papa, some of these animals sure are big. How did Noah get them on the ark?"

"Two at a time," Sean answered wisely.

"Where did he put the elephants?" Sean rubbed his chin stalling with the answer.

"On the lower deck for ballast, of course, so the boat wouldn't tip over in the big rainstorm." Sean sat up straighter, pleased with his answer.

Hannah unwrapped a piece of candy while she formulated her next question.

"How did the *giraffes* fit on the boat?"

"Noah cut a hole in the roof so they could put their necks through." Nicely done, thought Sean.

Hannah chewed thoughtfully on her licorice stick, taking care to put the chewy candy in the back, as to not disturb the wiggly tooth in the front while she worked on the next question.

"How did Noah keep the lions from eating the other animals?" she asked with a gleam in her eye.

Sean hung his head for a moment. He had run out of answers—and patience.

"Noah fed the lions a big lunch before he put them on the boat."

Hannah's jaw stopped in mid-chew, not sure whether too believe him or not. Sean gave her his best poker face. Strategically, before she could come up with another question he said, "Let's go to the reptile house. We'll see what alligators look like before they become boots."

After three hours, Sean thought his legs would break. They had seen the whole place in one afternoon. Gratefully, he found a bench and they sat and listened to street musicians. Sean gave Hannah a nickel to drop in the box. She then returned to the bench to greedily munch down a bag of popcorn he had bought for her.

"You look like a little chipmunk," Sean said with a smile.

Hannah pulled his neck down to kiss him. Her lips and fingers were greasy with butter. As she pulled away, she grinned at him. Sean knew in a few minutes, he would have to take her back to Sam's. This was not the childhood he had planned for her. But maybe, with a little luck, he could get it back. For that moment, his little girl was happy and when he laid down to sleep that night, he would see her face, shining with butter, curls in her eyes, smiling back at him. She was growing up so fast. He wished she could stay little, just a little longer. He faced the sun, now low in the sky, closed his eyes and willed himself to preserve that picture of her in his mind forever.

Chapter 19

He walked her back to Sam's house and returned to the hotel with a heavy heart. He began to worry about the envelope of cash. Anyone could find it and take it from his locker. When he was alone, he cut a slit in the mattress cover and shoved it under the ticking for safer keeping. But he knew with so many people coming and going to the bunk room, *it* still was not really safe.

When he went to bed that night, he closed his eyes and remembered the day he had spent with Hannah and smiled. But before he could sleep, thoughts of the past came flooding in–Molly and the baby, Andrew and Abby—all gone. He felt responsible, in some way, for all their deaths. Why hadn't he taken the ax from Andrew? Was it his fault that his wish for a son came true and killed his wife? And poor Abby. He felt like a coward for not rushing into the kitchen to save her, but he had to protect Hannah. It was a bitter choice he had to make. Sean knew deep down that none of their deaths were really his fault, but it didn't make him any less sorry for their passing—or less lonely. He thought about the mines closing and his struggle to feed the girls. He relived that afternoon with Abby dressing him as a woman for the first time. Then he saw himself snatching the envelope from the pants of the dead man in the club. Abby stalled Joey in the kitchen long enough for the two of them to escape. It was the past—the horrible past that haunted him. In a split second, he had lost his home and the life he had known. He began to wonder if he had lost his way altogether. He pulled a pillow tight around his ears to try to make the sound of his heart pounding in them go away. He tried to count his blessings, his health, his little girl and Abby's advice that sent them to Sam. Without him, they would surely be hungry by now and living on the street. For now, Sean had work and Hannah had food, a nice place to live and a family who took good care of her. S*he* was safe.

But Sean knew *he* was never safe. Even in another state, over a hundred miles away from Pottsville, as he lived and worked in a big hotel, he was not safe. Every time the bell rang, or the revolving doors spun open, he expected to see a man with dark hair and olive skin. He knew it would be *him*. Surely Joey would draw his pistol when he saw Sean, and kill him in cold blood. Poor Hannah would be orphaned and never understand why. And for what? Greed. That envelope was filled with blood money, stolen from innocent people. Sean knew there was no way to ever get it back to them. Over and over he tried to convince himself that he would put it to better use than those thugs ever could. Still, he felt guilty for having a pile of money he didn't earn, guilty for Abby's death and regret for turning his child's life upside down.

Sean did his best to act as if nothing were wrong. He worked as hard as he could to make tips and to convince Sam to keep him on—and it worked. Within a month, Sam gave Sean a supervisory position and assigned him to make out the work schedule for sixty-five men. Some of his men were drifters and left within a few weeks. Sean was constantly training the new recruits, some just in their teens. The younger ones had quit school to help support their families. At twenty-five, Sean was one of the oldest. And no wonder. Between the long hours and back breaking work, bell hopping was not for the chicken-hearted. Sean's promotion came with a raise, an extra fifteen cents an hour. Between the hopping, scheduling and training there was always plenty of work. And there were always big events on the weekends: weddings, parties and conventions. Sean soon learned the train schedule by when the dozens of people flooded into the lobby and rushed to check out.

Sean's hectic schedule was interrupted only by his weekly day off. He treasured his Tuesdays with Hannah. He slept late in the morning on those days and picked her up early from school. His favorite afternoons were spent with her at the docks, eating hotdogs and ice cream and strolling along the piers. He couldn't get enough of the boats he had dreamed about for so long. On their walks, they saw steamers, freighters, tugboats and even little rowboats. But Sean's heart belonged to the boats under *sail.*

The schooner with its long pointed bow and huge billowy sails, the *Nettie Allison,* sliced through the water like a knife. He couldn't believe all the cargo the stevedores pulled from her hull: bushels of oysters, clams and hundreds of pounds of fish. She brought in hogsheads of tobacco, bushels of corn, stacks of lumber, potatoes and just about anything from the farm or sea. The captain made his living bringing goods from the south and taking back goods from the city. This was the sort of life Sean wanted.

He loved the sound of the seabirds calling overhead and the smell of saltwater. No matter how hectic it was in the city, he could find calm at the water. When he stood at the farthest edge of the dock, for a few moments, he could forget about his past and his plight. When the wind came up, he and Hannah held out their arms to catch it, as if they had wings. Sean wondered that if a port on the river of the Bay is this glorious, what the mighty ocean must be like.

Sean and Hannah watched as a fisherman cleaned his catch on the back of his boat and tossed the heads and tails into the water. The seagulls squawked and fought each other over the booty. They even stole food from each others mouths in mid air. After the show, they realized they were hungry too and returned to the street to find some lunch. They stopped at the seafood market and found all sorts of delights never seen or heard of in Pennsylvania. They considered clam puffs and fried oysters, rockfish and spiced shrimp. The smell of the cloves, vinegar and cayenne made their mouths water. The air was so thick with the smell of fried fish sandwiches, French fries and smoked sausages, they could almost taste them. All Sean ever heard about from the other hops, was how delicious the crab cakes tasted "down at the pier." He knew he would probably never be able to afford to order the "best crab cakes in town" at the Lord Baltimore, so he bought two crab cakes with saltine crackers, some French fries and two Coca Colas at the water for he and Hannah to share. They devoured their feast with tartar sauce dripping down their faces. Sean loved everything about the water life. Even the smell of old fish being rinsed off the boats was perfume to his nose. He knew each day they were getting closer to *home*.

Hannah got along well with Sam and Flo. And she loved her new school in the city and the new dress that Flo had bought for her. But she looked forward to Tuesday afternoons with her father and was always sad when it was time for him to take her back.

"Papa, when can I live with you? When can *we* be a family again?" She clung tightly to his arm, as if they would never see each other again. It broke Sean's heart.

"Lamb chop, it won't be much longer. I'm doing better with my job everyday. Soon we'll have a place of our own and we can have dinner together *every* night, just like we used to. Now, don't look sad when you get back. It is so generous and kind for Cousin Sam and Flo to take you in until we can get back on our feet. Be a good girl and do as you are told. Keep your room clean and help Miss Flo set the table and clean up after supper. Smile and say 'thank you,' to her. She's doing us a big favor watching after you. You know that don't you?"

Hannah nodded reluctantly, tears glistened in her eyes.

"All right then. I'll come by after work tomorrow to see you if it's not too late. We'll be together again before you know it," Sean said enthusiastically.

Hannah wasn't convinced. She dragged her feet up the front stairs to Sam's house. Sean again remembered the envelope of cash that weighed heavy on his mind. If only he could use it to get them a place to live. Why me, Lord? Why me?

Ever since the stock market failed, the country remained in an abysmal economic state. While carrying their bags, Sean listened in as the guests talked about investments, stocks, bonds, real estate and big business. They discussed politics and financial trends at home and abroad. Sean had no idea how things worked outside Pottsville where everyone worked in the mine, a lumber mill or a brewery and lived from paycheck to paycheck. He eavesdropped on two businessmen while dragging their luggage to the elevator. Profit margins, interest rates, mortgages, expenditures—the big league. Sean knew almost nothing about it. He knew he was about to break a staff rule about speaking with patrons, but he had one big question he desperately needed answered. When there was a pause in their conversation, he mustered the courage to ask. "Excuse me, sirs. But if you don't mind me asking, what bank do you keep your money in?"

Both men chuckled. "Son, nobody puts their money in the banks anymore. Roosevelt has promised that the government will insure our money, but since the crash of '29, it's going to take a while for them to earn *my* trust back. If they failed once, they could fail again." Sean listened and watched nervously as the numbers lit up on the display as the elevator grew closer to their destination.

"I'm saving money so I can get my own apartment. Where should I keep it?" he asked earnestly.

"If I were you, I'd keep my money some place where I could keep an eye on it, check on it from time to time.

Some folks keep their money under a floor board, in a hole in the wall or a safe. I've even heard of people putting money in Mason jars and burying them under the tomatoes. Heck, you'd be better off to put it in a safe deposit box at the train station than keep it in the bank."

The men laughed at the joke, but Sean didn't. He knew what he had to do.

The first chance he got, he hid the envelope under his shirt and rode the street car to Penn Station. There he rented a safe deposit box and carefully placed the money inside. He slipped the key onto the chain that held Abby's locket and fastened it around his neck. A feeling of relief came over him. Keeping the envelope safe had been a constant worry. Now, instead of checking daily in his mattress, he could feel for the key around his neck whenever he wanted. Abby's chain comforted him as a remembrance of the past. In a way, she was still looking after him. As he held it between his fingers, Sean knew the key not only opened the door to the box, but someday it would open some doors for him and Hannah.

From that moment on, Sean knew he must educate himself in the ways of the world. He had to listen for advice to learn how to use that money the best way possible when the time was right. While standing quietly in the elevator, he learned about travel, money, and business, especially the shipping business. He learned about inflation, recession and the depression. Everyone seemed to have their own opinion on the economy, but one thing they all agreed on was that it had to get better. The more he listened the more he learned until one day he remembered something his father once said to him, "The more I know, the more I realize what I don't know." It seemed an incredible task.

One evening, a guest asked Sean to take his luggage upstairs to his room while he had supper with his wife. When Sean put the key in the lock, it pushed opened before he could turn it. He slowly pushed the door open wider. He heard a woman humming. It's just the maid, changing the sheets, he thought. As he leaned in the doorway, he enjoyed the sight of her youthful fig-ure while she worked and tried to peg the tune she was humming. A strange feeling came over him. His heart beat a little faster. His body froze. Then the hair stood up on the back of his neck. What was it? She stopped humming and became still, sensing his presence. As she slowly turned around, their eyes met. "I'll be finished in a minute," she said.

She pointed to the bags on his cart and offered, "You can bring those in. I'll be sure to lock the door behind me."

Warmth spread over his body. It started in his chest and worked its way down his arms and legs, his fingers and toes. His heart quickened some more. It's *her*, he thought. It's my *Maggie*.

His body relaxed as he stood watching her. She spoke again. He stared into her eyes, and watched her lips move. When he was satisfied, he looked her over from the top of her hat to her toes. He had made love to her a hundred times in his dreams. And here she was, standing before him, a blue-eyed, golden haired angel.

"Did you hear me? You can leave those. I'll be done in a minute," she said impatiently.

Sean never moved a muscle and stood grinning back at her, his stupid grin. She walked over to see what was wrong with him. Was he deaf or simple or….? Three steps towards him she stopped and covered her mouth with her hand. "Sean? Sean O'Connell? Is that really you?"

"I'm afraid so, lugging bags from floor to floor at this grand hotel."

"Oh, Sean, the police questioned us and there were rumors that you were involved in the shooting, somehow. But I didn't believe it. What happened?"

"It's a long story. I can't talk about it right now, but I'll tell you someday, I promise. How about you? What are you doing here?"

"The Shangri-La closed, so I had to find something else. I'm staying here in town with my Aunt Grace. I tried to get work as a waitress, but there weren't any spots open, so, I'm making beds instead. I would rather be in the restaurant making tips, but this was the best I could do. How long have you been here?"

"About two months. Do you like my uniform?"

"Yes, very classy. You look good in *pants*."

"Oh, and look at my stripe," Sean said pointing to the top of his shoulder. "I'm not just any bell hop, I'm the *chief* bell hop—the head monkey."

"And so you are," she said giggling.

"I've been here two weeks," she went on to say. "This place is so big, it's a wonder we found each other at all. My aunt knows the head of housekeeping, so I got hired. I got lucky. Jobs are scarce. How did you get on?"

"Oh, someone put in a good word for me," Sean replied putting his hands in his pockets and staring at his feet.

"This work is hard on your back, but it's steady. And no one has spilled a beer on me or grabbed me in the behind yet. How about you?" Maggie babbled nervously.

"Well, a little dog bit me once and I dropped a trunk on my big toe. It's still purple—the toe, not the dog. That's about it," Sean said trying to act casual, but he could barely stand being near her without touching her. He thought he would explode. "Maggie, I've thought about you ever since I left Pottsville."

"And I've thought about you once or twice too."

"Are you—*seeing* anyone?"

"Well, there aren't too many men standing in line to date a chamber maid," she said shaking her head.

"There's no shame to being a chamber maid. You're a victim of the times, like the rest of us. At least you have a job. I didn't think I could get a demotion from the mines. But, look at me. I look like a circus act."

"Well, I think your hat is very *chic*."

She teased him with her eyes, hoping to get a smile out of him. Instead, he put his arms around her and hugged her. He breathed a sigh of relief, when she hugged him back. She pushed him away all too soon. "Sean, think. Even though your dress is off, I mean your pants are on, I mean, you know what I mean. We can't do this now, not at work. The hotel looks down on fraternization between its employees. We could lose our jobs," she said frantically.

"You're right. We'll have to meet later, away from here. When *can* I see you?" he asked quietly

"I just started my shift. I won't get off work until around midnight—is that too late?" she whispered anxiously.

"Midnight is fine. I'll meet you around the corner from the lobby, in front of the B&O building." She nodded and returned to making the bed.

Sean knew he had to be back at work at sunrise. But he didn't care. He would gladly give up sleep to see Maggie again. For the rest of the day, he couldn't get the simple grin off his face. His mind raced. What were the chances that they would find work at the same hotel, in a different city? He knew she was from Maryland, but what were the odds? It couldn't be just chance. It was fate. "Thank you, Lord," he said under his breath as he looked out the window into the bright blue sky.

Sean buried himself in his work trying to make the time go faster. He grabbed every bag he could hoping at least one of them was bound for the twelfth floor where Maggie was working. The sight of her, just a glimpse gave him hope that he could find happiness. She seemed so familiar to him and put him at ease. It was like he'd known her his whole life, like they grew up together. He fell in love with her in Pottsville and thought he would never see her again after that fateful night. When he saw her in the maid's uniform, he fell in love all over again. Midnight couldn't come soon enough.

Chapter 20

The hours dragged unmercifully. Sean looked up at the brass clock over the front lobby doors so many times he got a crick in his neck. He thought to himself, how can you be so happy that you're miserable? Cupid's arrow had found him and he was powerless against it. He was in love.

His shift ended at six. He dreaded the next six long hours before midnight. He kept busy by making the work schedule for the next week. Then he slipped into the kitchen for a plate of food, but he could scarcely make himself eat it. His stomach was so full of butterflies there was no room for beef stew. He went to the staff's quarters to shower and change and even though he dawdled at shaving and dressing, there were still more hours to kill. He tried to interest himself in an article in a National Geographic magazine someone had left on the wash stand. He read the same words over and over unable to concentrate. It was no use. He put on his jacket and walked around outside the hotel. He paced the sidewalk back and forth until, Walt, the doorman gave him a dirty look. There were still more hours to kill. His stomach was in knots. Perhaps the water would calm him.

It was spring. The days were warmer, but when the sun dipped beneath the horizon, the air was brisk at the water's edge. A sliver of moon hung low in the sky.

And as the sky grew darker, the stars came out and twinkled. Sean thought of Maggie in his arms and his cheek against hers. And even though it was still too soon, he imagined asking her to be his wife. One day he would tell Hannah that the three of them were going to live together as a family—and that would be a happy day.

The smile faded from Sean's face as he began to have doubts. What if she said no? What if she didn't feel the same way about him? A sense of doom slowly consumed him. Maggie was so young and beautiful, a virtuous woman and no doubt came from a good family. Why should she settle for him, an out-of-work coal miner, who was homeless, widowed and had a child to care for. She could do better, he thought. Before long, he would have to tell her the whole truth about his past—and Joey. Surely she would think him a criminal or at least, cursed with bad luck. Maybe he was cursed. Sean's head hung low by the time he reached the front of the hotel. With thirty minutes more to wait, he gazed up at the towers. It truly was a grand hotel. He felt small beside it, small and worthless. The joy of seeing Maggie faded. Sean was so filled with doubt, he convinced himself he was not worthy of her. It would be easier to not meet her at all, than to be spurned by her. He couldn't stand the thought of her rejection. He had been through enough. Suddenly, he felt a chill and pulled his coat collar tightly around his neck. He couldn't go through with it. He glanced one last time to the hotel's penthouse, turned his back to it and took a few quick steps away.

Within seconds, he heard footsteps behind him. "Sir, can you help me?"

Sean turned to see a woman not much more than a teenager. She was thin and her eyes were sunken. There was no one on the streets this time of night. Where had she come from?

"Could you spare some *change?*" Sean was so startled by her, he couldn't speak or move.

"Anything, sir. A dime?" she begged.

Sean still stood motionless. No one had ever asked *him* for money.

When he didn't respond, the girl became nervous. "I'm sorry to bother you," she said as she quickly walked past him. Then it came to him. She's *hungry.*

"Wait," Sean called after her.

"Take this," he said as he put twenty-five cents in her hand. "Go and get something to eat."

"Thank you." Her face seemed to glow as she lifted her eyes to his. The woman tucked the change into her pocket and quickly made steps toward the diner at the corner. Sean looked after her, still astonished by the transformation of her face. He was still standing there, frozen when he heard a voice calling out to him.

"Sean, is that you? I got off a little early," said Maggie. She looked towards the woman as she made her way down the street. Her concerned eyes met Sean's. "Who was that?"

"Oh her, she needed some—help."

"Are you alright?"

Sean nodded without looking at her. Maggie slowly wrapped her arms around him. His body was stiff, unwilling to return her embrace. "What is it? You can tell me."

Sean hesitated with his reply, but slowly it came. "I've been thinking. What does a beautiful woman like you need with a washed up coal miner who's pretending to be a bellhop?"

"Well, that depends. What does a big strong coal miner want with a chamber maid?"

Her words didn't make him feel any better. He still stood like a stone. She lifted his chin and he lifted his eyes to hers. "Hey, I liked you when we were *both* waitresses."

She was chipping away at the wall around his heart, but he was afraid there was a chance she might chip straight through it. Gradually, he decided it was a chance he had to take. He had loved her from afar all this time. He longed to feel her next to him. Little by little, his arms crept around her shoulders. He pulled her closer and closer to him until finally he rested his face in her hair. It smelled sweet and tickled his nose. He pressed his cheek against hers, soft and warm. His arms drifted down to her waist, pulling her body still closer. He felt her heart beating nervously, pounding away. It made him smile. He listened to her breathe and felt her arms grow tighter across his shoulders. Her body fits mine perfectly, he thought. It is as if I have held her a hundred times, but this is our first real embrace. The hole in his heart that longed to be filled was healing. The aching of his body from another long week was soothed simply by her touch and warmth spread over him. A smile inched across his face as he realized, he was *home*. He glanced towards the diner where he saw the door swing open. The woman he had spoken to left with a paper bag in her hand. She looked towards Sean and smiled. Sean smiled back at her but she had already turned and walked hurriedly the other way. He realized the woman had stalled him just long enough to keep him from making a horrible mistake. He squeezed Maggie a little tighter and rested his head on her shoulder. He realized Maggie was trembling. Sean took her hands in his. They were ice.

"You're freezing," he said softly.

"I'm alright," she protested.

She's nervous, thought Sean and he smiled.

"Let's find someplace we can talk."

Sean put his arm around her shoulders and they started down the block when she stopped suddenly. "What time do you have to work tomorrow?"

Sean hesitated for a moment, not wanting to tell her and spoil a chance to spend time with her. Her eyes twinkled back at him. Calmly he said, "It doesn't matter. Men wait a lifetime to meet a woman like you."

Maggie smiled back at him.

"Will you let me buy you a cup of coffee?" he asked.

"I don't think that's a good idea," she replied.

Sean stopped in his tracks. The spell was broken. They were finished before they started. He knew it was too good to be true. He stared at the ground in horror. Then his eyes rose to meet hers. "Why not?" he asked guardedly.

"Because, I don't like coffee. I only drink *tea.*"

He pushed her away from him and waved his finger at her like as if she were a naughty child. "Don't scare me like that. My poor ticker can't take it."

After the scolding, Sean pulled her close to keep her warm—among other reasons. They walked to the diner without speaking, deep in their thoughts. They found a booth in the corner and slid into the seats.

"I guess you know the man who was shot in the club died," said Maggie.

"Yes, I know."

"And then, a widow was shot dead, right in her kitchen over in Cressona. Nobody's sure why. But the police think it was the same men. The whole town turned out for her funeral. It's scary when you're not even safe in your own home," she said as she sipped her tea. "The police know who did the club shooting."

Maggie chattered nervously during their first date. How awful that her conversation was about Sean's Abby, a woman she never met. She chatted casually about an event that still cut through his heart. It was a topic he hoped wouldn't come up until they got to know each other better. Sean's mind drifted as the horrible tragedy unfolded in his mind once more. He envisioned their little church, packed with standing room only parishioners and pall bearers carrying the casket to the hill where Andrew and Molly lay. He should have been there. No, he should have never allowed it to happen. He wondered if anyone was looking for them, him and Hannah. So many people had left that town looking for work. Maybe they figured he had left too. The pain crept from his chest into his neck. He was both sorrowful and angry at the same time. He discretely rubbed his face on his sleeve as Maggie talked away. He couldn't let Maggie see water in his eyes. After all, men weren't supposed to cry.

"You are awfully, quiet. Are you okay, Sean?"

"Yeah, I was just thinking about that night. I still have nightmares about it."

She leaned forward and took a sip from her cup.

"Just before Molly died with the baby, I watched her uncle die in my arms. There was nothing I could do for him, yet I felt guilty about it, like it was my fault. We never really liked each other, but I was sad when he was gone. I wasn't only sad for the loss of his life, I was disillusioned because life is so fragile and over so quickly. None of us knows how much time we have. But his death, at least, was peaceful and without suffering. He was old and he had a good life. It wasn't a bad way to go actually. But to die so violently, like the man in the club, with such hate and greed, surrounded by strangers, with a gun shoved in your face and your brains splattered, left lying in a puddle of blood as the life flows out of you—that's a bad way to go."

Maggie cupped her hands around the warm tea and stared through him off into the distance. He knew by the look on her face, she was replaying that night in her head too. Sean's mind drifted to the image of Abby lying in the kitchen floor. Then he thought of Molly and the baby. His bottom lip began to tremble. "But I can think of still worse ways."

They both stared into their cups.

Sean knew he had to change the subject of their conversation. It was far too serious and depressing, especially to share on a first date. Sean didn't want to drag her any further into his nightmare. They needed a fresh start.

Maggie began rocking in her seat nervously. "The paper named the lady that died, Abigail Ashe." Sean's heart skipped a beat. "Was that *your* Aunt Abby?"

Sean's face paled. He couldn't remember ever mentioning Abby to her, still, he knew he had to tell the truth. "Yes, *my* Aunt Abby."

Maggie sat back a little away from the table. "Your name and Hannah's were in the newspaper too."

Sean nervously turned a paper napkin over and over in his hand under the table. "Wait a minute. If you knew she *was* my aunt, why did you ask?"

"Sean, I had to see if you would tell me the truth. Can you blame me?"

Sean was glad he hadn't tried to mislead her. "Maggie, I want to explain," he said looking around the diner to see if anyone was listening. "You've got to believe me. I didn't shoot Abby," he whispered.

She leaned forward and reached across the table for his hand. "I know. A man doesn't put on a dress to feed his family and then shoot them. Besides, the article said there was a jar of money left by her head with a note that it should be used to bury her."

Sean swallowed hard. "What else did it say?"

"It said that you and Hannah were runaways. And that you tried to use a one-hundred dollar bill to buy a train ticket."

The face of the man at the ticket counter flashed across his eyes. Blabber mouth. He searched his mind for any other clues he may have left for the police.

"Maggie, when Vinnie was shot, I didn't run—right away. I was drawn to the blood, to get a better look at his wound. Curiosity got the best of me and I got caught. Joey and his men returned to the club and they saw me. They followed me home and figured out that I was really a man. While I tried to escape with Hannah, Abby did her best to stall them, but then they shot her. She was trying to buy me time to get away but instead, she bought a bullet." Sean looked at her pleadingly, "That's the truth."

"I know you're not a murderer. But why didn't you go to the police, Sean. Why are you still hiding?"

Sean couldn't answer her.

"Does it have something to do with the hundred dollar bill?"

Sean remained silent. He twisted the tea cup around in his hand. He knew he couldn't tell her that part, not yet. "Maggie, I don't want you to become involved in this mess. I promise to tell you the whole story, later, once I have straightened it out. If the local police find out about me, they'll lock me up. If Joey finds me, he'll kill me. Either way, Hannah will be left all alone in this world. I'll understand if you want nothing to do with me. You can walk away right now. But promise you'll keep my secret. Do it for Hannah."

"Let me help you," pleaded Maggie.

"No. I can't do that. I have to take care of this myself," Sean said. "I just need a little time," he said holding his hand out to hers. She gave him her hand and then rocked slightly back and forth in her seat thinking it over. When the rocking stopped, he knew she had made up her mind. Surely, she would get up and walk away and he would lose her, forever.

She broke the awkward silence. "I should probably go."

He knew it.

"But I can't. I believe you and well, I really *like* you.

The waitress returned with two slices of coconut cream pie. Maggie was famished and gratefully dipped her finger into the whipped cream and popped it into her mouth. Sean breathed a sigh of relief. She suddenly realized he was watching her. Their eyes met over the table and he shook his head at her for using her finger. She blushed as she wiped her hand on her napkin and reached for her fork. She turned it on its side and sliced into the pie for a big first bite. Sean smiled still shaking his head at her. She reminded him of Hannah. He handed her another napkin to wipe the corners of her mouth. More than ever, he wanted to know more about her.

"Miss Maggie, have you ever been engaged or even– *married?*"

She blushed again. "My goodness no. Well, on second thought, I was *nearly* engaged—once. But he wasn't the marrying kind. He was the restless sort. He dreamed of seeing the world, so he joined the Navy. We exchanged a few letters and when I realized he would never be happy in one place, I broke it off. It's been over a year. I still wonder about him from time to time, but I know it was for the best," she explained between bites of custard. Sean enjoyed watching her gobble it down.

"How well do you know Baltimore?" he asked.

"I've never really lived in Baltimore, only visited. My aunt lives here. She never married and I have spent a week with her every summer since I can remember. Even now, I'm just staying here because of this job. I plan on going home as often as I can."

"Then where is home?"

"I grew up south of here, in the next county, in a little town called Shady Side. My grandparents have a farm where they raise corn and vegetables and livestock. I help out in spring and summer, planting the crops and putting up the canning. My father and brothers have their own trade."

A warm feeling came over him as she spoke. She didn't come from a well-to-do family of lawyers or bankers or professors. Her people were farmers. She wasn't so different from him after all.

"Enough about me. What about you? What about your family?" she asked.

"I grew up near Pittsburgh. My father worked in the steel mill. But I landed in the coal mines on my way to see the Atlantic. That has always been my dream, to see the ocean and the ships that sail it. I want to build boats and own one some day. Before I got very far, I met Molly. It was love at first sight. We were married after knowing each other just two weeks. We were happy together. She gave me a beautiful daughter. Hannah is my family now and I'm thankful for that."

Maggie gently returned her hand over his as he spoke.

"We're getting by day by day. She's six now and looks more like her mother everyday. She's my sunshine and my reason for living these days."

"I would like to meet her."

"Really? I've been wondering about that. Doesn't it bother you that I'm a widower with a child?"

"Why should it? I can see that you adore her by the way your eyes light up every time you mention her. I bet she never gives you a minute's worry."

"I wouldn't be so sure about that."

"Nonsense. By the way, where is Hannah?"

"Remember when you asked me how I got the bell-hop job? Sam Mulligan, the general manager, is Abby's first cousin. That's how I wound up here. I guess you could say she put in a good word for me. When he found out Hannah and I needed a place to stay, he and his wife took her in. Flo dotes on her like she's her own. She's even got her in school here in the city. I see her after work whenever I can."

Maggie turned her head to look at the clock behind the counter. "Oh, my gosh. It's after one. My aunt will be worried sick. I have to go, Sean."

"Fine, I'll walk you home. It's not safe for you to walk alone at this hour."

Sean helped her into her jacket. The wind had returned and it became blustery. They walked quickly to her aunt's house with hardly a word. Sean wasn't sure if she wanted to be alone with her thoughts or if she was just exhausted. When they reached the door, Maggie stood on her toes and kissed him on the cheek. "Thank you for dessert and for walking me home."

"The pleasure is all *mine.*"

Sean gazed deep into her eyes. He could just make out her face by the light of the streetlamp. "Miss Margaret, when will you honor me with another visit?"

"How about tomorrow? I'm working. Same place and same time?"

"I'll be there."

He held her face in his hands and wondered if he should kiss her. He feared she might think him too forward. Instead, he softly kissed her on the forehead.

"Goodnight."

"Goodnight, Sean."

"Oh, and Maggie..."

"Yes?"

"Thanks for staying."

Chapter 21

Maggie gave him a tired smile and he watched as she closed the door before starting back to the hotel. On the way, he replayed every sentence that was spoken that evening and savored every word. He wanted to hear them over again in his head and to store them in his heart like small treasures.

That night, as he sank into slumber, instead of tossing and turning with nightmares about Joey, he dreamed of Maggie and their magical night. He finally had her all to himself, if only for an hour. When he closed his eyes, once again he could see her radiant face, her golden hair and sparkling eyes. In his mind, he kissed her forehead, her cheek, then her lips, for a long time. As he held her in his arms, they melted into one. He drifted off to sleep swimming in the warmth of her presence.

Sean hardly got four hours sleep. The next day dragged. It was the middle of the week and slow. Not many bags to carry or many tips to be had. After last night, it was good to have a break but the lack of rest made Sean feel eighty years old. As he headed to Sam's office to turn in the schedules for the coming week, it occurred to him that he should make his schedule like Maggie's so that they could work and be off at the same time. Then Sean thought to himself, who am I kidding? She is just infatuated. She will come to her senses soon enough. How could she ever love me? And if she ever did, she will surely leave me as soon as she learns how I took the envelope. She will be through with me soon enough.

Business was so slow that at three o'clock Sean took a break from his post to go to Hannah's school and walked her home to Sam's place. On the way, he bought them two hotdogs. They ate and talked as they sat on a bench along the street. Sean tried to keep the conversation light, but it was always the same song from the curly girl. "Papa, when are we going to live together?"

"Soon, kitten, soon."

"But when, Papa? It's taking so long. Miss Flo says if you want something really bad, you have got to talk to God about it. You have to put it in your prayers at night. That's the only way it will come true."

"Is that right?"

"Uh-huh."

Hannah talked with her mouth full, stopping occasionally to lick the mustard off her fingers. "Have you been asking God about it in your prayers?" she asked.

"Aye, that I have lassie."

"Well, she says you gotta be careful what you wish for and you gotta be careful what you say because there are angels all around us listening. So you better get your prayers straight the first time," she said with one hand on her hip.

He remembered that Abby called her Miss Priss.

"And have you *seen* any of these angels?" asked Sean.

"No, but I know what they look like," she said taking another bite.

"Really? And what do these angels look like?"

"Well, the ones in the picture books usually have blue eyes and blonde hair," she said rather matter-of-factly.

Sean thought of Maggie. She was the only blue-eyed angel he knew.

"And they have wings, and halos and big, fat, puffy cheeks."

Hannah looked like an angel with her cheeks puffed out with hotdog. She's not fat, but at least her clothes don't hang on her bones anymore.

"And, if an angel says something, you better listen. And if they want to give you something, you better take it. Or you could make them angry and be in big trouble."

Sean smiled and listened to her ramble on. He wiped the mustard from her upper lip with his thumb. He wished there *were* angels on Earth. He wanted nothing more than to get a place for him and Hannah. It broke his heart for them to live apart. He closed his eyes for a second and said a silent prayer for some help from an angel—in case there was such a thing.

When he kissed Hannah goodbye at Sam's door, she gave him her usual pout. He gave her a firm pat on the behind as he let her in the house. With that, she hopped like a robin into the foyer, happy to return to Flo's doting.

Sean's heart was light after seeing his little one. When he returned to the hotel, he reported to the lobby to finish his shift. The bell rang once. That meant there was a new guest checking in. Sean hurried to the front. Two older men stood at the counter with enough luggage for five people. Sean sighed, realizing this run was going to be a back breaker. He gathered his strength and donned a hospitable smile. "Hello, gentlemen. May I take your bags up for you?"

"Uh, just wait a minute there, boy. Let me get Charlie's key," said the taller one.

Boy? I'm a grown man and a father thought Sean. I could take this guy down in two swings.

The clerk handed over the key to the room and the guest motioned for Sean to take his bags. As Sean suspected, they weighed a ton, but he managed to get them all onto one cart. He pushed the load onto the elevator and waited–and waited. What could these guys be talking about? Couldn't they see he was holding the elevator for *them?* Sean called to them, "Gentlemen, I've got the elevator for you."

"We're not ready yet. Let that one go," said the same man.

Let it go? Who knew how long it would take to get another one. Did he think they were the only guests at the hotel? Sean pulled the heavy cart off the elevator and gestured to the operator to go ahead without them. Just as the doors closed, the man and his friend called to Sean.

"Sonny, haven't you gotten us an elevator yet? We need you to take our bags upstairs."

What? He's got to be kidding, thought Sean. He just told me to let the elevator go. Is this guy crazy? Sean's blood boiled up into his neck and his face began to perspire. Sean swallowed his anger and answered him civilly, "No sir, but I'll get you one *now.*" It was all he could do to keep from raising his voice to him.

The three of them stood for an eternity waiting for the next elevator. The silence was deafening. These two will stiff me for sure, thought Sean. Finally, the doors slid open and Sean dragged the cart back onto the elevator once more. As he held the door open for the two of them Sean looked over at the operator. It was Willie. His face was stony and he looked straight ahead, as always. It was going to be a long ride up.

By the third floor, the taller man was talking about some problem at the harbor. "It's getting worse everyday, Charlie. The crime is terrific on the waterfront. The unions have their hands full with these cargo ships."

"It's the times, Frank. There's no work. People are desperate. They're hungry," answered Charlie.

"Yeah, well if they're hungry, why don't they steal food? They're stealing alcohol and tobacco and anything else that can be sold on the black market," said Frank. "No, these aren't homeless people. They're just crooks and they're greedy. One of my sloops has been broken into three times. I'm nearly ruined. There's a pack of wharf rats out there and I'm gonna set a trap."

"Have you gotten the police involved?" asked Charlie.

"What a joke. Those guys couldn't catch a crook if he was already handcuffed to them. What do they care if my boat is getting robbed? They don't even go near the private piers after dark. Maybe *they* are afraid of getting mugged," joked Frank.

Sean remembered what Lizzie had told him about the Shangri-La.

"Or maybe they've been paid off," he said without turning to face the men. Willie stared at him sternly for breaking the rules and talking to guests out of turn.

"What?"

"Begging your pardon, sir, but it sounds to me like they know what they are doing. Maybe the cops are turning their heads because they are getting a piece of the action or maybe they're afraid of retaliation. It could be a ring," offered Sean.

"Maybe the cops around here *are* crooked. Those knuckleheads sure as hell haven't done anything to protect me," said Frank as he made a ridiculous face.

Charlie covered his mouth and snickered, "Hey Frank, why don't you put a man out there on your own? Forget the police. Just use a guy in plain clothes, someone who can blend in with the surroundings, like he's a drunk or a bum. Don't let them know they're being watched," said Charlie.

Frank's eyes widened. "Yeah, yeah, like a security guard or an undercover cop. That's the ticket. But where am I gonna find somebody like that? Where am I going to find a man who knows his way around the dock and isn't afraid to work long hours? I need somebody who's going to stand up to these guys. He's got to be in pretty good shape."

Sean stood up a little straighter. Willie looked at him with a frown.

"Yep, and he's got to know his way around a gun too," said Charlie.

When they arrived at the nineteenth floor, Sean shoved the cart down the hall.

"Hey, do you know anyone who's looking for a job like that?" asked Frank.

"Pardon me?" asked Sean.

"I asked if you knew someone looking for a job around the dock."

"No. No, sir."

Frank unlocked the door then scratched his head while Sean unloaded the bags into Charlie's room. "Do you know how to shoot a gun?" asked Frank. Sean was surprised at his question and answered cautiously.

"Yes sir. I've taken out a few squirrels and rabbits with a shot gun."

Frank let out a low chuckle. "Baltimore squirrels?"

"No sir, I'm from Pottsville, really Cressona, Pennsylvania."

"Is that next to Podunk?" joked Frank.

"He'll need a pistol," advised Charlie in a serious tone.

Frank swung around to face Charlie then back to Sean. "Wait a minute. Were you a bellhop in Cressona?" asked Frank.

"No. I was a coal miner."

"He's never shot a pistol, then," said Charlie.

"Have you ever shot a pistol?" asked Frank.

"I'm afraid your friend was right."

Frank was disappointed yet continued to scratch his head while he mulled it over. "Well, if you can hit a squirrel with a shotgun, you ought to be able to hit one of those bastards with a pistol, don't you think?" asked Frank lightheartedly.

Charlie kept a stern look on his face while he nodded in agreement. Sean didn't like the way the conversation was headed. "Begging your pardon, sir, but I don't know anything about being a security guard."

"What's to know? You catch them stealing, you shoot them," said Frank. "Who's going to give you any trouble? The police? Those nitwits should be thankful you're doing their job for them."

"I don't know," Sean said staring at the floor in search of an answer. It sounded dangerous. What would happen to Hannah if *he* got shot?

"C'mon. What are they paying you here?" asked Frank.

"Well, it's not the pay. It's the tips."

"Okay, so what do you make a day with tips?"

"I usually make anywhere from four to five dollars a day. Sometimes, on a really good day, I might clear six."

Frank laughed out loud. Charlie gave Frank a disapproving look. "I'm sorry, son. I'm not laughing at you. That's a fine daily take, nothing to be ashamed of. But, how about if I give you six dollars *every* day?"

Sean thought for a moment. Every dollar got him closer to a home with Hannah. But he still had his doubts. "Thank you for your offer, sir. But I'll have to talk to my boss. He was good enough to give me this job. I need to discuss it with him first. I couldn't leave without giving him some notice." At the very least he needed to buy some time to think about it. He wanted to get Sam's advice about this proposition.

"What do you think, Charlie? Common sense and loyalty," asked Frank.

"It's a rare combination."

"That's what I'm thinking."

Sean pushed the cart away from the door and Frank handed Charlie the keys to the room. "Charlie, are you all set here?" asked Frank.

"Yep.

"I'll see you and the missus for dinner around six."

"Ill see you then."

Frank looked over at Sean and said, "Come with me."

He rested his hand on Sean's shoulder and steered him towards a meeting room. Frank carefully pushed open the door to find no one in the room. They walked to the window and Frank released the catch and swung it open. He squeezed through the window and stepped onto the roof.

"Wait a minute. I don't think you should be out there," warned Sean.

"It's okay. I'm not afraid of heights. C'mon out here. Take a good look at that view," he motioned for Sean to join him. He had always wanted to see the harbor from the roof and couldn't resist the offer.

"Look at that water. Goes for miles, doesn't it?"

Sean nodded, his jaw gaped in awe. He could see the rooftops of houses, the blue bottle and clock face of the Bromo Seltzer tower, the Washington monument and the green dome of the Basilica. All over, the fields were greening up and the trees were blooming. The water did seem endless.

"Amazing, isn't it? But one man's heaven is another man's hell. Four people jumped to their death from this very roof just after the crash in '29. It was all taken away from them–all their money, that is. They took their *own* lives. The nineteenth floor is haunted by their tormented souls. They walk the halls and walk through walls, mostly late at night."

Sean carefully stepped backward toward the window and climbed back through.

"What's your name, son?" Frank asked as he climbed back through behind Sean.

"Sean O'Connell."

"Pleased to meet you, Sean," he said extending his hand. "Do you believe in ghosts?"

Sean's lips never moved, but his pale face gave his answer.

"Don't worry, son. There aren't really any ghosts walking through these halls or angels making the beds for that matter," said Frank with a chuckle as he patted Sean on the back. Sean had his doubts. He had already seen *one* angel making the beds.

Frank and Sean rode the elevator back to the lobby.

"Okay, Sean O'Connell. Here's the plan. You talk to your boss. You tell him Mr. Frank is going to pay you *ten* dollars a day to watch the docks for him. And you tell him you have to start tomorrow or there's no deal. See what he says."

Sean couldn't believe his ears. *Ten dollars a day.* He had only dreamed of making that kind of money. "Yes, sir."

"It's settled, then. I'll see you in my office bright and early.

Here's my card:

Francis J. DiAngelo
DiAngelo Shipping Co.
Port of Baltimore
212 Pratt St.

"Thank you, Mr. DiAngelo." It was the first time anyone had offered Sean a business card. He quickly memorized the address and tried to hand it back.

"No, you keep it. And Mr. DiAngelo sounds so formal. You're working for me now so you can call me Frank." He reached over for Sean's hand and put a rolled up wad of money in it.

"Here's sixty bucks, your first week's pay to seal the deal. I've got five boats on that harbor that are getting broken into. If you can stop it, you'll be worth every cent."

Frank folded Sean's fingers over the cash with one hand and firmly gripped Sean's shoulder with the other to prevent him from trying to hand it back. Frank's hand was strong and warm, yet Sean felt a chill go up his spine. When the elevator door opened, Frank bolted to the lobby. Sean was in a daze, unable to speak or move. His arm was still frozen, holding the money in front of him grasping the cash until his knuckles were white. He watched Frank enter the revolving door and swing around into the street. In an instant, he was gone.

Chapter 22

Sean hardly knew this man, Frank. What was there about him that made him so convincing? Maybe it was his authoritative way of talking or his business card or the sixty dollars he gave him. It all happened so fast. At first he was rude and Sean pegged him for a jackass. Sean could have never guessed he was the owner of a shipping company. Frank knew nothing about Sean and yet offered him a job. One minute Sean wanted to punch him and the next he couldn't wait to work for him.

When Maggie came on duty at three, Sean sneaked up to the twelfth floor and found her unloading the linen. "I can't understand it. He doesn't even know me, offers me a job and gives me a week's advance on the spot," he said as he pulled the money from his pocket to show her.

"Good Lord, Sean. What else do you need? Your luck is changing. It's a *sign*. Take the job with Mr. DiAngelo. How long can you last as a bellboy? There's nothing to decide. Explain it to Sam. You've worked hard for him. He'll understand. And now you and Hannah can get a place of your own. She'll be so happy to have her daddy back. You two belong together."

"But I'll have to work nights."

"So?"

"When will I see you?"

She paused for a moment with a stack of towels in her arms to think it over. "Oh, I don't know right now, but I'm sure we'll find a way."

"I haven't even looked for a place. I don't know where to start."

"Let me talk to my aunt. She's lived here all her life. Maybe she knows someone who has a room to let."

"Thank you, Maggie."

Sean gave her a hug around the waist while her arms were still loaded down.

"Now you stop that, Sean. You are going to get me fired," she said as she looked around to see if anyone was watching.

When he decided no one was looking, Sean took full advantage of the opportunity and gave her a smooch on the cheek too. She slammed the towels down on the cart. "Damn you. Now get out of here and tell Sam," she said pushing him away from her.

Sean didn't try to hide his simple grin. It had been too long since he felt this way. Maggie tried to act annoyed with him, but he knew she loved the attention.

The grin quickly left his face as he neared Sam's desk. He felt like a child who had been sent to the principal's office for fighting—again. He didn't want to upset Sam. They both knew bell hopping would be a temporary stint, but Sean hadn't realized *how* temporary. He trusted Sam and had doubts about giving up a sure thing for a shaky one. He knew his life was about to change again in a split second. Just forty-eight hours earlier he was depressed and had no idea which way his life was headed. Then he found Maggie and this strange man came out of nowhere and offered him a job. It was almost too good to be true. Doubt tightened his stomach into a knot. He remembered Maggie's words, "It's a *sign.*" Still he feared the bottom was about to fall out—again.

Sean gathered his courage and told Sam about his unusual meeting on the elevator. He handed him Frank's business card. Sam put on his reading glasses and studied it for a moment. He turned it over and looked at the back for a second and then studied the front again. His face never changed. Was he angry? Did he think Sean was ungrateful for all he had done for him and Hannah? Sean's heart sank. I've let him down, he thought. It seemed an eternity passed before Sam spoke.

"I thought I knew every captain on that dock, but I've never heard of Mr. DiAngelo. But he's right. Something has got to be done about the robberies. They are hurting business and giving Baltimore a bad name. Folks are going to spend their money elsewhere. The early part of January we had a big reception here. It was the first wedding we had after booze was legal again. Three cases of champagne, special ordered from France, were heisted from the dock. The father of the bride had to toast with ginger ale. It was positively embarrassing, but there was nothing I could do about it."

He handed the card back to Sean. "Well, I'm sure you'll make a fine night watchman and it is certainly more than I can pay you."

A wave of relief came over Sean. "Thank you, Sam."

"Uh, Sean–have you ever used a gun?"

"Like I told Mr. DiAngelo, I've shot some rabbits and deer…"

Sam chuckled and shook his head. "Well, my boy, you may know your way around a firearm in the woods, but it's a little different when you are waving that thing around people. I saw a man get shot once. You never forget it."

Sean bit his tongue.

"Just don't go getting yourself killed. Where would Hannah be if something happened to you? Have you given that any thought?"

Sean's eyes fell to the floor. Sam was right. Maybe this was a harebrained scheme after all. It was a dangerous job, perhaps a little too dangerous. He had to make sure Hannah was taken care of. Sean was about to tell Sam he had decided to stay on at the Lord Baltimore after all when Sam offered some advice.

"Sean, you can't stop a bullet, but if you use your head, maybe it won't come to that. I'm sure Mr. DiAngelo is going to outfit you with a weapon, but keep it in your pocket. Use it only as a last resort. *He who lives by the sword shall die by the sword.* Proverbs. Use your head first, then your fists and save the gun for an emergency. Something's got to be done about the crime down there. You're as good a man for the job as any. This place has never run smoother since you have been making the schedule and working overtime. You are a cracker-jack at supervising the staff to get folks in and out. You have an eye for the big picture. Have some confidence in yourself. A little faith goes a long way."

"Thanks for everything," said Sean twisting his hat in his hand.

"You know, if you stay with us a little longer, I might be able to offer you something in middle management. Course, I don't know exactly when that will be."

"I appreciate it, Sam. I sort of agreed to do this. I don't want to let him down."

"Then go with your gut. Sometimes it's all we have to go on. You're a good man, Sean. I knew you wouldn't stay long. This was just a stepping stone for you, but if this new job doesn't work out, you know where to find me. Oh, and Miss Hannah can stay as long as she likes. She's kinda grows on you. She likes to share her stories from school at the dinner table. We look forward to them as our nightly entertainment. She's a—catbird."

"You mean a *chatterbox*."

"That she is. But sometimes she says things beyond her years, like she's really a little old lady impersonating a six year old."

Sean knew only too well. "You and Flo have been so kind to take care of her. How can I ever repay you?"

"No payment needed. We're family," said Sam as he shook hands.

For the next few hours, an uncertain future weighed on Sean's mind. Finally, it came to him and he knew what he had to do. At the end of his shift, he walked past the front desk and took a piece of paper and a pen. He went to an empty banquet room, sat at a table and began to write. It was hard to find the words, but he was able to get down a few. When he finished, he changed out of his uniform and headed for the train station. When he got there, he took the note from his pocket and read it over once more:

To Mr. Sam Mulligan:

If you are reading this letter, it means I am dead. Abby paid with her life for this money so Hannah and I could have a better future. Please use it to take care of Hannah and make sure she finishes school. If possible, I want her to go to college. I know you'll do right by her. Tell her that her mother and I loved her.

Yours truly,
Sean O'Connell

Sean's hands trembled as he folded it over and slid the note into the safe deposit box with the envelope of money.

He rode the streetcar to the dock. This time when he looked at the boats, he saw them with different eyes. He tried to find a vantage point to get the best view of them. Like a shepherd watching over his sheep, soon they would be his charge. He walked around for a couple of hours and when his legs grew tired found a seat on a park bench. He scanned the piers for anything that looked amiss but as evening fell, the people cleared out, one by one, until he was alone.

Sean walked back to the hotel. Maggie finished her shift just before midnight. When he saw her, he wrapped his arms around her and they stood together embracing for a moment. Then Sean slowly rocked her back and forth. Finally, her curiosity got the better of her. "Well, tell me. What did Sam say?"

"He thinks I should take the job and said Hannah can stay as long as she likes."

"I told you he wouldn't be angry. Soon, you and Hannah will be together again. Aunt Grace promised to ask the ladies at church if anyone would take a boarder with a little girl." Maggie's face beamed. Sean's head was still spinning.

They held hands as they walked to the diner. There was a spring to Maggie's step. But Sean couldn't take his eyes off the sidewalk. The risk involved with his new job weighed heavy on his mind. Maggie chattered between bites of cherry pie. Sean listened, mostly. Then she asked where he was headed, before he met Molly. "All I ever wanted was the ocean and to see where Grandda landed. I was on my way to New York City. Then I planned to travel south along the shore until I found a place that felt right. Instead, seven years later, I landed in Baltimore. I had never seen the water or seafaring boats, until now."

"You mean you've never seen the Atlantic?"

"Nope, never made it that far east. I was distracted by a pair of brown eyes," he said with a tired smile.

"It's just a couple of hours away by train or you could get there by boat. You're not that far off. In fact, you are almost there," she said as she lifted her cup to her lips.

"I've been thinking the same thing. I just have a few more things to take care of before I go," he said with a far off stare.

Maggie glanced at the clock on the wall. "My goodness, look at the time. My aunt will be waiting up for me. Sean, will you walk me home?"

"I would be honored."

It was warmer that night with hardly a breeze. They walked arm in arm. Maggie rested her head against his shoulder. The day had finally caught up with her too. Sean held her hand in his pocket. It was small and soft. He didn't want that night to end. He wanted to tell her he loved her, to go upstairs with her to feel her body next to his and sleep a long deep sleep. If he woke up beside her, he would know it wasn't just a dream.

When they got to her house, she turned to face him. "Well, this is it. I should go in. Goodnight, Sean." She turned to put her key in the door.

"Wait."

Sean took both her hands and pulled her close to him. He held her face in his hands. He closed his eyes and put his lips to hers. He kissed her for a long time and surprise, she kissed *him* back. Sean couldn't feel his feet. He was suspended somewhere between heaven and earth. When he pulled away, he studied her face. Her eyes were still closed. He kissed her again. Then he put his arms around her and embraced her tightly, her cheek against his. He rocked her back and forth in his arms. He thought his heart would burst. He wanted to tell her that he loved her, but knew it was too soon.

He whispered in her ear, "Maggie..."

"Yes?"

"I love–d seeing you tonight. When can I see you again?"

She slowly pulled away from him. Then she nervously fumbled with the collar of his shirt. "Tomorrow is your day off and I don't have to be at work until four. My aunt wants to meet you. Can you come for lunch?"

"What time?"

"A little before noon, we eat at twelve sharp." She implored with her starry eyes. Sean couldn't have said no even if he wanted to.

"I'll be here with bells on, me lady," he said and kissed her hand goodnight.

Chapter 23

Sean hardly slept a wink. He was uneasy about meeting Maggie's family and even more worried about taking on a job as a night watchman. He couldn't stand to toss in bed any longer so he dressed and headed down to the docks. He hoped to survey the situation a little before his new boss got there. There was a lot to think about in the two hours he had to kill. Just after the clock tower struck seven, he saw a dark sedan pull up. "Sean, my boy. You look bright eyed and bushy tailed."

"I have to confess, I'm a little nervous about this."

"Nonsense, a strapping lad like yourself? Why you're perfect for the job."

"Thank you, Mr. DiAngelo. "

"Now stop with the *Mr. DiAngelo*, call me Frank."

They walked through the harbor onto the pier. Sean's heart quickened as they stepped aboard a stately schooner. He felt the boat rock gently back and forth under his feet and grinned as he imagined the sails filling and the bow slicing through the waves. "Are you all right, son?" said Frank noticing Sean's expression.

"Yes, sir. She's a beauty. I bet when the wind catches her canvas, she flies."

"My good man, she's got wings," said Frank reaching into his pocket.

"Here's the key to the boathouse. It's mostly skiffs, oars and extra sails. I just thought you might need to have a place to get out of the rain or use the head."

Sean stared blankly at him. "What? You never heard of a head? It's what we call the privy on a boat. You better get used to the lingo if you are going to work on the water."

"Thank you, sir."

"Oh. Almost forgot. Here's the pistol I promised you. Are you sure you never used one of these?"

"I'm sure."

Frank showed Sean how to cock it. Frank pulled the trigger a couple of times before he loaded it. "I've got a holster but I think it'll give you away if you carry it on your hip."

Sean nodded slowly a little overwhelmed by the whole thing.

"Maybe you should put it in a coat pocket so you can get to it handy like."

"Yes sir."

Sean fumbled with the gun as he tucked it into his coat. "Uh, are you sure you're up to this?" asked Frank.

"Yeah, I'm sure. I'll give it my best shot."

"Best *shot*. That's a good one. You gotta sense of humor, at least. You gotta be able to laugh at yourself, don't you? All right. You can get started tonight. Maybe *I* can get some sleep for a change," he said as he patted Sean on the shoulder.

Frank turned on his heel and walked back to his car. Sean walked around the harbor and the piers for a while. When it was nearly noon, he headed back towards town, to meet Maggie's aunt. When he rang the bell, Maggie greeted him at the door. She was radiant. She wore a light blue dress that matched her eyes and a long string of beads around her neck. "Well, I *heard* a bell, but I don't *see* any," she said as she inspected Sean from head to toe.

"Well then, you haven't searched *everywhere*, now have ya?"

"You are a devil," said Maggie as she pinched his arm.

"That I am." Sean leaned over and stole a kiss from her lips.

"Damn you. What will the neighbors say?" she asked as she first pushed him away then took him by the hand.

"It's probably the most excitement they've gotten all week," Sean mumbled as Maggie dragged him into the kitchen.

"Goodness, Margaret. Shouldn't you show your guest to the parlor?" asked her aunt.

"It's quite alright, madam. The kitchen is the heart of the home and my favorite place. I smelled your cooking the minute Margaret opened the door. I want to see for myself what is making my mouth water. I hope I'm not imposing."

Maggie's aunt blushed and offered her hand. "I'm Margaret's Aunt Grace."

"Sean O'Connell at your service ma'am. Thank you for your luncheon invitation," he said kissing her hand.

"Delightful, isn't he?" Aunt Grace giggled.

"Oh, he's a real charmer alright," said Maggie. "A regular Valentino."

The women had prepared a table with an embroidered table cloth and good china. "Isn't this lovely," remarked Sean.

"It might be a little pretentious for leftovers but it will do," replied Aunt Grace.

Leftovers meant open-faced sandwiches with hot pork roast and gravy. Grace served small bowls of kale, cooked with bacon and seasoned with vinegar on the side. Sean hadn't eaten home cooking like this since Abby.

When he was nearly finished, Sean asked, "Can you cook like this Maggie?"

Her aunt smiled. "She's a fine cook, it's the dishes she could do without."

"Oh, stop it. Sean will think I'm a lazy bag of bones," pouted Maggie.

"Oh, there's no chance of that. I've seen her in action. She knows how to work. I *like* to watch her work."

"Oh, Sean, now *you* stop."

Maggie folded her hands and laid them on the table. She gave a glance to her aunt and then her eyes twinkled back at Sean's. She couldn't wait to share her secret. "Aunt Grace knows a lady at her church that needs a boarder."

"Mrs. Arnista," added Grace.

"She's from Poland. Her English isn't very good but her cooking is. She's a widow and only has one room to let but it's close to the hotel. It's small, but you and Hannah could be together. She's had a few boarders since her husband passed."

"Sean, she is the sweetest lady and I know she's lonely. It would do her good to have a little one around," offered Aunt Grace.

"I think we should go see her this afternoon," said Maggie. She handed Sean a slip of paper with a name and address.

Aunt Grace brought a cake to the table on a large glass plate. Sean argued that he didn't think he could eat another bite. Still, she cut a slice and set it before him. "What's this?"

"It's the latest thing–pineapple upside down cake. You put the pineapple on the bottom of the pan and pour the batter on top. When it's finished, you flip it upside down so the fruit is on top," explained Maggie.

"My goodness, you ladies are going to have to put me in a wheelbarrow and roll me out of here." Both women giggled, happy to feed Maggie's new beau.

After lunch, Sean helped Maggie with the dishes. He nibbled at her ear and kissed her on the neck when Aunt Grace was out of sight. Maggie squirmed and complained, unable to get away from him with her arms in the dishpan and suds up to her elbow. When Sean took Maggie's jacket from the hook by the door, he heard her aunt whisper to her, "Margaret, I saw the way he looked at you. Don't let this one get away."

Sean smiled. It was his intention to keep *Maggie* from getting away. He thanked Aunt Grace for lunch then he and Maggie walked to Mrs. Arnista's house. It was a row house, just a few blocks away. Sean knocked at the door and when it was opened, the air was thick with the heavenly aroma of this lady's cooking. Mrs. Arnista smiled as she greeted them. "Welcome. Welcome. You are the niece from Grace, yes?" she asked.

"Yes, I'm Maggie and this is Sean."

"Yes. Sean. Nice boy. Where is little girl?" she asked looking behind them.

"Hannah's in school," answered Sean.

She lifted her hand and nodded her head. "Yes, of course, school. Hannah, is her name, yes?"

The landlady motioned for them to follow her. The house was neat and clean. There were African violets at every window and most were in bloom. She showed them a room with twin beds and a dresser. The room was so small there was barely enough room to walk between them. There was a window that looked onto the garden behind the house. Sean had his doubts when he saw the size of the room but then a cat slinked up and curled itself round and round his leg.

"She is my pussy cat, Isabella. I call her Izzy. Busy Izzy. Go now, scat cat."

"Does Hannah like kitties?" asked Maggie innocently.

"A little," said Sean teasing her back.

Mrs. Arnista's English was broken at best. And Sean knew no Polish. Sometimes there were awkward silences where they just smiled and nodded. Finally, Sean asked how much she wanted for the room. He feared he wouldn't be able to afford anything in the big city. She smiled but obviously didn't understand. Sean held up a few dollars. Her eyes squinted to get a good look at them, but then she shook her head no." Sean wasn't sure if he offered her too little or too much. "Mrs. Arnista, I will be working strange hours. I need someone to help me look after Hannah. I need a room—and a babysitter. She's a good girl, not much trouble. But I want to make sure we understand each other."

Mrs. Arnista nodded her head and smiled some more. "Grace has told me this."

The landlady led them into the kitchen. The smell of her cooking grew stronger. "You eat my food," she said in a stern voice.

Maggie's eyes met Sean's. "Uh, Maggie and I just had lunch with her Aunt Grace. I'm sorry, but we can't eat another bite."

"Baloney. Always more room for food. I am old lady. You must do what I say," she said shaking her finger at them.

She ladled a spoonful of cabbage and half a sausage onto a saucer and gave them two forks. Maggie and Sean each took a bite. The spices were different than they were used to, but it was delicious. Sean finished the plate, returned it to the table and said, "Thank you. It was very good."

Mrs. Arnista pointed to the pants pocket that held Sean's money. Sean reached in and pulled out few bills. He fanned them out so she could see them.

"I will cook." She pulled out a bill.

"And wash clothes." She pulled out another bill

"*And keep Hannah.*" She said softly as she pulled out one more.

She folded over the money and put it in her apron. Then put out her hand to shake Sean's. At first, Sean was startled at the amount of money she took. She gave Sean a warm smile. As he held her hand, he got the feeling that Hannah would be well cared for by this widow and no one could put a price on that.

After they said their goodbyes to Mrs. Arnista, Sean put his arm around Maggie. "Miss Margaret, it's time you met my curly girl. Shall we give her the good news together?"

"Well, that depends."

"Depends on what?"

"Depends on if you will let me buy her a tin roof."

"That's bribery."

"In its purest form."

The two walked a little more. Curiosity got the best of Sean. "What's a tin roof?"

"A sundae with vanilla ice cream, chocolate syrup and red-skinned Spanish peanuts."

"Hmmmm, then that depends."

"Depends on what?"

"Depends on if I get one too. Hannah's not the only one who likes ice cream."

"Sean, you must be ready to pop. You've already eaten lunch—twice."

"*Always more room for food*," said Sean with a phony Polish accent.

"Sean O'Connell, I think you're just a big kid yourself."

"Are you just now figuring that out?" Maggie punched his arm.

When they got to Hannah's school, she was the first one out the door when the bell rang. "Papa, Papa. It's Friday. No school tomorrow and no homework either."

She dropped her lunch box and primer to the ground and Sean lifted her from the waist and swung her round and round. He buried his face in her curls and kissed the top of her head. Her arms hugged his neck then he lowered her to her feet. Suddenly Sean remembered Maggie was patiently waiting to be introduced. "I'm sorry, Maggie."

"Don't be. I think it's wonderful."

"Hannah, this is Miss Schmidt. She's my–*friend.*"

"I'm pleased to meet you, Hannah. My whole name is Margaret Ann Schmidt. But you can call me Miss Maggie," she said offering Hannah her hand.

Margaret *Ann.* It has a nice ring to it, thought Sean. Hannah and Maggie surveyed each other. Sean was happy to have these two finally meet and hoped they would get along. But Hannah wore a concerned face.

"You mean *girlfriend,*" said Hannah, "or else you wouldn't be holding her hand. Bobby Rogers tried to hold my hand, but I punched him good. He chews gum he finds stuck under the desk. I don't want to be *his* girlfriend."

"Is it all right? I mean, that Papa has a girlfriend?" asked Maggie.

Hannah knitted her eyebrows. "Well, I don't have a mama anymore and Papa needs a new wife. So I guess it's okay. When are you two getting married?"

Maggie blushed.

"Whoa, whoa. Wait a minute. Don't marry us off just yet. We haven't talked about that. We've only been holding hands a short while," explained Sean.

"Well, what are you waiting for? She's nice isn't she? And she's pretty enough. I think you two should get married so we can get a house and all live together," said Hannah as she folded her arms across her chest.

"We *are* going to live together, *you and me.* Maggie found us a nice place to live not far from here. We're going to Sam's to get your things now. Are you ready?"

"Ready? I've been ready. What took you so long? Come on. Let's go."

Hannah squeezed in between Sean and Maggie and took Sean's hand. Then she glanced up at Maggie and took her hand too. Sean smiled as they walked to Sam's. Maybe this was going to work out, the *three* of them.

On the way to Sam's they stopped for ice cream as promised. Hannah decided to pass on the tin roof with peanuts on account of her loose tooth and had a hot fudge sundae instead. She ate the cherry first and then all the whipped cream. There was so much fudge on her face, it looked like a beard. Maggie and Sean shared a black cow. Thank goodness it was more root beer than ice cream because their bellies were still full. Hannah turned to Sean and asked, "How come we never had this before?"

"I never heard of a hot fudge sundae," Sean admitted. "This is Maggie's doing."

"Hmmmmmmm. Maggie huh? When *are* you getting married?" she teased.

Sean tickled her ribs under the table until she was out of breath. "Do you see what you're getting into?" he whispered to Maggie.

"I'm afraid so."

They gathered Hannah's things at Sam's. Her departure was bittersweet. "Don't forget about us," Flo said as she bent down to hug Hannah.

Hannah wrapped her arms around her neck and hugged her back. Flo's eyes met Sean's. They were welled with tears and her chin was trembling. Flo had become quite attached to the little one. "You will call on us from time to time won't you?" she asked.

"Yes ma'am. And thank you for everything," Sean said and kissed her hand.

When they were settled at Mrs. Arnista's, Sean put Hannah down for a nap. Sean's eyelids were heavy as well. "You should get some sleep too. You have to work in a few hours and stay up all night. I can make it back on my own," said Maggie.

"Are you sure?"

"Positive."

She gave him a peck on the cheek but he wasn't about to let her get away that easily. Sean pulled her to him and rested his hands on her waist. "I don't know what I would do without you," he said.

She gently removed his hands from her waist, squeezed them in hers and gave him a smile. "Sleep. I'll see you tomorrow."

A few hours later, Sean awakened to the smell of supper. Mrs. Arnista had made pirogues stuffed with potatoes and cheese. Hannah was already sitting at the table. Sean dined with her watching as she ate an entire plate of them. Then she noticed something from the corner of her eye. She hopped down from the table to pet the cat. "Look Papa, this place even comes with a kitty," she beamed.

"We've met," he said gently pulling the cat's tail. "I've got to get to work, now. I'll be back in the morning. Make sure you wash up and go to bed when Mrs. Arnista tells you."

Hannah only half listened as she continued to tease Izzy. Hannah used both arms but had difficulty lifting her. The cat had had enough of her attention and struggled to get away. Sean searched Mrs. Arnista's face and wondered if he should leave these two alone so soon. "Go, go. It's all okay. All okay," she said sensing his reluctance.

"Thank you for everything. The dumplings were delicious."

He kissed Hannah goodbye and Mrs. Arnista smiled and waved him off.

Sean spent that evening patrolling the boat pier. He tried to vary his position from time to time in case anyone was watching him. He searched for anything that seemed suspicious. He saw one man with a cart checking trashcans for soda pop bottles. He saw another man checking the trashcan for food. It made him sick to his stomach. He'd been hungry, really hungry, but he had never had to eat from a trash can. He remembered the soup kitchen and thought of telling the man about it. As he watched, he decided the man was mentally ill. He smelled a dead fish someone had left on the dock. A stray cat hissed as Sean drew near. He backed off to watch her. Then two rats tried to horn in on her dinner. She kept them at bay with threats of claws and teeth. The rats were nearly as big as she was. A third rat joined them. Suddenly, the odds were too great. Sean managed to scare the rats away. The stray cat seemed grateful for his help and carried the fish away.

As the hours passed, Sean's thoughts drifted to Maggie. He wanted to be with her every minute. How could they possibly see each other when she worked all day and he worked all night? He wondered how he had let himself get talked into taking this job. Frank was persuasive and wouldn't take no for an answer. No one could steal all that cargo alone, thought Sean. There had to be a lookout and at least one other or maybe two others to carry away the loot. Sean slid his hand into his breast pocket to feel for his gun. He must have felt for it every fifteen minutes. His gun was ready, but when the time came, would he be ready? He wrestled with that question the rest of the night.

Sunrise couldn't come soon enough. Sean couldn't keep his eyes open any longer. He waited for Frank to arrive, so he could give him a report before heading home. "How was your first night?"

"I didn't see a thing."

"Good work, my boy. That's the kind of news I like. I had a great night. Slept like a baby. Fine work," said Frank patting him on the back.

Sean felt empty on the walk home. What had he expected? He was terrified that he might see a thief, but then was disappointed when he didn't. He stripped off his shirt and pants and climbed into bed and slept until two in the afternoon. He awakened disoriented, slid on his trousers and dragged himself to the kitchen. "Night owl," said Mrs. Arnista as she set a plate of food on the table before him.

"Thank you, kind lady."

The food smelled good, but his stomach wasn't quite awake yet. He held his fork in his hand hesitating. The sun came out from behind a cloud and shone through the kitchen window. It nearly blinded him. He scooted his chair and plate around the table. His head throbbed. He couldn't seem to wake up.

"Papa, what are we going to do today?" asked Hannah.

Sean put his hand over his ear nearest her. "Talk a little softer, lamb chop. I've got a headache."

Sean felt like he'd been drinking whiskey all night. It was already mid-afternoon—half the day was over. In just a few hours, he would be back at the docks. What had he gotten himself into? He took a deep breath and tried to get his bearings. "What have you got on your mind, lassie?"

"Well, the sun is out today. I was thinking we might go for a little walk."

"And where should we walk?"

"I was thinking maybe we should walk on the street that goes by my school."

"Walk to school? On a Saturday?"

"Well, not all the way to school. I was wondering if we could take a rest before we got there and maybe…"

"And maybe what?"

"And maybe have another one of those hot fudge sundaes."

"Ahaaaaaaaaaaaaaaa. Now I get it."

Sean forced himself to take a bite from his plate– and made her wait a little for his answer. "Ice cream? Hmmmmm, only good girls get ice cream."

Sean took another bite and chewed slowly. Hannah leaned in towards him and gave him her best puppy dog eyes. "Have you been good?" asked Sean as he glanced towards Mrs. Arnista for the answer.

Hannah looked her way too, hoping for approval. Mrs. Arnista grinned and put her hand over her mouth to hide her smile. This was, after all, a serious matter. "Uh-huh. I mean, yes sir," said Hannah.

"You don't sound too sure about that."

Sean gave Mrs. Arnista a wink. She tightened her hand over her mouth, but her eyes were smiling and her chest was bouncing with suppressed laughter. "I was quiet all morning so you could sleep, wasn't I?" asked Hannah.

There was distress in her voice. She could see her ice cream slipping away. "That you were and I am most grateful," he replied.

By now, Sean's stomach had settled and he stuffed his mouth with brown bread and butter. He sneaked a sideways glance at Hannah from the corner of his eye and could barely keep from laughing himself. A little suffering and teasing was good for the soul–especially if he was not the one on the receiving end. Hannah nervously awaited his answer as he swallowed down the last of his milk. He rested his glass on the table and slowly turned to face her. His expression was blank. He could hear Mrs. Arnista snickering behind him. He stared at Hannah for a long time. She looked down at the table with a most sorrowful face. "Young lady…"

Her face saddened some more. There would be no ice cream today. "Are you brushing your teeth? Tooth fairy doesn't take teeth with cavities."

"Uh huh, and look how wiggly it's getting." She pushed the loose tooth back and forth with her tongue." Mrs. Arnista grimaced.

"In that case, we should invite Maggie for ice cream too."

"Yes sir," she squealed and nearly choked her father with a hug.

Sean turned to look at Mrs. Arnista. She took her hand away from her mouth and laughed too. "Shame on you, Papa," she said wagging her finger and clearing his plate.

"Get your sweater, lamb chop."

Chapter 24

For the next two weeks, Sean watched as boats tied up for the night and shop owners closed their stores. Automobiles bounced past and people grew fewer on the sidewalks. He listened to the bells of the streetcars and to the clip-clop of the fruit vendor's horse. Lovers took their last evening strolls and the colors in the sky changed from gold, to red, purple and then gray as the sun sank low over the city. This was the time he thought most about Maggie, from sunset until the last rays of light faded away, quiet time. Hardly anyone walked the piers after dark and there was seldom a policeman in sight. Sean was already growing weary of this schedule and struggled to stay awake. Night work made it difficult to spend time with Hannah or Maggie during the day. The lack of sleep made his head throb until he saw spots in front of his eyes. Every muscle in his body ached and there was a dull buzz in his ear that never ceased.

Sean never thought he would find anything good to say about the mines, but back then he was in bed by dark and got up with the birds, the same as everyone else. Keeping these new hours was madness. He lived in a continuous state of fatigue and confusion and fought to stay awake to see Hannah, but often, the best he could do is nap with her when she got home from school. He was comforted by her little heart beating next to his, but even this sleep was not always restful. The room became too warm with the afternoon sun. Instead of sleeping, his brain struggled with puzzles and unsettling dreams caused his legs to jerk. He could never fully relax for fear that he would oversleep.

It was tough to court Maggie through all of this. With their crazy hours, sometimes they only had time for a short walk or a piece of pie after work. Sometimes it was too difficult for him to choose between spending time with Maggie or Hannah. That's when he took them both on a *double* date. He was sorry he hadn't ever found time to take Maggie to dinner or a show and thankful she had never complained. Sean knew he was lucky this job had found him and grateful for the ten dollars a day–he couldn't pay rent without it. Every payday he socked a little more money away for the future. But he was tired of living in his current state of hell somewhere between consciousness and sleep.

Saturday morning, Frank met him at the dock to give him his wages. Even though he felt lousy, Sean gave Frank the most convincing smile he could muster. Still, Frank saw through his tired eyes. "How's it going?"

"Well, I haven't caught any big ones, or little ones. Heck I haven't even had any nibbles. I guess that's good."

"Why that's stupendous. Seeing nothing is exactly what I'm happy to pay you to do. A job well done, wouldn't you say?"

Sean nodded, half-heartedly.

Frank watched him for a moment, reading the disappointment in his face. "Oh Sean, you're used to loading a coal car and at the end of the day it's full. You can *see* what you've done. That's easy. Now you are being paid to keep your eyes open to see nothing. Well, it's worth every penny to me. Life is that way. Seeing is believing, but the hard part is believing what you're not seeing. Are you following me, there, Sean?"

"I guess…"

Frank took a deep breath in preparation to give Sean some fatherly advice. Sean's shoulders slumped a little. His head was splitting but he knew he couldn't escape the lecture that was coming his way. "You see son…"

Sean braced himself.

"Sometimes life is smooth sailing and that's great. But you've got to be prepared for when it isn't. A smart captain won't cast off when a storm is brewing. And sometimes you shove off in clear skies and get hit with a squall from out of nowhere and you've got to fight to stay afloat. That's what separates the men from the boys. Yes sir, when it looks like you are losing the battle, that's when you've got to fight harder. There's no giving up or giving in when you are out at sea. You've got to have faith and believe you are going to survive or you won't. And when you think you haven't got any fight left, that's when you have to find courage and fight the hardest. Unfortunately, it's got to get to that point before most of us will ask for *help*," he said pointing into the sky.

Sean wondered if Frank used to be a preacher. "He hears all prayers and he answers all prayers. Sometimes we don't like the answer we get. That's life. Nobody said life was fair. "

Sean thought about how angry he was when *He* let Molly and the baby die. "Only He knows the whole story. *He* wrote the book."

It was then Sean realized he wasn't angry anymore. Now he just wanted to understand. He wanted to be rid of that envelope of money, of looking over his shoulder. He wanted the noise in his head to go away. At this moment, most of all, he wanted Frank to shut up. "Nobody down here gets to skip to the last to see how it's going to turn out. We've got to muddle through page by page and hope for a happy ending. Do you believe in happy endings, Sean?"

"I believe it's possible. It just seems like a long time coming."

Frank grabbed his belly and laughed. "A long time coming, he says. How old are you, twenty-five or so?" Sean nodded.

"Why, you haven't even *started* living yet. Wait until your legs give out and your eyes fail. Wait until you start praying you can make it across the road or make it to the toilet in time. That's when you get religion. Believe me, you've had it easy so far."

Easy. He has no idea what I have been through, thought Sean.

The two stood for a moment collecting their thoughts. Suddenly, they were hit by a gust of wind. It swept the ground fiercely and forced upward against them. They covered their faces against the flying debris from the ground. There wasn't a cloud in the sky. Sean used his sleeve to rub the dust from his eyes. Frank pulled a handkerchief from his coat to wipe his face. "Do you believe in heaven, Sean?" Frank shouted over the wind. His eyes peered into Sean's, as if he could see through to his soul.

"I used to. But lately, I have my doubts."

"Well let me assure you, there is a heaven. And you don't have to see it with your eyes to believe it. All the loved ones you've lost are there looking down on you right now. They're all rooting for you, my boy. You've only got a little while down here. Get some living in while you're still alive."

The wind stopped as suddenly as it started.

"Sooner of later, you will face stormy seas. Stay sharp, captain." Frank said shaking his finger sternly at Sean. He made a few great strides, got into his sedan and drove off.

Sean walked home. What a strange man, he thought. One minute, Sean was swept up by his speech and the next he was sure he was a lunatic. How did *he* know there was a heaven? It probably got beaten into him by nuns at some—*Catholic* school. How did anyone know if there was a heaven until they died? And dead men told no tales.

Sean tried to sleep but his slumber was fraught with strange dreams. He couldn't get used to sleeping in daylight and his conflict about what to do with the money made it that much worse. When he awakened, his head was swimming. He knew he had to find something to take his mind off his problems. He decided to take Hannah and Maggie to a matinee. Hannah loved the cartoons and the Marx brothers had them all in stitches. When they stopped for ice cream, Hannah asked for a banana split—twenty-five cents. Sean put his foot down. He knew her eyes were bigger than her stomach. And anyway, who would squander a whole quarter on an ice cream? She settled for a root beer float and slurped the very last drop of the foam from the bottom of the glass with her straw. They walked her home to Mrs. Arnista and she was so exhausted that she was asleep by the time her head hit the pillow.

Mrs. Arnista caught Sean and Maggie kissing in the kitchen. "You two, lovebirds, go. Get out of here. Go and have dinner. I watch while she sleeps," she insisted shooing them with her hands.

They strolled along the downtown sidewalks gazing into the windows of the shops and restaurants. It was magical. For once, they didn't have to watch the clock for work. When the sun sank low, they ordered dinner in a little café. And for the first time since the end of Prohibition, they ordered wine. Sean thought Maggie was amazing. Her eyes shone like diamonds back at his and her hand was soft and warm. Her glance at him made his heart swell. He wished that the night would never end. I want her all to myself, he thought. He wanted to ask her to marry him, but it was too soon—he still had unfinished business.

After dinner, Sean walked her home. They sat on the porch swing for a long time, just holding each other, gently swinging to and fro and not saying a word. They were satisfied with each other's company and that was enough. Finally, Sean gave her a warm kiss and let her go. He walked home slowly, smiling and thinking about that glorious day.

As he neared the house, he could make out Mrs. Arnista standing on the stoop. She waved her arms at him in distress. "Mr. Sean, Mr. Sean. Come quick. It is the little one."

Sean's thoughts raced. What could it possibly be? Did Hannah skin her knee or bump her head? Did the cat scratch her?

"Hannah is sick. She is so hot, so hot. I give to her cool water and give her cool bath. She is still so hot. She needs the doctor."

Sean found Hannah lying in bed, pale with beads of sweat on her forehead. She gave a faint little cough when Sean entered. Mrs. Arnista dipped a cloth into a basin of cold water, wrung it out carefully folded it and rested it on Hannah's forehead.

"What's wrong my curly girl? What's the matter?"

"Papa, my legs hurt. They feel so heavy and jumpy."

Sean looked to Mrs. Arnista for an answer. "It's the fever," she offered.

"She must drink." Mrs. Arnista handed Sean a glass of water. He slid his hand beneath Hannah's head to lift her to the glass. Her hair was matted, soaked in perspiration. Hannah took two sips and closed her eyes. How could she become ill so quickly? She was fine a few hours ago when he left her.

"Call a doctor," said Mrs. Arnista frantically. Sean saw the anxious look on her face. Did she suspect it was some terrible illness? Sean lost his faith in doctors with the passing of Molly. But Mrs. Arnista was right. He had to do something. He ran back to Maggie's house. Maybe her aunt knew a doctor nearby. What could it be? Measles? Mumps? The flu? Could it be–*polio*? After all, it was spring and she had a fever. Then he remembered she complained about heavy legs. Please, God–not polio, he prayed under his breath. When he got there, Aunt Grace answered the door.

"I'm sorry to call so late at night, but it's Hannah."

"What is it? Is she sick?"

319

"Yes, I wonder if you can tell me where I can find a doctor."

"You'll not find a doctor at this hour. Does she have any rashes or a sore throat?"

"I don't think so."

"Is she sneezing or does she have a runny nose?"

"No. I don't think so. I really don't know."

By now, Maggie stood behind Grace, with her bathrobe pulled tightly around her.

"Oh, it's hard to tell what she's got. I have a bottle of aspirin you can try. That should help bring down the fever. Crush up a tablet and put it in a spoonful of jam or syrup. Make her swallow one down whenever the fever creeps back up. Keep her drinking. Give her ginger ale or weak tea with a little sugar. She's got to have plenty of fluids to sweat out the fever," said Grace.

"Sean, do you want me to come with you?" asked Maggie.

"No, Mrs. Arnista and I will handle this. Besides, you've got to work tomorrow. There's no point in all of us losing sleep."

Aunt Grace handed him a small bottle of aspirin and a large green bottle of ginger ale. Sean thanked her and rushed home to do exactly as she instructed. Within an hour, Hannah's fever broke. She sat up and drank some tea. An hour later, her fever crept up again. Sean knew he needed to sleep but he couldn't stop worrying about Hannah. He stayed up the whole night watching over her. Finally, by mid-morning, he couldn't keep his eyes open any longer. Mrs. Arnista rubbed his shoulder.

"Go lay down in the front room. Sleep. I watch her."

He gave her another dose of aspirin before passing out on the sofa. The smell of fried onions awakened him in late afternoon. Mrs. Arnista had been cooking while she kept an eye on Hannah. She sat Sean at the table and presented him with a large plate of kielbasa and potatoes. "I can't eat now. I need to check on Hannah," protested Sean.

"No. Eat. You must eat before you go working. Hannah sleeps now. Eat."

Sean knew she was right and he was starving. He covered his plate with salt and ketchup and ate every bite. He pulled on a clean shirt and headed for the front door.

"I'll be back in a couple of hours to check on her," he called back to the kitchen.

"No, stay with your job. I send for you when I need you."

Sean thought better of leaving so soon and crept back to Hannah's room one last time. The turn at the doorknob made her stir. He pulled back her sheet. It was drenched and her curls stuck to the side of her face. The fever had broken again.

"Papa, where are you going?" she said with a pout.

"Lamb chop, I have to go to work now and keep an eye on Mr. Frank's boats," he said as he gently brushed her hair away with his hand.

"When are you coming home?"

"I'll be home when the sun comes up and kisses you on the cheek."

He leaned over and pressed his lips on her moist face. "Will you be a good girl for me and get well while I'm gone?"

She stared at him with glassy eyes. "I'm thirsty, Papa."

"That's my girl."

Mrs. Arnista handed her a glass of ginger ale. She swallowed it down quickly.

"Slowly, slowly. Too much for the stomach," Mrs. Arnista warned.

The color returned to her cheeks.

"Go. Go now. I watch her. Go."

Sean watched as Mrs. Arnista pulled up a chair and sat next to the bed. She gave her the Sunday comics and Hannah sat up to get a better look at them. It was a good sign. Sean hated to leave her, but he must.

It was a long night on the docks. Sean couldn't stop worrying about Hannah. He didn't see anything unusual that night except a drunk relieving himself on a tree. When the milk man came through, he quickly headed home. When he got there, he quietly pushed open Hannah's door.

"How is she?" asked Sean softly. Mrs. Arnista was still sitting in the same chair.

"Won't eat anything. She drinks water, that's all. The fever comes and comes. I give her aspirin, like you show me. She is better and then the fever, she comes again." Mrs. Arnista looked terrible. It had been a long night for her too. She had faithfully stood her watch and cared for his baby. He put his hand on her shoulder. "Thank you for watching her. I am wide awake. You go and sleep."

She nodded and headed to her room. Sean pressed a cold damp cloth to Hannah's forehead and she awakened. Her eyes were wide and bright but her face was expressionless. "It must be morning. You're home."

"Yes, cupcake. Papa is here."

"Did you catch any bad guys?"

"No, not tonight."

"What will you do with them when you catch them?"

What a question? Sean was still wondering about that himself. "Take them to the police–to jail, I guess."

"That's okay. The bad guys will still go to heaven when they die."

"What makes you say that?"

"Cousin Flo says even bad people go to heaven, everybody does, if they believe." As usual, Hannah spoke with great authority. For the moment, Sean was relieved. His chatterbox was back. "Sick people go to heaven too. I'm gonna go to heaven when I die."

"Lamb chop, please, don't talk like that. You are *not* going to die. You are not going anywhere. You are going to get well and go to school and teach the teachers a thing or two. Do you hear me?"

She nodded. A sad look came over her face. "I'm so tired, Papa. My eyes hurt."

Sean lowered the window shade as far as it would go, but the morning sun still shone brightly into the room. He took the hat from his head, put it on hers and tilted it down over her eyes. He felt her cheeks with the back of his hand. Warm, but not hot. He wasn't sure if her temperature was going up or coming down. She drifted back off to sleep. Sean took the gun from his coat pocket and slipped it into the top drawer of the dresser. Then he joined her in slumber for the next couple of hours, seated in the chair next to her.

Sean awakened to the sound of Hannah's crying. Her legs were thrashing about, tangled in the blanket and sheets. She screamed with her eyes shut tight.

"What is it, Hannah? What is it?" Sean asked grabbing her by the arms.

Mrs. Arnista heard the cries and rushed to the room. She stood at the door wringing her hands helplessly. "It's the fever again. She has a bad dream."

"Hannah, Hannah, wake up, darling. It's just a bad dream. Papa is here. We are here," he shouted over her screaming.

She slowly opened her eyes and wept softly. Sean rubbed her back to comfort her. "Hannah, you were just having a bad dream."

Her skin was on fire and cheeks were bright red. Her lips were cracked and the sheets were dry.

"I make a cool bath," said Mrs. Arnista as she hurried towards the bathroom.

Sean poured a glass of water from the pitcher on the nightstand. "Drink this."

"I don't want it," she whimpered.

He sat her up in bed and supported her with his arm.

"Hannah, please baby, drink a little for Papa."

Her eyes began to close as she faded back off to sleep.

"Hannah. Hannah Jane. Drink this right now," he ordered.

Fear struck at Sean's heart. The thought of losing his little girl terrified him. He must get her fever down with water like Aunt Grace advised. Hannah managed to take a tiny sip and then her head fell forward in sleep.

"Hannah. Wake up. Wake up and drink. You've got to drink." By now, Sean was frantic and shouting so loudly Mrs. Arnista heard him over the running water. She went back to Hannah's room to see what had happened.

Sean grabbed the back of Hannah's hair and tilted her head slightly backwards. When her mouth gaped, he poured in a little water. She choked and sputtered. Most of it ran down the front of her gown, but some of it went down her throat.

"Please, Mrs. Arnista. Can you get me an aspirin in a spoonful of jam?" She nodded and hurried to the kitchen.

Hannah faded away again. Sean carried her into the bathroom and stripped the clothes off her. He put her down under the cold running water. She screamed. "No, Papa, no!"

Her lips turned blue and her bottom lip trembled. Her skin became gooseflesh.

"Drink some more water, and I'll make the bath warmer for you."

"But I'm freezing."

Sean got on his knees and lifted the glass to her lips. "Drink it now."

She leaned forward, closed her eyes and drank. "Atta girl, keep going," said Sean now smiling. She gulped down half of it by the time Mrs. Arnista arrived with the aspirin and a kettle of hot water. She began to pour the hot water into the opposite end of the tub. Sean stopped her. "Not until she finishes drinking." Hannah whined, but drank the rest of the glass. Mrs. Arnista handed over the spoon with medicine then emptied the kettle. Sean swished the warm water around Hannah with his hand. Hannah was still shaking. He held the spoon of aspirin and jam to her lips. She knew better than to disobey his orders. Reluctantly, she cleaned the spoon with her lips and then held the concoction in her mouth.

"Swallow it," said Sean sternly.

After a moment, Hannah obeyed, but winced and gave her father a sour face.

"Good girl."

When Sean stood, his legs shook like horse flesh, but he wasn't cold. It was the adrenaline. His eyes met Mrs. Arnista's. He felt guilty about yelling at Hannah and looked to the landlady for her approval. She patted him on the shoulder and smiled. "You are a good father. I watch her now," she said as she handed him the kettle.

Sean returned the kettle to the stove and poured himself a glass of milk. The clock in the parlor chimed. It was five o'clock. Another day gone and he missed it. He wondered how much longer he could keep these hours–and where he would be without Mrs. Arnista. She had been a blessing, watching over both of them. His stomach growled. The landlady must be starving too, he thought. It was time to take care of her for a change. Carefully, he turned the gas on at the stove and lit the burner with a match. He adjusted the blue flame then slid on a skillet. When the butter sizzled, he scrambled four eggs and put two slices of bread in the electric toaster. He thought of Sunday breakfasts in Pottsville and of Abby. He missed her, but not splitting wood for the stoves. His mind drifted and he wondered if she would have liked the luxuries of the city, gas stoves and electric appliances. It was going to be another long night, so he fumbled with Mrs. Arnista's percolator to brew them a pot of coffee. By the time it started to sputter, Hannah tiptoed into the kitchen with one towel wrapped around her head and another wrapped around her chest. She looked like a little kewpie doll. She stood next to the stove to get warm while Mrs. Arnista changed her sheets.

The landlady smiled when she joined them in the kitchen. "She feels cooler now. A little better," she said as she pulled a fresh nightgown over Hannah's head. "Okay. Back in bed, little one," she ordered.

"Wait a minute."

Sean poured the last of the ginger ale for Hannah and handed it to her.

"Drink it all, young lady."

"Yes sir."

"She looks better," said Mrs. Arnista guardedly. "But the fever, she will come again."

Mrs. Arnista peeked into the frying pan. "Ahhhhh, a man in the kitchen. Wonderful. I am very hungry."

She pulled two cold ham slices from the icebox and carefully laid them in the skillet too. As they finished their eggs, there was a knock at the door.

"Maggie, what are you doing here?" asked Sean.

"I told Sam that Hannah was sick. He wanted a report, so I thought I would sneak over and check on our little patient."

Sean gave her a peck on the cheek and let her in but he hung in the doorway to take a long look at the sky. It was getting black faster than the sun was setting. The smell of rain was in the air.

"Mrs. Arnista, you look exhausted. Are you alright?" asked Maggie.

Mrs. Arnista smoothed back the hair from her face and reset a couple of hairpins. "Long night with the little one. I'm all okay."

"Can I see her?" asked Maggie.

Maggie and Sean crept into the little bedroom. Hannah was sleeping again, but it was fretful sleep. Her chest moved up and down quickly with shallow breaths. Sean pressed his ear to her chest. Her little heart was beating away. He pressed his lips to her forehead. Burning up—again. Mrs. Arnista was right. The fever was back. Maggie rested the back of her hand on Hannah's cheek and looked up at Sean. They stepped back into the kitchen.

"Mrs. Arnista, can you give me another aspirin with jam?"

"She has fever again?"

"I'm afraid so."

"But she has medicine only one hour ago."

"I know, but we aren't going to put her in the tub again, not yet. We have to try again with the aspirin." She nodded and set to work.

"Sean, she's a firecracker," said Maggie.

"That's what we've been dealing with for two days."

Mrs. Arnista gazed up at the clock in the hall. "Sean, you must go. You are late."

"I can't leave her again. Not when she is like this."

"Go, I can do it," she insisted.

"What if she gets worse? You can't leave her to find me," Sean argued.

"I can come back and check on her in couple of hours," offered Maggie.

"Yes, we will be okay."

Sean hated to leave this to the women. A wave of guilt came over him and he hesitated when pulling on his jacket. Mrs. Arnista must have sensed it. "It's okay. It is all okay," she said pushing him out the door.

"Be back in a minute," he said looking toward Maggie.

Quietly, he slipped into the bedroom to check on Hannah once more. He wished there was something more he could do. It was hard trying to be a father–and a mother. He longed for Molly. He decided he wasn't angry with God anymore. It was time to make peace. Maybe Frank was right about giving it your best fight and then getting on your knees and asking for help. Sean closed the door behind him and kneeled on the floor next to Hannah. He put his palms together and rested his elbows on the bed. He closed his eyes and softly prayed:

"Dear Lord, have mercy on my little girl. Break this fever and make her well again. I've done everything I know and I need your help. Humbly, I ask you to give her back to me. She is all I have left. Amen."

He kissed her on the cheek. "Get well," he said softly, wiping the water from his eye. He watched her sleep a moment then quietly closed the door behind him. When he and Maggie reached the street, Sean put his arm around her but was still deep in thought. "Worried about Hannah?"

"Yep. But there's something else. I have a funny feeling, like something strange is going to happen."

"It's the storm that's rolling in. You can feel the electricity in the air."

"Maybe. Would it be alright if I don't walk you back to the hotel? I've got to get to the dock."

Maggie nodded. He held her face in his hands and stared into her eyes. He reached down his shirt collar for the chain.

"If anything ever happens to me, give this key to Sam. It unlocks a safe deposit box at the train station. There's something for Hannah in there. He'll know what to do."

Maggie looked confused. "But what's going to happen?"

"I'm not sure. But I'll be alright–I have *faith*." He kissed her fingers that held the chain and gave her a backwards parting glance. His stride got bigger until he began to run toward the docks.

The sky grew darker and the wind stronger as the storm drew near. Sean surveyed the harbor and walked down every pier. His eyes searched the boats and the loading docks for anything amiss, but he found nothing. He unlocked the boathouse, flipped on the light and took a look around. Everything was in its place. He patrolled the whole area once more. As he finished the second sweep, his apprehension subsided. A little voice in his head tried to convince him there was nothing to worry about. Hannah's fever, Frank's rants and the storm rolling in had taken their toll and made him wary. He had only *imagined* the worst.

Poor Sean hadn't gotten more than five or six hours sleep in the last two days and it was fitful sleep at that. Once he convinced himself there was nothing to fear his eyelids grew heavy. For now, the winds had calmed so he moved back towards the street where he could get a better view of the moorings. He rested on a bench and pulled some newspapers over him as if he were homeless. He knew better than to sleep on the job and he had never done it before, but he couldn't hold his eyes open another minute. It was growing colder. I won't stay here long, thought Sean. When it starts raining, I'll move into the boathouse. Within minutes, he drifted off into the world of twilight, somewhere near sleep. He envisioned Maggie with her eyes shining the way they had the night before. He remembered kissing the fingers that held the key to their future. He kissed her cheek and her lips and was about to kiss her neck when he was startled by a clap of thunder. His eyes popped open and the sky was completely black. The wind raced across the water and blew the newspapers off him.

A pair of headlights approached. He thought better of craning his neck to see who it was and instead he crept behind a cargo box to watch and listen. His heart quickened. A lone man walked onto the pier holding his hat with one hand against the wind. He boarded one of Frank's boats, climbed down into the hull and then returned to the deck. A minute later, a truck pulled up. Sean moved closer crawling behind the cargo boxes.

"Where the hell have you guys been? You're late. Double time." The voice sounded familiar.

"C'mon, get these boxes in the truck. We haven't got all night," he urged as the two other men climbed into a cargo hold. They struggled off the boat with a large wooden crate and loaded it onto the truck. Then they returned to the boat. They seemed to know exactly what they were after and where to get it. Their heist will be done in minutes, thought Sean. I must stop them.

He reached into his breast pocket for his gun. But it wasn't there. He quickly patted down his coat and pants. Nothing. Panic set in. Then he remembered. He had never put it back in his coat. It was still in the dresser drawer. A chill raced down his spine. How would he stop them without a gun? His mind raced. Maybe he could at least stop one of them he thought. As the two movers got to the truck with another crate, he yelled, "Stop thief." They dropped the crate and looked Sean's way into the darkness, but they couldn't see him.

Sean yelled again, "Put your hands up."

"Cops! Let's get outta here." They jumped into the truck and sped away.

The third man was still in the cargo hold. Sean ran towards the pier knowing all he had was two fists and the element of surprise. The thief's flashlight shone brightly on the deck and he peered into the darkness with it. "Hey, Vito? Freddy? Where the hell did everybody go?"

Sean lunged towards him. When he turned to face the man, the hair stood up on the back of Sean's neck. It was *Joey*. Sean knocked the flashlight out of his hands and got in two swings before Joey's eyes adjusted to the darkness. He wrestled him to the deck of the boat, but somehow Joey broke free and reached into his coat. He stood over Sean, pointing his gun in his face. Sean realized he must have landed a couple of good punches because Joey was wobbly on his feet. Still, Sean knew he was no match for a bullet. Joey hesitated and stared down at Sean as he tried to steady himself and catch his breath. He squinted and leaned in closer to Sean to get a better look at his face.

"You! You're the son of a bitch that took *my* money. That was supposed to be a clean job. But no, you had to go and ruin it. I've got every cop in the country looking for me and I'm in hot water with the boss too, because of you, you *queer.* You lose ten grand and they don't soon forget. I was working my way up the line and you had to go and ruin it for me. Now I'm pulling these shitty little jobs. I'm all washed up. Thanks to you, the sissy that wears dresses. This is going to be sweet."

A sickening, evil grin spread across his face. Sean heard the click as he cocked his pistol. "Say your prayers, weirdo."

Sean never took his eyes off Joey looking for a way to get the gun away from him. "Help me, Lord," he whispered under his breath.

Joey hesitated. "What did you say?"

Suddenly, there was a flash of lightning. For a split second, Sean saw the determined look, the look of hate on Joey's face. Thunder shook the boat and startled them both. Joey regained his stance and tightened his grip on the pistol. He yelled over the wind, "Say your prayers, you piece of shit."

Then Abby spoke to Sean, "The devil be damned. *Get him.*"

Sean lunged towards him grabbing his legs. Joey's knees buckled and he fell backwards. Sean grabbed his wrist and got in one quick jab to the chin, shaking Joey enough to lose control of his gun. As it fell from his fingers, they both scrambled for it, but it bounced overboard.

Joey struggled to get to his feet. "Damn it. Now you really pissed me off," he said reaching into his pocket.

He pulled out a knife and tripped the spring that released the switchblade. Lightning crackled overhead. The light reflected off the silver edge and flashed in Sean's eyes, but he never blinked. He still struggled for another chance at Joey. By now, Joey's right eye was nearly swollen shut. Blood streamed down his chin from a laceration in his bottom lip. His breath was labored and he fought to stay on his feet. Sean saw his chance and rushed him once more to get the knife and finish it once and for all. Joey stabbed Sean's hand when he grabbed for his wrist. Sean forced him to the ground and got in three swift jabs to his face. Joey hardly fought back. Sean hit him one last time and he was out. Sean searched the deck for rope to tie his hands before he came to. Somehow, Sean had to get Joey to the police. Suddenly, Sean worried that Joey would blab about the money. But there was no time to think about that. He had to find some rope. He found a piece tied to a cleat near the edge of the deck. He dropped to his knees and went to work with Joey's knife to cut off a length. Sean could hear Joey grunting. He couldn't let him get up again. He sawed with the blade as fast as he could but before he could finish Joey got to his feet and reached into his pocket. It occurred to Sean that he had never searched him for another gun. Joey smiled as he pointed a large pistol Sean's way. There was no chance for Sean to lunge forward again. He was too far away from him and on his knees. His life flashed before his eyes as he waited for the bullet to pierce his brain. Dear God, it's over, he thought. Joey cocked his pistol and took aim. Swiftly, a gust of wind caught the boom. The rope that secured it had been cut down to a thread by Sean seconds earlier. The rope snapped instantly. The loud pop made Sean drop his head and cover it with his arms. The boom swung around with terrific force over Sean. It continued in its course hitting Joey square in the forehead. It made a loud cracking noise, like at the ballpark when the baseball splits the bat, as it shattered his skull. It swung wide over the edge of the deck knocking Joey overboard. Afraid the boom may swing back along its original path, Sean crawled on his knees and elbows. He hung his head over the side of the boat to see if he could catch a glimpse of Joey. He stared into the rough, murky water for what seemed an eternity but Joey never returned to the surface. The water churned and finally when the sky opened up, rain fell by buckets. Even if the crack on the head hadn't killed him, Sean knew he would never survive the waves of the fierce storm. When the wind died down it took all of Sean's might to refasten the boom's rope. When he was finished, he crawled to the middle of the deck, lay on his belly next to the mast and rested with the rain drenching his skin. It is over–I can finally stop looking over my shoulder, he thought. The man who has dominated my thoughts and dreams is no more.

Every part of his body began to shake. He was soaked through. Was it the cold rain? No, he had seen yet another man die. His stomach grew queasy. He had to get off the boat before he fell overboard too. His legs were jelly and he could barely walk. Then he remembered Hannah. Poor Hannah. He had left her burning up with fever. He had to get home to his baby.

Chapter 25

Sean got his second wind and ran as fast as his legs could carry him through the storm towards home. The rain came down so fiercely, it stung has face and hands and he could scarcely see his way. When he got there, a light was still shining in the window. Mrs. Arnista heard him and met him at the door.

"Mr. Sean, Mr. Sean—come quick. Come and see!"

"Dear God. Have mercy. Not Hannah too," Sean prayed under his breath as he shed his soaking wet coat and shoes.

"Bubbles, bubbles. Beautiful bubbles," shouted Mrs. Arnista smiling.

"Bubbles?" A bubble bath in the middle of the night?

"Yes, the beautiful pink bubbles. Come and see."

When he got to Hannah's room, she was awake and eating a bowl of chicken noodle soup in bed. As he got closer, he could see pink blisters all over her and she was slathered with some kind of white paste.

"I don't understand."

"She gets the pink bubbles when you are away. They are itching her. I make the medicine on her and put on the socks to stop the scratching."

Then Sean noticed the white cotton socks over her hands like mittens. He was still standing there, confused. Mrs. Arnista was desperate to make him understand.

"Cluck, cluck, cluck. The fever is no more. We got the chicken pox."

Sean then realized by the joy in her voice that Hannah was going to be alright.

He put his hands in his armpits and flapped his wings and clucked like a chicken too. "The beautiful *bubbles*. We got the chicken pox. Cock-a-doodle-doo," he shouted.

He hugged Mrs. Arnista and lifted her at the waist. He spun her around and around getting her soaking wet too in the process. She didn't mind and was just as caught up in the moment. They both laughed maniacally. Hannah shook her head and growled. "Hey, what's so funny? When can I take these socks off my hands? I'm itching like crazy. "

"No, no scratching. It makes the marks. No scratching. Rub, rub," Mrs. Arnista said as she rubbed Hannah's back.

"Oh, Hannah, show your father. Mr. Sean, we almost forgot."

Hannah smiled wide with her teeth clenched together. There was a small opening in the bottom row where she had lost a tooth. She pushed her tongue against the gap so that it looked like a pink worm sticking its head through the hole.

"When did that happen?" asked Sean

"When I woke up. I wiggled it and it finally came out. Mrs. Arnista has it ready for the tooth fairy," she said happily pointing to a match box on the dresser.

"And how much is the tooth fairy paying for teeth these days?"

"Well, some kids get a nickel, but some get a dime."

"A dime?"

Sean looked over at Mrs. Arnista and she shook her head. "The world has gone crazy," she said with a serious look.

"Let's see what happens tonight when you put it under your pillow, *snaggletooth.*"

Mrs. Arnista smiled at Sean once more, happy that the Hannah crisis had come to an end. Suddenly, her expression changed, "Sean, what happens to your face? You are bleeding."

"Oh, I fell on the boat. The water was rough out there."

She lifted his right hand and surveyed his wounded knuckles. "Yes, water is rough out there," she said dubiously. He took a quick glance in the mirror over the kitchen sink and rinsed his face and hands in cool water. As he dried off with a towel, he heard the clock in the parlor. It was half past eleven. Maggie would be off soon.

"Mrs. Arnista, I've got to tell Maggie that Hannah is alright."

"Go, go to her. Tell her. She is worried. We are all okay."

Sean looked back at Hannah who was slurping noodles through the hole in her smile.

"And, you *need* your woman," she added.

The rain was slowing down to soft, fat drops as he hurried to the hotel. He went in through the back and took the staff elevator to the twelfth floor. He couldn't find Maggie. The floor clerk told him she had been assigned to the fifth floor because they were short staffed. He was too impatient to wait for another the elevator.

He raced down seven flights to find her. When he did, she was loading her cart to quit for the night. He tapped her on the shoulder.

"Hey, beautiful."

When she turned, he kissed her square on the mouth. She pushed him away. "Are you crazy? We could get fired."

"We could, except I don't work here anymore and you were off five minutes ago."

He kissed her again and she still she fought him off. "You are soaked to the skin."

"I know."

"Not here. Not in front of the guests."

"What guests? It's almost midnight. They are all in bed. Come with me. I need to talk to you."

He took her by the hand and down two flights of stairs. When they got to the third floor, he carefully opened the door to the Calvert Ballroom. There was no one there. He walked across the room and turned on one light. It was the most beautiful room she had ever seen, even grander than the lobby. There was a balcony on three sides, crystal chandeliers, high arches, and gilding everywhere. It looked like a princess should dance here—and tonight, *she will,* thought Sean.

"Sean. What are you doing?"

He returned to her and put his arms around her. He gave her a small kiss on the cheek and then pulled her close to him. He started to sway back and forth with her.

"What are you doing?"

"Dancing."

"But there's no music."

"I hear music."

She gave in and followed his lead–still talking.

"How's Hannah?"

"She's wonderful. The fever broke. She's got the chickenpox."

"I guess there are worse things. I'm glad she's better."

"Hannah's better and now everything is going to get better."

"Sean, what's come over you?"

"I don't know."

"Did something happen tonight, at the dock?"

"Yes, but I don't want to talk about it tonight."

"Why not?"

"Because—I'm in love."

She smiled, laid her head against his shoulder and melted in his arms. By now, her clothes were almost as wet as his. She gently whispered in his ear, "I love you too."

* * *

The next day, Sean told Frank about what happened on his boat, the attempted theft, and Joey's demise and he left it at that. A day later, Joey's body was found washed onto shore 500 yards down stream. The story made the front page of the Baltimore newspaper. "Benito Joseph Rossi was wanted in three states for theft, fraud, gambling, pandering and murder. He was the nephew of Carmine Rossi, the leader of one of the five big crime families." Sean could still hear the newspaper boys shouting the headlines all the way to the dock.

341

Once Sean knew about Joey's past, he felt he owed Frank more of an explanation, starting with the shooting at the Shangri-La. "I was working in a beer joint in Pottsville when Joey rushed in with his boys and shot a man in cold blood. Like you said, it's something you never forget."

Frank nodded. "What was his beef? Power, a dame, money?

"Money."

Sean hesitated a moment, not sure if he should tell Frank about the envelope.

"What was his vendetta with you? A couple dozen people witnessed that murder. Why you?" asked Frank.

Sean felt the blood rush into his face. He knew he had to tell him the *whole* truth. "Joey left the guy lying there dying in a pool of his own blood. Everybody beat it out of there and I was the only one left. I had never seen a man shot so I walked over to get a better look. Curiosity got the best of me—I felt like a little kid. I wanted to see the hole in his head and the brains splattered on the chair. Then I gave him a little shove with my foot to make sure he was really dead. And, well, I heard something."

"What? What did you hear? Did he say something? Did he make a confession?"

"No."

"Well, what was it?"

"A rattle."

Frank paused for a moment. He rubbed the side of his face with the back of his hand, thinking. "What do you mean, *a rattle?* Like a baby rattle–or do you mean a *death rattle?* I've heard about the death rattle. I didn't know it really made a sound."

"No. I mean a rustle, a crackle, like he was lying on a newspaper."

"And?"

"And, I rolled him over, rubbed my hand over his back and he had an envelope shoved down his pants."

"Well, so you went down the dead man's pants. What was in the envelope? Stocks? Bonds? A will? What?"

"Cash."

"*Cash?* How much cash?"

Sean wavered, but he was already in too deep.

"Well? Don't leave me hanging. Spill your guts, man," laughed Frank.

"Ten thousand dollars," mumbled Sean.

"What? I thought you said ten thousand dollars."

"I did. After Joey shot Vinnie, his boys searched the front of his coat, but couldn't find the money. So they searched Vinnie's car. When they couldn't find it there either, Joey came back into the beer joint. That's when he found me standing over the body and told me to get out of there. He didn't know I found the envelope."

"He saw another *man* standing over the body and told you to leave without searching you?"

"Well, sorta."

"What do you mean, *sorta?*"

"Well, I wasn't a *man.*"

Frank took one step back away from Sean and gave him a strange look. "I was with you up until now, but you lost me, son."

"There weren't any jobs at the beer joint for men, just women, as waitresses. My family was starving. There was no work. There was nothing else I could do."

Frank stood and stared at Sean for a long while with a blank expression. Then a smile peeled across his face.

Finally, he grabbed his belly and doubled over with laughter. "Now I've heard everything. A man dresses like a woman to feed his family, sees a man get knocked off and takes the dough off the dead man. Next he works as a bell hop for pocket change when he's got ten thousand dollars in cold hard cash. Then he gets a job as a security guard and kills the guy that's looking for him, in the line of duty, three hundred miles away. Unbelievable," roared Frank.

"I didn't kill him," said Sean angrily.

"I know, I know. I'm sorry. You're right. But if you have ten thousand dollars, why work for peanuts in a hotel carrying bags?"

"Because when I tried to buy a train ticket, the man at the counter couldn't make change for a one-hundred dollar bill. He asked me if it was counterfeit. Then he asked if it was *stolen*. I got scared. I couldn't risk getting found out, not with what I had been through. It was my only chance to get out from under. I knew I had better put it away until things settled down. I did it for Hannah."

"And a wise man you are. Jesus, O'Connell. You've been through the wringer my boy."

Frank reached out, grabbed Sean by the shoulders and shook him gently back and forth. Then he gave him a little pat on the back. The two stood for a moment in silence. Frank put his hands in his pockets and began scratching in the dirt with his shoe. He seemed nervous. "Sean, you know what you have to do, don't you?"

"What?"

"You've got to turn that money in. It's not yours. It's stolen, dirty money. If you don't, you'll be looking over your shoulder the rest of your life. But you won't be looking for Joey anymore. He's dead. You'll be looking for *you*."

Sean stared at Frank perplexed.

"A man's moral fiber, his character, is his most valuable asset. Without that, he's nothing." As much as he hated to admit it, Sean knew he was right.

"And if you don't, your conscience is going to eat you alive."

Sean's stomach tightened into a knot.

"You've got to go to the closest police station and turn it in, *all* of it. And make sure you tell them about your run-ins with Mr. Benito Joseph Rossi—*both* of them."

Sean's eyes searched down at the ground for an answer but couldn't find one. He could feel Frank's eyes piercing the top of his head. He still had all the money from the envelope, well, *almost* all of it. One thing he knew for sure, he was done with nights and with being a security guard. "Mr. DiAngelo, I think your boat yard is safe, at least for now. And anyway, I don't think I'm cut out for this kind of work."

"What do you mean, not cut out for this? You did a fine job. All you needed was courage and a little *faith*." Sean returned the pistol to him and realized that despite all that had happened, he never even used it.

"What will you do now?" asked Frank with a concerned tone.

"I'm not sure. I've got a little money saved, thanks to you. I need to get my life back, spend some time with my girls–and look for another job. Maybe I'll go back to the hotel."

Frank smiled back at him. "*After* you turn in the money?"

"Absolutely," said Sean still not sure about it.

Frank sensed his indecision and said firmly, "I know you'll do the *right* thing."

Sean held out his hand to shake Frank's. "Thank you, Mr. DiAngelo, for everything."

When they finished shaking, Frank reached in his pocket. "Oh, I almost forgot. Here's what I owe you for this week," he said as he counted out the bills. Sean put them into his pocket. Then Frank held out one more bill. "This is for you too. A little *bonus*. You earned it." He held out a one-hundred dollar bill.

"I can't."

"I insist," he said as he curled Sean's fingers around the bill.

Frank explained, "Funny thing. I was at Penn Station yesterday, and a cleaning lady came up to me and asked me if I could change a hundred dollar bill. So I helped her out and gave her some smaller bills. Now where would a cleaning lady get a hundred dollar bill? I can't stop thinking about it."

Sean's face paled.

Frank turned Sean towards home and patted him on the back once more. When Sean got a few yards away, Frank shouted after him. When Sean turned to face him, the morning sun had peeked out from behind the clouds and shone directly into his eyes. Sean tried to block the rays with his hand but all he could see of Frank was his silhouette.

"Make sure you turn in that money, *all* of it. You will be rewarded for your good deed. And Sean, there's still time for that son you've been praying for."

Sean nodded and turned around without speaking, his eyes watering from the brightness. He took a few more steps towards town and then it occurred to him. How did he know he was praying for a son? He spun on his heel to ask Frank, but he was gone.

Sean tried to walk home but his feet were clay. He started and stopped half a dozen times. It was like he had forgotten how to get there. He knew there was something he must do. It was time. At Lexington Street, he stopped in front of a jewelry store and stared in the window. He didn't realize how long he was standing there until a sales clerk opened the front door and asked him to come in. A few minutes later, he walked out with a gold band inscribed with little spring flowers and set with tiny diamond chips. Finally, his feet remembered the way home. When he got there, he found Hannah playing with Izzy on the sidewalk, teasing the cat with a piece of ribbon.

Sean poked his head in the door and asked, "Mrs. Arnista, is it alright for her to play outside?"

"Yes, yes. Fever is gone. She eats everything. She is okay now."

"Oh, Papa. Look." Hannah reached into her pocket and pulled out the matchbox. There, wrapped in tissue paper, was a shiny dime. "Look what tooth fairy brought!"

Sean's heart sank. He forgot all about it. So much had happened he just couldn't keep up with it all. Thank goodness Mrs. Arnista remembered. Sean smiled back at Hannah. "You made quite a haul there. Tooth fairy must love you." Sean gave her a squeeze. Hannah and

Sean sat on the stoop together. He rested his head in his hands and leaned on his elbows.

"What's the matter, Papa?"

"I was thinking about asking Maggie to marry me, but I'm not sure what to do."

"What do you mean? It's easy. You just get down on your knee and show her the ring and then you'll live happily ever after."

"That's all there is to it?"

"Yep. Easy as pie."

Hannah stopped playing with the cat and the two of them sat deep in thought. A look of concern came over Hannah's face. "Do you think she'll marry *us*?" she asked.

"What do you think?" Sean took the box from his pocket and showed her the ring.

Her jaw dropped and her eyes grew bigger as she looked it over. "Papa, it's so pretty. *I'd* even marry you for that ring."

"It's settled. Go and get your shoes on, lamb chop. We've got a job to do."

Sean propped open the door with his foot and called into the house. "Mrs. Arnista, Hannah and I are going to ask Maggie to marry us."

Startled, Mrs. Arnista hurried to the door. "Marry *us?*"

"Yep, I guess we are a package. Double or nothing."

"Oh, she takes both," she said confidently.

Hannah hopped out of the house and skipped down the sidewalk ahead of him.

"Thank you for being the tooth fairy last night," Sean whispered to the landlady.

Her eyes watered. "I am only glad she is okay, all okay."

Hannah chattered the whole way to Maggie's house, but Sean scarcely heard a word. His heart pounded and his feet were ice. What if she said, no? He couldn't bear to think about that possibility. He knew what he wanted. He just hoped that's what she wanted too.

Hannah insisted on ringing the bell and Aunt Grace answered the door. She looked down at Hannah covered with scabs and dots of calamine lotion. Grace giggled at her. "Oh my goodness. Aren't you a sight little missy. What are you doing out of bed?"

"Can we talk to Maggie?" asked Hannah. "We wanna know if she'll marry us?"

Sean stared at the ground and shook his head. "That's my girl–so much for a surprise." He had to laugh.

Aunt Grace covered her mouth with her hand. Her eyes met Sean's. "Is it true?" she whispered. Sean nodded.

"Oh and look, I lost a tooth," said Hannah through her snaggletooth grin. "The tooth fairy brought me a dime–enough for ice cream. Can we get some today, Papa?"

Grace was ready to burst with the news and could scarcely take in what Hannah was saying. "Margaret Ann. Margaret Ann. You have visitors," she cried as she hurried back into the house.

"Thanks a lot for spilling the beans, Miss Priss. Now will you let me do the talking?" asked Sean.

Hannah giggled and wrapped her arms around his waist. She hung on him until they nearly fell off the step. "What about that ice cream?"

"Not today. That dime will have to burn a hole in your pocket a little longer. Can you hold onto the tooth fairy news until I pop the big question to Maggie?"

"I'll try, but it won't be easy."

Maggie came to the door in her maid's uniform, ready for work. Aunt Grace stood close behind her, determined to not miss a thing. Maggie tried to look surprised, but she knew these two were up to something. Sean took off his hat and got down on one knee. He took the ring box from his pocket and lifted it for her to see. "Margaret Ann Schmidt, will you marry me?"

"Marry us, Papa, you mean *marry us.*"

"Margaret Ann Schmidt, will you *marry us?*"

Tears welled in Maggie's eyes. They welled in Grace's too. Hannah smiled and swung her arms back and forth still trying to figure out how to get that ice cream.

"Well, what's it gonna be? You love us, don't you?" asked Hannah impatiently.

"Yes, I love you. And yes, I'll marry you. I'll marry you *both.*"

Sean put his arms around Maggie and held her tight. Home. When he felt his arms slide around her waist, he knew he was finally home. He felt her arms tighten around his shoulders. He wanted this moment to last forever. But it ended too soon when he felt someone tugging on his pants leg.

"Hey, what about me? I'm a part of this deal too, you know."

He crouched down, wrapped his arm around Hannah's knees and lifted her to their level. She wrapped an arm around each of them.

"Are you sure you want to do this? Are you sure you want to spend the rest of your life with me and the chicken pox kid?"

"I'm sure," said Maggie softly.

Maggie wrapped her arm tightly around Hannah. Suddenly, they were all startled by the popping noise that came from Hannah's dress.

"My seeds, my seeds," she said with a look of surprise.

Hannah reached into her pocket and pulled out a spent pod, rolled up at the edges and four dark shiny seeds. "They're ready. Mr. Jack told me I would know when they're ready if I kept them in my pocket."

"Have you had that pod in your pocket ever since that train ride?"

"Uh-huh. Except for when I was sick. Then Mrs. Arnista kept them in her pocket for me."

"Like a little mother hen watching over her chicks," said Sean shaking his head.

"Papa, we have to get a house soon, so I can plant them in the garden."

"Aye, lassie. I'm working on it. I'm working on it."

"Oh, Miss Maggie. I lost a tooth," said Hannah as she forced a grin once more.

"You promised," scolded Sean.

"You said to wait until after you popped the question. You popped it, didn't you?"

That night, Sean met Maggie after work. He took her down to the water and told her the whole truth about that night at the club and the envelope. He watched the wheels turn in her head as she took it all in.

"But if you found money in the envelope, why did you take a job as a bell hop?"

"I was a miner. I thought people would get suspicious if I started to throw around money like that. It was all in hundred dollar bills."

"Hundred dollar bills? If you don't mind my asking, how many are there?"

"One hundred."

She knitted her eyebrows and tried to do the math in her head.

"Ten thousand dollars," Sean offered.

"Oh my, I hope you have it in a good bank."

"No bank. Everyone said not to trust the banks."

He reached for the chain around her neck and lifted the key with his finger.

She glanced down at the key then back at Sean "Ten thousand dollars in cash is sitting in a safe deposit box at the train station?" she whispered with wide eyes.

"That's right," answered Sean softly.

She blinked at him several times and then threw her arms around him "Oh, Sean. Let's get out of here. Let's go to Shady Side and live on the farm. I want to go home."

"Okay, but I have one more job to do. I have to go there early in the morning. Will you come with me?" Sean asked.

She had a concerned and doubtful look on her face. "Sure–I'll go."

Chapter 26

The next morning, Sean met Maggie at seven. They rode the street car to Penn Station and took the money from the safe deposit box. Sean stuffed the envelope into the front of his pants and covered it with his jacket. Maggie grew nervous as they walked to the nearest police station. "Are you going to tell the police about Joey?"

"Uh-huh."

When they arrived at the station, a policeman came to the counter. He was an older man, probably in his late fifties. His head was bald and he had a round face and apples for cheeks. A tiny gray mustache under his nose looked like Charlie Chaplin's. His belly was round too and it pressed against the counter as he stood at it. He greeted Sean and Maggie as they drew near. "Well, aren't we the early birds? What can I do for you folks this morning? Officer O'Shea at your service," he said with a thick accent.

"I would like to report a crime. It happened in Pottsville," Sean stammered.

"Oh, you'll have to report that to the Pennsylvania authorities."

"Well, officer, I don't think I'll be going to Pennsylvania again anytime soon. This man was wanted in several states. The FBI was looking for him and anyway, now *he's dead.*"

"It sounds like this is a matter for the higher authorities. Can you come back later when my supervisor is here?"

"No. No sir. I need to get this off my chest. I've carried it too long."

"Have you got a confession, son? Wait just a minute. Let me get it all down." Maggie and Sean watched as he searched every desk drawer for a pencil and paper. "Very well then, tell me what happened."

"On Wednesday, March 14, I witnessed Benito Joseph Rossi shoot and kill a man named Vinnie."

Officer O'Shea stared back at him. He didn't bother writing down a single thing. "That's it? That story has been all over the papers. I'm sorry to burst your bubble, lad. But that's not exactly news."

"This is what got him killed." Sean reached into his pocket, pulled out the hundred dollar bill that Frank gave him and put it in the envelope.

Maggie grabbed Sean by the elbow, "Sean, no. What are you doing?"

"I've got to Maggie. I can't live like this anymore."

She anxiously watched as Sean slid the envelope across the counter to the officer.

"Are you crazy?" asked Maggie.

O'Shea's eyes were fixed on Sean's. "What have we got here?"

O'Shea opened the envelope and peered in with one eye closed.

"That's ten thousand dollars. It's all there. You can count it," offered Sean.

O'Shea quickly closed the envelope and stood up straight. "Jesus, Joseph and Mary! Excuse me, Miss, but lad, have you been walking around with this since March?"

"Yes sir. And I want to turn it in."

"Why has it taken so long for you to come forward with it?"

Sean was ashamed to answer him.

"Your conscience got the better of you, didn't it?"

"I wasn't sure what I should do then. But I'm sure now," Sean said confidently.

Maggie let out a soft moan.

"Well now, I'll have to contact the FBI on this one," said O'Shea with a smile and an air of deep satisfaction. "Those boys will have to come over this way and see what we've got for them. Thank you folks for stopping by. I'll take care of this."

"Sir, there's more," said Sean.

"More? Like what?"

"I watched Mr. Rossi get killed."

"Great day in the morning, boy, you sure know how to be in the wrong place at the right time. Say, are you reporting a murder? Did *you* kill him?" asked O'Shea as he leaned over the counter towards Sean.

"No. No. I didn't kill him. It wasn't like that."

"Then who did?"

"I was watching over some boats for my boss, kind of a night patrolman job and Joey and his men were stealing from the cargo hold of a ship."

"So you did kill him," shouted O'Shea.

"Sean would never do that," defended Maggie.

"Please, just hear me out, officer. I got a couple of punches in and then he pulled a gun on me. He was wobbly on his feet from the blows to the head. I got the gun away but it fell overboard. He pulled a knife on me, but before he could use it the boom got caught by the wind and swung around and cracked him in the head. He went into the drink. I never saw him again," Sean explained nervously.

Officer O'Shea looked back at him with a cynical expression on his face. "That's one of the most cockamamie stories I've ever heard. How do I know you didn't smack him in the head with a board? Were there any witnesses?"

"There was only *God* as my witness," Sean mumbled.

What had he gotten himself into? He just gave away the money he had worked so hard to keep. He confessed his involvement in Joey's death and now this policeman was going to arrest him for murder. "Can anyone verify that you were on duty that night as a patrolman?"

"Yes sir. I was working for a man who owns a shipping company. But I don't work for him anymore. I'm not really sure how to find him, but I know where he keeps his boats."

"You don't know how to find him because he doesn't exist, does he?" asked O'Shea.

Maggie panicked. "I can vouch for him. He really was working in the boatyard that night."

O'Shea held up his hand to silence her. "Begging your pardon, I need to hear it from him, Miss."

"Did you go to the police after this *accidental* death occurred on the boat?" O'Shea interrogated.

Sean's head dropped. "Ah-haaaaaa. That's because you killed him, isn't it?"

"No, no. It wasn't like that. I just needed some time to clear my head."

"Some time to get your story straight you mean. I'm going to have to keep you for questioning until we can get some things squared away. This story is just a little too far-fetched. You understand, don't you?" asked O'Shea as he pulled out a pair of handcuffs.

Sean nodded as he put his wrists together in front of him.

"Sean, no. This can't be happening. You're a hero. You can't go to jail. Lord please help us," pleaded Maggie.

As O'Shea secured the cuffs, Sean mumbled, "Where is Frank DiAngelo when I need him?"

Officer O'Shea froze. "Did you say, Frank DiAngelo?"

"Yes, I worked for him. He hired me to watch over his boats."

"*His* boats?"

The officer took off the cuffs and laughed until his belly shook. "Now I've heard everything. Those aren't his boats. He's a detective working for the city. His job was to break up a theft ring on the docks. Moonlighting, he is, and they have been paying him plenty. Frank told me about a kid he hired to do his dirty work for him so he could sleep at night and still report to his desk. You learned to shoot picking off squirrels, did you?"

"That's right," said Sean thoroughly confused.

"Frank and I were cadets together at the police academy. We were in school at St. Joe's before that. I guess you could say we were in school. We spent most of the time in Father Tony's office. We drove Sister Mary Agnes crazy."

I knew he was Catholic, thought Sean.

"Frank even thought about joining the priesthood once or twice, but he couldn't stay out of trouble long enough to get there. Can you believe it?"

"Yes, I can believe it," said Sean with a serious tone.

"Well, I'm sure Frank will vouch for you if any further interrogation is in order. I guess that makes you a free man, doesn't it?"

"Absolutely," answered Maggie.

"Still, those ships are tied down pretty tight in port, regulation. I wonder how that boom got loose."

Sean gave his best poker face.

"No matter. That Francis, what a corker. *His* boats. You won't be getting arrested today, son. But I will need your statement. Could you write down what happened in your own words?"

"Yes, sir."

He reached around behind him into a file cabinet drawer. "Just fill out the top of this form, with your name and address so I can get the paperwork going for the reward."

"The *reward?*" asked Sean.

"Yeah, if we get the forms out today, we should have a certified check here for you in about a week."

"The *reward,*" repeated Sean.

"Yes, laddie. The reward for the capture of Benito Joseph Rossi—dead or alive. He was wanted by the U.S. Marshall. Don't you read the newspaper?"

"Well, no."

"Sweet Jesus. Just fill it out and we'll get you your check."

Sean scribbled in his name and address and a few words about what happened. He looked over at Maggie.

Her eyes were shining. He quickly passed the form back over the counter to O'Shea.

"Well, then. Stop back by here in about a week. I should have a check for you. I'll be looking for you. Nice meeting you," he said as he turned his back to them. Sean took Maggie's arm and headed for the door.

"Well?" she asked.

"Well, what?"

"Aren't you going to ask him?"

Sean was still in a state of shock. Finally, he realized what she was asking.

"I can't. I just can't."

Maggie stopped in her tracks. "Well, I can."

She dragged Sean back to the counter.

"Excuse me, sir. Begging your pardon, Officer O'Shea, but can you tell me, how much *is* the reward?"

"Madam, you must not read the paper either. The reward amount is five thousand dollars."

Postscript

It's been three years since we left Baltimore and moved to Shady Side. Within a couple of weeks of arriving, Maggie and I exchanged vows at Oakland Methodist, her family's church. From the minute I saw her home, I realized I wasn't the only one who had been keeping secrets. Maggie had been keeping some too, like where her home *was.* Her family lived on a farm all right, a farm next to the water—on the West River of the Chesapeake Bay. "You told me your people were farmers," I complained when I saw her home for the first time.

"We are. At least the women are. My father and brothers fish and build boats."

"Build *boats?* Maggie, how many times have I told you I want to work on the water and build and sail boats?"

"Once or twice."

"Well why didn't you tell me?"

"I wanted to make sure it was *me* you loved, not just where I lived. When I was sure, I waited a little longer. I wanted it to be a surprise."

And what a surprise it was.

Shortly after I proposed marriage, Aunt Grace drove us south in her Ford. We crossed over the Patapsco and then the Severn River and I got to see the skyline of Annapolis and the Naval Academy. When we got to the new South River Bridge, a boat was waiting to go up river. The lights flashed and the bells sounded. A gate came down and the drawbridge slowly opened. We watched in amazement as a tall-masted sail boat crossed in front of us. The June sky was bright blue and without a cloud. The water was like a mirror and I marveled at the huge trees and small summer cottages that dotted the shore. When the boat passed, the bridge closed and we waved at the bridge-keeper in his booth as we drove across.

The roads that followed were winding and lined with cattle and horses in pastures, fields of corn and tobacco, barns and ponds. Farm houses sat at the end of long dirt roads overlooking the fields. The ruts in the road made for a bumpy ride, but we didn't mind. Maggie was excited about going home and nervous about introducing me to her family. Hannah bounced along on my lap, hanging her face out the window and letting her long curls sail behind her.

It took us the best part of the morning to get there, but as we turned into the lane my eyes widened. The house was two stories, white clapboard with green shutters, a porch and a rose garden on the side. The lawn was bright green and newly mowed. Then I saw it. I saw the sun sparkling on the water behind her house. There was a pier around the point and boats for fishing and oystering. There was a vegetable garden across from their home and a boathouse near the dock. I rolled down the car window even further to smell the air. I inhaled deeply at saltwater and freshly cut grass. I heard the seagulls and the gentle lapping of the waves against the shore. It was the place of my dreams.

When I first met Maggie's father, he looked me over like a piece of livestock. He shook my hand and grabbed my arm to feel for the muscle. Then he rolled my hand around in his. "I guess these hands will fit around a pair of oyster tongs," he said as he and his sons had a good laugh.

I had no idea what he was talking about then, but I know only too well now.

In spring, we fish. In summer we crab. In winter, we tong for oysters. The tongs will break your back after a few hours, but at the end of the day you can *see* what you've done. Working the bay is hard, but I have the water and sky all around me and the roll and pitch of the boat. When the weather is too bad, we don't go out at all. Sometimes the snow or sleet keeps us ashore. Sometimes it is so cold, the creek freezes solid and the icebreakers can't even get in. That's when we build a fire in the woodstove and work in the boathouse on our latest project. We build skiffs and bugeyes quickly, but an oyster boat, like a skipjack could take a year. Some fishing boats take longer. We build some for ourselves and some to sell.

The first meal Maggie's mother cooked for us was fried soft crabs. Hannah was wary at first. They looked like giant spiders. But one bite of the sweet and crunchy claw, and she was a believer. I loved every morsel. Now every June when the locust trees are in bloom, we take a shallow skiff and pole along the marshes and scoop up the freshly shed crabs with a dip net. When there are plenty, we even eat them for breakfast. Every time I eat a soft crab, I remember that first night.

By, now I've eaten everything that comes out of the bay: oysters in stew or fried with green tomato pickle relish or even raw with horseradish and ketchup. I've tried my hand at picking the meat out of hard blue crabs with their sharp points and cayenne pepper. I'll leave that to Maggie. She and her mother pick them out like machines. I'll take crab cakes with mayonnaise, a fat slice of summer tomato and salt and pepper instead. I have eaten sweet rockfish stuffed with sage dressing and smoked blues. We fry spots, croakers and white perch in warm weather.

The vegetable garden has tomatoes and peppers and corn. Maggie's mother pickles cucumbers and beets and heads of green cabbage are shredded and covered with salt to ferment. She keeps a couple of hogs in a pen nearby to eat the garden waste. A hog is slaughtered every winter. I have never eaten so much pork and sauerkraut in my life. There's a small orchard with fruit and nut trees. Cherries and apples are canned for pies. "Eat what you can and can what you can't," is the family motto. Fish heads are turned in with the compost for fertilizer. Oyster shells line the driveway. The men do the tilling but the women do most of the gardening. And Hannah has become a little farmer too. I built a new trellis on the side of the house for Maggie's climbing roses, but before she could plant them, Hannah planted her seeds from the gator-killer, Jack. The wisteria vines have grown like weeds and she has already gotten a few flowers, pale purple, that look like bunches of grapes that bloom in spring as promised.

I bought a little piece of land from Maggie's grandfather, a point with water on three sides. Grandpa nearly gave it away. "You can't even get a potato to grow on that sandbar," he said. "You two are crazy."

But, I don't want to plant potatoes, I want the sea. I want to see it, smell it, hear it and wade into it whenever

I want. On occasion, I even dip my hand into the brackish water and taste it. I bought the land and the lumber to build the house with part of the reward money. Maggie's brothers and father helped me build it. It has two stories and an indoor bathroom. We've got kerosene heat and an electric stove and hot water tank. I don't have to bring in wood unless Maggie wants a fire in the hearth. And there's no coal to shovel. We are so far back in the country that there are no trains or streetcars or even taxicabs. So I bought a second-hand automobile, a big sedan. I can drive Maggie any place she wants to go.

I sometimes wonder that my life has changed so much in just three years. There is a seasonal rhythm here unlike any other I've ever known. It hasn't been easy to learn, but now I understand. I'm a waterman now, like the other men in the family. We oyster in the hardest weather, winter. We tong in months with an "r," September to April. We sort our catch on our boat and throw the culls back into the same beds for seeding in the coming years. We are territorial, guarding our own beds from year to year and tending over them from generation to generation. In spring, the fish return from the ocean to the bay to spawn, mainly rocks and blues. We fish to eat, fish to sell and fish for men to take fishing, on our charter boat, the *Suzette*. There is no limit to how many fish can be pulled from the water. And we crabbers are a serious bunch, carefully repairing our pots and painting our floats. Each crabber has his own colors to identify his pots. We have favorite hunting grounds and are nearly as territorial with our pots as our oyster beds. From May until October, we are out before dawn,

JOAN LEHMANN

fishing our pots and re-baiting them with fish heads and salted eel. There is a stern law about emptying another man's pots. There could be a fine or even jail time. But the best deterrent is the shot gun we keep below deck. We finish by noon then have to quickly get our catch to its destination before the crabs die in the summer heat. They might find their way to a fish market in Annapolis, a restaurant, a roadside stand or a packing house where the crabs are steamed and picked by dozens of women.

Though I have a new life in Shady Side, I have never forgotten the lives I left behind. I took Hannah back to see Flo as promised and Sam was glad to see me too. The hotel business is booming. When we visited and the doorman put out his hand, I gave him a tip–as well as a shake. On our way out of town, I left a donation for the shelter that gave Hannah and me soup and bread that first night we arrived. I haven't forgotten the hungry or what it's like to be that way.

My girls and I visit Cressona every year in spring, to take care of the graves and pay our respects. It still hurts to stand by the grave of Molly and my son. But I know they are in a wonderful place. Abby left the house to me in her will, as promised, but I didn't have the heart to sell it. I rent it out. The mines have re-opened and a coal miner, his wife and six children live in that house. Seems every time I see him, his wife is with child again. I tease, "Kiss her goodnight, already. Haven't you figured out where baby's come from? Keep your breeches buttoned, man." They struggle, like we did, but they seem happy.

We made a trip to Ocean City. Hannah loved the boardwalk with the cotton candy and carnival rides.

But I wanted the Atlantic. The emerald water stretched as far as the eye could see. The sound of the waves lapping the shore *was* like a lullaby. The tide, the wind and the smell of real saltwater were intoxicating. Ireland, the home of my forefathers, was just across on the opposite shore. Hannah and I stood on the beach and faced the mighty ocean. We lifted our faces to the wind and then lifted our arms to catch it. Maggie giggled when we pretended to fly. But *we* knew we had wings.

I took off my shoes and felt the sand and sea foam under my feet. It wasn't enough. Then I waded into the same water my Grandda Joseph had waded. It still wasn't enough. I took Hannah's hand and we jumped in with all our clothes on. Maggie scolded us for not changing first. But I had waited a lifetime for this day. There was no time for changing. This was my dream. Hannah and I swam and splashed around like fish. Maggie refused to come in. She said she couldn't swim. But she couldn't stand being left out either. Carefully, she waded in a little deeper with each wave, until a large one caught her by surprise and soaked her skirt. The lure of the warm water overcame her and she jumped in to swim with us between the swells.

I have thought a lot about that day and how wonderful it was. And I now realize that swimming is a lot like walking. Everyone can do it. You just have to have the courage to take the first step—or stroke. And life is like the ocean. You can't just wade in a little at a time. You might as well dive in head first because you are eventually going to get wet anyway. And I now believe that everyone can find happiness. You just have to be strong enough to get through the hard times and believe long enough until you find good ones.

The bay is a whole world unto its own. The sunrise is different everyday and sometimes the colors will take your breath away. I have learned to identify every waterfowl by its silhouette in the sky. When Canada geese fly overhead in a v-formation, I have to stop to watch them. I admire the large gander in the lead and listen to all of the geese honking to him from behind. "Back seat drivers," Maggie's father calls them. And I marvel at the children skating on the creek when it freezes over. Even as I dreamed of the water as a child, I never really knew what it would be like to live here. I guess some would complain about the isolation of the countryside, being too far out in the boonies. But not me. This is where I belong. This is where I have *always* belonged.

The bay is my home, but I know my back can't take the oyster tongs forever. I've got my sights set on a boat, a big one. I've thought about a steamer, with a big smoke stack and paddle wheel, to transport passengers and cargo to Baltimore and back, like the *Emma Giles*. But I think I'd rather captain a boat under sail, a schooner, like the *Nettie Allison* and live by my wits and the mercy of the winds. It's riskier, I know, but I would tire of all the noise and smoke and the dusty coal of a steamer. I'd much rather be left with the sound of the wind flapping on the canvas and the tides. I would need only a small crew and the stevedores to unload the cargo, the bushels of crabs and oysters, tomatoes and hogsheads of tobacco. I've done enough sailing with my father-in-law to have a good idea about sails, winds, ropes and booms, *now*. I've thought about a dozen names for my boat, but I keep coming back to just one, the *Hannah Jo.*

I've already got one customer lined up, The Lord Baltimore. Sam says he'll take all the oysters, clams and crabmeat I can carry. I'll even bring a little shad roe, just for him. I would never grow tired of taking a boat from the West River, past Annapolis and the Thomas Point lighthouse to the Patapsco down into the Baltimore Harbor. I'll earn the cash to build the boat myself. I won't touch another cent of the reward money. It's put away in a safe place so our children can get a proper education. Maybe they'll go to college in Baltimore or further up north. It doesn't really matter to me as long as they go to school. I don't want them to have to work or worry like I did. Life is too short and I still remember only too well how hard it can be.

Hannah is spending this long summer Sunday playing with her cat, a calico, named Ginger. Santa Claus never forgot her wish and brought it on his sled after all. But her favorite playmate is her little brother, *Joseph.* He's nearly two now. He's got blond hair and freckles, like Maggie, but my boy's got *my* green eyes. He and Hannah play on the beach collecting feathers and shells and building sandcastles. She bullies him one minute and dotes on him the next. She is his *other* mother.

When I look at the faces of my children, I see the past. Hannah looks more like Molly everyday. In my son, I see my father and his father. When I look into their eyes, I see the future, full of promise and grandchildren and great-grandchildren. I know they were sent from heaven. I now believe in angels here on earth: Sam and Flo, Mrs. Arnista and Maggie. And I know there are angels in heaven watching over me. But they don't have wings and they don't play harps. No, they are doing what they like best. Abby has got a chicken in the oven and Andrew is still chasing her around the kitchen table. Molly is rocking our son and singing him to sleep. And I believe that God forgives. Joey is drinking beer and playing cards with Vinnie. When I get there, I'll be eight years old wading in the sea of Ireland looking for mussels for supper with Grandda Joseph.

But heaven will have to wait a while for me. I am still meeting angels down here. My lovely Maggie is with child again. I'm watching the miracle in her belly grow a little each day. If it's a girl, we'll name her Abigail, after the courageous great-aunt she never knew. If it's a boy, we'll name that little devil, *Frank*.

Joan Lehmann is a family physician and works in an ER near Baltimore. Writing is her second career. She writes for local newspapers and is completing another book, *Don't Move Lily*. She and her family live in Pasadena near the Chesapeake Bay. Visit her website at www.JoanLehmannMD.com.

Made in the USA